They were the Donner People— slaves of an unspeakable desire

The starving pioneers talked as they worked, laying the green wood down on the snow for a fire. It was Christmas Eve, but there was no Christmas feast—there was no food.

"Through the centuries, man has eaten almost everything on Earth . . . but he has had to kill it first. We haven't even seen a coyote or an owl to kill," Uncle Billy wheezed as he hunched down to light the ice-covered wood.

The men and women of the Donner-Reid party glanced furtively at one another as the fire began to blaze. A pall of silence hung over them, broken only by the crackling of the burning branches, as each man sat lost in his own thoughts . . . did the other plan to butcher him like an ox, or slit his throat like a sheep? Even family members began to ponder the hungry look in the eyes of their kin.

A terrified whimpering sound rose and grew from the direction of Harriet Pike, who sat clutching a tattered blanket to her emaciated body.

Starting with Harriet's scarecrow frame, Patrick Dolan's eyes continued to move around the circle with a glittering, half-crazed stare.

"It's true we have no coyotes, no owls . . ." Patrick's voice broke tremulously through the silence, "but we do have each other . . ."

THE DONNER PEOPLE

Lee Davis Willoughby

A DELL/BRYANS BOOK

Published by
Dell Publishing Co., Inc.
1 Dag Hammarskjold Plaza
New York, New York 10017

Dell ® TM 681510, Dell Publishing Co., Inc.

ISBN: 0-440-02084-0

Printed in the United States of America

First printing—January 1982

1

THE PETITE GOLDEN-HAIRED woman directed the boys in the placement of the barrels and planks. From the wagons young girls brought cotton pads and lace tablecloths. Benches for twelve were unstrapped from beneath the conestoga wagons and put on the ground. Upon the lace tablecloth was laid out a table setting of china, crystal and silver. At the head and foot of the makeshift table were set high-backed Queen Charlotte chairs. Over all wafted the aroma of frying brook trout, roasting beef, baking biscuits and boiling rice.

It was no feast day nor special celebration. George and Jacob Donner had dined this way each evening with their families since departing Springfield, Illinois.

The brothers, into their sixties, saw no reason to change their life style just because they were making another trek westward. Their father had done much

5

the same in their moves from North Carolina to Kentucky, and thence to Indiana and to Illinois. The Donner heritage could be maintained as well on plank boards as around a prosperous Illinois farm table. George Donner's five daughters by his second and third marriage deserved just as much civilization as did his elder children and grandchildren left at home in Illinois.

The same principle applied for his sixty-five year old elder brother Jacob. "Uncle Jake," however, insisted upon this nightly ritual more than "Uncle George." He possessed two rascally teenage boys by his wife's first marriage, and four boys and a girl by his present marriage to Elizabeth.

"Boys," he had often maintained during his six and a half decades, "should be treated like a litter of unwanted puppies. Drowned!"

Then his pinched, tired face would expand into a loving grin. Children of all ages were his special joy in life. During the day he would allow the children of both families to be brash, devil-may-care and mischievous. But during his dinner prayer, which sometimes could ramble into an hour-long sermon, the children were quick to learn that Uncle Jake's watery gray eyes missed very little. They loved him all the more because of it.

It was hard to say that the children loved Uncle George, even his own. Back home in Illinois the prosperous farmer was considered a gentle, charitable spirit. For strangers, it was a positive pleasure for him to do a kind act.

To the children he was exactly as he looked: a towering, gray-bearded Biblical patriarch, who could tear you apart with the glint of his hazel eyes.

Two women saw him as a granite-faced handsome man at sixty-two: his wife and sister-in-law. Tamsen

Donner and Eliabeth Donner were each forty-five. The petite Tamsen hardly looked thirty and the stout Elizabeth far above her real age. Between the two women was little love—except the love both felt for the same man. Elizabeth Donner was the sister of George's second wife. She had believed it was her right to become number three on the death of her sister. George had gone after the spry and beautiful schoolteacher, Tamsen, in Springfield. Furious, Elizabeth had latched onto the widower brother just to stay within the Donner clan. But, give her a chance to best Tamsen in front of George and she became a devil in corsets and petticoats.

Elizabeth's greatest weapon against Tamsen was her absolute avoidance of all work.

"Lupins, Aunt Tammy. Would you like Leanna and me to centerpiece some of them?"

Despite her gloomy and dispirited feeling, Tamsen Donner smiled at fourteen-year-old Elitha. Elitha and twelve-year-old Leanna were her step-daughters, but by mutual agreement she had become "Aunt Tammy." As a former school teacher she was more concerned with their minds than their beauty. They had very good minds; their beauty was from within.

"I would like that, and perhaps some willows from the creek."

Willows and lupins, she thought. That's all there is to Little Sandy Creek, except some yellowish sand and grass trampled down by the oxen.

Against her better judgment, she raised her golden head again, the hair bleached as near white as the canvas tops of the wagons. She hated herself for looking away toward buttes and snow-capped mountains in the distance. She kept her clear blue eyes to the left. The cutoff road to Fort Bridger seemed hardly used at all. The road to the right, she was well aware, was deeply rutted after four years of emigrants travelling to Oregon. But she refused to look at the wagons crawling over that sagebrush country.

She felt as though death had visited her and taken someone away. Many "someones." Strangers at first, on the easily travelled roadbeds from Springfield to the Missouri. Then it had become a substantial community of six hundred souls.

Oh, her husband had carped about the people they were forced to associate with, and the children had grown tired of the uneventful and tedious miles across the Great Plains.

But, to her, size had been security. No band of Indians were about to attack such a large throng.

"Seems a long time for them to pass from view."

Tamsen turned, an instant smile lighting her face. Even at fourteen, Solomon E. Hook stood near six feet. The sun had bleached his brown hair sandy, because he refused to wear a hat, and his eyebrows bonewhite. His long, youthfully handsome face had turned as chestnut brown as his eyes. Despite the fact that he was Elizabeth Donner's eldest son by her first marriage—a marriage that was not discussed in mixed company—he was a favorite nephew to Tamsen. Although both Donner families possessed servants for the trip, Sol was an energetic worker and Tamsen's chief aide.

"I suppose we have appeared the same to mountainmen and Indian scouts, Sol. An armada of land ships sailing the grasslands."

Solomon laughed. Because his voice was changing it ranged between baritone and alto. He loved to hear Tamsen talk. His puppy-love for her went back seven years when she was his second-grade school teacher. He had at first been crushed and resentful when she married George Donner. Then, when his own mother had married Jacob, the blow had been somewhat softened. He suddenly realized that Tamsen would then be part of his family forever. This trip had changed puppy-love to real love—but not for Tamsen.

"I wish I were with them, Aunt Tammy."

She put her arm about his waist and drew him close. She had thought his heart would break during the farewells. To everyone on the wagon train it was quite obvious that he had lost his heart to Governor Boggs' daughter Ellen. But as a boy of fourteen, and she as a woman, had no say in the decision to split the train.

"I, too, longed for Oregon, Sol."

It was little solace. "California," he scoffed. "What do we know of it, except what you have read in Mr. Hastings' guide and now his letter to meet him at Fort Bridger? Do you really think the Mexicans will attack, now that we are at war?"

Tamsen laughed, but it was not a reassuring sound. "Sol, my knowledge of geography is only as good as the maps I have seen, but I would say that the Mexican city of San Antonio is a good seven to eight hundred miles to the south. Our own Antonio doesn't seem to be concerned by it, and he is from that country. Besides, we are people of peace and not of war."

"Substantial," he scoffed again. "That's what Mr. Reed said when the messenger brought us the letter at South Pass. What did he mean that we had a different manifest destiny than the Boggs and Thornton people? And what does it mean, anyway?"

"Whoa!" she chuckled. "You want a full lecture when supper is almost on the table."

He frowned. There was a certain puzzlement on his handsome face when he frowned. It came near to being a sulk. "Who else takes the time to discuss things with the women and children? The men sit in the camp council and say 'do.' You are the only one who tells us why we must do this or that."

Tamsen looked back. James Noah, who doubled as teamster and cook, didn't seem nearly ready. Catching enough trout out of the shallow, clear creek waters had put him far behind.

Still, she was hesitant to give her thoughts on the subject as opposed to those of James Frazier Reed. He could consider a majority of the Springfield party substantial people, but hardly himself. The forty-five year old man announced his vast wealth through an enormous and elaborate wardrobe for his family, the custom-built design of his wagons, the number of servants and a haughty snobbery toward all men and all women.

Only silk shirts and silk underclothing ever touched his skin. As it was mid-July his jackets were all linen with velvet trim. Hot water had to be prepared each morning so that Eliza Williams could lather his lantern jaw for a shave. She was not allowed to touch his upper lip. He alone, as she held a hand mirror, would trim the pencil-thin mustache. Many times it would take as long as a half hour, because James Frazier Reed loved to view his own reflection. He was of the singular impression that no other man on earth had been granted such handsomeness.

Only one person on earth did he love more than himself and that was his spoiled, pampered step-daughter Virginia. The thirteen year old girl already possessed a womanly body fuller-bosomed than that of forty-five-year-old Tamsen. She had a delicate, glowing beauty that she did not quite comprehend, and Reed kept her almost exclusively to himself.

Tamsen found the man insufferable, but did not presume to impose her thoughts on Solomon Hook.

"First, Sol, I think you had best know exactly what the journalist John L. O'Sullivan penned to start this whole matter. '. . . Nothing must interfere with the fulfillment of our *manifest destiny* to overspread the continent allotted by Providence for the free development of our yearly multiplying millions.' Sol, like you, the majority of those millions don't even know what the words mean. It vaguely suggests that somewhere between Mexico and Russian Alaska is alluring land. Land that is May in December. Land that it is America's bounden duty to settle with a large influx of emigrants."

"Mr. Reed says it will bring nothing but the ne'er-do-wells, the rolling stones, the fugitives from justice, the poor white farmers who have ruined the east and now wish to ruin the west."

"Oh, Sol, they are still people with a dream. Maybe that is the simplest way of defining what Mr. O'Sullivan wrote. The dream is out there, so go seize it and make it come true. Perhaps that is also what Mr. Reed meant. We also have a dream, but it is based on past accomplishments. The Donners left no ruined farmland, but grown children to care for family property. We are farmers and businessmen seeking a new field of endeavor, but take substantial possessions with us to bring it about."

The sulk became almost fierce. "I hate farming. I hope it is not my field of endeavor forever."

She laughed gaily. "It does not have to be, Sol. Look, your stepfather was more adept at running his milling and grinding business than he was to growing wheat. A new farm area will also require all manner of new businesses around it."

This brought the sulk back to a sly smile. "Even a school?"

"That is our little secret, Sol. Your Uncle George would be furious if he knew what we had done."

In seven years of marriage, it had been the only time she had raised her voice to George Donner. He had thought her idea foolish and wagon space too limited. Their three wagons were required for foodstuffs, household goods for the new home, gew-gaws to be given as presents to the Indians, and laces, silks,

and rich stuffs to be traded with the Mexicans for
California lands.

Tamsen had thought differently and had gone
against her husband's wishes. She had shorted herself on personal clothing, and, with the help of Sol,
had stuffed the back half of a dozen drawers with
books, school supplies, even watercolors and oils,
everything necessary for the founding of a young ladies' seminary for her daughters in an unknown new
land.

They were drawers that Tamsen knew her husband
would not open until journey's end. Fancy clothes
would not be needed until a homesite was established.
The Jacob Donner family could dress as fancily as
Elizabeth desired, but the George Donner family
would wear sturdy homespuns on the trail. His wealth
would not be advertised. Nor would it be carried in
a chest as it was in the case of Jacob Donner.

That was the other reason Tamsen knew her husband would not be entering the dresser drawers. For
months, before the trip began, Tamsen had worked
on a modest-looking quilt that would not be used
until placed on their new bed. When completed, she
had carefully stowed it away in one of the drawers.
Only George and Tamsen were aware that each night
during the quilt-making, she was secretly sewing
within the quilt bills that totaled ten thousand dollars.

Noah James came to the long dinner table and
rang a little silver bell. It was always the grimmest
moment of the day for the freckle-faced twenty-year-
old man. Since becoming an orphan at ten he had
been raised on the Donner Illinois farm as a herder
of the dairy cattle and a cook for the other herders
and milkers. As such, his life had been quite simple
and with little contact with the family or the main
house. He had not been asked to come on the journey, he had been ordered.

After ten years of taking orders from George Donner and his eldest sons, he had not balked. He had nearly balked when he learned that the food he cooked had to go upon silver platters and within silver covered dishes and tureens. He had balked when Elizabeth Donner began to carp about his simple cooking and insisted that a dinner bell be rung fifteen minutes before serving.

George Donner flatly refused to listen to the young man's complaint. It was a woman's matter.

Tamsen, as usual, had to be the peacemaker. Quietly, she began to coach Noah in the usage of spices and the preparation of different dishes—in exchange for his agreeing to ring the stupid bell before each evening meal.

Tamsen won him over, as she did most people. Even when they didn't like what they had to do—such as ringing a silly bell—they did it out of personal loyalty to this charming lady.

"I doubt that your mother would have heard that half-hearted tinkle, Sol," she laughed. "You'd best go over and fetch her. She spent the afternoon with Margaret Reed."

Sol brightened. His true love may have just departed on the Oregon Trail, but that did not mean that his fourteen-year-old eyes still couldn't enjoy feasting themselves on Eliza Williams.

For the Reed family, the twenty-five-year-old Irish lass was a woman of all purposes: cook, governess, washer of clothing, butter-churner, seamstress, barber, dresser, lady-in-waiting and nurse for all of Margaret Reed's real and mostly imagined aches and pains.

Eliza was an indentured servant from the north Ireland estates of Reed's uncle. Like Noah James, she had been given no choice in the matter of coming west.

Two years of servitude remained before her debt

was cancelled. Two years to further enhance her own personal *manifest destiny*. She was determined not to remain a hired girl forever—nor marry the wrong kind of lad.

It was not conceit that told her of her dark beauty, it was the look in men's eyes. They would sparkle so with lust that they would mirror her coal-black curly hair, eyebrows like cunningly inverted vee's and eyes of such an equally dark yet brilliant hue that the pupil points were like a single sparkling evening star.

Even on the trip, James Frazier Reed made her wear maid's uniforms of black, with white duster cap, starched apron and lace dickey. As an excellent seamstress she made sure that the bodice was always tightly sewn to mold about her perfect, round breasts and display the smallest waist on the wagon train.

But within Eliza Williams was also a playful Irish devil. When the Donners began to dine formally, James and Margaret Reed insisted upon the same degree of elegance.

As the Reed table required only six settings, Eliza secured help from her twenty-four-year-old brother, Baylis, also an indentured servant from Ireland, to bring out the round oak table top from the household goods wagon and secure it upon a flour barrel. It, too, was set with china, silver, crystal and silver, but only for the weekdays. Solid gold service was used for the Sabbath meal.

Her secret intention, however, was not to outshine the Donner table. It was to make the Reeds look pompous and arrogant for trying to outshine them.

Margaret Reed she silently pitied. James Reed she mistrusted and almost feared. For twenty-five years she had fought to keep her virginity for "barter" on the proper marriage contract. Reed had an imperious, aristocratic notion that servant girls also had nightly chores to perform. She had three years accumulation of black and blue pinch marks to attest to that notion, but had subtly avoided her employer at every turning.

Now, she thought, as she saw Solomon Hook approach, if that one were just a few years older I might be showing him a bit of ankle.

Oddly, Tamsen Donner was having a similar thought. Because Elizabeth Donner had nearly broken her neck to make friends with Margaret Reed, Tamsen had steered fairly clear of that family group.

Two weeks before she'd had to coordinate the Fourth of July celebration with Eliza. James Reed had in mind to toast the occasion with wine and fine old brandy he had carried in his stores for a thousand miles. George and Jacob had offered the food.

Noah James had been awestruck being that close to Eliza Williams for the first time. Eliza had treated him with a more imperious attitude than James Reed might have. But to the unmarried young bucks of the Boggs and Thornton party, who had brought back fresh deer meat from the Rocky Mountains, she was all charm and grace and discreet flirtation.

Tamsen glowered at the way in which Eliza now greeted Sol to the Reed wagons. She knew it was Elizabeth's duty to warn her own son about such designing women, but knew that chore would more than likely fall back on her shoulders as well.

And therein was the sole flaw in the character of Tamsen Donner—she could also be a bit of a snob. Her great experience in handling servants made them love and respect her, but she was of the solid opinion that servants and family members were unthinkable as marriage partners.

She watched Sol closely until he approached the main Reed wagon. Only once, on the first day of the journey, had she been invited within its interior.

It loomed over all the others and had to be pulled by an oxen yoke of four. It was gigantic, as James Reed had intended. It had been custom-built, as had his other wagons, in his furniture factory in Springfield—before it had gone bankrupt. Comfort was what he demanded for his 'ailing' wife and her mother, Mrs. Keyes.

Unlike the other canvas-topped wagons, with entrances front and rear, this mansion on wheels had easy steps at the side, which led into a room amidships. Here were spring seats such as the most fashionable Eastern coaches used, bolted-down tables and rose-glass hooded lamps dangling from chains. To each side of one table were chaise-longues for Margaret and Mrs. Keyes.

At each end of the amidship room was a door and pull-down ladder. Two-storied? To be sure! Forward on the second floor, because James Reed did refer to it as his 'ship,' were mattress areas for his four children and Eliza Williams. Aft had been divided into two compartments; one for himself and his wife; the other for his mother-in-law. Upon the flooring of each had been laid triple thick feather mattresses.

Mrs. Keyes must have felt that at her advanced age such comfort should not be given up lightly; three weeks out of Springfield she began an eternal sleep.

Thereafter, James and Margaret went back to separate bedrooms.

Below the 'master bedrooms', on the first floor, were storage compartments for the vast wardrobe for the whole family and a dressing compartment.

Beneath the children's compartment were built-in cupboards and preparation area for 'family food.' Family food meaning that which Eliza would prepare amidship on the sheet-iron stove, with its pipe carefully conveyed through the canvas top.

The stove also provided warmth for the compartment and the women who would come to sit cozily and comfortably to chat with Margaret as the wagon moved along.

Since the morning departure, all that was left was Elizabeth Donner. There were five Springfield family parties: two Donners, Reed, Eddy and Murphy.

At first, except for one, Margaret had tried to include them all into her little 'social gatherings.'

Eleanor Eddy she had found naively young at twenty-five, too quiet and too mysterious about herself and her husband. Margaret thrived only on gossip were never given so much as an initial invitation.

Lavina Murphy and her two married daughters were never given so much as an initial inivtation.

Margaret marked them as "poor" the first night out when she got the report that they dined on salt pork, beans, hominy and Dutch oven baked bread. Her own personal tastes ran toward fresh churned butter, cold ham and pickles, cheese, dried fruit, and tea, coffee, or milk to wash down delicately broiled antelope steaks.

Besides, in her opinion, a widow woman of fifty, with five unmarried children, and two married, had no right to impose their shiftless, lazy, boorish, moronic lack of morals upon the likes of herself and her children.

"Imagine," she had gossiped to Elizabeth, Isabella Boggs and Hazel Thorton. "They do little more than sit around their campfire and eat off of wooden plates with only spoons. Utterly backwoodish!"

The Boggs and Thornton families had eaten in quite the same manner, but the women justified their temporary dining arrangements—they were saving their good service for when they set up new homesites.

To them "old widow Murphy" was large, boisterous and uncouth. Well onto two hundred pounds, her breasts hung near to her waist, her mousy brown-gray hair refused to stay back in a bun and stuck out of her skull like the pelt of a frightened porcupine. The other family wagons had hired "bull-whackers" to urge on the oxen. Her sons-in-law she left to tend her dairy cattle. In brogans of a man's size, she strode alongside her oxen pulled wagons, bellowing and cracking the whip, in language that was colorful if somewhat smarting to more sensitive ears.

On the trail her heavy-jowled face could become as fierce as her language. At night, by the campfire glow, it could soften to take on the aspect of an aging Madonna. That was a time when it was only seen by her immediate family.

The women who shunned her never saw her loving nature. William Pike and William Foster, her sons-in-law, and hence called by her just Pike and Foster, were young and abundantly energetic. But Lavina Murphy was wise to men. Her husband had died in the bed of another woman, leaving her with John, Mary, Lemuel, William and Simon, ranging stairsteps from fifteen down to ten. She also knew Pike and Foster to be young scalawags who would pant after a change in pace at the drop of a pantaloon.

Perhaps she could never change those two, but she could get the younger ones away from the finger-pointing gossips of Springfield.

As far as the 'uppity' women in the fine wagons, Lavina never gave a thought to not being invited to sit among them. It had never happened in Springfield, so she never questioned why it was not happening now.

But one who had been invited but a single time had given Margaret Reed nothing but worry since. Tamsen Donner was just too intelligent for Margaret to cope with.

Reed was incorrect—even in north Ireland, though it was the name used by James's father and uncle since his boyhood. They were actually exiled Polish nobles by the name of Reedowsky. Exiled because of a murderous plot against the crown. James's fierce and haughty Polish nature had not been subdued by the mingling into his blood stream that of his stiff-necked and restless Scotch-Irish mother.

In America he had tried to overcome his Polish past, even serving in the Black Hawk campaign with a lanky young man from Illinois by the name of Abe Lincoln. But the millions of rubles the Reedowsky family had taken from Poland were now considered Russian property, and the agents of the Czar were relentless.

James Frazier Reed was on the run, just like the common outlaws that he scoffed at.

Although Margaret Reed found Elizabeth to be horribly boorish, she had befriended her just to keep Tamsen away. And, after all, Elizabeth was the only socially acceptable woman available to invite within the wagon.

"Solomon," Elizabeth snapped, "you intrude!"

"The dinner bell, mother," he gulped.

"Really," she sniffed, "as the wife of Jacob, and thus senior female member of the family, we shall dine when he escorts me to the table and not when some servant decides to ring a little bell. Intolerable. Well, dear Margaret, my thanks for the fantastic afternoon. You do know how to make these dreary hours speed. Solomon, your arm. I have yet to dress before dinner."

Margaret Reed smiled to herself. Yes, she thought, this dowdy woman might scream a lot in private, but carried a very small stick in public. She was, Margaret determined, just as cautious and fearful of Tamsen Donner as she was herself.

And for the life of her, Margaret Reed could not

determine why she really feared her. Tamsen was a mere whiffet: barely five feet and less than a hundred pounds. True, she shepherded the Donner brood like an all-seeing-Diana, with her intense physical vitality. There was the touch of the aristocrat about her. Perhaps that was it.

Elizabeth was like a flour sack with lace sewn about the edging to make it frilly. Frumpy and soft. A follower and not a leader. Since Springfield Elizabeth's leader had been Margaret.

They marched to the table by rank of family and age. George Donner had decreed this out of respect for his brother. Elizabeth 'paraded' to daily underscore the fact to the entire camp. There wasn't much camp to parade before that night.

Scrubbed, brushed and with travel boots polished came the handsome Hook brothers: Solomon and twelve-year-old William.

Everyone fully agreed that they favored their father rather than mother, next in the parade line, ranging from nine down to three, came "Young" George, Mary, Isaac, Samuel and Lewis, each as soft and round and dumpling-shaped as Elizabeth.

George Donner arrived at the table with his daughters by his second wife on each arm: Elitha left and Leanna right.

Tamsen and the three younger daughters came like a possum with its young. Tamsen was most successful with other children; her own were clinging-vine problems. Tears still streaked six-year-old Frances' face face from the dreaded ordeal of having her hair brushed. Four-year-old Georgia was a troublesome eater and her face suggested she was ready to make a great deal of trouble that evening. The face of the "baby" couldn't even be seen. It was a nightly ritual for three-year-old Eliza Pauline to hide her face within the folds of her mother's gown and have to be tugged along by the arm.

It was a habit which had developed only since the start of the trip and one which Tamsen had vowed to break with dire threats. She had been soundly overruled by her husband. As stern as he could be with the older children and servants, George Donner was a softy when it came to his three "baby" daughters.

It was Elizabeth's second grandest moment of each day. Everyone, but especially her "dear, dear" George, could see what well mannered children she was rearing while Tamsen had nothing but a parcel of spoiled, ill-tempered brats.

Her third grandest moment of each day was about to begin. Jacob would surely have something to say about the three children in his prayer, for he was scowling fiercely.

Jacob Donner's scowl had nothing to do with Tamsen children. A horse and pony were galloping directly at them at a dangerous pace. He knew exactly who it was and what the man would want. He had been approached that morning by James Frazier Reed and had wisely not discussed that conversation with his brother.

Reed looked more attired for the English countryside. His gray cutaway was a good match for his prized gray racing mare. Amazingly, his tight-fitting white breeches, tucked into knee-high gray boots, did not suggest that he and his daughter had been cantering over the plains for the entire afternoon. The dyed beaver tophat he raised in a tally-ho gesture as he pulled the mare into a cloud raising stop.

Virgina Backenstoe raced right on by, showering the dinner table with a further cloud of dust. Although getting a little large for the pony, she insisted upon riding Billy side-saddle. Like her stepfather, girl and pony were overdressed for the scene. A perky velvet-veiled hat sat atop her many bouncing brunette curls. The flowing riding gown, pony trappings, elbow-length gauntlet gloves and even jauntily held parasol were in light lavender velvet and white trim.

Although her face could not be seen beneath the shadowing veil, her pert little head turned for just a second toward the table as she galloped by. Solomon Hook blushed scarlet, knowing what she was about. The attention that he had shown Ellen Boggs had uncovered a jealous streak in Virginia. At every opportunity presented to her she now stuck her tongue out at Solomon in defiance.

James Frazier Reed did not alight. He smiled so broadly that it gave a faintly mephitic look to his pencil-thin mustache.

"Dear Jacob," he said expansively, "have you made arrangements for the meeting?"

"Have not," Uncle Jake said curtly, keeping his seat as though welded to it. If the man was so impolite not to come off his horse to address him, then he was damned if he would rise.

Glaucus made a rude noise and voided himself.

The children had to stifle their snickers.

"What meeting?" George demanded.

James Frazier, which he preferred to be called rather than just James because it made it sound more like "Sir James" or "Lord James," sighed in open disgust. However, it had nothing to do with the natural discharge of his horse after such a long ride.

"As we shall now need a train captain, I asked your brother to arrange a council meeting for this evening."

"Forgot!" Jacob snapped and locked his jaw. That was not all that James Frazier had asked of him.

'Small matter,' George said, sensing that his normally jolly brother was not saying all he knew. "We are just under fifty now and can easily round everyone up after dinner."

"Hardly necessary," Reed said pompously. "In my opinion the vote for captain should be decided solely by the household heads."

George toyed with the square bottom cut of his beard. On leaving the Missouri, Governor Boggs had wished every man, woman and child to have a say in matters. James Frazier had launched such a tirade on the matter that the women and children had been excluded. Boggs had won out on the bullwhackers because they would be the main fighting arm of the unit as well as teamsters.

"That narrows it somewhat," George mused.

"Exactly. Five of us. Mrs. Murphy will just have to get one of her sons-in-law to speak for that whole parcel."

"Got a candidate in mind?"

"Well," James Frazier drawled, "I do believe that it must be a man of physical vigor, with an active mind, and with great experience in handling men. Not to boast, but I do possess those qualities and am a man of quick decisions and decisive action."

Jacob's face was suddenly as black as a thundercloud. It was James Frazier who had lobbied them into taking this nearer way. He had done that mainly by boasting of his personal knowledge of Hastings, his vast military experience, his full regalia as a Master Mason and to thwart the fear of an attack by the Mexicans produced a certificate addressed to any Mexican official it might concern, attesting to his character, signed by the governor of Illinois and duly stamped with the eagle, shield, and sun of the Great Seal of Illinois.

George was quick to speak before Jacob exploded. "James," he said, deliberately not giving him the affected full title, "we shall discuss your qualifications for candidacy over dinner. Thank you for letting us know that you are running."

"Well, there is hardly any other but you and I with wealth and position—Jacob being too old, of course."

"Stand for prayer," George said suddenly, nearly toppling his own chair in his rush to rise. By family ritual no other discussion could take place after he had made that announcement.

James Frazier spurred Glaucus into a Tennessee Walk. He was most pleased with himself. He had never counted on Jacob's vote, but coupling George's with William Eddy's and his own, it was a foregone conclusion. He hadn't even wasted his breath talking with old widow Murphy.

Then, as Walter Herron came running to take the mare from him, he smiled. It seemed a most proper occasion for him to wear his Master Mason uniform.

"Dear Heavenly Father," Jacob intoned in a voice four times louder than usual, "'we thank Thee for this day and what we are about to receive from Your bountiful nature. Lord, because you know all, please make some men of wealth and position see that other men insist that their possessor should act as if he were one of the crowd. And Lord, forgive the poor humble beast Glaucus her droppings, because the mare can't be responsible for a master that names it in fine defiance of Latin gender. But Lord, let Noah James, Sam Shoemaker or John Denton hear my voice to get this damn manure out of here before it draws flies. And speaking of flies, Lord, may you let one land on the insolent tongue of Miss Virginia and defecate. Amen."

George Donner cautiously opened his eyes. It was the shortest prayer he had ever heard his brother utter. He wanted to roar with laughter but dared not, for every child's eyes were glued on him for a reaction. Tamsen stared straight ahead, her jaw tight to hold in her mirth. Elizabeth's jaw was also tight, but from mortification. How could she ever dare face Margaret Reed again after what her husband had just prayed?

Jacob looked quite content, his eyes still closed. He would keep them closed until he heard a flat shovel scrape across the ground.

Everyone had heard the prayer, or heard of it before the meeting was called. The manner of voting did not set well with the bullwhackers and cattle herders. Hired hands or not, they were men and this was supposed to be a democracy. To spite James Frazier Reed they were the first to arrive in front of the side steps to his gigantic wagon.

The short, rough-and-ready William Eddy was the next to arrive. The quiet twenty-eight-year-old man was well liked by the teamsters and herders. Among them all he was the best hunter and the most skilled in the arts of the frontiersman. Early in the trip they had learned that he was no man to be trifled with in a quarrel. Single-handed he had broken up a fight between the Boggs and Thornton teamsters. Therefore, these teamsters felt they could count on him in a pinch.

"Gonna go that way anyhow, boys," he drawled, "cause I ain't wanting the job."

He was being straight-forward and enterprising. A carriage-maker by trade from Northern Illinois, he would require more finances than he now possessed to start a new shop. James Frazier had subtly suggested that he might be of big help to William Eddy someday in exchange for a "little" nomination now. Besides, he could no longer get lost in the crowd now that it had dwindled from six hundred. He was like a man constantly looking over his shoulder.

"Who says it is gonna go that way?"

Lavina Murphy stepped into the circle, squired by William Foster and William Pike. All three bore rifles tucked under their arms. Even without the rifles there was something about Foster and Pike that commanded respect. Tall, lanky and full muscled on their big-boned frames. Their ruggedly handsome faces and coloring could almost have made them brothers. Jaunty and easy going, they wore their hats to the back of their heads, their holsters low on the hip and were constantly jawing on a blade of grass or length of thistle.

"Evening, Miz Murphy," Eddy said, doffing his hat, "Who else might we be having? Your boys have their hands full with their own wagons and herds."

"Now if that ain't a hoot," she chuckled. Then she tilted back her head and roared until more loose ends of her mousey gray-brown hair sprang up. "I wouldn't let Foster and Pike lead me to the privvy, if'n we had one. They might just be tempted to drop me down to hear the splash."

This brought a deep-throated roar from the two young men. Hellions when they wished to be, they respected Lavina unmeasurably.

"But, Eddy," she said, suddenly sobered, "my vote would go for George Donner—even though Foster says he is too patriarchal and Pike thinks him too gentle."

"If you had a vote."

Just as James Frazier came onto the steps to make this cutting statement, George and Jacob joined the group.

There were several seconds of stunned, open-mouthed gaping. Rather than looking regal, James Frazier looked somewhat ridiculous in the long navy-blue frock coat with its beribboned neckpiece and jeweled badges. Because he knew he looked so handsome and commanding he took off the plumed cock-hat and posed with it across his chest.

"I repeat," he said, as though addressing a gathering as a monarch, "if you had a vote, Mrs. Murphy."

"What be the rules?" she asked sweetly, having already heard them when Antonio came over to cadge a plate of beans because he couldn't stomach the Donner food.

"The Donners and I agreed that each household head would have a vote."

The other men grumbled in their throats, but Antonio broke into a gold-toothed grin. He claimed to speak very little English. The darkly handsome twenty-three-year-old claimed many things, but expounded upon very few of them. George Donner had hired him because he claimed to have great experience in herding cattle along the Oregon Trail. That he was an excellent cowhand no one could deny, but not until they were beyond Independence Rock did any of the terrain seem familiar to him. After that everyone seemed to be an expert on everything, so he reverted to speaking "leetle Ingles," except for when he wanted Murphy beans.

It had not taken Antonio long to smell the aroma and learn that William Foster as a child had migrated with his family down to Texas. Growing up he had not taken to dry-land farming, but had taken to chili peppers. They had become a regular personal crop on his return to Illinois. Antonio was well satisfied that Foster had ample dried to keep him happy until the wagon train reached California. He was also satisfied that James Frazier Reed had just been caught in a trap of his own making.

The widow smiled slyly. "Well, sir, I be a household head."

"One of them will handle your vote," Reed said snidely.

Lavina shook her head until her heavy jowls wobbled like twin lumps of jelly.

"They," she said gently, "be household heads themselves. Each with wife, children, their own wagon, oxen, horses and share of cattle herd. Got the same, if not more, than Eddy here."

"And that's a fact," Jacob growled.

Reed stiffened.

"I will grant that, but must still disallow them from casting a vote."

"Disallow?" Jacob bellowed. "Who has given you the right to grant or disallow anything?"

George knew it was time for him to become peacemaker. Reed was his friend and associate in putting together the Springfield group, although he could be a very different and trying man at times. But everything had been of a very friendly nature all the way from Springfield and they still had a long way to go.

"Now, now, Jacob," he soothed, "someone has to get the meeting started now that Boggs is no longer our captain. Still, James if we are going to consider a wagon as a household, she has a point. She be man and woman, bullwhacker, cook and the whole shebang of that outfit."

"And you be my choice for captain, George Donner," she insisted.

That brought a silence among the hired hands. They had come prepared to fight for their rights. They knew that a captain of a train of this sort had little real power. That on all important issues the whole company would have a voice. But a George Donner might give them more of a voice than a "Sir James."

Reed opened his mouth and then closed it again. A quick mental calculation told him that if Donner decided to become his rival for the captaincy the vote could quickly become five to two. He considered allowing the hired hands the chance to vote, but was not sure his own would fully support him. He even considered ptting off the vote until breakfast time, but logic told him that there was no way he was going to be able to beg, bribe or steal back the Murphy, Foster and Pike votes.

It was a devastating moment for his ego, but he was aristocrat enough to save face.

His head came up proudly. There was a flare about his fine nostrils. His final decision would still keep a woman from having a vote among men.

"As we have no spokesman to run our meeting, I would strongly suggest that we all agree that we designate our wagon train the George Donner party."

The sudden shout of agreement so startled him that he sharply turned and marched back into his wagon. His imperious nature took it as a rebuff. Had he been a trifle less stiff-necked he would have seen that his gesture had added greatly to his prestige as a man and graceful loser.

Margaret was near to tears as he entered the amidship room.

"Horrible, horrible, people," she sobbed.

"It matters not, my dear," he said aloofly. "Hastings will change it all when he takes over as guide at Fort Bridger."

2

DURING THE NIGHT and early morning hours changes came that he had not anticipated.

"The nearer way" had changed some minds after departing for Oregon.

The apple-faced and jolly Peggy Breen had changed the mind of her Patrick. Only two years of their four decades had been spent in America. The brogue was still full-flowered on their lips and with true Irish prodigality they proudly boasted a brood of seven, ranging downward from an already hefty man-boy of fourteen to a baby girl of one.

That his loins had produced six sons to one daughter added to the ruddy freckle-faced, banty-rooster nature of Patrick. All, including mother and father, were as coppery hued as pegged and polished frying pans.

Patrick was in love with life, in love with his wife,

in love with his children, in love with America. America had been very good to him. He still owned his two-year-old farm in Iowa, three wagons for this trip, seven yoke of oxen, a herd of twenty cows, riding horses and Towser.

Even though Paddy Breen possessed as much wealth as a Donner or Reed, his real pride centered around his dog, Towser, and another accomplishment that was no mean feat for an Irishman of that day, or a man of forty. Since coming to America, Paddy had taught himself to read and write, and had taught the English sheepdog how to herd cattle—although on the plains Towser had tried to herd buffalo and had received a gimpy leg for his efforts.

"Howdy! Howdy! Howdy! 'Tis dawn and not a lad or colleen about to see me cavort and dance."

No one could really overlook the return of this Patrick. The light-hearted bachelor had attached himself to the Breens in Iowa and had kept them laughing all across the Great Plains.

From somewhere, no one was sure where, he had secured reindeer sleigh bells for his oxen, a sky-blue canvas covering for his wagon, an enormous box of hand-made toys that delighted children of all ages, and a tail-gate on his wagon that would drop down into a stage with built-in reflectors and candle-holders.

He claimed not to be a showman, although he could do a breakdown or an Irish jig on his little stage after a day of far journeying. His lanky, double-jointed body could make people laugh and forget that the next day would be little different than the one just past.

He was more homely than handsome, but that was his secret weapon in remaining unmarried and yet quite a ladies' man.

Tamsen had once made a comment about the man, and now repeated it:

"Every wagon train should have a Patrick Dolan!"
James Frazier was more caustic as he peeked out
of his wagon flap:

"Damn foreigners have returned."

His comment was pointed more at the other
wagons coming in rather than the Breen and Dolan
arrivals. As they were Irish he could abide them. It
was the "Dutch" that rankled him.

Actually they were not Dutch but German.

Margaret crawled into her husband's compartment
and peeked out beside him, her heart prayerful. Her
prayer was instantly answered.

Johanna Wolfinger sat the first wagon as though not
having lost an instant of sleep throughout the night.
No one was quite sure what age to put upon her and
her husband Wolfgang. They were below forty and
a striking couple with their similar blondeness, statu-
esque poise and haughty demeanor.

Margaret smiled to herself. She enjoyed the woman
for her sparkling conversation and beautiful singing
voice, but knew that Elizabeth was most envious of
Mrs. Wolfinger's rich clothes and jewelry.

In the children's compartment Eliza Williams also
smiled to herself. It had nothing to do with the Wolfingers. It had to do with the following two wagons
which carried the partners, Spitzer and Reinhardt.

The thirty-year-old German men were indeed great
opportunities for her. Each single. Each seemingly
well-to-do. Neither overly handsome, but not unattrac-
tive either. Neither well used to this mode of travel,
they had employed "old man" Hardkoop as teamster,
cook and handyman. Hardkoop was all the sixty year
old man went by, as his full name was too hard to
pronounce and remember. Eliza had several times
used the old man as her entree to the bachelors. He
would thank her kindly for the leftover Reed food,

but as yet had received only smiling nods from Spitzer and Reinhardt.

Eliza had all the way to California to change that. Then she heard a screeching scream that sent her hair ends rising.

James Frazier Reed bolted from his wagon in his nightdress, waving his arms and bellowing like a maniac.

"No! No! We banished you! You brought enough trouble upon this train! Turn back!"

Lewis Keseberg motioned for his teamster, Karl "Dutch Charley" Burger, to halt the two wagons. With deliberate calm the tall German from Westphalia came down out of his saddle.

The six-foot-four-inch blond took off his hat and waited for James Frazier's approach. The handsome Nordic face expressed no emotion, although the piercing blue eyes had caught a glimpse of George Donner's approach as well. Inside the rippling muscular body many emotions were seething. It had been largely through the urging of Reed that he, his wife and children, wagons and teamster had been banished.

At the time he had been called an uneducated farmer and a thief.

Actually, the thirty-two-year-old giant spoke four languages, possessed a degree in theology, and kept the amount of his wealth and where it came from a very private matter.

Other than his reason for banishment, he was not well-liked. He treated people as though they were responsible for some tragedy in his life and he was paying off a grudge against the world.

At this moment, for the sake of his one- and three-year-old children, he would swallow his fierce pride and be humble.

"Mr. Reed, I wish to—"

"Shut up!" James Frazier screeched.

Despite his own considerable height he had to look up to bellow into the emotionless face. That's what riled James Frazier most about the man. He was cold-blooded.

"What's this all about?" George asked.

"What's this all about?" James Frazier mimicked. "You know damn well what it is all about, Donner! Can you forget that he and that damn teamster of his robbed an Indian burial-place and made off with the buffalo robes from the body? I am still scandalized and terrified at that insult to the Sioux. We are still not out of their territory and they do have friends among the other tribes."

"Mr. Donner, may I speak?"

"No, he may not! Out! Out!" James Frazier shouted.

"Speak your mind, son," said George Donner.

James Frazier turned scarlet. If he were captain he would have no interest in what the man said.

"We have done as the council ordered. Dutch Charley and I went back to the Platte and placed the dead warrior again wrapped upon his scaffold. I ask once more for the protection of the train."

"Protection!" James Frazier bawled. "You are going to bring the Sioux right down upon our necks!"

"I think not," he said quietly. "A Sioux war party watched us replace the robes and then rode away. Haven't seen them since."

A single horseman rode right up to them and nearly fell out of his saddle from illness or fatigue.

Donner and Keseberg rushed to help him down.

James Frazier forgot Keseberg for the moment, for here was a new victim to attack.

"What is Boggs doing? Sending back to us all the misfits and sick ones?"

"Sorry, Mr. Donner," Luke Halloran said weakly,

"been keeping it a secret since the Rockies. Mrs. Thornton tried to nurse me, but her man said they could no longer accommodate me. Guess I ain't no good on horseback anymore, either."

George Donner had lost two wives to consumption and was looking at it again.

"Well," James Frazier growled, "you will just have to ride, Mr. Halloran, for we have no ambulance wagons."

"No, but we have charity for strangers in distress," Donner said sternly. The twenty-five-year-old man was so gaunt and weak that George doubted he could even walk. As the new captain he decided to solve three problems at once.

"Lewis, I would be obliged if you would carry Luke to my wagons and ask my woman to prepare a bed for him. No need for your teamster to unhitch as we will be on our way after breakfast. James, I think you'd best get some clothes on. The dew is heavy this morning and I want to start while it is still cool. Boggs said we better not tarry, because we would be reduced to only about ten miles or less a day."

James Frazier did not protest. He had been under other officers and orders he felt were grossly incorrect, but he had obeyed. Obeyed until he could scheme to get the orders changed.

He would save his scheming for Fort Bridger.

For eight days nothing seemed much different than the hard and monotonous days since Independence, except for the land. The upland country was sagebrush scattered and barren. The late July winds were blistering hot in the day and chilling at night.

Buffalo, which none had really liked, was replaced with the meat of the antelope or mountain sheep.

The holiday atmosphere prevailed, made even more

so by the nightly cavorting of Patrick Dolan. Because they were in the period of the longest days of the year he seldom had to burn his candles.

The evenings with their colorful sunsets were a show in themselves. The older people would sit and watch in quiet contentment. They were facing west and that was all that mattered.

The late setting sun gave the children a greater amount of time to run and play and stretch their legs after so many hours within the wagons.

Therein was a strange oddity. The Hastings guide warned of the country being aswarm with rattlesnakes, so concerned parents ordered their children to ride. But after supper, those same parents never gave a single thought about rattlesnakes as the air was filled with happy screaming and yelling youngsters.

Therein was another strange oddity. The "American" family wagons stayed fairly separate on the trail and in the campsites, except for Johanna Wolfinger, who generally rode alongside her friend, Margaret Reed.

But in the evening, except for the Reed children, playtime for the other children broke down all barriers.

Because his children were not in the pack of "little Indians," it mattered not to James Frazier. Because of the fierce afternoon heat, he and Virginia now took their canter in the cool of the evening.

During the day he would ride within the wagon, sipping at a brandy snifter. No scheme ran through his head.

Schemes ran through other heads.

Deliberately, Eliza made an extra apple pie and took it to the Spitzer-Reinhardt wagons. It was accepted with nods and smiles, but no invitation to visit.

The next morning Hardkoop returned the pie tin and offered to sharpen her knives. He had been a cutler by trade his whole life and had more knives, razors, grinding stones and instruments in the bags on his pack mule than he did food. That's why he had taken the job as cook and handyman.

"What is wrong with those two?"

"Nothing's wrong."

"But they never speak."

"Don't know more'n half-dozen English words."

Idiot, Eliza scolded herself. She pondered the problem for a couple of days and then developed a solution. A German man would wish a German-speaking wife.

Phillipine Keseberg troubled over the request. She would not have even let Eliza sit down beside her campfire had not Lewis and Dutch Charley been off hunting. But the thirty-two-year-old woman was starved for friendship. A bride of two years, although Ada was three, she had resigned herself to spinster-hood until the handsome young pastor-trainee had come to the Westphalia community. The Baron and Baroness Keseberg had not wished their promising son to "wear the cloth," especially not with such an outstanding marriage in store for him. Stubborn and determined he thought himself quite capable of handling both, although the heiress Ernestine Grimm was just as stubborn and determined to draw him away from the church once they were married.

For a year he had to train in one little mountain community church after another. In the full vigor of young manhood he found that innkeeper's daughters were the best warming pans for cold winter nights, and Phillipine was one of them.

For nearly two years he fought church and family against an unwanted marriage and child. Church and family won. He railed even louder—and mainly against God. Still stubborn and determined he cursed the church as he left it and cursed his family as he left them—but was wise enough to take along the money his father offered to get him started in America.

He wanted a farm, a large farm, far away from everyone. He wanted to hide Phillipine away so no one would identify her as his wife, and thus forbade her to associate with anyone on the wagon train.

"I am with little English, myself," she said shyly. "I am most sorry."

Eliza leaned closer. There was a deep bruise mark above the right eye of the pinched little face.

"Did you hurt yourself?"

Phillipine blanched as though not knowing how to answer.

"Yes," she stammered. "Accident. Please, I go look in on my babies."

"And the lessons?"

She started to quickly refuse and hesitated. So much was stored up inside of her—things that only another woman would understand. If she did not talk it out soon she knew she was going to lose her mind.

"Maybe . . . sometime . . . only . . . only when my husband away."

She darted up the back steps of the wagon and was gone.

For the moment Eliza accepted the accident story. Her mind was on another matter. If such a plain, simple, shy creature could capture the manly likes of Lewis Keseberg for a husband, then she shouldn't feel she was setting her sights too high in aiming for one of the bachelors.

Another in the wagon train was scheming, but in a more child-like vein. Virginia's tongue was having no effect on Solomon. He just ignored her all the more. Besides, he just couldn't pull himself out of his own gloomy mood to notice much of anything. When he heard the wagons returning he was just sure in his heart that one of them would carry Ellen Boggs. It hadn't.

To make him notice her, Virginia resorted to trying to make him jealous. When no one was watching but Solomon she would flirt outrageously with John Breen. The red-headed, freckle-faced strapping youth was perhaps her worst choice. He may have been fourteen in age, but hardly in mind or body. Since then he had had the urging of a man, and in four years since had had many opportunities to put those urgings to experience.

He hid his knowledge behind a most innocent boyish mask and was quietly wise. The little flirt was too often with her stepfather. John would just bide his time until he could catch her all alone.

In the meantime he could debate on whether he wanted to make "good" friends with Elitha Donner or Mary Murphy.

"Rider coming! Rider coming!"

They were less than two miles from Fort Bridger. James Frazier and Virginia had ridden on ahead, dressed as though the military personnel at the fort would be greeting them in full dress parade.

Nor was this a messenger from the fort. The rider was coming on their tail from the east. Nor did he seem in any hurry to catch up with them. His horse just seemed to lope easily along as though riding the crest of the rising heat waves.

Because he thought it was his responsibility as captain to greet any such stranger George Donner turned his horse and rode back along the train.

Several times during those eight days he had counted his blessings, and they had been intoned in Jacob's dinner prayers. The train had run most smoothly, with only a minor thing here or there that could wait for repair at the fort. Keseberg and Reed had stayed as far apart as a cobra and a mongoose.

The children had been most mindful, including his three youngest and there had not been a single quarrel of any nature.

He had even come to respect the many skills of William Eddy and Lavina Murphy. They each had a knack for forgetting the comforts of civilization and trying to adapt to this more natural environment.

For a moment he was a very contented man.

"Howdy-do!"

The stranger rode with one leg thrown back up over the saddle horn and his lanky body totally relaxed. His skin was so near the shade of his buckskins that it was hard to see a separation point. Perched jauntily on the back of a mass of sandy curls was an otter skin cap in the same style that George had worn as a boy in Kentucky made out of coon skins. Below it was a square face that came into a cleft chin. Except for a scraggly mustache the face was clean-shaven and openly friendly. Beneath craggy, sandy eyebrows were eyes so softly brown that they gave the impression that the man was very comfortable with himself and life in general.

George lifted his hat in greeting. "Welcome. I am George Donner, captain of this train."

"Pleastahmeecha," the man grinned, thrusting out a beefy paw. "Name's Thornburg. Doolittle Thornburg. Mos' call me Thorny. Goin' to the fort?"

"Yes, we are, Mr. Thornburg."

"You'll see it from the next rise. Ain't far now."

"You've been there before?"

"Las' week."

"But you were coming from the east."

The man chuckled drily. "Mountain men and trappers don't travel in straight lines, sir."

George Donner listened carefully. His ear had

picked up something very strange. The man seemed to purposely give his voice a very slow, country drawl, although there was a faint accent underneath. The accent had been most polished and very British.

"And you have furs to trade at the fort?"

"Yep. Ain't got many, though. Summer coats on critters ain't near as good as fall and winter coats."

In truth, Doolittle Thornburg had no furs on his pack horse. He was lucky to have the fur on his head and scalp. His luck of late had been miserable, as though his seven years of good luck had been used up and the reversal was beginning to take place. For seven years, since jumping ship in New Orleans, he had done right nicely trapping in the Arapahoe and Sioux territories. He had only wanted pelts, not land, so was quite welcome in every village visited. Then his tastes began to expand. In the next few years he used his "golden lance" on too many Sioux and Arapahoe maidens, the last being the fourteen year old third wife of a chief, who he had taken by force.

That had been in June. He had been a hunted man, pursued by the chief's warriors ever since. He had thought just to let things cool down and they would forget it all. But from an Indian scout at Fort Bridger he learned that the young wife had killed herself by jumping off a cliff. They would never forget Doolittle Thornburg.

For a month he stayed at the fort trying to get any manner of job with the departing Hastings train. The Indian scouts, who cursed his brutal act, made sure he was known as a bad omen.

His only choice, as he saw it was to try to sneak back over the Rockies to different trapping grounds.

He had seen the Donner Party heading west, but they had not observed him. Then, a half day later he saw the Sioux war party, and made sure that they did not see him. Slowly and cautiously he made it back to the Donner train and what protection it might afford him until once again at the fort.

Logically, he assumed the Sioux were after him. It was the same party that had watched Lewis and Dutch Charley return the buffalo robe. For the moment the warriors had been pleased, for their brother could ride the hunting trails of *Seyan* with all his personal possessions.

Then they became highly suspicious. No white man returned, he only took. What greater thing than a buffalo robe did they wish to take? The war party followed the Keseberg wagons back to the Little Sandy.

There the Reed wagon made their suspicions grow even more. Such a wagon could carry off a great store of treasure, and even though they were greatly outnumbered they continued to follow.

For them it was a rather easy journey. These white men were most wasteful. Each day they would leave behind the best part of their antelope hunt: the entrails, the brains, the hides—and articles that someone would forget to repack each morning.

They didn't care how long the trailing went on, they were having great benefits.

"But . . . but . . ." Donner stammered, making the rise. "Where is the fort?"

"That's it," Thornburg said.

"But where is the stockade and the military buildings?"

"Never's been any. Bridger just calls it a fort to make his place sound more impressive. Only thing that will impress you here is his sky-high prices. Unless you go north to Fort Hall, to get back on the Oregon Trail, or go right straight down to the Pacific, there isn't another thing in between."

Donner was bitterly disappointed, as though he had been cruelly duped by the Hastings guide. He had expected a fort, like Laramie, with a blacksmith shop, a trading post and a military officer to tell them of the Indian situation.

All he saw in the valley were two long squat log cabins joined by a horse corral. Where the river broke into channels a couple of hundred oxen grazed.

A short distance from the log cabins sat an Indian tepee. Well, Donner mused on a wry thought, at least the children will get to see their first Indian.

They did, but not in the tepee. The tepee was the blacksmith shop. It had been easier to put up than another log cabin and had cost Bridger only a gallon of his bad whiskey.

Donner's next disappointment was more serious. He had fully expected to see sixty to eighty wagons preparing to leave with Hastings. He saw four in the whole valley, and one was going nowhere for a long time.

"Where is Hastings?" He asked more of himself than of Thornburg.

"Left already."

"But what of us?"

Doolittle opened his mouth and immediately shut it. He was well aware that Hastings had left directions for any who wished to follow him, but he was not about to have the Indian Scouts ruin his chances again. He would just bide his time until he could worm his way into the party. Better to go forward to California than eastward to a scalping.

The Reed wagon passed to roll gently down into the valley and he could not help but gawk. The flaps were thrown back to give a breath of air to the entire amidships room. Margaret reclined on the chaise longue in a flowing silk afternoon dress.

Seated at the table were Johanna Wolfinger and Elizabeth Donner. Before them was a full silver tea service and a tray of finger sandwiches.

On a hassock next to his mother sat nine-year-old Young George Donner, gently pulling on a rope that activated a peacock fan that stirred the air over the chaise and table. George was more prone to sit and listen to ladies' gossip than to play with children his own age.

Serving them, in afternoon uniform of sparkling white, from dust cap to high button shoes, was Eliza. The tufts of black hair peeking from beneath the cap, eyebrows and eyes made quite a sharp contrast against the uniform.

"Lordamercy!" Thornburg gasped, and wasn't sure if it was because of her breathtaking beauty or all that luxury here in the uplands. A scene like this he had not seen since leaving England, and there only because his mother was a maid to Lady Crandell.

A woman such as the maid he had not seen since New Orleans, if even there he had seen one to match her loveliness.

His gasped comment had made Eliza look up. When their eyes met, Doolittle winked. She gave him a cold stare, a saucy flip of her head and continued pouring tea.

But before the wagon was too far beyond she peeked back up through her eyelashes. Never before had she seen a man in buckskins—and buckskins that molded his body so well that it left little doubt as to what his muscular frame would look like without them. There was no doubt that he was one of the most spectacular-looking men she had ever beheld.

But she had knowledge of the men who wore buckskins, if not the opportunity to see one.

James Frazier Reed had lectured them all before leaving Springfield, right from Hastings' guide.

Mountain men and trappers were dirty, uncouth, lice-ridden old men who couldn't be trusted as guides. Their buckskins never came off, even when they were in a tepee with a squaw (He quickly skipped over the reason they might be in the tepee in the first place). Only bought furs and robes at trading posts. Mountain men cheated you blind and wasted the money on bad whiskey. They are penniless wanderers, little better than the Injuns.

Knowing that most mountain men could not read, Hastings had never feared of them learning of his attack. Nor was it really personal. He had found the "nearer way" and was trying to be a good businessman and keep all of the guide business for himself or his own hired guides. Jim Bridger and his men had done the same for several years in bringing people out from Independence.

But his writings and what Eliza saw didn't quite jibe. Still, one phrase stuck in her mind—"penniless wanderers." If her Ma and Pa had not married poor then she and Baylis would not be in America working off their debts.

No, a man could be molded in the image of a Greek God, which this one nearly was, and she would turn away if he was "marriage poor."

As they began to make camp, Doolittle Thornburg didn't think any of them "marriage poor." Even the Murphy clan was prosperous in his eyes. He had seen many a wagon train come west, but nothing to equal this.

But when he saw the Donner and the Reeds sit down for dinner, he was then fully determined that he had to join this train, one way or another. There had to be some "real" money to be made off of this outfit.

James Frazier felt as out-of-place as he looked. His elaborate and gaily colored costume did not match his mood.

"The man should be shot," Margaret said to soothe him.

"The man had his reasons, mother," Virginia spoke right up.

Margaret gave her a scathing look that was to still her to silence. For once Virginia would not be daunted. She had been in on the conversation and had seen the logic of it, even if her stepfather had not.

"Father, make her see reason. The man had sixty-six wagons and the season is getting late."

"Do not intrude, Virginia," Margaret barked.

"She does not intrude," James Frazier said calmly. "She was there and heard all from Bridger."

"And I see no problem," Virginia said haughtily. "He said that the route is three hundred and fifty to four hundred miles shorter. We will have no bad canyons to cross and the going will be smooth, hard and level."

"But husband," Margaret protested, as though he had given the information, "we are still a small group. Can we protect ourselves against Indians?"

He barely whispered. "Bridger claims we will have no danger from the Piutes and Diggers in the area."

"Well," Margaret was quick to change sides, "wherein then is the problem?"

Virginia smiled to herself. "Mr. Bridger wishes us all to join the Hastings train, plus some people who have straggled down from Fort Hall."

"More low life," James Frazier gruffed. "More of the same sort we have been stuck with for a hundred miles."

"I would hardly call Johanna low life," Margaret sniffed. "Can't the "better" families just leave on their own?"

Virginia giggled. Those were very nearly the same words her stepfather had used and received a severe tongue lashing in return for. People were people to Jim Bridges, as long as they could pay his prices.

"The whole matter, Margaret," James Frazier said, with a note of defeat in his voice, "is being taken up by Mr. Bridger with the train captain."

All of James Frazier's scheming had been for naught. Again, he would have to wait until they joined up with Hastings to make his voice heard.

George Donner found Bridger and his partner Vasquez to be charming and accommodating gentlemen, and the fort, despite its ramshackle exterior, to possess just as many services for the traveler as Laramie.

"Recruited oxen? I am sorry, sir, but I do not understand."

Bridger pointed toward the pastured oxen. "Once they were broken-down animals coming down off the South Pass. Rest and good grass have restored them. Turn in your broken-down animals and for a cash consideration you leave with fresh teams."

It was a suggestion well taken, as were the excellent ones made by the blacksmith. To accomplish all the needed repairs would take him four days.

George Donner felt it was time well spent, although James Frazier silently cursed the further delay.

It was a welcome respite. Four whole days without a wagon moving beneath them. Four whole days for the herds to graze at will. Four whole days for wagon tires to be reset, bedding aired, stores refurbished and a team to be replaced.

One of the waiting party had decided that east was a better direction than west and hired a Donner teamster away at a higher price. The only problem being that Hiram Miller didn't tell George Donner he was leaving.

Before Doolittle Thornburg got wind of it, Donner had already hired a Bridger recommendation. Jean Baptiste Trubode was the twenty-three-year-old offspring of a French trapper and a Mexican mother. His Mexican was so fluent that it made Antonio think that more Indian blood flowed in his veins than Spanish.

George Donner's next problem was the McCutchen family.

William "Mac" McCutchen was the owner of the wagon that was going nowhere. It was amazing that the broken down wagon had made it this far.

Donner was a compassionate man, but the six-foot-six man of powerful proportions had a picturesque vocabulary that turned even Donner's patient ears red.

"I can only suggest, Mac, that you approach Lavina Murphy. She's a widow woman with three wagons keeping her jumping. As there's just you and your wife and baby, she might consider transport in exchange for teamster help."

Lavina Murphy was willing. As Amanda McCutchen was still nursing little Harriet, she could see to all the children. Lavina's daughters then could take over all the cooking and housekeeping chores.

Amazingly, Mac was able to figure a way of getting all his goods and stores onto the already overflowing Murphy wagons.

The MacDuff party was easier to handle. Mary Florence McDuff had come down from the Red River Colony of Manitoba with two wagons and an ailing husband. Pioneer life was nothing new to the flaming red-haired beauty of twenty-eight. Proud to be a relative of Lord Selkirk, she still maintained the aristocratic demeanor although secretly penniless.

There was a determination in the proud, high-cheekboned face and deep sparkle to the hazel-green eyes that George Donner had liked at once.

"We shall be no burden, Mr. Donner. Even though

my Canadian teamsters have departed, I have acquired the services of two unattached travelers. May I present Charles Tyler Stanton of Chicago who was on horseback and James Smith who was afoot."

Charles Stanton, diminutive in stature, stuck out a work-hardened hand for Donner to shake. At thirty-five he seemed hardly the emigrant type, and in some respects wasn't. He had trained himself in geology and botany, and had been slowly travelling west to practice these fields. A shrunken belly, and a few close scrapes with Indians had convinced him that a wagon train was his best bet.

James Smith smiled sheepishly at Donner. Donner smiled slyly back at the stocky twenty-five-year-old. Smith had been a Reed teamster out of Independence until he had been fired over a matter George felt was most petty. In his charitable way he had earlier secured him a position with Governor Boggs.

"Didn't work, sir," he mumbled. "Miss Ellen Boggs tried to get me to steal horses to bring her back down to your nephew Solomon. When I told her I couldn't be doing no such she said some mighty nasty things against me and got me kicked out on foot."

George Donner prided himself on knowing when a man was telling him a lie. Smith's open, homely face was truthful.

"I am glad that you can be of service to Mrs. Mac-Duff, James. But I would ask of you two favors, please. Keep the story of Miss Ellen to yourself. I do not want that love-sick puppy running off after the Boggs party. And . . . avoid Mr. Reed, if you can. He has just replaced two yoke of oxen that he still maintains you caused to die by letting them drink bad water."

Smith nodded, but smarted over the reminder. They had not even been the oxen he had been bullwhacking, they were two of the extras that Milt Elliott had teamed for the big wagon. Strangely, Milford Milton

Elliott had remained most silent on the whole matter.

Smith didn't rightly want to see either man.

But he had been seen by Milt Elliott, who went on the run for James Frazier Reed.

His face was suddenly bleak.

"I thought we had settled that matter."

"You know the saying about bad pennies, Mr. Reed."

"Milt, we've been together a long time. You'll go back to making furniture again once we get settled. You know I appreciated you taking those oxen to the stagnant pond, even if you did take the wrong two. No more mistakes, Milt. It may have been accidental him coming across me that day . . . but . . . but I can't let him get close to Virginia or my wife." He stopped, glancing warily at the barrel-chested young man.

"What do you wish?" he asked ominously.

Reed pondered. James Smith had not thrown the day in his face when he had been fired. Perhaps it had been an accident and the man had seen nothing.

Up to that point it had been one of the most thrilling and exciting days for him. It was a glorious June day. Their canter along the cottonwood lined North Platte had reminded him of the south. At a wide bend in the river was a tree-shaded natural pool. It was so pastoral a setting that he had paid no heed to the grazing and watering oxen along the bank.

When Virginia asked permission to swim he considered the smooth-running, shallow water safe enough and took the horses farther along to give her privacy. But once they were shackled for grazing his mind became a torture chamber of thoughts he was constantly trying to push away.

She had been but a child of four when he married Margaret. Her beauty had captivated him then, but he considered it step-fatherly love. But with each passing year he had placed her on a higher and higher shrine of adoration and had fought more and more against his desires.

At that moment, he told himself, that he wished only one small thing—a little peek to see what manner of woman she was developing into.

But he had been unable to tear his eyes away as the last garment came off and she prepared to step into the water. She was a poolside nymph with long, creamy legs, so delicate a waist and youthful breasts so round and firm that it made his throat go dry.

For uncounted minutes he watched her gracefully swim about and bathe. He was hardly aware of how great his desire had become or that he had actually unleashed himself. He was caught up in a fantasy.

Then the bubble burst. A man came crashing through the underbrush calling for the oxen. For a moment he had stared at Smith without recognizing him. Then Reed had sheepishly realized he still held himself within his hand.

He had quickly given the reasonable excuse of being there to relieve himself. It was accepted with a shrug and Smith moved on to round up the oxen.

At the sound of Smith's approach, Virginia had dived beneath the water and come up under an overhanging branch. After Smith's departure she had swum back and prepared to clothe herself.

Their eyes had met and locked. Never had she seen such fear and confusion, nor did she understand it.

He had turned and fled back to the horses, so guilt-ridden that he could hardly think. Oddly, all that would cross his mind was the name Milt Elliott.

Milt would know how to handle the problem. Milt had handled the problem for him before—many times.

There had always been young girls working in Reed's furniture factory as polishers who would fall madly for Reed's virile good looks. Milt could always arrange a quiet place for them to meet the boss. He could also quietly arrange for them to be fired when they became too demanding or indiscreet.

But this was different. Would Milt understand the problem?

Milt understood. He understood everything about James Frazier Reed and thought the man could do no wrong. He would do anything in the world for him.

"What do I wish?" Reed slowly repeated the man's question. "For the moment, Milt, let's just keep our eyes and ears open. One false move on his part and then we will have to figure out a way to silence him."

He nodded, but as he turned away his face was a study in joy. Every little favor he did for James Frazier Reed made him a richer man.

"Hello, I am Tamsen Donner. My husband tells me that you have an ill husband, Mrs. MacDuff. Can I be of any help?"

"How kind of you," she smiled warmly, "and shall we make it Mary Florence, Tamsen? We shall be together for a few weeks."

"As you wish. Have you been here long?"

"Nearly two weeks. There was a Dr. Gooding in the Hastings party and he thought my Harlan a little too ill to depart with them, but he is most improved."

"That is good news. My husband says you're from Canada. This must be quite a change."

Mary Florence laughed gaily. "Most have the impression, Tamsen, that we are snow and ice the year around. It is marvelous green country and most dear to me. But a good wife goes where a husband wishes to lead."

Tamsen could well understand that statement. "At least you do not have a parcel of children to drag behind."

Mary Florence smiled a little sadly. "They'll come in time. We want to be well settled before starting a family. My husband carries with him a land grant from the Mexican government. He thought it best to take advantage of it before this war ruined his chances. Oh, here comes the best medicine in the world for him."

Tamsen turned to follow her gaze and saw nothing but four of Bridger's Indian servants coming down the trail with large sacks on their backs.

Despite herself Tamsen began to giggle. "Forgive me. It is just that my children have waited so long to see these so-called savage Indians and Mr. Bridger's are certainly not. What medicine are they carrying?"

This made Mary Florence laugh. "Tamsen, it is nothing more than chunks of glacier ice from the mountains nearby. He charges dearly for it, but it reduces Harlan's fever."

"Well, I never," Tamsen gasped. "Ice in the dead middle of summer."

Mary Florence frowned. "End of July, Tamsen. I know mountains—and fall comes early. I'm glad we depart in the morning."

Tamsen started. That was news to her. Where had the four days vanished? It seemed like just yesterday that she had heard from George about the ill Mr. MacDuff. Well, she could understand how a patient consumed time. Luke Halloran tried not to be a bother, but she had her hands full nursing him.

And who else but she could inventory the supplies with Noah? Imagine $20 for a barrel of coarse milled Mexican flour. She had paid $4 a barrel in Independence for rich brown whole wheat.

Then the Solomon problem had taken quite a bit of time. Time she had not discussed with her husband, and perhaps should have.

Solomon was no dummy. He pinned Smith down on his return like a rabbitskin being pegged up to dry. He was already packed to leave and catch up with the

Boggs wagon train, but made a fatal mistake. He could not leave without saying goodbye to Tamsen.

Calmly she sat and listened to the reasons why he had to rush off after Ellen Boggs.

At teaching from a textbook, she was an expert, at teaching from experience she was a trifle shy. She was a mother of all young girls, but something prompted her to say:

"It is lust, Sol."

"What is lust?"

Tamsen relaxed. She was at least starting off with the stronger hand of knowledge—or so she hoped.

She was still convinced that his interest in Ellen was mainly just youthful lust and not love.

Then she giggled again as the Indian dropped an ice sack by the MacDuff wagon and Mary Florence began to search around in a thin leather pouch for coins.

"I should get some of that to cool down a young man in our wagons. Again, may I be of help to you?"

"I thank you, but no," Mary Florence smiled. "Harlan is a bear when he is ill, and I wouldn't subject a stranger to his bad temper. But, Tamsen, thank you for your friendliness. It is rather lonely being the only woman on the trail for two months coming from Manitoba. I look forward to the rest of the journey."

"As do I," Tamsen smiled and turned away. She was a very observing woman. It seemed an inordinately large sack of glacier ice, and the leather money pouch seemed exceptionally thin. She had expected to find another regal Margaret with the woman's noble background. She had found a beautiful, warm and yet somewhat troubled young woman. Financial troubles only?

But this was a husband and wife, quite alone, and with him quite ill. Well, she could shepherd them as well, if need be.

Mary Florence allowed Charles Stanton to heft the ice bag up onto the back of the wagon and then sent him on other errands.

With the flap down a certain hardness entered her face. She pulled the sack back to the middle of the wagon and opened it.

Harlan MacDuff lay still and white upon the wooden bunk attached to the wagon side.

She looked down at him, her face taut and still.

"Never should have left," she whispered, placing chunks of ice on either side of his gaunt frame. "And now we can't go back."

"It's almost funny, Harlan. You are the one who growled and complained so about the wintry ice and snow. And now it's the only thing that's keeping you . . . alive."

He didn't respond or move.

From the sack she took chunks to pack along the inside and outside of his legs and then covered his body with layers upon layers of quilts to hold in the coolness.

"Did you hear me lie to her?" she laughed. "It was almost as convincing as when you first told me the tale. I do think that she believed as I once did. Then, you always were one who could spin a tall tale."

She drew the stool close and sat down. She put out a thin hand and stroked the hair back off his forehead.

"Now comes the tallest tale of your whole career, Harlan. You have lied, cheated, gambled and womanized on me for the last time. You owe me now. Hastings wouldn't take us because the doctor said you were a dying man."

"Well, you are dead, Harlan. You died this morning, but I am determined to keep you alive in the eyes of others until I am out of this godforsaken place. Oh, you are an unforgivable bastard! You owe me this much for an empty jewel case, a money chest that doesn't even rattle and a family that I forsook for your love. Five years of marriage to you has taught me much, Harlan. I can survive. Oh, God yes, I am going to survive! You pulled me down into your gutter and I was hopeful enough that this move was a climb back up. Well, I will climb alone. I will not crawl back to my family and let them remind me of what you became. You will play the part of a living, breathing man—and your corpse will serve me as the live Harlan never did."

3

GEORGE DONNER WAS EXALTED. He had been exalted before in his sixty-two years, but never like this. Moving out of Fort Bridger were twenty fully repaired wagons, a contingent of seventy-four well-rested men, women and children, with herds of lowing cattle and ample recruited oxen for each yoke.

They moved smartly according to the train plan he had commanded. He was beginning to feel that he was indeed a seasoned train captain. The four-day layover in Fort Bridger still gave them time to catch Hastings.

Others had felt the four days had been too short:

John Breen had not been able to catch Virginia alone.

Milt Elliott had wanted to settle the James Smith matter before leaving.

Eliza had wished at least one German lesson and had received none.

Solomon Hook wanted a few more days to determine if he should run away or not.

Margaret, Elizabeth and Johanna wanted a few more days without moving, although they rode in the greatest comfort.

Doolittle Thornburg wanted nothing more than to go with them, but Bridger's Indian Scouts had kept a watchful eye on his every move. He had purposely not made contact with a single soul in the train, although he had made some mental notes from a distance. Eliza was beautiful, unmarried, and trying to win the favor of the German bachelors.

Tamsen was beautiful, though older, married, but a soft touch if he had to play that game.

These two were the only women in the Donner-Reed train really interested him. As far as work went it all looked quite bleak for Thornburg.

Bridger had been unable to get a single Indian scout to go with the party because they smelled death among the group. Doolittle pegged it to be Harlan MacDuff, a sick man whose wife was quite a looker. A woman like that was going to need more of a man on the trail than her two misfit teamsters.

So, with a jaunty air, he headed back east as the train took off toward the southwest. No one watched him, nor observed his deception. For his eastward journey was really a slow circling back toward the Wasatch and the Donner-Reed wagons. He was in no hurry. He wanted to make sure his tracks were not being followed by anyone.

Those of the Donner-Reed party who had been awestruck at their first sighting of mountains at the Continental Divide, now stood in fear of this rough country with its deep ravines and peaked granite mountains—and no guide to tell them what the next turning might bring.

"Brake, Tamsen, brake!" Noah James hollered, slic-the bullwhip over the oxen heads to get them to do the same.

What had appeared as a gently rolling tundra was in fact a fifteen percent drop of nearly a thousand feet. A quarter of the way down the oxen had begun to snort and their sleepy eyes flared with fright. The wagon was beginning to push them.

Tamsen pulled on the brake lever until she felt either it or her arms would break. But the momentum built up by the wheels would not brake. They continued to turn and grind into the heavy leather brake strips, heating and cooking the hide until it sent up clouds of blue-black smoke.

"It's doing no good!" she screamed.

"Hold it anyway!" he called back, now standing directly in front of the team and pushing backwards on the center of the yoke.

"I can't do it alone!" she cried, feeling that truthfulness was better than bravery at that moment.

The other five Donner wagons were finding they couldn't do it alone either. The teamsters were pulling them out of line and beginning to run upon a parallel course. Now they didn't even have the simple ruts made by the Hastings wagons to follow. Rocks and dead stumps became a peril. As though they were propelled by some form of engine they all put up a plume of smoke. The brake shoes would not last for the entire descent—instead of slithering and bouncing along they would plummet over the oxen to disaster.

"Hold back the rest!" George bellowed. "And send every rider down on the double."

Herds were forgotten and most of the men on horseback galloped down the dangerous hillside. Most, because James Frazier motioned for his men to sit tight, and the Keseberg and Murphy wagons were oddly heading northwest along the crest of the hill.

A wagon at a time they could have easily handled. Six at one time was quite a task.

Ropes were secured to the backs of the wagons and men and horses dug in to brake them down, slowly making the hillside look like a plowed field. Sticks, twigs and even rocks were forced into where the brakeshoes were burning out.

They concentrated first on the wagons bearing the women and children. Once they were down to a safe speed they were taken off to walk and lighten the load.

Now other men could jump from horseback and apply muscle and shoulder to bring the huge back wheels to enough of a stop so that the spokes could be lashed to the sidearms of the wagon bed. Still the wagons kept moving down the grade, some of the rope lashing snapping, and some of the spokes cracking.

Blankets were brought out to hood the heads of the oxen. In rebellion they began to lock their powerful legs and refuse to move. The weight of the wagons kept pushing them forward, but they bristled and fought back. Slowly, the entire line was brought to a stop.

There had to be a better way to lock the rear wheels for the other wagons yet to descend, but for these six they would have to make do with rope lashings until they had eased them down into the riverbed bottom.

"Take them down one at a time," George advised. "I want no mishaps. Jacob, you take charge. I'll go back up to see that the others are better prepared."

It was a torturous climb back up for his horse. The beast was smarter than man and kept trying to turn to the left or right. George stubbornly held the reins tight to force the animal forward. When the horse stumbled and nearly threw him, he stopped to let it rest a moment.

He, too, needed a moment of rest. As agile as he was at sixty-two, his heart was nearly thumping out of his chest and his brow was covered with salty sweat. He had just seen his entire family almost smashed into oblivion.

He looked down to check on their progress. It was going slowly, but safely. The men had to urge the hooded beasts to take forward steps, but this was wise. The oxen would step and plant, step and plant, keeping the weight of the wagons from overpowering them and causing the locked wheels to slide along rather than roll.

Then he looked up to the crest. To his disgust everyone in the Reed entourage just stood about watching the action below as though it were a great sideshow.

Then movement on his left caught his eye. He had not worried about the departing Keseberg and Murphy wagons at the time, because the safety of his family was all he could think upon. But now he watched them with growing curiosity as they switched back and forth on the side of the mountain.

Slow and tedious, he thought, but began to apply the same principle for the rest of his climb. Now the horse did not balk, for it had wished to climb this way by instinct all along.

It had not been instinct which made Lewis Keseberg suggest this method of decent to Mac McCutchen. In his youth he had traversed the Alps on wooden slated skis in the same fashion.

"Thank you for your help," George said sarcastically when he reached the Reed wagons. "We are supposed to be a train, you know."

"My men were busy," James Frazier Reed shrugged.

George turned to the others, controlling his temper.

"Follow the lead of Keseberg. Keep in his track and make the same turnings. It may be longer and slower, but it seems a lot safer."

"I advise against it," James Frazier declared. "It is not the way Hastings went."

"Damnation!" George growled. "I am beginning to wonder if your wonderful guide ever explored this route or Bridger ever saw it. Smooth and hard and level, my horse's hind-end! You haven't been on that hillside, Reed, so don't argue with me about its incline. I say we follow the lead of Keseberg."

"Not my wagons," Reed insisted haughtily. "I will be the judge of how best to get them into the canyon. I divorce myself from this train."

George Donner knew he had that right, even though the man was being stubbornly wrong.

"As you wish, James. I would just advise that you have the women and children walk down. It's rough enough on a regular wagon, let alone your monster."

James Frazier took it as a personal insult.

"They ride," he snarled, and turned to give orders on the preparation of his two supply wagons.

"Johanna," Wolfinger barked at his wife, "you come wid me!" He winked at George. "We go slow down."

Without comment, she followed her husband to where the other wagons were waiting, as did the Breens, MacDuff, Spitzer and Reinhardt parties.

Elizabeth Donner turned away from Margaret and fluttered her eyelids at George.

"What must I do, dear, dear George?"

"Walk," he said curtly and turned his horse about to go help the wagons get started.

"Well, I never," Elizabeth gasped, her hand flying to her throat.

"Never mind," Margaret Reed soothed, "come right

on back and ride with me. I have no intention of walking a single step on this journey."

"Oh, Margaret, I am so embarrassed. George was such a sweet and kind and considerate man until he married Tamsen. She has just changed him into such an unspeakable thing."

Milt Elliott had watched the Donner wagons and figured out their problem.

"Gotta brake right from the top, Mr. Reed. To save our brake shoes I got two men cutting down aspen saplings to stick right through both back wheels and secure them tight."

"Try it with the two supply wagons first, Milt."

The other wagons were in their first turning when the Reed wagons were ready to descend. Far below the Keseberg group were back on a northwest course; and even farther below the Donner wagons were inching straight downward.

Milt Elliott began chuckling to himself a quarter of the way down. "What was their problem? This is easy."

He and Walter Herron had not hooded the oxen, as they thought that foolish. The heavily braked back wheels were all that they needed, making deep furrows in their skid and holding them back.

But they were two teamsters alone without riders constantly checking the wagon. James Frazier had held back his herders and other teamsters to prepare his personal wagon.

The wagons skidded down the hillside, but the back wheels were constantly being forced against their natural design to turn. They strained against the sapling through their spokes, putting enormous pressure on the rope lashings. The hemp fibers began to stretch and snap one by one. Each strand loosened slowly gave more play to the four-inch-thick sapling.

Being green timber it could take a great deal of give and take without giving any warning to the driver.

A following horseman would have been able to see beneath the Herron driven wagon that the sapling began to look like an Indian bow being strung, but there were none and they were too far along for it to be noticed from the top of the hill.

It split like the crack of rifle fire, followed by little explosions as it ate out the fourteen spokes of the right wheel in rapid order.

Before Walt Herron could think, the axle assembly dug into the turf and spun the wagon parallel with the downward slope. The unknowing oxen continued to pull forward, forcing the tongue to a hard right angle.

With a scream he jumped free just as the left wheel spokes began to shatter.

The wagon quivered in place for a second before slowly rolling over onto its side, with a sound like dozens of eggs being crushed.

The oxen strained against the unusual motion, but the wagon had the downhill grade to help it roll again and again and again: tossing the ton-heavy animals about as though they were weightless. The mountainside echoed with their death cries as the hillside became strewn with the wagon contents, and still it rolled down until it lay in a tangled mass of ruin.

Milt Elliott reined and reined on the oxen to prevent a similar fate. His oxen did not respond. The death cries from their fellow beasts had unnerved them. Even if it was to destruction, they were trying to race.

Fearful sweat broke out on his brow as he heard his own sapling brake give four loud explosions. From the high perch he could not look back to see that it had broken in such a manner to cause no harm to the spokes, but was allowing the rear wheels to turn at the speed the weight of the wagon and the angle of the down hill slope demanded. In his fright he never once thought to reach over and pull back on the brake lever.

Faster and faster the wagon began to career down the hillside, until his own oxen began to bellow against the pressure against their pounding legs.

To those below it sounded like the fatal approach of an avalanche.

"Jesus!" Jacob gasped. "To horse! To horse! Head off that damn idiot or wreck him before he plows right through us all!"

The horsemen had more trouble getting back up to the wagon than the wagon did in getting to them. Before they had had three-quarters of the mountainside to bring the Donner wagons under control. Now it was less than a quarter.

Arrogantly, Milt Elliott kept screaming at the riders who were trying to help him:

"Don't wreck it! Don't wreck it! Move your damn wagons out of the way!"

Jacob Donner was trying to do just that, but he did not want runaways on his hands, either. At slow angles he was trying to fan out the six wagons and provide several alleys for Elliott to race through.

Oxen had proven to be excellent hauling beasts for the westward movement because they were by nature following beasts. Short-sighted, they reacted to movement ahead. Unfortunately none in the Donner party trying to head them off were aware of the fact. Horses that darted in front of them to ward them off only caused them to grow confused as to whom to follow. The oxen were nearly stumbling over themselves in trying to go left and right and forward.

James Smith, who had been among the first to answer George Donner's summons, rode up alongside John Denton.

"They've gone crazy!" he bellowed, brandishing his hunting knife. "Only way to stop them! You left and I right!"

The Englishman turned pale. He had never killed a thing in his life, let alone anything so large.

"Why not shoot them?" he hollered back.

"No good," came back the answer, "they would collapse and roll the wagon down like the other."

Denton didn't understand, but he would follow Smith's example. He almost changed his mind when he saw the young man jump from his horse and onto the back of the oxen. That seemed the most dangerous part of all.

For Smith the dangerous part was just starting. He had to straddle the wide-shouldered beast just behind the hump, secure a left hand hold in the coarse fur and lean over to get an angle to plunge the knife into the rib-cage and try to reach the heart.

On his second plunge he saw that Denton had gained the courage to follow his lead, but before either could plunge again they came under attack from a different quarter.

The bullwhip began to lash at their backs and arms.

"Get off! Get off!" Milt screeched, whipping the bull hide back and forth like a maniac. "These are the property of James Frazier Reed!"

"Devil take him!" Smith screamed, without looking back and began plunging again. All he got as a reward was a sticky arm and another stinging bite across his back.

But between his legs he could feel a tremor. The quivering was becoming like an earthquake and the beasts were slowing.

"Do it! Do it now," he shouted at Denton, and leaned over for another plunge.

The whiplashes made John Denton want to give

up at once, but he leaned over and began to stab the beast.

Milt Elliot was near insane with hatred. He saw it only as a vengeful act on the part of James Smith. He forgot the reins and stood to take the whip in both hands to give it the full force of his crack.

He did not hear the fierce Mexican yell or the whine of the rope slicing the air. The lariat came down about his arms and closed tightly. A second later he was airborne off the wagon and Antonio didn't even look back to see where he might land. He had instantly dropped his riata and whistled up Jean Baptiste. For the moment they could be brothers with past experience shared. They rode close to the dying oxen to be ready as pick-up men for Smith and Denton.

Only at the last minute did they think they would slide over behind them on the saddle. The Donner wagons were getting dangerously close and the Reed supply wagon was careening back and forth without a driver. In its erratic course it could still destroy a couple of wagons.

Then, first one oxen's leg and then another buckled, and a jaw hit the turf and began to plow. The men jumped free. Then the powerful back legs could no longer push forward and sank. One ton and then two tons of dying flesh pulled down the tongue and began to act as a front braking system. But it was not immediate. Normally the wagon would carry two thousand five hundred pounds of freight. James Frazier had it packed with nearly four thousand pounds.

It stopped within three feet of Tamsen's wagon. Ironically, she could think of only one thing. They would not have to bury the poor oxen, they had done so themselves by plowing around them a mound of mountainside.

* * *

James Frazier Reed was livid with rage. Everyone was at fault for this disaster but himself. Had he been the captain nothing like this would ever have come about. His rage turned to near mouth frothing when he learned it was James Smith who had slaughtered his oxen.

"Ya!" he ranted, "I will make him pay for this, Donner."

"He saved one of your supply wagons, Reed."

"No! He is out to kill off all my oxen. I demand that he be banished."

"From what?" George grinned slyly.

"From this damn wagon train!" he shrieked.

"Well," George drawled, having the first enjoyable minute of that day, "as you divorced yourself from it, I don't see how you can demand much, Reed."

Reed's eyes narrowed and his pencil-mustache twitched.

"Get my wagon off this mountain, *Captain*," he snarled. "You've got an obligation."

George hesitated. Sometimes charitable men had to be hard. "My obligation rests with the wagons down the hill."

"But you have an obligation to get your sister-in-law down."

"No," he said drily. "She's got an obligation to her legs to get her there by supper time."

Elizabeth Donner nearly went into the vapors within the Reed wagon. Margaret did not have time to soothe her this time. She was in a near state of shock over the ruined supply wagon. And like her husband, everyone was to blame for it but themselves.

And for all his expertise in the handling of men, James Frazier stood silent, perplexed as to what to do. No way would he allow his self-designed wagon to go down the hill and encounter the same fate as his two supply wagons, although he had been reassured that the one was still in excellent condition. Nor did he trust taking it down the Keseberg path. It was so long and tall that he feared it tipping at most every turning.

He was stuck on the mountain crest with nowhere to go.

The pine woods came right down to the river on the opposite bank and Lewis, Mac and Lavina looked at the next mistake of Lance Hastings.

To the amazement of Donner, they had been the first down the mountain.

"Canyon's so damn narrow their wheel tracks scarcely had room this side of the river," Mac growled.

Lewis shielded his eyes and looked toward where the canyon angled out of view. "Nor did they seem to do much about it."

"But we must," Lavina said firmly. "I reckon its about a mile to that angle, Mac. No reason the women and children can't bend a little muscle to pile us up a rock road."

"Got plenty of men for that," Lewis insisted.

Lavina took off her battered old man's hat and looked back up the mountain. "Gonna take every man jack of you to get Reed's ship down for launching. Heavy damn brute."

Even in four days of travel Mac McCutchen had measured James Frazier Reed well.

"Man's a jackass not to figure the problem out yet. All he needs do is rig a windlass at the top of the ridge and let her down gently with ropes."

Lavina chuckled. "I'm not knowing what you mean, but think we'd best find George Donner with your suggestion."

But George was still with the last party coming down the switchbacks. Jacob was still in charge. Even Lavina felt a swift surge of pity at the sight of the old man. The day had been rough on him. His gait was halting and feeble.

"Can you rig such a device?" he asked tiredly.

The giant man beamed. "With enough help and rope, sir."

"I leave you to issue what orders you desire, Mr. McCutchen. I will be—"

Tamsen ran forward and caught him by the arm. "You will be right here, Uncle Jake, directing Mrs. Murphy's worthy project. You used to build the best roads on the farm."

"Poppycock!" he snorted. "McCutchen will need every man of us."

"Not really, sir," Mac lied.

Lavina picked up on his tone. "Women and children can gather the rocks from the riverbed, but someone has to know how to place them.'

George rode up, with the wagons following. The narrow shelf at the bottom of the mountain was already congested. The wagons would have to be lined up in single file and pushed through the canyon. The shadows were already lengthening and this was hardly a good camping site.

"No," he said gruffly, upon hearing of the windlass plan. "The man has divorced himself from the train and the problem is his alone."

Tamsen could hardly believe that it was her husband speaking thusly. Others had gathered and heard. They had also heard James Frazier. They had greatly mixed emotions.

"Mr. Donner," Lavina said quietly, which was such a change from her normal gruff bellow that everyone hushed to listen. "I know that man thinks right highly of himself and ain't been the friendly type, but even our Lord Jesus didn't turn his back on the likes of him."

"Amen!" Jacob sighed.

George scratched at his square beard, while beneath it his lips broke into a grin. Everything in Hastings guide had proven most false, except for the point the widow has just brought out. A train was like a big family, with squabbles, hurt pride and differences of opinion. But it had to have a father-leader and it had to become loving and caring of everyone's needs.

"Tell me what you wish of me, Mr. McCutchen," he said, then caught sight of the blood-splattered James Smith. He didn't want him back up the mountainside. "Oh, lad, we got the second MacDuff wagon down safely. Now, I've another chore for you. If this road is to be built, we need to know for how long. I'm obliged if you would scout the canyon for us."

"Good as done," Smith beamed, proud of the honor. He was not aware why Donner was sending him away.

"And I'll tell Mrs. MacDuff," Tamsen offered, not seeing her in the crowd. "Someone should check to see how her husband made the trip down, anyway."

"And, ladies," Lavina said, returning to the bellow, "bring your children over by that big rock. Uncle Jake will tell us what to do."

Mac McCutchen had already figured in his mind the men he would need, counting in Reed's men still at the top. To the disgust of Sol, his brother Billy and John Breen, they were considered children for road work.

4

By the time Tamsen reached her, Mary Florence was in tears. She knew that she could not afford to be caught—that, indeed, she had to hold out for a few days more—but try as she would, she could not manage it. The ice had lasted but a few hours out of Fort Bridger. She was thankful that the nights were cool and crisp, that the streams provided cold water to pour over the blanket shroud. But this hot August day had been the worst. It had been a blessing in disguise that James Smith had been taken away and she was forced to drive one wagon and Charles Stanton the other. Only her nostrils were then subjected to the strong odor of decomposing flesh that was beginning to waft from the wagon. Now she couldn't keep the woman away without being rude.

Tamsen interpreted the young redhead's tears as worry over her husband's illness.

"My husband has sent Jimmy Smith to scout the upper end of the canyon for us. Some of the men are going to bring down the Reed wagon and the women and children are going to make the road more passable."

Mary Florence nodded without speaking.

Then she felt Tamsen's fingers, fierce suddenly upon her arm.

"Oh, Mary Florence," she whispered. "Oh, Mary Florence, how terrible! Your—your husband . . . ?"

She nodded again, for she could no longer live with the lie.

Tamsen turned and looked at her, seeing her face pale, her lips tremble visibly, though her teary eyes seemed quite determined. But she did not sense grief.

The wind shifted and Tamsen nearly gagged.

"How long?" she asked grimly.

Again Mary Florence saw no reason to lie. It was over. They would just have Smith and Stanton lead her back to Fort Bridger.

"Six days . . . counting today."

"Before we even left?" Tamsen gasped.

"The reason for the ice," she said dully. "I feared your husband would be like Mr. Hastings and not take me along. That's why I had to make it appear that Harlan was almost well."

"Oh, Mary Florence, my husband would have understood."

She shrugged. "The question is, will he understand now. We are still close enough to Fort Bridger for him to send me back for such a lie."

"I don't consider it a lie. You were doing what you thought was best for your survival."

Real tears of grief were there in the hazel-green eyes now. For the first time it was really dawning on her that Harlan was dead. For six days she had talked to him to keep him alive in her mind—and for the ears of others. Miserably, she shook her head.

"What do I do now?"

"I'm pondering that. Unfortunately we have a few gossips that will be horribly shocked at your deed and not understand your reasons. Fortunately, the two worst ones are still on the mountainside. So, I think we must act quickly."

"To do what?"

"To bury your husband!" Tamsen said flatly.

"But he is in but blanket shrouds. They will smell that—"

"They will smell nothing! My brother-in-law is a far-sighted man. We carry with us a pine coffin half-filled with fragrant cedar chips. Of course, Elizabeth stores her best dresses atop them, but that's her bad luck. You prepare your husband and I'll go arrange the rest."

"But," Mary Florence wept, "what will you tell them?"

"Tell them? The simple truth. Your husband has died."

Jacob Donner was most gracious in giving up his coffin. An hour before he had thought he would be lying within it by sundown. But sitting on the flat rock, giving nothing but directions, had revived him. Nor was it just the rest that had stilled his beating pulse and heart.

He was a man who loved to see honest industry in people. He had raised his older children to love God and His earth. Elizabeth had the greatest say on raising this second family of children and he had never been too pleased with the results, until that moment.

Young George had pouted and complained bitterly to Lavina.

"My mother would not approve of me doing this."

"Now is that a fact?" Lavina started, in mock surprise. "Why then don't you just run right on up the hill and ask her permission. Come, children!"

Jacob marveled that she was capable of turning the whole thing into play, and that after a long sulk Young George joined in. He also marveled that the huge woman knew as much about the placement of the rocks to form a rough roadbed as he. Yes, he loved industry, especially in a woman. Once he had feared a widow woman and children would be a burden on the wagon train. His fears had begun to evaporate as they had come across the Great Plains and Continental Divide. Now they were turned to pure admiration.

She was pure gold, such as Tamsen. For that girl he would give the last penny out of his pocket and never ask the reason for her need—it would be a sound one.

The lead weights of burden to the train, in his opinion, were obvious by their absence or previous actions: Elizabeth, Margaret, Virginia, because they were still on the hillside; Johanna Wolfinger, who flat refused; Phillipine Keseberg, because her husband declared she was not available; Spitzer and Reinhardt, who claimed they must do repairs on their wagons; Luke Halloran, who was ill; and John Breen, who stubbornly followed the men up the hill, invited or not.

The doers and don't-ers were being prepared in his mind for his dinner prayer.

Then he smiled with pride on a couple of the "doers."

Solomon and Billy Hook had complained not once at the request to dig a grave on the mountainside, to carry the coffin to the MacDuff wagon, to respectfully depart while Tamsen and Mrs. MacDuff did women's work with the dead, then come on call with John Murphy, Pat Dolan and Charles Denton to carry the coffin and lower it into the dug grave.

It had not been asked of Uncle Jake, but he stood upon the flat rock and signalled Lavina for a moment of work stoppage. He had no fear that his voice would carry to the gravesite and to God.

"Lord, I knew not this man we send you this day, other than he was Scottish and thus must have been a fine gentleman. He leaves in our care a fine figure of a woman. Lord, you know we look out for our own, so don't you be worrying over her. You know I got me some other names on my mind, but right now you just get ready to welcome Harlan MacDuff. I'll talk to you about the others at supper time."

That evening's supper time and prayer were unusual from preceding ones. Because the land was such the wagons had to remain parked where stopped and communal cooking fires built on the narrow, sandy river bank. No Donner table, silver or china was forthcoming. They sat and ate on rocks and logs like all the rest. No child complained about going to bed that night; they were bushed. Lavina didn't have the heart to tell them that the next day, and possibly the day after, would be mostly the same.

Uncle Jake didn't mind bringing it up in his prayer, although decided to leave out quite a lot, too.

"Lord, bless the children who toiled and must toil again. Bless the men on the mountain who still toil and give Brother Reed sense enough to have fed them, which I seriously doubt. Thank you, Lord, for keeping us from disaster today, except for Brother Harlan who you took home today from natural causes. I've got a list of others here you could take away for any cause whatsoever, but we'll talk about that later. Thank you for the safe return of Brother Smith and his good report on Your wide canyon ahead. Wish you could have done the same here, but you didn't. so we're doing a little improvement on your work. Amen!"

Mary Florence sat up suddenly, nearly knocking the dinner plate from her lap. Tamsen had insisted that she and Charles Stanton eat dinner with the Donners.

"Harlan must be laughing," she said a little bitterly. "Twice Mr. Donner has given him a beautiful introduction before the Pearly Gates, but he would hardly be there to enter."

After Sol and Billy had closed the grave, Tamsen had stayed beside it with Mary Florence. As though it too had to be buried beneath the earth, the whole history of the MacDuff married life had come flowing out of the woman. Tamsen had listened, although she was not one who really cherished listening to such confessions. At the time she had not commented.

"He's dead," she said quietly, "and Jacob, without knowing it, has made sure there will be no questions. Whether he stands before Saint Peter or the Devil no longer matters. You've got to start thinking of a new life for yourself."

"I thought that's what I was doing," she scoffed, "but I wasn't." Then she laughed wryly. "Oh, Tamsen, I'm in for it now. His illness gave me an excuse to decline Margaret Reed's invitations."

"You may still decline. No one voted her queen of the wagon train."

Many on the hillside that afternoon and evening might have challenged that statement. Although they were there to see her and her wagon down to safety she was rude, arrogant and totally uncooperative.

James Frazier was little better. He had no sooner accepted the windlass as a workable scheme, than he gave orders for his men to bring down his herd and see to the salvage of the two supply wagons—and took off for a canter with Virginia.

Amazingly, it was the tough-tongued McCutchen who made the other men see that it was a blessing to be rid of the man. The felling of the trees to make the windlass scaffold, the splicing of the many ropes into longer lengths, the choice of a tree of adequate girth to roll before the front tires to control its descent—all had gone well until Margaret decided to take a hand in the matter, via Eliza.

Because Spitzer, Reinhardt and Hardkoop were not in the group, Eliza felt she could be as imperious as her master or mistress.

"The delay is intolerable," she snapped at Lewis Keseberg, as though the words were her own. "Our foodstuffs, except for minor supplies, are all down below. We demand to be down there by dinner time."

"Demand?" he said testily. Few, male or female, had the courage to demand of Lewis Keseberg. But instead of flaring back, he stood and admired her spunk. He had been admiring much more about her in the past several days, but from a far distance. With Phillipine, since the birth of Lewis, Jr., he had forced himself to dampen his passions. Every sighting of Eliza was like a bellows blowing on embers that had been half-extinguished. It was the first time he had been this close. The wrath in her face made her more beautiful. Phillipine always smelled of baby puke, sour milk and sweaty hair. Eliza smelled of scented water and fresh, ironed aprons. He reverted to gentle insistence. "Do you know what you demand, *Fraulein* Williams? Our manpower is halved, with the Reed men taken away. We strive for safety, not speed."

Eliza was taken aback. "You know my name?"

Lewis grinned, bringing his face to its most handsome state. "I am also aware that it is Eliza. In German we would call it *Elisa*." He pronounced it *Ell-ee-saw*, soft and purring.

Despite herself Eliza felt a shuddering thrill. It was more of a German lesson than she had gained from his wife. But that, in itself, was also a sobering thought. As attractive a man as he might be, he was not within her consideration, due to his married state.

"Interesting," she murmured, because she couldn't think of anything else to say. "I once asked your wife to help me learn German, but I have seen little of her since."

Lewis stiffened and then thought better of his sudden anger. Perhaps a friendship between Phillipine and the dark beauty would afford him a better chance with her.

"The babies keep her busy, you know. But I shall be glad to raise the subject anew with her, *Fraulein Elisa.*"

Eliza hid the surprise in her face. She had almost been told in so many words not to come around unless Lewis was away, which had not happened since leaving Fort Bridger. She had also nearly determined in her mind that he was a wife-beater. But she had to cancel all thoughts, for this was the first time she'd talked to him in person and she found him most charming and exciting.

"Thank you. I would appreciate that."

"And I would appreciate you calming Mrs. Reed. I am from a family, *Fraulein*, who have many servants. The best, always, carry the message of the master in tone and meaning. You have done well. We are doing our best. May I suggest you soothe your mistress not only with my words but a fresh bowl of wild raspberries? I have seen many such bushes up that draw where I have been felling trees for the windlass. If you have held back a pitcher of cream before the herd went down the hill, it will add to the soothing."

Eliza turned back to the wagon perplexed. In every aspect of her wildest dreams, except one, she had just been talking with *the* man she had molded out of fantasy. Handsome, sophisticated, suave, educated, moneyed, manly, gentle, understanding—but, alas, *married.*

There always had to be a fly in the ointment, but still she handled Margaret as he had suggested. To her utter amazement it worked.

"Now there is a most considerate man," Margaret simpered to a pouting Elizabeth Donner. "He is doing his best for us and still considered our comfort. Well, girl, why do you stand idle? The raspberries! The raspberries!"

Eliza flung herself wildly down out of the wagon and then hesitated. Was he being just a considerate man or was this some form of male-trap? She was even more perplexed, not knowing if she even really cared.

"Come on," she scolded herself, "this is not like you, Elizabeth Marie Helen O'Williams." The "O" as well as the "beth" had been dropped on coming to America. Now all that would echo in her ears was the softer German "*Elisa.*"

"Fool," she muttered, and snatched a basket from beneath the wagon.

Climbing into the draw she felt guilty having thought such evil of Lewis Keseberg. To left and right was the sound of axes and saws. Men of the Donner Party coming to their rescue. That thought gave her a moment of pause. They were really not a part of this party. They had stood arrogant and aloof, but once in real trouble the others had come back to rescue them. Nor was it really being appreciated.

"Holy Saint Paddy," she gasped, "I'm becoming like the worst of the whole lot."

"If you mean the Reed clan," a laugh came from behind a bush, "that I doubt."

"Oh, no!" her throat said, as Keseberg himself stepped out of the bushes, as her heart said: "Oh, yes!"

With a grand gesture he indicated a huge pile of berries on a pile of leaves.

"I have saved you some time—" he began.

Eliza started for them, then drew back.

"Your tree!" she said. "Is it felled?"

"*Ja!* Long since, *danke.* Honestly, since before we talked. I pick berries since."

"Why?"

"Because I know you come for them."

"Oh, no," she moaned, "then it was a trap."

"Trap?" he said, wagging his big head. "I set no trap. If you had not come I would have brought the berries to you."

She backed away from him, sensing the lie. She chided herself for having pulled off her maid's cap coming up the draw. Her black hair now hung loose about her shoulders, soft-curling, as though she had wished to present him with such a picture. And had she not?

"You are most beautiful," he murmured, "and I do not mean offense in the statement."

It threw her off guard. One moment declaring it was not a trap and then speaking of her beauty.

"I-I am not offended."

"Good, for my guilt is great making such a statement as a married man. But in my country when one sees beauty it is considered proper to speak of it."

"I-I thank you." Now she was really perplexed. He had been the one to comment on his marital status, and that should have calmed her. But it had a tendency to excite her. She was quite aware of Phillipine's plainness.

"But, honestly speaking, my desire to kiss you goes beyond my marriage vows. It will be almost spiritual . . ."

Perhaps, Eliza reflected, it would be . . . for his eyes were almost saintly.

She went up on tiptoe, her dark eyes closing. Her arms stole upward around his massive neck, and her lips caressed his, warm and quivering. Never in twenty-five years had she tasted of male lips. He made no threatening motion, and his lips were almost spiritual. She felt no fear, but only a tingling sensation of enjoyment. It was so natural, as though meant to be. Soft and loving. She brought her hands down and cradled his face between them, lingering over the caress.

She had given him too much an indication of her inner emotions. The swift, backward motion of her head was almost brutal—for his mouth became fierce with lust, his big hands fiercely moving savagely over every curve of her body.

He was too powerful. He held her mouth imprisoned, unable to scream—and a scream she determined would bring little more than embarrassment. Then for a moment she thought she was free.

But the moment was all that he needed to scoop her up in his massive arms and push through the tangled underbrush. Her fists were now free to hammer away at his head, neck and chest.

"*Ja!*" he chortled. "You beat on Lewis all you wish, tiger-cat. He feel nothing."

She began to weep when they came into a little clearing. He had planned well. The chips from the tree he had felled had been gathered together into a crude bed under a bower and covered with pine branches.

To her surprise he put her down gently, then sat beside her and smoothed her hair back off the forehead.

"I did not mean to frighten."

"Well," she stammered, bringing her sobs under control, "you have. Now, please just let me go."

"Any time that you desire, *Fraulein*."

This added to her surprise. Free to leave, she suddenly had no desire to run in fright. He certainly wasn't like James Frazier Reed. Given this much opportunity she would have been already stripped of her clothing.

"Thank you," she murmured. "Perhaps I misread your intentions."

Lewis laughed drily. "I think not. I changed them when it came to me that you had never laid with a man before."

"Or when you recalled that you were married?"

The laugh now turned bitter. "It is loveless. Perhaps I should leave the train when over these mountains and go to the place of the people who fight with Jim Bridger. I am told that with them a man can have as many wives as he can support. I could support many."

She sat up and studied him quite differently. The statement had not been made in jest.

"But I wonder how the women feel about that?"

He suddenly grinned. "We could go and ask them."

She giggled. Here she had been determining whether it would be Spitzer or Reinhardt she would go after, and was now being asked to share one man with another woman. It was insane.

He took her hand, palm up, and studied it. Then he smothered it in kisses. Despite herself she thrilled. The desire was there to replace her palm with her lips if only it wouldn't mean going any farther.

Reading her quiver correctly he pulled her close and kissed her as before. So gentle and soft and undemanding.

Just as gentle were his hands, stirring up fires within her that she was not aware could burst so suddenly to flame. Her breasts took on a life of their own—swelling to full roundness and the nipples almost painful in their own desire to have his hand caress them once again.

He held himself in check until her lips quivered on a note of passion. Only once since the wedding had he tasted of Phillipine's cold indifference. He wanted these hot, demanding lips upon his own. He wanted to feel them welded as one, but not if it meant only a single time. With this woman, he had to show love to get love in return.

Then, suddenly, twenty-five years of resistance were gone. She, too, had heard of the Mormons at the fort. She, too, had heard of the growing ratio of men to women in the west. But those would be marriages possibly just as loveless as the one Lewis was now burdened with. She wanted a husband she could love, even if she might have to share him.

She laid back on the boughs and closed her eyes. She sensed his bulk descending.

"It will be all right, Miss Margaret," Eliza soothed. "I will help you down the mountain."

But Margaret Reed continued her fierce crying and screaming. Her entire body was racked with hatred. It didn't matter to Eliza that they would have to vacate the wagon. She could have floated down the mountain. She had never realized what a marvellous sensation love could be, this kind of love. She had not feared, even when it started with agonizing pain. For so large a man he was most gentle in his teaching and his loving. How could anyone believe that he beat his wife? Slowly, inexorably, he had brought her to full womanhood and planted dreams in her head. Lewis figured it would take them a week to get to the lake of salty water. A week for her to make good friends with Phillipine. Oh, yes, for German lessons. Now that she was to become the second wife of Lewis Keseberg, German was more important than ever. *Elisa.* She loved it.

Margaret's wail turned into a piercing screech.

James Frazier came up the wagon steps with Virginia in his arms. Her hair was tangled and hatless; her riding dress tattered and torn from her body. She was frightfully white and her eyes stared glassily.

"Mountain lion shied the pony," he said, his voice full of fright, and his face badly scratched. "I gave chase and we were both knocked off by the tree branches. Nothing is broken. She is just frightened and shook up. Eliza, get her into a bath, a change and rest. Send the other children down so she will not be disturbed."

"They are not here!" Margaret wailed. "That damnable George Donner has them walking down with Elizabeth. I refused to move until you returned."

"I will see to it," he sighed, setting Virginia down on her feet. As though she had been held against her will, she spun away and dashed up the compartment stairs.

"Aah!" he snorted in self-disgust and went back down the steps.

Eliza took the kettle from the stove. The water was still hot from the tea she had fixed to go with the raspberries and cream. That was before George Donner had broken up the jolly little party with his quiet demand. Quiet in Eliza's opinion, but not quiet in Margaret's mind.

Elizabeth had come to see the danger involved and had taken the three young Reeds along, though she dreaded the walk with a passion.

The chore, at least, would take her away from the woman's wailing.

Margaret did what Margaret did best—she collapsed on her chaise longue and bemoaned her fate among all these heathens.

"That does change matters," George said with genuine sympathy. "Sorry for the gal, but you will have to take responsibility for her riding in the wagon,

James. As is, we may have to shore it up half-way down and finish in the morning."

"Why is that?" he asked inanely, his worries still centered on Virginia. After it had happened she had been so white and still. There had been no shaking, no crying, no talk. She had been so limp that he had had to carry her in his lap.

"Rope, mainly. Enough for half-way down and then we will have to take down the windlass and reconstruct it. Be too dark within a couple hours to do much more today."

"Torches," James Frazier mumbled. "I will get my men to make torches to work by."

"They're all below," George grunted. "Ain't been no help to us at all."

James Frazier looked at him as though it were startling news to him. "Then why in the hell am I paying them a wage? How many do you need? I'll ride down and get them."

"Need 'em all," George said sourly. "These men need a break and some chow. Ain't a one of them had a bite of supper."

"Did you ask?" he snorted, as though he had left orders that had not been carried out.

"Did that, James. Your woman said she had nothing in this wagon."

"You must not have made your intentions well known. The wagon has ham, beef jerky and all manner of materials. I will have Eliza start cooking the moment she is finished with my daughter."

"Don't bother. I asked the young lady to let the fire go out. Don't want an accident with it on this grade. Wagon will be problem enough."

"But food for the men?" James Frazier insisted, as though it had been his original concern and must be settled.

"Have your men gather up from our folk below. Another half hour of growling bellies won't hurt them."

"I will see to it at once!"

The sudden cooperation and speed in which he zig-zagged down the mountain was surprising. George Donner tried not to be a suspicious man. He could feel sorry for Virginia and her accident, but could not help but feel that the sudden action was caused by Margaret Reed. Never in his life had a woman blistered him with such a tirade of abuse over such a simple matter as walking. Well, if the woman wanted to take her chances in the wagon it mattered not to him. The whole operation was consuming far more time than he had wished and it had been a tiring day to begin with.

James Frazier's cooperation had nothing to do with Margaret, and only in part because of Virginia. His head ached sharply and the wind ate into his face scratches and made them sting. But he felt none of it. He felt only shame and remorse. He had to keep busy to lock out of his brain the sight of Virginia's eyes. In a single second they had turned from teasing, laughing gaiety to dull hate.

I mustn't think about it, he told himself. I must get her off this mountain and through that canyon. Beyond are vast valleys in which to canter. Not here—not now. It had to be a place where today could be forgotten and things could be returned to as they were before.

Undressing her was like dealing with an uncooperative rag doll. Eliza would give her instructions on how she could help, but Virginia remained limp and uncommunicative. The eyes were just too glassy and dull. No broken bones to be sure, but Eliza began to fear something else. Her brother Baylis had once been kicked in the head by a bull and had never quite been the same since. On the excuse that she was trying to untangle the matted hair she carefully felt of every inch of the skull. But there was not a single knot or bump and never once did Virginia cry out in pain.

Then, taking away the rest of the tattered skirt and pulling off the petticoat, Eliza feared again. The pantaloons were dyed black with dried blood. She didn't try to tug them off the hips, but got snips to cut them away from the body and legs. The youthful pout of hair was matted tightly and the dried blood down her legs looked like sun-parched desert land.

Gingerly, Eliza felt along to find the abrasion, but could find none and Virginia refused to tell her where she hurt. Cleaning away the dried blood would give her her only clue, but the matted hair suggested that the poor girl might have split herself in the fall.

The china basin was dark red by the time Eliza had her cleaned well enough for a further examination. The long, creamy legs were without flaw, so that blood had to come from the spurting of a higher up wound.

Eliza thought nothing immoral in examining with fingertips the flesh beneath the hair. To the Reed children she had been nurse, as well as everything else.

But her first touch brought a flinch and a deep moan. Gently, she probed, finding the flesh like a heating stove, and puffy. The limp body began to stiffen by degrees, but the eyes remained glassy and dull.

Eliza began to frown when she determined that neither end of the cleft had been split. This time she probed downward along each side of the seam and it caused Virginia's head to flay back and forth on the pillow and little discharges of blood to seep out and rewet the hair.

Eliza sponged the area dry, spread the legs farther

apart and placed a fresh towel between them. As though the action reminded Virginia of something, she sat directly up and stared down between her legs.

"What are you doing?"

Eliza looked up. The glassy eyes were now ringed with fear and mistrust.

"I fear, Virginia, that the damage is internal. It feels to me like there is still quite a bit of blood in there that has to come out and is probably blocked by a clot. Don't be afraid, but what I must do will only hurt for a second."

A slow, sly smile crept over her lips, as though she had just recently heard those words before. She started to tell Eliza not to proceed, but the act had already commenced.

She winced and fell back on the pillow. The pain was the same. She knew she would never forget that pain as long as she lived. But this pain was short-lived in comparison. The other pain had gone on and on and on—as she felt her whole insides ripped and torn. It had been so horrible—not the later action—but that ghastly feeling of the hot, sticky blood. It had so sickened her that she had had to turn her head away as her stomach started to revolt. But there had been nothing but dry heaves and sobbing. She had turned her head back, hatred in her eyes. Hatred over the fact that she could not be sick and get rid of that horrible feeling.

James Frazier was panting, a silly grin on his face. He was laughing at her because she could not get sick! Her eyes had narrowed into slits and she pushed him away. Then, upon trying to sit up, the loss of blood made her light-headed. She fell back limp.

As though in a dream she heard him growl and the rending of cloth. Before it had been a teasing matter that she had gone along with until the pain and the blood. Now he was an animal in bringing back the pain. Somehow, before she fanted, she got her hands up to his face and her fingernails into his flesh.

The next she knew she was in his lap upon the horse. She still wanted to be sick so remained silent.

Now the feeling was back. The probing finger had not brought it about, that was almost pleasant. It was that horrible, bloody feeling again.

"I'm going to be sick," she wailed.

Eliza quickly cleaned her hand and got the basin from her own nightstand. She put it between Virginia's legs, sat her erect and held her forehead as she soothed the back of her neck.

Again it was only dry heaves.

Eliza poured her a cup of water and made her drink it down in a single gulp. Now something would come up. Again and again she made her drink and discharge it. She wanted her cleaned out at both ends. What had been within the discharged blood clot had told her more than she really wanted to know.

At first she didn't want to think on it at all and told herself it wasn't possible. She had hardly bled at all that afternoon. But her giant had been gentle. Her internal examination told her how savage had been this attack.

She wanted to be sick right along with Virginia.

"Bastard!" she growled. "I could kill him for this!"

"For what?" Virginia asked innocently, falling back on the pillow. The sickness was gone and she felt much better, although terribly weak.

"For what he did to you!" she flared. "It is unnatural and unthinkable."

Virginia yawned. "I don't know what you are talking about. Please finish cleaning me. I am so terribly, terribly tired."

Eliza gaped. Could this be possible? She could fully believe that James Frazier Reed would attempt such a shameful assault, but for Virginia to play innocent about the matter she could not believe.

Oh, yes, she had put herself in the path of God's wrath that day. But she saw marriage at the end of the path as her salvation. Virginia had no such choice. Eliza was really perplexed as to what she should do.

Virginia wasn't. If it meant this much blood each time she never, ever wanted to do it again. She had already determined coming back on the horse that she never, ever wanted to do it again with her step-father. She had teased him into it just so she could learn. She had learned. She had learned that men seemed to get a strange sort of enjoyment out of the act. Perhaps, she thought because they don't have to bleed.

Well she now had the knowledge she sought to have a real tool to make Solomon Hook jealous. She could tease John Breen in the same manner, but never let him get to the point that she had her step-father.

Eliza finished cleaning her and threw a fresh sheet over her nudity. She stretched, like the mountain lion they had never seen.

No, she thought, even though John Breen has been panting around all day, I will wait awhile. I have plenty of time to taunt John and Sol. Unnatural and unthinkable, she mused. Interesting? Perhaps she would just lie abed for a few days and really put a scare into her step-father. Billy was getting too short for her. She really did require a much finer mount. How much did unnatural and unthinkable silence cost?

5

THEY WORKED throughout the night because James Frazier was the new ramrod. He was everywhere, shirking no task, but asking for help rather than demanding it. If a change had overcome James Frazier Reed, they would all wait to see how long it would last.

He was unaware of his fatigue until they had the huge wagon down by the riverside. He waded to the center and sat down facing upstream. He let the cold torrent pour over him, trying to reduce his fear and fever more than cleanse the sweaty body and ruined suit. It was refreshing for body but not for mind.

Lavina had had the women and children back to work since sun-up. Today it was work and not play. Their muscles ached and many had swollen blisters on their hands.

Yesterday she had been a fun companion. Today they looked on her as a mean slave-driver. Jacob's admiration for her grew. She allowed no one to shirk or lollygag about. Well, almost no one.

She had put into effect Tamsen's suggestion that everyone said wouldn't work. All of the younger children were put in the care of Phillipine Keseberg. At first she had timidly balked, but once she had all the under five children gathered about her it gave her a sense of pride that someone thought she was worth something to the whole group.

Nor had Lewis balked when the Reed wagon was down. He gave her a tired smile and went up into the wagon to collapse for sleep.

Tamsen and Mary Florence were new recruits, as was the returned James Smith. The Wolfingers, Spitzer and Reinhardt still held out with excuses.

James Frazier slowly rose on near-frozen legs and stood dripping. His fatigue had vanished watching them. For nearly a half mile they had widened the riverbank where necessary. He waded to the first excavation point, stepped up and paced it off to the edge of the trees.

At any other time he would have begun bellowing over his find. But wordlessly he returned to the river and started lugging back rocks. The path was fine for the regular wagons, but a trifle short for his large wagon.

George Donner sat sipping a cup of coffee and watching. He was almost too tired to get the cup of coffee to his lips. He knew exactly what James Frazier was about.

"Why don't he get his men to help him?" Jacob asked.

"They worked right hard last night," George said admiringly.

"More than I can say for some." Elizabeth had claimed swollen legs from the walk and refused to get out of bed that morning.

Clumsily, George got to his feet. There were some words that just had to be said.

"Hear me!" he shouted. "Any family who do not work on the road will not be allowed to pass upon it."

Hans Wolfinger looked up from where he was saddle-soaping reins. "You cannot do that. You must leave it for all who come behind."

"I don't see why," James Frazier shouted curtly. "Hastings didn't even leave us the sweat smell of his balls to follow. I'm going last, German, and will crowbar it back into the river if need be."

Wolfinger fumed. "And what about that German?" he demanded, pointing at the Keseberg wagons.

At any other time it would have galled James Frazier to champion Lewis Keseberg, but he was hardly himself that morning.

"Are you blind? They have worked the day and night and now his woman works to free other women."

Wolfinger grinned. "We work when we see *your* woman work."

It was a stalemate. Everyone knew that Margaret would not budge herself from the wagon—and no Margaret meant no Johanna.

But Old Man Hardkoop held a fierce conference in strident German that had Phillipine blushing from overhearing. She would never be able to repeat what he had uttered, but within a few moments Wolfinger, Spitzer, Reinhardt and Hardkoop were at work on the road. Johanna sulked in her wagon, afraid to be seen going to sit with Margaret.

As the day wore on, Lavina noticed that James Frazier was working much more slowly. Hardkoop had passed him, and now others of the German party were ahead. Like the rest of the Reed party, except for

Margaret and the ailing Virginia, Eliza was also at work on the road.

"Miss," Lavina said, "I think your bossman needs a rest."

Personally, Eliza wished he would drop dead in his tracks. But the last thing in the world she wanted was for anyone else in the train to learn what he had done.

Eliza nodded and went back along the river. But he did not look up at her approach.

"Rider coming down!" she heard someone call from the wagon area.

"Mrs. Murphy thinks you need rest," she explained.

James Frazier swayed dizzily, and for a moment Eliza thought he was going to fall. But he straightened up wearily, and when he spoke, his voice was but a whisper.

"Yes. For a little while. Must get through this canyon."

Muddy, wet and tired as he was, he stumbled down the river rather than the road. Despite what he had done, Eliza followed to catch him if he fell.

They walked right by where the rider was being greeted by the Donner brothers.

"Well, hello again," Doolittle Thornburg called cheerily and jumped from his saddle.

Eliza's head turned toward the greeting, but for the moment saw only an unrecognizable man in buckskins. She just barely nodded and continued on after James Frazier.

Margaret began to scream the moment he brought all that mud into her amidship room. He ignored her and sank down on the other chaise longue.

"Get those filthy things off him!" Margaret demanded.

"He is your husband," Eliza said grimly. "I have work to do on the road."

Margaret came erect instantly on her own chaise longue.

"What is that you said to me?" she stammered, but saw that she was talking to thin air. Eliza had vanished just as quickly as she had come.

"Well, I never," she gasped. "James Frazier, I want that impudent girl fired."

His only reply was a loud snore. He had worked his mind and body to a point where it could sleep without thinking.

She looked at him with total disgust. It was ridiculous for a man of his bearing to work like a slavehand. She was not about to touch him. He could just sleep in his wet filth for all she cared. She laid back on the chaise longue and gave way to a new storm of weeping.

"Oh, Eliza," George Donner called, rested from his own nap, "Mr. Bridger has sent this Doolittle Thornburg out to see if we might have use for a guide. Would you kindly call Mr. Reed back out for a short discussion on the matter?"

"I'm afraid, Mr. Donner, that he is all done in."

"You're the captain, George," Jacob growled. "You just make the decision."

"I suppose—"

"I don't mind waiting," Doolittle cut him short. "Miss Eliza can just come and fetch me when the man is awake."

She looked at him quietly. Now she recalled his wink and her own thoughts that he was one of the most spectacular men she had ever seen. He was still that, but she now had Lewis Keseberg as a comparison. For the moment, she determined there was no comparison.

"I shall be busy at work, sir."

"Then I shall help," he said enthusiastically. "What

do you need? Water fetched, meal ground? I'm good at most anything."

"How are you at road work?" she laughed. "For that is what I am about."

"Well," he grinned, "I'll be along shortly. I'd best settle matters first with Mr. Donner."

Lavina Murphy waddled up proudly, followed by her contingent of workers.

"Except for a couple of spots, Mr. Donner, we are about ready to go on."

"Praise be to the Lord! My friends, this be Doolittle Thornburg. Mr. Bridger says he knows the country and Indians hereabout right well. He's going to be helping us along our way to Hastings. Well, Mr. Thornburg, shall we prepare?"

Doolittle hesitated, looking up at the sun and cloudless sky. He had only a vague idea of what lay to the west.

"Might be best if I scout ahead."

"Been done. Good canyon just a mile or so ahead."

"And," Jacob added on, "we are all of a mind to vacate this spot."

There was general agreement. Doolittle found he had to "do little" for them at the moment.

They reacted as though they had been camped for days of rest and play. The herders took through the cattle, extra oxen and horses, then came back to help.

They, and the older children, walked the river with long poles to chuck back in the rocks that the wheels and heavy loads would push out in passing.

One by one, the wagons inched along until again in a straight line. Still, it was the better part of the whole afternoon and early evening to get them over the makeshift road.

The Reed wagons were last, and still problem children. What had been salvaged from the wreck was now a greater weight for the two. Because James Frazier slept through it all, and no one dared ask Margaret and Virginia to walk, that added to the weight of the big wagon.

But because they were moving again no one seemed to mind the extra effort put into getting those wagons through.

But the change in worlds in a simple mile and a half was awesome. Trees and mountainsides were exchanged for towering red cliffs with wind-carved statue like facings and tops. Because it was dusk when they were finally all gathered together the deep canyon was already night-like and the exit portal in the far distance a seemingly black hole for them to enter.

The oddly shaped cliffs reminded the Germans of gargoyles staring down at them. Because of the shadows constantly moving through them from the setting sun they actually seemed to move about and frightened the smaller children.

Communication was no problem. The least sneeze, whisper or dropped utensil reechoed back a dozen-fold times.

Preparations for dinner sounded like the inside of an asylum with the inmates revolting.

It was nerve-wracking at first, but the dinner was more important than the racket. As though it could close out all that had transpired they wished it to be the same as usual.

Water, which had been their icy companion for two days, was no more in this canyon, except for a soda-spring.

"Ugh!" William Pike kidded. "That is horrible, Harriet. Your beans taste bad enough without cooking them in that."

"Is that a fact now?" she flared, looking for something to throw at him.

Playfully he grabbed for her wrist and tried to force

her to drink some soda-water from the tin cup. At twenty-one Harriet Murphy Pike was already built just like her mother—large everywhere. She spun away on a laugh and gave him a belt to the shoulder.

"Stop it, you!" Sarah Murphy Foster scolded. "I need water for cooking and help, Miss Priss."

Harriet spun back. As sisters they were as different in temperament as size. Sour Sarah was thin as a willow reed and looked a good ten years beyond her twenty-five. She felt that life was a lodestone and made sure everyone knew her feeling on the matter.

"And where am I supposed to be getting water?" Harriet carped.

"Same's the rest," she said sourly. "They been goin' the mile back to the river spring."

That had been another wonder for their eyes. The water poured right out of the mountainside from an underground river. It was like magic.

"I'll go get it," Pike volunteered. "I'll lash a barrel onto the side of the saddle."

Sarah looked at him as though this were magic, too. She was under the strong impression that she did all the cooking and womanly chores and her husband Foster was left with all the manly chores.

"I'll go to help," Harriet chirped.

"You'll go no farther than that coffee-grinder," Sarah snarled.

"What about Amanda McCutchen?"

Sarah gave her younger sister a look that ended the matter.

Pike smiled gleefully to himself, and set to work. For the first time ever he had something to thank his sister-in-law for. He had not wished his wife to accompany him.

He had volunteered because he had seen Charles Stanton lash a barrel on one of the MacDuff horses and the "new widow" lead it back down the canyon.

Others had done near the same, including the new guide and his pack horse with empty leather bags on the rack, but his only interest was in Mary Florence MacDuff.

Several times he had tried to get close to her while working on the road. He had heard Tamsen Donner call her by name and had repeated it over and over so he wouldn't forget it.

As a married woman he hadn't given her much thought. He had once tasted buckshot in his behind from an irate husband. But since she had "planted" her husband, he viewed her quite differently. He grinned to himself again. He and Foster shared most everything in life, except their wives and other women. Other women were their battleground—although in a very funny, loving way. When either were interested in a new conquest they would share all the information they could gather on her and then connive and sneak to see which could first get their hand beneath her pantaloons.

Pike felt real sneaky. Foster had gone to the other end of the canyon with James Smith. There was no grazing or water within the canyon for the cattle and they had asked the new guide how far they had to go for new pasture land.

Doolittle had shrugged, his mind on other matters. He had just seen Eliza and Baylis Williams depart for water and wanted to follow.

Doolittle had not seen the angry scowl on Eliza's face. Every time she needed help from one of the hired Reed men they were no-where to be found. Baylis she didn't trust sending alone, he was becoming more child-like with each passing day.

Pike whistled along, contented that he would get in the first strike.

The rifle shot magnified itself from the other end of

the canyon and rolled itself over and over again into prairie like thunder. He shrugged. Above the cliffs the sky was rosy-gray and cloudless.

"Someone got a mountain goat," he mused and kept whistling along.

They heard the whistle of lead before the rifle report and echo.

"Duck," Foster shouted.

James Smith started to react and felt a slight burning sensation in his shoulder. Then, on the rock canyon floor the bullet that had eaten through his flesh pinged and whistled off at an angle.

"Ricochet!" Foster called again.. "Stand down!"

He crawled from the saddle and went flat as the tiny ball of lead bounced from canyon wall to floor to canyon wall, with a re-echoed banshee wail. It faded slowly into an eerie silence.

Foster spun and sat up. There were no further shots.

"Damn idiot, whoever he was, for hunting in this canyon."

"Got the wrong meat," Smith grunted.

"You're hit!" Foster said, concern in his voice.

"Flesh wound," Smith growled. "I'm fine till we get back."

Oddly, he too felt it was just a wild bullet from a hunter's gun from the party. He was unaware what a fear he had become for James Frazier Reed, and thus a fear and enemy of Milt Elliott.

"Damn," Milt growled, high up in the rocks. "Thought you were such an expert marksman, Herron!"

"Hey, Milt, that's a helluva distance. Winged him, didn't I?"

"Winged, shit! You saw what the bastard did to our oxen! I want him just as dead!"

Sometimes things moved just too fast for Walter

Herron's slow mind. "Taught a lesson," was all he could recall Elliott telling him of this little venture.

In the camp not much attention was paid to the rifle shot at the time. It was a mark of their inexperience that no one even thought that it might be an Indian ambush.

Things were moving too slow for Pike. Below the rivermade waterfall out of the side of the mountain the pool was like a town watering hole.

Tamsen was being aided by Sol Hook; Peggy Breen had her son John. The quiet Bill Eddy filled two canvas bags and departed. Old Man Hardkoop didn't mind gathering water for Spitzer, Reinhardt and Wolfinger; he was enjoying the easy talk of the women.

Eliza left Baylis to gather most of the Reed water, while she devoted herself to helping Phillipine, who had come alone. The chore of caring for the small children had begun to bring her out of her shell and Eliza wanted to start building the friendship for her own purposes.

Mary Florence had been filling her own barrel before the arrival of Doolittle. Seeing that he would be intruding upon Tamsen, Eliza and Phillipine's chatter, he offered his services to Mary Florence.

It was not done because she was a beautiful woman, which he agreed that she was; but because he wanted to show Eliza that he could be a gentlemanly fellow.

Mary Florence accepted on a smile—a slow, quiet smile. She would dip the two wooden buckets into the pool and he would carry them back to the horse and barrel.

"Mr. Thornburg," she said at last, "were you ever in the Red River country?"

Doolittle considered the question. He had spent a marvelous summer with a rolypoly Indian maid somewhere thereabouts.

"Well," he said, "don't reckon I was ever that far north, ma'am."

Mary Florence thought not. In and around the colony she had been quite used to the mountain men and trapper types. Something of Doolittle's sensitive line of face was all wrong, although the body was rugged enough. Clean-shaven, she thought. Perhaps that is what makes him seem different. And clean buckskins and hands. Ah, now she knew! The nails were just too clean.

She shivered as with sudden cold, knowing the feeling that here was something unusual yet thrilling, reminding her somehow of the ancient Scottish warlords, manly-trunked and lean-fleshed and, despite all their immense size, clean cut gentlemen.

"Perhaps you didn't miss much."

"Is that why you and the mister left?"

He saw her mouth tighten; an expression of fear was reflected briefly in the water surface her pupils had caught. Doolittle bent close so the others couldn't hear.

"That was damn foolish of me, ma'am. I'm sorry if I made you think of your recent grief."

"Thank you . . ." she began, her eyes searching his face, moving in odd darts, as though memorizing it inch by inch. "I don't mind the mention of it. We can't change what has happened, can we?"

"Well," he smiled, "it does leave you most alone."

"Perhaps I was always alone," she answered sharply, almost savagely, and turning, dipped the buckets into the water.

He quietly accepted them as she scolded herself.

Fool, she mused. You'll never be catching yourself a new man with such a sharp tongue and mind. She almost laughed. Harlan hardly in his grave and she was thinking thoughts that a week ago she said she would never think. New man? Well, it would hardly be a wandering mountain man. This time it was going to be someone solid and dependable.

A bucket hit the water at a wrong angle and splashed. She started.

"Oh, sorry Miz MacDuff," Pike grinned. "Didn't mean to wet you."

Throwing back her head she laughed aloud. It was the first time she had made such a sound since leaving the Red River, and even a long time before that.

"Actually it felt quite refreshing. You're the Murphy they call Pike, aren't you?"

It was enough to really inflate his ego. "Well, Miz MacDuff, I ain't really a Murphy. I be William Pike. Foster be my brother-in-law, but he be a William, too."

"Oh, I understand. Then you two are the husbands of the Murphy girls?"

That was information he didn't want her pondering on. "Well, I reckon, such as they are."

It was such an odd statement that Mary Florence blinked.

Slowly, Pike pulled the bucket from the pool. He looked at her calmly, waiting for her to speak. That opening line with a woman usually brought some response. "My wife is the big fat one," he said at last.

Her surprise was now such that she was left speechless.

"And not a very good lover," he added suddenly.

Mary Florence stiffened. His face was not keeping the secret of what his words were implying. It was a grinning mask of lust and conquest.

This type of man had also been at the Red River colony, where every woman looked better to him than his own.

"One more bucket will fill your barrel," Doolittle said.

Pike stomped back to his own horse and barrel,

nearly spilling half the bucket in his fury of dumping it. The intrusion had come at the worst possible moment. Now he would have to start all over and just when he was sure that he almost had her in his grasp. He had taken her quietness as growing sympathy.

"Ma'am," Doolittle said quietly, "I couldn't help but overhear his last words and I'd be careful of him, if I were you."

"I am capable of taking care of myself, sir," she snapped, then hated her sharp tongue immediately.

Reflected in the pool she could see the shake of his head in a gesture of half-expressed doubt. Then the image was shattered by Pike's redipped bucket.

She stood and turned to Doolittle suddenly, handing him the bucket.

"I owe you, Doolittle," she said, surprised at her own boldness, "and the least you can do is accept supper with my teamsters and I."

"I-I don't know. Mr. Donner said the families would share me around, as part of my keep." And he wanted to eat with Eliza first.

"Then, I guess I am the first to share you, *Doolittle*." She gave his name a real, purring Scottish burr.

That she was calling him by his first name infuriated Pike. "He could eat with us," he quickly suggested, as the only thing he could think of to get rid of the man.

Doolittle was trapped. "Well," he drawled, "the lady did ask first."

"I think," Mary Florence said, "that we'd better go back now so I can start cooking."

"Why?" Pike flared. "I ain't finished talkin' tah you yet!"

She gave him the sweetest, most gracious smile she could muster.

"Why, William Pike, that is most true," she cooed, "and I shall look forward to its continuation."

She locked her arm in Doolittle's and quickly guided him back toward the horses.

"Whee!" he whispered. "You can take care of yourself, lady."

"I'm sorry. I used you, Doolittle, just to get away from him, but the supper invitation still stands, if you like."

He stared down at her profile, her honesty of words reflected in her eyes. Honesty in women was something he had almost forgotten about. Because he was so different from the bucks the Indian maidens had pulled every deceitful trick in the book to look upon his golden body and manhood.

"Supper stands, but how did you know my whole name?"

She laughed. "I was there when you were introduced."

"Kind of you to remember."

"Hardly," she murmured, pulling closer to his arm. "You are the type man one doesn't forget things about."

Her intent was to put on a good show for the eyes of William Pike, but the tremble in his arm at her words gave her a new thought. As a new man in her life she doubted it, although his ego could be played upon very easily. But as a "protection" of her "new widowhood" from the "lusting wolves" might not be a bad idea.

"Although," she continued in a soft voice, "I still know so little about you . . . so very little."

It was Doolittle's turn to be speechless and silent. He was well used to Indian maidens chasing after him, but had never been really chased by one of his own race. He felt a little out of his element.

Then his face relaxed slowly on a new thought of his own. It was really a stroke of good luck. Let the maid know that she was not the only filly in the corral. This was a real lady.

"I'll need time to change once we are back, ma'am."

"It's Mary Florence and I don't mind those clothes at all."

"I do," he said firmly. "They ain't the only ones I own, you know."

But again he was not thinking of anything but Eliza. He wanted her to see him in something different *at* someone else's camp fire.

Having been a sailor he knew how to roll his clothes so that they did not wrinkle. Still, two years not wearing them had made a difference in the man and not the clothes. The beige flannel trousers fit him like a kid glove and the open-throated silk shirt he was just barely able to button. The boots hurt his feet and he decided to stay with moccasins.

Proudly he walked by the Donner camp and then the Reed camp, a curse rising in his mind. To dine in such luxury should have been his fate. He could hardly believe his eyes at the beauty of those table settings.

Then his eyes popped.

Mary Florence MacDuff had been most aware of the manner in which others dined on the wagon train. Such she had thought very unnecessary for just herself, James Smith and Charles Stanton.

But that night was different. She wanted Doolittle Thornburg to see her in a different light. She cared not what others thought.

The heavy plate Selkirk emblemed dinnerware was unwrapped from lengths of wool, delicate crystal removed from cotton wadding. From a distance Hardkoop gaped at the handsomeness of the bone-handled cutlery laid out upon Swiss lace. The others had finery; this was old world elegance.

In unpacking her last worldly treasures, she had stumbled upon a Harlan MacDuff secret: several wax-sealed bottles of Madeira wine and two earthen jugs of Scotch whiskey.

With such, for gentlemen diners, she could out-Donner the Donners, if not out-Reed the Reeds.

At first the sling-armed James Smith and the shy Charles Stanton felt a little out of place, but Mary Florence was in a mood to make even William Pike feel welcome at her table.

Her greatest pride, even when Harlan was never home to partake of it, was her cookery. On thin metal rods she had skewered Manitoba potato quarters, chunks of antelope, onion sections and whole carrots. As they slowly roasted on forked branches above the fire, she unwrapped another clay jar as though it were her greatest treasure of all.

It had taken her eight of her twenty-eight years to taste the first peaches off her own trees. All she had to show for such patience were six identical preserve jars and a dozen burlap-wrapped cuttings that she kept faithfully moist.

The men, at that time, were not aware of the honor she was bestowing upon them. The juice from the peaches was slowly poured, time after time, over the cooking meat and vegetables. The fruit would serve for dessert.

A simple meal, but filling and tasty for hungry men.

With each comfortably granted a Scotch goblet in hand, she excused herself for a few moments before she served dinner. The talk turned to matters of the day, with a short break to hear Jacob Donner's dinner prayer echo and reecho through the canyon.

He was getting back into fine fettle and rambled for a full twenty minutes. His concern over the health of James Smith was not excluded.

"Funny," Charles Stanton mused, "ain't a man in the camp that was out hunting."

"Well, I sure as hell didn't shoot myself to get out of work," Smith grumbled.

"What do you think of it, Mr. Thornburg?"

He had thought little on it. "Not Indians," he said logically, and with reason. "They would have caught us in ambush and kept firing until they got what they wanted. No, from what you say about the way that ole bullet kept ricocheting around it could have come from a mountain man a good mile or so away who missed his mark. Just your bad luck, Smith, that one of the ricochets came back to bite you."

"Why do you say one of the ricochets?"

"Knowledge," he said expansively. "Direct hit would have knocked his whole shoulder off."

Smith accepted it as fact, for the flesh wound was really too minor for the sling, but the attention he had received over the whole matter was almost as rewarding as his single day as a scout.

A sound from the back of the wagon made him turn. It was a different Mary Florence who stepped down. Her red hair had been pulled to one side and flowed over her right shoulder like a cascade, making the ruffle-front blouse even whiter. She swept to them in an exquisitely tailored tartan skirt of navy blue, forest green and blood red. Her proud face was aglow with excitement, the smiling lips shell-pink and the hazel-green eyes soft and velvety.

Damn it all! Doolittle thought. I didn't expect her to be this lovely all dolled up. Across an open space he could see Eliza serving dinner to the Reed family, sans Virginia. In maid's black and white, by candle-light, she was equally lovely. But clearly there was an unexpected factor in the matter now, for this woman was including him in on the luxury and Eliza was still only a servant of it.

＊　＊　＊

"I had those filthy rags burned," Margaret said smugly. "You have hired men to do that sort of labor, James Frazier."

Who can't follow orders, he was thinking. A hell of a mess Milt Elliott almost got them into, but he smiled and nodded his agreement.

"Now on another point," Margaret went on. "A woman in my position, undeservedly, has been made mockery of, sir. Envy, I call it, unfortunately. Imagine, forcing *my* maid to do such work and thus go against my personal wishes. It shall not happen again, sir. My needs, of course, shall prevail."

She lowered her voice to a tense, conspiratorial whisper, all the time keeping an eye out for Eliza's advance back toward the table.

"You, unfortunately, slept through most of my trauma. I wish for you to have a sound talk with Eliza and days added to her service for those that have been stolen away from me. Her place was really here with Virginia, if not with me."

Margaret, seeing his slight start, thought mockingly: It was your place to be by her side, too.

"Briefly, sir," she went on, looking toward the Mac-Duff camp, "I do not like our children being subjected to that sort of thing. You don't see Elizabeth Donner allowing their hired hands to sit at the table as equals. That woman is showing her true colors by entertaining three men at once. Of course, I can't fault the new guide. You were asleep and couldn't give him proper instructions."

James Frazier nodded. Donner had come and told him about the man. He had quickly agreed to the hiring. Anything to get them out of there and his life with Virginia back to normal. Doolittle Thornburg had been on his mind ever since.

"You are quite right, my dear," he said. "I have already suggested to George Donner that the most valid service the man could perform for us would be to scout ahead and learn how close we are to Lance Hastings."

Margaret's watery eyes sparkled. This would solve her own envy problem quite nicely. She knew that the Scotswoman was "putting on the dog" for one man alone, but the woman's table was putting her own to shame.

After dinner Eliza had planned on casually ambling over to the Keseberg wagons, but James Frazier caught her before she could get away.

She listened to him, but knew the words were Margaret's. Her eyes widened, then a slow flush of anger stole over her pretty face.

"Damned presumptuous of you, I'd say," she muttered grimly. "Did not you agree to the rule that no wagon would go through without work on the road?"

"That is beside the point, Eliza. Your concern should have been for Virginia, and Mrs. Reed."

Eliza smiled a slow, enigmatic smile.

"What of your own concern?" she said wickedly.

"My concern over the accident is great."

"Accident," she said mockingly, "is hardly what I would call it."

"What do you mean by that?" he gulped, his voice hoarse and unnatural.

"I had to clean her up, remember? If I had not been there Mrs. Reed would have learned of the 'accident' immediately."

He jerked away from her like a puppet on twisted strings, his mind boggled. James Smith was a petty little fear in comparison to the knowledge that Eliza possessed. No, there would be no days added to her service with the family. If anything they would be greatly shortened—one way or another. But this time he would not discuss it with Milt Elliot. It was a matter he had to carefully think out and handle quite on his own.

The matter put to Doolittle by George Donner he did not have to carefully think out. He didn't like it. To be separated from the wagon train again meant not seeing Eliza and missing out on a return invitation for dinner with Mary Florence. With the time lost at Fort Bridger and on the mountainside, he easily figured the Hastings party to be a good two weeks ahead. That long on the trail alone was not to his liking, but he had to start living the lie that he had created.

He tried to stall on the matter, but George Donner shooed him away at daybreak. Even before he left the canyon mouth he could hear the train begin to rattle along its way. He had been in the saddle for an hour, riding easily along. He figured a good two hours for the wagons to come the same distance. His horse could pick and choose its footing on the stone floor as the awesome canyon narrowed, the wagons would have to roll over the scattered rocks or have them pushed aside.

He sat and listened to the echos for a few moments. It was like a shoemaker's hammer rat-atat-tatting through leather onto a metal lath. The wagons were rolling directly over the stones and sending the weird sounds into the deep ravines and back out again.

The canyon floor rose slightly and then was no more.

Again as if by magic he was instantly transported into a different world. The vista below was unmeasurable and so black with wooded terrain that only here and there did he glimpse a silver flash of a northwest flowing stream.

From the crude Lance Hastings map he had seen at Fort Bridger he rightly guessed that what he saw was the Red Fork of the Weber River that ran down into the Great Salt Lake.

Again he sat for a long time, but looking, not listening. There was enough mountain man in him to let his eyes travel very slowly over the forest tops below, rising just as slowly as the valley evaporated into the far distant Weber canyon.

"Just your luck, Doolittle," he grumbled. "Not a single dust cloud or puff of smoke. You might just as well be the first man to set eyes on this virgin land."

Winding down off the height he soon knew that to be a falsehood. The forest carpet of deep pine needles had been severely etched by the sixty-seven Hastings wagons. Here, where the trees were still quite widely scattered, he could follow the ruts with no difficulty and knew Donner would have no trouble finding them as well.

At riverside he was just as surprised. At this point the Red Fork ambled along, as though it knew it was going against nature by flowing northwest. Over the centuries it had produced wide, hard gravel banks, of a width double the size of the Reed monster.

To his chagrin it stayed this way for four miles. Chagrin, because it threw his calculation on the speed of the Hastings train way off. If this continued they would be making a good ten to twelve miles a day to the Donners one to two miles.

Then the forest suddenly closed in on the fork and turned it into a rapids. Wheel tracks turned into the water as though going for a swim. But the opposite bank told the story of the difficulty of emerging. Picks and shovels had been used to make ramps in the steeper banks. The depth of the ruts suggested to Thornburg that many days and a great deal of manpower had been expended on the effort. The tightly trunked forest beyond told of further difficulties. Hastings had tried to take his party through without wasting further time on cutting a road. One high tree branch still possessed its banner of victory—the bows and canvas right off the top of a wagon.

"Well," Doolittle drawled to himself, "this is going to bring us closer together in location but not time. Here, now, what's this?"

Stuck in a bush at the top of the river bank cuts was a leather pouch tied closed by a length of red cloth. Within was a letter from Lance Hastings. Even though it was brief Doolittle read it twice, once on each side of the river. He had been correct in thinking they might be close to each other in location, but figured the time element was something for only George Donner to determine. He looked upstream and shrugged. He would wait and let George Donner make a determination on campsite, as well.

"What the . . ." He came awake with a sharp kick to his moccasin clad sole by a heavy boot. Milt Elliott towered over him with James Frazier at his side.

"I am not wasting my portion of your guide fee on sleep, Mr. Thornburg."

He sat up, rubbing the sleep from his eyes. "I wasn't going to stand around waiting with a finger up my ass," he growled. "There's a letter."

James Frazier saw the indicated pouch on the ground and quickly snatched it up. To Doolittle's amazement he smiled on reading the message.

"How do you see this, Thornburg?"

"Most like he said," slowly rising. "Weber canyon is very bad. If he fears that his own party might not get through it, our luck would be worse. He's got the manpower from sixty-seven wagons."

James Frazier pondered. "Well, I am glad now that you didn't ride to overtake him."

"Weren't my place. Will still go if Mr. Donner tells me."

Reed smiled quizzically. "Matter for the whole company to decide." Then he looked knowingly at Milt Elliott. "Go hustle them along, Milt. The party that goes after Hastings to bring him back should get started right away. Three of us, I would suggest."

Doolittle took it to mean that he would be the third with those two. He saw no reason for it, but saw no reason against it.

Milt Elliott bolted back to his horse. He saw a lot of reason behind it and anticipated that James Smith would be the third going out with them.

After the easy ride out of the canyon and down Red Fork the news was vastly disappointing. They were only seven days out of Fort Bridger and being forced to stop again.

"Well," George drawled, "I can see sense in sending a messenger to find Hastings and bring him back to guide us, but I can't see sense in his stating he will guide us across the mountains by a better and shorter route than that down the canyon. Why didn't he guide his own people that way?"

"That is something," James Frazier said, with overdue politeness, "that we can only learn from the man himself. I have been across the river, waiting for you to arrive, and it is rough. I would suggest that we send three men out. Their trail is bad and one man alone would kill himself hacking through the undergrowth."

"Excellent suggestion, James. Now, who shall we send with Thornburg?"

James Frazier pondered as though he didn't have it all worked out in his mind. "The best horses to get them there have to be considered too, George. I do not mean to boast that I have two of the finest in my mount and that of Milt Elliott's. I think I speak for Milt when I say that we would be glad to go. But as for Thornburg, it has just come to me that he could be of greater service by staying behind. If there is a better and shorter route over this mountain, can he not be looking for it while we are gone?"

It was met with a mumble of agreement from all. Only Jacob Donner wondered in the back of his mind why James Frazier was being so cooperative.

"Then who for the third?" he mumbled.

"I thought Smith," Reed said, almost too quickly. "He proved he is not a half bad scout."

"With two good arms," Mary Florence snorted. "Do you forget he is slinged, man?"

Before he could protest that a woman had raised the objection another raise an objection of her own.

"James Frazier," Margaret hissed from the wagon steps, "you and Milt both can't go and leave me manless."

"And I shall be glad to go in place of Smith," Charles Stanton quickly got in. "My knowledge of botany could be of service in helping to find where they have broken trail."

James Frazier quietly and quickly realigned his thinking. His whole pie was being reduced to a third, but he was still the most important third to get to Lance Hastings first.

"You are quite right, my dear, I was unthinking. Milt will stay, of course. Stanton, glad to have you along."

Big Mac McCutchen cleared his voice. "Horse is good, but my arms are better. I can axe through for two men, if I am needed."

"Needed and accepted," James Frazier grinned. Now that he had narrowed the mission into his own self-interest, the two would be excellent to help get him through. Smith he would let Milt worry about, and Eliza wasn't going anywhere.

6

MARY FLORENCE hadn't raised any objection to the departure of Charles Stanton and her being reduced to a single wounded helped. She automatically assumed she could fall back on Doolittle Thornburg.

George Donner had taken James Frazier's suggestion too much to heart. Even though it was just after high noon, Doolittle was sent off to live up to his boast of knowing the country and its Indians.

It didn't take him the whole afternoon to learn two things: a man could get hopelessly and aimlessly lost in this dense forest where the sky was only a mere slit overhead *unless* they stayed to some well defined and well traveled trails through the woods. Nor were there deer trails. The markings in the dirt were of unshod Indian ponies, and the newness made him keep his own mount's horseshoe markings safely off the path.

Keeping parallel to the Indian trail he was quickly "across Hastings mountain," but looked into another canyon valley and a mountain even higher. Far below, in an aspen glen, a spiral of smoke rose and the sound brought back to him was most familiar—Indian women beginning the erection of tepees. No matter the tribe, he knew those heavy laboring women did not take the large buffalo hide canvas covering and poles off the travois for a single night's stay.

Women, children and a camp meant a war party somewhere about.

He slowly circled back and found a safe spot to put down his bedroll for the night. There was no question in his mind that the trio would not be back the next day.

The same was thought in the camp.

Eliza laughed gaily and tried the word again. Her laughter was not so much over the manner in which her tongue got twisted on the word as it was nervousness over the dangerous game she was playing. They had sat three-abreast on a log before the camp fire, with her in the middle. Lewis had sat quietly puffing on a Bavarian carved pipe that amazingly had all the facial features of George Donner—right down to the square beard. Phillipine was in a state of happy bliss. Lewis had opened a long-closed door for her in allowing her to teach Eliza German. He was the one most qualified to do the teaching, she was well aware, but it was an opportunity for her to make a woman friend with his blessing.

The simple words Eliza learned quite handily. A few times Lewis had grunted over minor mistakes and she repeated correctly. Then, as though in reward, she felt his hand come to rest between them and then slowly inch out to touch her thigh. In a casual gesture she turned more toward Phillipine, let her right hand fall down upon Lewis's and spread her skirt out to cover the action. Their fingers intwined and now a squeeze was a reward for each correct word.

"Ach! That baby is always hungry. I am a few moments, please."

Phillipine no sooner was within the wagon than Lewis turned and stole a quick kiss. It was all so thrilling and dangerous. He looked at her with awed tenderness.

"*Elisa*," he said huskily, "you-you think on us?"

Slowly she nodded her head.

"All of the time," she said.

"And you will become—"

"Your woman? That's what I do think about all the time."

His sigh was gusty with relief.

"Just over these mountains is the lake and settlement of these Mormon people."

"I know," she said, and a note of sadness crept into her voice. "Working on the road I was able to find out much about them from Tamsen. Their city of Nauvoo wasn't too far from the Donner Illinois farm. They were not a loved people there, Lewis. Their leader was killed and they were burned out. Their settlement here is only a few months old."

"Good. That will mean plenty of fine land left."

"Church land, Lewis. They claim the whole basin and to become one of them you must share all you possess. I—I can't be responsible for you having to do that."

He looked at her with renewed interest. As much as he hated to think about involving himself with an organized church again, he had begun to build all of his thoughts about the future around her.

"We will do what we must do, *kindlein*."

"We would be fools," she said. "I thought that was our only answer in the eyes of the world—that it would ease my Catholic mind. This trip is teaching me quite a bit about myself. I loved to think of the day I would marry and have a home of my own. I still do. But now I know that *loving* is the biggest part. I look at Augustus Spitzer and Joseph Reinhardt and know that I could never be a wife to either. I can look at you and know that Salt Lake is not the answer, either. It would be like putting a fence around a wild bull at mating season. I am your woman now. You—can take me wherever life will be best for us . . ."

She stared at him in wide-eyed surprise, as though someone else had spoken the words.

"I—your woman," she whispered. "Oh, Lewis, this will be dreadful for Phillipine!"

"No," he said gruffly, "it will be wonderful for her!"

"I wonder if I would like being Phillipine," she said bitterly.

"I don't blame you the thought," he said gently. "You are two different women to me. Many men would just run off and desert her. I thought of such in Germany." He scoffed. "Perhaps God still has not fully released my soul to the devil. With this next rule I break he probably shall. We go on to California, *Elisa.* I shall some way find the manner to take you also as wife, and the sin will be mine."

She gazed at him tenderly. For such a promised future she could put up with the Reeds for awhile longer.

After she left he turned the matter over in his mind. Eliza he did not want as a mistress, he thought angrily. He wished for her under him constantly, and not with guilt attached. He had to find a way to make her his wife.

Phillipine came and sat daintily on the log, smiling softly and secretly to herself, as though finding life enjoyable for a change.

"Phillipine," he said hoarsely, "we must talk of the future."

Never before had Lewis talked of the future with her, he had just ordered what it would be.

"As you wish," she said softly.

"What think you of *Elisa?*"

"I think her most lovely and most friendly a being."

"What think you of her joining our party in California?"

"Whatever you desire, husband."

Her words suggested that he had to explain his desires no further. She sat with a quiet glow of triumph on her face. Ever since he had come down off the windlass crew there had been a not-so-subtle change in him. The almost nightly beatings she had experienced across the Great Plains had ceased. Something, or someone, had tended to civilize him. Not until that evening had she realized that it was Eliza.

Well, she could accept that. She could accept anything that would stave off the beatings. But she felt sorry for Eliza. When things didn't quite go the way Lewis wished them, he could grow quite fierce. In the meantime she would make a friend of Eliza, because she needed her mentally just as desperately as Lewis desired her physically.

In the middle of the morning Doolittle Thornburg rode back into camp, a report of sorts formulated in his mind. High above a group of Ute warriors watched him and the camp. They smiled to themselves patiently and knowingly. They were just returning from nearly two weeks of tracking the other wagon train. If this one followed their lead then they were no fear to the Utes either.

They had become almost bored in the mile to mile and a half a day progress of the Hastings group. They could not understand such stupidity. The wagons had tried to go through portions of the canyon that were even wholly impassable for Indian travois. Cliffs that the Utes avoided, the white men had spent days in bodily lifting up their wagons by block and tackle and windlass. Some had not made it up to the precipice and lay as smashed ruins seventy-five feet below.

But they were no longer a concern to the Utes. That group was now out on the plains of the Great Salt Lake, beyond their territory. Let this group do the same and they would be of no worry. But let a single tree be felled for a log cabin clearing and they would be greatly concerned.

Had Doolittle gone down into their camp, as was his normal custom, he might have learned this fact.

"Not even a well defined animal trail," he told George Donner, "but I did get to the summit. Beyond I saw the plains."

He failed to say that he saw another canyon valley and mountain in between.

"Did you blaze it?"

"No need. It's rough but must be Hastings' other route."

"Well, he should be here shortly with Reed. That will give us time to plan and leave in the morning."

But no one arrived back that day or the next.

"The youngsters love the idle play," Lavina Murphy scowled, "but I'm beginning to fear they ran into Indians."

"I saw signs of none," Doolittle said casually, but he now sensed that their every move was being watched. And it was, in utter confusion. Finally, the war party chief could stand it no more and sent a group of warriors out to see what mishap may have befallen the three men from this party. He was not pleased with the site of his own camp being so near, but wished the white wagons to move first.

White Eagle shuddered each time he heard the report of their hunting rifles. He feared that the white men might have run across some of his tracking party and would force him into attacking the train. He was hardly a coward and his warriors knew that as fact. But the Utes were stretched thin fighting an enemy older than the white man. The war with Mexico was forcing the Comanche into Ute territory and this they would not stand.

"What of this?"

White Eagle's attention was diverted to the banks of the Red Fork just above the wagon camp.

A young woman, on a small pony, and in head-to-toe ensemble of flaming red velvet, was riding upstream quite alone.

"Do not let harm befall her," White Eagle snapped. "I do not wish problems with these people, although they give me many."

He was not the only one to see Virginia Backenstoe Reed ride off alone.

John Breen saw and it turned his stomach into a mass of quivering jelly. He had waited so long to catch her without James Frazier being about that he could hardly believe it. He went to where the Breen horses were tethered and jumped upon one without saddling the animal.

Eliza had not only seen but been an unwilling participant in Virginia's departure.

"I question if she is strong enough."

"Nonsense!" Margaret carped. "She is the picture of health and I'm delighted she is up and about. It is boorish to have to eat dinner with only the younger children."

And twice as boorish to serve it, Eliza thought.

Virginia was well aware of what she was doing. She had watched camp events quite carefully that morning. Only when she saw Sol Hook departing by foot did she spring into action.

Jean Baptiste had persuaded Sol to go hunting, he'd gloomily agreed only after Tamsen thought it a good idea. But all the way into the woods he was tortured by memories, griefs and decisions. Because they would be gone the better part of the day Jean Baptiste had suggested they take a sling pack of extra food. Sol had felt guilty in taking extra jerky and dried fruit without telling Tamsen. He had finally come to the conclusion that he must go after the Boggs train alone. He had seen the Bridger map but once, but knew that after the Hastings "nearer way" was the original Fort Hall trail. A man on foot, he determined, could make it through these woods ten times faster than the wagons. Going up the stream bank he had walked at a pace that maddened Jean Baptiste. Hunting was not a chore that he enjoyed and wished it quickly over. A quarter mile from the camp they began their climb into the woods. Sol began looking for the right spot to slip away from the young French-Mexican.

Virginia let the pony pick its way at will along the river side. She had marked in her mind the spot the two young men had entered the woods and was in no hurry to catch up too fast. She was also waiting for the other element in her plan. She didn't have to wait long to hear the clatter of hoofbeats on the river bank stones. Nor did she have to look around to see who was pursuing her.

"Virginia, wait for me!"

She ignored the call until he had the saddle-less horse abreast and was grinning down at her.

"I thought you might like company for your ride."

She looked at him strangely, as though not recognizing him. "I'm sorry, but since my accident I seem to have a hard time remembering some things. Who are you?"

He took her statement for fact. "I'm John Breen."

She smiled weakly as Bayles some days smiled, "Hello, John Breen."

She said no more and continued to ride slowly. She wanted him to get a good close-up look at her. For him she had decked herself out in splendor, glowing, radiantly if too strikingly beautiful, and for Sol the colorful red so it could be seen at a goodly distance.

Gad, he thought, what a gal! Ever since he had started mooning over her he had been the brunt of his younger brothers' jokes and ribbing. Now he would show them that he wasn't too coarse and vulgar for her.

"I am turning here."

"Doesn't look too good a spot for a ride."

"Because of the accident I do not wish to ride too fast or too far."

John followed. A slow pace was to his liking to give him a better opportunity to feast his eyes upon her and get her into a meaningful conversation.

It was cool in the woods under the tree shade. Virginia managed the well-trained pony with expert skill. They went straight up the wooded mountainside, Virginia keeping her eyes alert for signs that Sol and Jean Baptiste had come the same way.

John's horse was skittish. It didn't like the feel of a human directly upon its back. It snorted and pawed and fought the rope reins.

Virginia said nothing until she saw the recognizable orange of Jean Baptiste's tam ahead of them through the trees.

"Perhaps we should walk, before your horse decides to cause another accident. Do you ride bareback much?"

It was an opening John was not going to let pass. He slipped from his horse and went around to assist her out of the sidesaddle.

"Did all the time back on the farm, but not with this horse. My favorite Paw sold off before we left. You would have liked that old mare."

Willingly, she allowed him to lift her down. Instead of being clumsy, as she had expected, he was strong and brought her down with a slow ease.

His slowness was on purpose to look her over closely. He missed nothing: the pearly translucence of her, the sheen to her curls, the redness of her lips, and the full-blown youthfulness of her bosom and figure.

"Thank you," she smiled sweetly. "And why would I have liked your horse?"

"She liked to be ridden double," he chuckled. "She could always tell when I had a pretty girl on her back and would neigh each time I would try to steal a kiss."

"Did she neigh much?" Virginia asked, timidly.

"Nearly got a sore throat one day," he chortled.

Virginia smiled, and her smile was knowing and excited. She had John Breen doing exactly as she had anticipated he would do. She tucked Billy's bridle into the saddle loop, for he was trained to follow wherever she walked.

"This ground is rough. You may have to take my hand, John Breen."

It was an invitation he quickly accepted. He was not even aware when she had taken off the right riding gauntlet. He glowed and trembled at his touch of her bare hand. So long had he daydreamed of such a moment and the moments that were to follow that his youthful arousal was immediate.

Because he was still growing too fast for his clothing, Virginia could not help but notice. But he was moving a little too fast for her plan. Sol hadn't even noticed them following yet.

"Eeeek!" she shrieked, grabbing onto his arm with her free hand. "Something is crawling beneath my skirt!"

She began to stomp and let out little eruptions of high pierced sound.

"On that rock! Sit on the rock and we will shake it out! What does it feel like?"

"Something as big as you," she wailed. She quickly obeyed and hoped he had gotten her double meaning. All that concerned her was that the noise she had made was bringing feet pounding back through the woods.

Jean Baptiste started at the unexpected sight.

He knew she was a girl of breeding, and mistakenly suspected that her call was due to the mésalliance with the uncouth boy shaking so at her skirts that bare calves and thighs were showing above the red riding boots.

"*Mon Dieu!* What is this?"

John Breen started at the unexpected sound of his voice. He spun so quickly that he lost his balance and sat down hard on the ground.

"Something up her skirt," he stammered.

Jean Baptiste suspected it had been a spidery hand. He screwed up his face until he looked like a benevolent old chaperone. But the girl's eyes confused him. There was no trace of fear, but they sparkled as though bordering on anger. Had he blundered in where he was not wanted?

"It's all right now," Virginia pouted. "I do not feel it crawling on my leg anymore."

What she really wanted to do was demand why Sol Hook had not come running back to her aide and catch her with John, but then her whole plan would be out in the open.

"Fine," Jean Baptiste grumbled, "but less noise, please. Over this rise is a little glen with grazing antelope, if not scared away already. My hunting partner is waiting for them to come closer up to us. Kindly go in another direction."

"Sure, why not?" John agreed.

Virginia sat silent as the teamster went back through the woods. Mention of the glen and antelope had given her a new thought and a much better plan for Sol to see them together.

She got up, brushed down her skirt and held out her hand for John to take it again.

"I like the idea. One glen suggests there must be others. You might even teach me how to ride bareback. I've never done it before, you know."

Again she gave double meaning to her words. More and more confused, John gazed at her as he took her hand. He, too, had seen the bare calves and thighs— and much more than Jean Baptiste. Beneath the red velvet was not a single inch of petticoat or pantaloon material. He had been incredulous, but greatly intoxicated at the find. Now he had to find another excuse for shaking out her skirt.

They walked in silence, each working out their own plans. John directed them on a rising angle away from the hunters. When they reached the rise there was another aspen glen a short distance down and a long narrow clearing.

"Did you mean it about barebacking?" John gulped, when they were through the aspen trees.

"Why not?" she shrugged, trying to be indifferent. "Although I would be afraid to try it alone."

John had been suffering excruciating torment that she would not utter those words.

"Good as done," he chuckled, grabbing her about the waist. "Just relax, as up you go."

The first attempt didn't work. Virginia tried to automatically sit side-saddle.

"You'll just keep slipping off that way. This time as I lift swing your leg over and pull up your skirt."

The view he got as she swung her leg over the broad back nearly made him drop her.

"I'm up and comfortable," she giggled, bunching the skirt into her lap and down each leg as well as she could.

The horse looked back wide-eyed, as though he disagreed with her statement.

With an agile leap John sprang up in front of her.

"We made it. Now wrap your arms about my waist and scoot up close."

The horse continued to stare in disbelief. It gave a snort of utter disgust.

"Why don't you try to make it neigh?" she giggled again.

Her head was on one side, her hands clasped about his middle. He turned his head, but the angle was such that he could only give her a peck on the side of the mouth.

"He didn't neigh," he said.

"Maybe because it wasn't a real kiss and wasn't stolen."

John's Adam's apple jerked in his muscular young throat. The invitation was there but the next kiss had to come without warning. Slowly, if somewhat reluctantly, he got the horse to start moving. Billy came trotting up and gave the horse a jealous leer. The horse jerked its head up proudly, as though fully understanding. Because the pace was just an amble it suddenly didn't mind the weight.

For half of the clearing Virginia kept her head directly behind John's broad red neck. This was not the clearing or glen she wished to really perform within. When she had her head to the side she had already determined that only another stand of aspen separated them from the grazing antelope. And as no shots had rang out, it meant that Sol was still watching them.

Without warning John tilted to the side, swung his arm back about her waist and drew her close. Before she could protest his lips were upon hers. Not only was it surprising and quick, but a little harsh and bruising.

In a little bit of a stunned daze, she said the first thing that came to her mind.

"Still didn't neigh."

"Because it still isn't the way I normally kiss."

Virginia frowned. The aspen stand was still a little ways away. If she stalled him now she might not be able to get him to kiss her again for Sol's benefit. She might just have to be punished with two more of the bruising encounters.

"How is normal?"

Again without warning he drew his right leg up and onto the horse's neck. Before the horse knew what was taking place, and Virginia as well, he nimbly stood erect on the one leg, twisted about and sat down facing her. He grabbed behind each thigh, lifted her legs over his own and pulled her forward.

It happened so quickly that she remained relaxed. "I—" she started to say, but his face loomed right before her eyes and his paws closed over her ears.

To her utter amazement his hands were gentle and his lips just barely touched her own again and again as though sampling them.

Just as gently one of the paws slipped to the nape of her neck as the other dropped and stole around her slim waist. This time the lips stayed, but were not demanding and harsh. Something soft and moist ran quickly across the crack of her lips. An electric thrill shot up her spine and made her hair ends tingle.

John was using every bit of kissing expertise he had

learned from the older farm girls. Once he had been as brusque as the first two stolen kisses. Then, when he was thirteen, a daring girl of twenty had shown him how much farther a young man could get in being subtle until the girl reacted one way or another. A few times his face had stung from the reaction, but he did not anticipate a face slap that day.

She was gazing at him almost eagerly, with shyness and surprise, for all her determined restraint to hold off for the next clearing.

Again he let his tongue just lightly play along her lips until they trembled under his touch.

Then, without conscious volition, her arms flew up around his neck, and she pulled him farther forward, locking her mouth to his in a savage kiss. He had his reaction. While her fingers crawled through his hair, his crawled down to bunch the skirt even higher up onto her waist and back off her legs. She didn't feel the coolness because his legs beneath her own were like raging furnaces.

Then, against her pelvis she felt something else just as raging. As long as it was still shrouded in pants cloth she did not fear it or the bleeding it would bring about. Besides, the other sensations running through her body were giving her enough emotions to cope with. Each kiss seemed so different and startling and exciting.

The hot noonday sun was quickly exchanged for cooling aspen shadows. She shivered, but because of his words.

"Let's get down here and do this thing proper."

Now she did have to stall. It was only twenty to thirty feet through the stand.

"No," she gasped, "in the sun. I'm freezing in here."

To make her point even stronger she pulled him back into another savage embrace.

John didn't care where, he was as far from freezing

and being most subtle. He had won the battle by undoing a button at a time without her knowing, now all that was left was to win the war.

With her hands and mind busy demanding more of his kisses, he reached around her and let his hands come to rest on each of her butt cheeks.

With a single jerk he pulled her forward and entered without problem at a slight upward angle. When her mouth gaped open in surprise he thrust his tongue deep to keep her from screaming out.

The scream stayed in her mind because the pain was there and gone before it even registered. She stiffened, locking him in tight. He was not as manly endowed as James Frazier, but that was not what made her turn almost to statue-stone. She knew that at the first trickle of blood down her thigh she would lose her breakfast all over him.

But there was no rumbling in her stomach. They both sat perfectly still, hugging tightly. The only motion was the left to right to left sway of the horse, but motion enough to make John grow in excitement and size.

Foolishly, Virginia thought that he had her so tightly plugged that the blood could not escape. To keep it thus she pulled him into an even tighter embrace.

John took it as another reaction and slowly moved his hips in the opposite direction as the horse's sway. Virginia feared it would cause him to release and fought against the motion.

John was being pulled from side to side, creating sensitivity never before aroused. He was being transported beyond the point of even thinking.

The hot sun beat down again upon them and he was not aware. The horse neighed at something ahead in the clearing and he did not hear it. His only senses lay centered between his legs.

Virginia felt and heard and drew her mouth away

to rest her chin and head onto his shoulder. For the moment she would allow their waists to remain locked because it was becoming most pleasurable.

As though they belonged in a most different setting, she watched the dozen antelope raise their heads one at a time and sniff at the air. Then, as though hearing a starter's gun, they leaped in unison and began bounding northeastward across the clearing and away from the hidden hunters.

Jean Baptiste jumped up to shout at the intruders and stood silent with his mouth gaping. Because of his well traveled life at twenty-three he thought his eyes were telling him correctly what was transpiring upon the horse, but never had his eyes viewed such a happening.

"*Caramba!*" he gasped. "This Jean Baptiste Trubode must someday try."

Sol Hook rose angrily. Because of his inexperience he was not really aware of what was happening below, or even really watching. All he could think about were the escaping antelope. They, he had determined, were his best avenue of escape away from the teamster. He had waited for one to be felled by a shot and then Jean Baptiste running down to slit its throat and bleed it. Time enough for him to be well away before his absence was questioned. Now this!

"Get out of there, you damn fools!"

The shout carried down to Virginia but John hardly heard it, he was so near fruition that his ears were ringing.

The shout brought Virginia back to her original plan. Sol had seen them and that's all that mattered to her now. She got a hand onto each shoulder round and harshly pushed back.

"What the—" John started to protest, but the push was sending them off the side of the horse. Virginia started to scream as they fell.

John had been thrown from a horse many times and knew how to roll onto the ground and not get hurt. This was a different matter. They were still joined. He wrapped his arms about her head and tried to roll her into a ball. It gave her more fright than anything and she was fighting him back even before they thudded into the tall grass.

"*Mi Dieu!*" Jean Baptiste oddly mixed Mexican and French in his excitement. "He is still putting his length to her!"

Sol stiffened, as though he had been struck by lightning. Her piercing scream moved his body before his mind. He pounded down the hillside out of gentlemanly concern for her womanhood and not jealousy. She was not the tongue-taunting Virginia Reed at that moment, but any young girl in a similar circumstance.

Virigina had greatly miscalculated his arrival in her mind. In fantasy he was supposed to be instantly upon them with raging jealousy. In fact, John was ready to fully spend himself before Sol made it to the edge of the clearing.

He collapsed atop her exhausted. Equally exhausted she lay most rigid and utterly confused. Something bizarre had happened to her after the scream. She had been filled with the warmest, most compelling desire to stay that way forever and ever.

Sol Hook ended up causing her more pain than John Breen.

Embarrassed at the sight of them and furious at John for being such a lustful animal, he took him by the scuff of the neck and threw him off to the side.

Virginia let out a painful yelp and sat up. Stunned, John rolled in the grass and tried to shake off his exhausted state. From somewhere in the back of his mind he recalled Jean Baptiste and scrambled up, ex-

pecting to have to fight the little French-Mexican for
intruding again.

It took him a moment to focus his eyes and then
he roared with mirth. Sol was standing in a very un-
gainly, inexperienced boxer's stance. Sol was hardly
any match for him. He had him in size by a good
head, length of arm reach and well used muscles. Sol
stood as though transfixed by the chuckle. John Breen
was also experienced at barnyard scuffles. He would
let the enemy make the first move to weigh his worth.

Virginia sat seeing neither of them, her eyes glued
upon her creamy white thighs that stayed creamy and
white and bloodless. This was as bizarre as her feeling of never wanting him to exit. Where was all of
the blood that she feared would make her sick? She
just continued to stare at it not being there.

John watched Sol begin to circle, pure joy lighting
up his blue eyes. He kept his hands down at his sides,
until Sol made his first clumsy lunge forward. At the
last possible instant, John moved his head aside a
little, the motion graceful, exactly timed, so that he
scarcely seemed to have moved a single muscle. The
tight fist whistled over his shoulder inches from his
ear, and Sol was thrown off balance and landed
heavily against him.

John still did not raise a hand, but Sol was suddenly doubled over and screaming in terrible agony.
From the edge of the clearing Jean Baptiste had seen
John's knee come up and catch Sol squarely between
the thighs.

But even as he began to run to give Sol some aid,
John did begin to use his fists, chopping away at Sol's
bent over neck and back. Sol went sprawling in the
grass face-down. All of John's bully instincts came
surging to the surface and he began to kick at the
downed figure with his boot toes and heels.

Jean Baptiste in many respects was even smaller

and more wirey than Sol, but he had an equalizer against John. Using a most odd mixture of French and Spanish curses, he stopped short and shouldered his two-barreled shotgun. He drew the hammers back one at a time, and Virginia knew that she had never in all her life heard a more threatening sound.

"Stop it!" she shrieked. "Stop it, all of you!"

Sol rolled over and sat up on a moan.

"They started it!" John insisted hotly.

Jean Baptiste grinned wickedly. "And finished it, *señor bambino*."

John glowered. He did not know what he had been called, but he took it as an insult.

"Put down the weapon and we'll see who finishes what."

"Haven't you done enough?" Virginia screamed. "Get out of here, John Breen. I never want to set eyes on you again, you dirty, nasty creature. Oh, Sol, what did the bully do to you?"

John stood for a moment stunned, unused to a girl with such quickly changing moods. He walked to the horse, but then he turned, quivering with rage.

"You were a part of it too, girl!" he got out. "A man does not do that thing all by himself!"

"Move!" Jean Baptiste snarled, even though he knew the boy spoke the truth. Still, he shuddered at what this would do to the wagon train. He had seen family feuds break out over such a happening. "And if you know what is good for you, keep your mouth shut!"

John flung himself up onto the horse but didn't move for a moment. Oddly, he somehow expected Virginia to ride back with him.

Virginia scrambled to her feet. She had one last act to perform for his benefit. She raced over, squatted down and threw her arms about Sol's shoulders.

"Oh, Sol, I am so sorry. I didn't mean to make you jealous by riding out with that cowardly nothing."

The blood rose and beat about John Breen's ears. He heeled the horse about and into a gallop without ever hearing Sol's answer.

"Jealous? Of what? I thought you were in trouble and came the same as I would have for Elitha or Leanna."

Virginia's face was a turmoil of emotions. Hate struggled to master uncertainty or be commanded by vanity. Vanity won out.

"Did I hear wrong?" she inquired sweetly. "Surely you came because you realized it was me?"

Sol could feel the horrible beads of sweat pop out on his forehead, his fingers dug into the grass. "I think I'm going to be sick."

He pushed her away, not out of rudeness, but to keep her from getting dirtied by his churning stomach.

Virginia jumped up, taking it as a most insulting answer to her question. No one dared treat her like that and get away with it. She now wished that John had pounded and kicked at him a great deal more.

"Not jealous," she mumbled, clawing her way back into Billy's side-saddle without benefit of the wagon steps. "I'll make you wish you had been jealous, Sol Hook. Good and jealous."

Jean Baptiste was too busy to pay her any mind. The knee to the groin and the kicks to the stomach were finally having a terrible effect on Sol. He wretched and wretched so hard that he was starting to spit up blood. On that he started to gag, lose his breath and turn blue.

The teamster forced him down flat on the ground, grabbed him by the back of the belt and shook him up and down until he coughed out the blood and phlegm.

Then he dropped him and let him rest. It would be a little time before he had strength enough to walk back to camp.

John Breen charged through the camp, making sparks fly from the horseshoes. The sides of the Reed wagon were thrown back and he turned the horse sharply to the left in front of the steps and glowered in on the tea-drinking ladies.

"I just caught Sol Hook raping your daughter and had to give him a bit of my knee and boots. The Mex was in on it, too!"

Margaret half raised off her chaise and fell back in a dead faint. Elizabeth Donner struggled to her feet, fighting disbelief and total embarrassment. That a being who came out of her womb could have done such a dastardly thing was so crushing that she stumbled down the steps and fled in a panic back toward the Donner wagons. She could never, ever again, show her face in public. Sol had ruined all the rest of her life and it was really Tamsen's fault. She had always felt that the woman was a horrible influence and this was just living proof of the matter.

Johanna Wolfinger sat with little or no reaction to the news, for she very seldom reacted very strongly to anything. But at times such as that she did not want to be a participant, either. Regally she rose, adjusted the heavy necklace of rubies on her shelf-like bosom and marched sedately down the steps.

Only one person in the amidship room questioned John's bold announcement and why he had not escorted Virginia back if such had been the case. Something smelled very amiss to Eliza. She stood quite silent by the bolted-down tea table watching the departure of the two women, ignoring the third—because faints, real or otherwise, were quite common with Margaret—but giving most of her attention to the rapid gallop of the pony down the riverside bank.

Virginia came riding in too belligerent and fierce of face for someone under the stress and trauma of the time before. Eliza's suspicions mounted.

She held her silence as Virginia jumped down from Billy and stomped up the stairs.

"What is this?" she demanded, stopping short at the sight of her mother.

"You tell us," Eliza said quietly. "John Breen has just come back with a most damaging story against Sol Hook."

Virginia started. This was better than if she had planned it herself. To save himself, John had given her all the ammunition she needed to ruin Sol for not being jealous. Now she could really begin play-acting. She ran and threw herself down across her prone mother.

"Mommy! Mommy!" she wept. "He has ruined me! He is such a beast!"

It did not surprise Eliza that Margaret sat up instantly and gathered her daughter into a soothing hug. She had suspected a fake faint all along.

"Hush, my sweet baby," she crooned, "Mommy is here. This never would have happened if your step-father had not deserted us at our darkest hour. Just don't fret about it—don't fret at all. Eliza will come up with you to see that there is . . . well, no trouble from all of this."

Virginia rose as though her mother had said nothing more than 'good-night' and turned to go up the ladder steps, but Eliza did not move.

"Eliza," she called over her shoulder, "you heard mother, didn't you?"

Eliza turned toward her wonderingly. For one who had just been raped she was just too calm, too cool, too collected.

"Most everyone saw John Breen ride out after you,"

Eliza said, on a frown. "How did you meet up with Sol Hook for this to happen?"

"I do not wish to discuss it, for it won't help matters, will it?" She disappeared into the top of the wagon.

Eliza knew that it wouldn't harm matters to know the whole truth, and hadn't the slightest idea, at the moment, how to get the truth out of Virginia. She wondered if they were having the same doubts at the Breen and Donner wagons.

Virginia threw herself across her mattress bed and grinned. She was enjoying herself hugely.

John Breen, for the moment, was the toast of his brothers' Eddie and Patrick, and the pride of his mother for being so heroic. Paddy Breen, like Eliza, was suspicious. He knew his son too well and had heard too many tales about his youthful female conquests back in Iowa. Then he had chuckled over them, boasting to his friends that "Johnnie was certainly a chip off of his old man's most important block." Now he did not want to chuckle or boast of John being a hero, not until he could be sure of all the facts. Donner was the captain of the train and this involved his nephew and the snobby Reed family. Either one of them, and both combined, could cause big problems for him.

He looked to where Patrick Dolan was sitting. The jolly clown was not laughing or bragging on John. That made Patrick Breen Sr. really start to worry. The man with a ready song or dance was like a second father to John, knowing just about everything there was to know about the fourteen-year-old strutting about in a man's body.

Patrick Dolan also knew John Breen's greatest weakness—he was a compulsive liar and Dolan was forever covering up for him with the Breen family.

At that moment his angular face was a tragic and not comic mask. This lie, which he felt deep in his soul was a lie, because John had let him know too strongly of late his interest in the Reed girl, was one he did not feel he could help upon. He was an overly lustful man himself, but gained his conquests through clever funning and not force.

Paddy Breen read his face exactly and it made him feel worse. He, too, knew that to discuss the matter with his son wouldn't help it at all. His only recourse was to sit back and let matters take their own course.

Elizabeth Donner would not let the matter lie dormant, even when she saw the abuse her son had suffered when Jean Baptiste came dragging him in.

She had already spread the ugly rumor and used her vindictive tongue against Tamsen until she was nearly hoarse.

Tamsen had taken it all quietly, because she was stunned into disbelief—disbelief also over her husband saying nothing whatsoever, and Jacob turning horribly ashen.

Sol heard the thin squeak of his mother's hysteria the moment they were on the edge of camp, and he was also stunned into disbelief, and only wanted to go somewhere to lie down in his misery.

"He has defamed us all!" Elizabeth was screeching at the family gathering, not caring if the young ones understood what she was ranting about or not. "He has taken that poor, sweet, innocent child by force and thus deprived me of my truest and dearest friend. I disown him forevermore."

For all his injuries, Sol moved to face his mother with a staunch pride.

"From whom have you heard this lie?" he asked. His voice was very quiet, but so deep with hatred Elizabeth could feel it.

It was a moment before Elizabeth recognized his swollen face with the badly broken nose from a boot kick.

"'Lie,' he says! I hear no denials coming from the Reed wagon. I hear nothing from there and probably never shall ever again. I should have known that you would turn out to be just as lustful as your real father. I suppose you even have William thinking along the same dirty lines."

"I said, it is a lie!"

"Enough on the matter," Tamsen snarled. "Come, Sol, I will see to your wounds."

"Didn't I tell you that she would take his side?" Elizabeth hissed. "Didn't I, just?"

"I will help," Jacob said, concern in his voice. "Let me have a look at that nose." He stretched out his hand but Sol pulled away from him.

"Later," he growled. "If you do not believe me, ask Jean Baptiste. Where did he go?"

"I need not ask him anything," Jacob said sternly, knowing full well the man had slipped away so as not to get involved in a family matter. "Your word is all I need, Solomon."

George Donner cleared his throat ominously. "But how do we handle the situation, Jacob?"

"Lordy, lordy, George," Uncle Jake sighed. "At your age you should know that you handle a rumor like you do the grasshopper. You can't beat it out or burn it out or ignore that it is there. You just have to let it eat itself out and glut itself to death on its own greed."

"Has no one listened to a single word that I have said?" Elizabeth demanded.

"Hardly," Jacob said drily, taking Sol by the arm to lead him to Tamsen's wagon.

Elizabeth's face froze in a hateful mask. Her opinion

was firmly set and it would take a mountain to fall on her for it to change.

She was not alone. An invisible line was drawn and sides taken, especially among the teamsters.

Jean Baptiste told the whole story to Antonio in Spanish. For the moment Antonio advised that they keep their silence and out of the trouble.

Milt Elliott took it upon himself to turn it into bigger trouble. Belligerently the Reed teamsters armed themselves and waited in their wagons as though expecting a mass assault upon the women.

Finally, Jean Baptiste had to tell the truth to the other Donner teamsters so they could arm accordingly.

Bill Eddy, still hoping for financial favors from James Frazier in California, came to offer his services to Margaret until her husband returned.

Mary Florence believed the truth from Tamsen, as Tamsen knew the truth. She did not have to enlist James Smith to side with the Donner cause—he would not have sided with the Reed faction even if Sol had been guilty as sin.

Doolittle Thornburg stayed neutral. To side with Eliza would lose him a meal ticket with Mary Florence, and to side with Mary Florence might ruin whatever chance he had with Eliza.

Old man Hardkoop lost his job with Spitzer and Reinhardt over the matter and oddly enough went right to work for Lewis Keseberg.

Keseberg's attitude amazed many.

"This is bad," he muttered, "very bad. Thank you for telling Philline and me your thoughts, *Elisa*. I have been many things, but never one to side with a lie. If it causes you trouble, you come to us at once."

It caused Eliza severe inconvenience, if not trouble. Margaret Donner flew into a rage when she heard of

Keseberg's siding from Johanna Wolfinger. Eliza was denied permission from seeing those nasty-minded people.

The Breens also tried to stay neutral, although John strutted about like a banty rooster.

Lavina Murphy crushed her shapeless hat upon her head and stalked up and down in front of the family fire. Pike wanted to side with the Donners, because Mary Florence had sided with them, but Foster was for going the other way. His reasoning was personal and kept that way. For a long time he'd had his eye on Virginia and now that she had been had once, he might stand a chance.

"We will go by my gut feeling," she growled. "Peggy Breen ain't set foot over here since she first came to brag on her hero. Ain't like her. Ain't like her not to be over here a hundred dozen times a day to borrow a cup of this or a pinch of that. Shamed to show her face, I'd say. Pike? Foster? You boys may be hell-raising wild oat sowers, but you be men enough to fess up to your mistakes. Nobody's fessin' up proper here, from there and there. I said me say. Amandie, your man ain't here, so you'll have to do the sayin' for the McCutchen family."

"I've been a-thinkin' on it," Mrs. McCutchen muttered. She looked into Lavina's face and added: "That boy is all right. We talked with his uncle 'bout us at Fort Bridger and Mr. Donner had him bring us to you. My Mac would stand up for him if he were here."

The three absent men came more and more into the various conversations as the days began to pass.

"Snakes or Utes got them," Jean Baptiste declared, because he claimed to know all about Indians.

"Guide says none about," Hardkoop scoffed. "He should know. Goes out each day to check."

Doolittle did go out each day, but only far enough

to check on the Indian village. To his chagrin it was still there.

"Supplies are getting low, Paddy," Peggy Breen said on a worried note. "If we don't get going soon we'll be in trouble."

"Can't you borrow or buy? We got cash silver."

"Can't you get your son to tell the truth so I can show my shamed face?"

Patrick Breen shook his head sadly. He had done everything but thrash the boy, but as long as Virginia stayed with her story John felt safe staying with his. Also, it gave him the false notion that Virginia was protecting him so that they could be together again.

"This is becoming intolerable," Hans Wolfinger carped. "Did you see the higher mountains this morning? Dusted with snow like a strudel. What manner of man is this Hastings to lead us into such an impossible situation. I say someone should tell George Donner to take us back to Fort Bridger."

"Why don't you tell him yourself?"

"You know full well the reason why I am not speaking to that family."

But Eliza could speak to them, when she could sneak a message through Lewis Keseberg.

The shadowy figures moved cautiously to the sleeping forms just beyond the Donner and MacDuff wagons. The teamsters and herders were only supposed to be scared off for working for Donner, except for one.

Milt Elliott had been very sure exactly where James Smith put down his bedroll each night. He was just as sure that he would never rise from it.

He gave a low, soft whistle and shovels and mattocks were raised.

"Yeoww! I think I broke my blasted arm!"

The yell had not come from one of the bedrolls but from one of the attackers.

The noise of the assault diminished as the attackers discovered that all they pounded into were rocks and logs. They stood a little confused and dumbfounded.

From the near woods came snickers and catcalls. Once warned of the pending attack, George Donner had not been above trickery, but refused to allow a direct confrontation.

He, too, was growing greatly concerned. The next day would be the eleventh of August—five days since the three men had gone after Hastings. With Jacob he had concluded that a determination had to be made the next morning, without a bunch of bashed skulls to get in the way. Warring camp or not, they were going to need each other to get over Doolittle's mountain route or back to Fort Bridger.

The Reed men, except for Milt, began to snicker and give catcalls back. Then they began to roar with laughter over the joke that had been played on them.

"What the hell we doing here?" the slow-witted Walt Herron chortled, indicating he wasn't really that dull. "Reed should be here to handle his own dirty work."

Milt flew into a rage. "Then you are all fired, as of right now."

"Does that include me," Baylis giggled, "for only Mr. Reed can do that."

"And to the rest of us," Herron insisted. "Hey, you bullwhackers in the trees. I've still got me a jug of Jim Bridger's firewater. Come on out and we'll celebrate getting fired."

Only Milt stomped away.

As much as George Donner was against his men drinking, he closed his mind to it that night.

James Smith looked down at his bedroll, a horrible sickness beginning to crawl through his stomach. It was slashed and torn as though really brutally attacked. He didn't have to reason out that he would be dead if

they had not been warned. The wound in his shoulder
hurt, as though reminding him that, too, might not
have been an accident.

But just over a couple of dead oxen . . . ? It came to
him that Milt Elliott had been standing above his
bedroll as he fired the Reed men. Then, because the
present problem centered around Virginia, another
picture flashed vividly through his mind . . . because
the story Jean Baptiste told about the bareback ride
was also most vivid.

At the time he had thought nothing of Virginia
swimming or Reed being close by. He was, after all,
the girl's step-father. He had even accepted the story
that Reed was relieving himself, because he was not
the type of man who had any desire to look upon
another man. Now he wondered if he had stumbled
onto something, and they thought he had seen more
than he actually had seen?

He shivered and could not shake off the horrible
feeling that he would never see the end of that
journey.

"Sometimes, Milton," Margaret sneered the next
morning, "you can be a pig-headed lout. Fired? How
in hell do you expect us to get out of this god-forsaken
place without men? Oh, forget it! James Reed will
handle the matter when he returns. You escort Virginia
on a ride this morning."

"Do you think that wise?"

"I would not suggest it," she said testily, "unless I
thought it wise. Elizabeth has sent word that she
wishes to speak to me. I gather that her son has
finally confessed and I don't wish for Virginia to hear
all the sordid details."

Eliza turned from the stove and blinked at her. The
woman was impossible. She went about acting as
though Virginia had not been on the scene when the

sordid little details all happened. Details that Virginia still refused to discuss. The whole situation was beginning to grate on Eliza's nerves. She wanted to scream out the truth, but knew that Margaret would just sweep that under the carpet in her impossible way as well.

Virginia gaily came down for her ride in a pure white riding habit. Eliza nearly laughed aloud. She was hardly the virginal innocent any longer.

Milt reluctantly took her from the wagon and stopped short. A blurry-eyed Walt Herron stood with Billy and Milt's horse.

"What are you doing with them?" he snarled.

"Just as Mrs. Reed ordered me to do," he yawned and turned away to underscore that there was still a higher authority around than Milt.

Almost roughly he picked Virginia up by the waist and threw her up onto Billy's saddle. Then flung himself up into the saddle and rode off with a scowl.

Virginia smiled her secret little smile. She had not been aware that Milt Elliott was so strong. As a matter of fact she had hardly been aware of Milt Elliott, although he had worked for her step-father for years. Perhaps "common men" like John Breen were far more interesting than "little boys" like Sol Hook.

Still, as she rode regally by the Donner wagon, she could not help but stick out her tongue at Jacob Donner. To her utter amazement and disgust, he stuck his tongue right back out at her.

The council meeting was a total failure. Without James Frazier there the Reed faction would not vote or budge, even though the meeting had been called to appease Hans Wolfinger.

In a way they would agree that there wasn't any going back. By the time they would get back to Fort

Bridger and the long way around through Fort Hall, the snows would be flying in the Sierras.

"Give Reed one more day," William Eddy insisted.

"And one more and one more," Keseberg growled, "until winter clicks down around us like a sprung trap I know winter in the mountains from Germany. It is not like winter in your flat farmlands. Thornburg, how long to get over your mountain?"

Doolittle shrugged.

"What is that supposed to mean?" Keseberg demanded. "You have been up there each day. Have you not blazed a trail?"

"Naturally not," Doolittle said quietly, and he thought logically. "Any stray Indian scout might find it and think to turn it into an ambush." He shrugged again. "I know the way when the time comes."

The hardest way.

The morning ride stretched into noon. The hours had passed without Milt hardly being aware. His mind was in a turmoil. As well as he had served James Frazier in the past, he had now failed him twice when it came to Smith. And now there was the Sol Hook matter. That really stumped him. The whole thing had an air of suspicion about it that he was incapable of judging without James Frazier.

"Milt, slow down! It's getting hot and Billy and I are getting tired. I want another drink from your canteen."

"You just had one five minutes ago."

"And I wish another one. Boy, are you an old sourpuss today."

"Bad night," he gruffed.

"So I heard Walt tell mother this morning. Did you really fire them all?"

He gazed at her blankly. "Done to protect you,

mainly. Don't want Smith telling what he saw at the pool that day."

Virginia felt a queer embarrassment. "What do you know about it?" she asked lightly.

Milt fumbled for words, knitting his heavy brows as he concentrated. "Well, miss, I suppose it's this way: if your Paw wants something done, he gives me all the reasons why he wants it done."

Virginia was startled. She eyed the man searchingly. "Then the hunting accident was no accident."

"Again to protect you."

From what? she thought bitterly. So her step-father could nearly kill her by making her practically bleed to death. She smiled grimly.

"Then why haven't you done anything to protect me from Sol Hook?"

"Miss Virginia," said Milt, with an unusual softness in his voice, "I'm right sorry that happened to you and I'm just waiting for Mr. Reed to come back and tell me what to do about it all. Given the word I'll make that young whelp regret touching you."

"What if I gave you the word?"

"I-I suppose, I could figure out something."

Impulsively, she reached over and laid her hand on his saddled leg. "I might do anything you desired in exchange for the favor, Milt."

Surprised at this, but immensely delighted to be of service to her, he grinned. "I wouldn't desire anything, Miss Virginia."

The strangest thought came to her: I can make any man desire me if I put my mind to it.

"It's early. Why don't we take the saddle off of Ranger and go for a bareback ride?"

"Bareback," he chuckled. "I haven't ridden bareback since—" He stopped and his mouth tightened. "Why do you say bareback?"

"That's how I rode," she giggled. "That's how I would like to ride today . . . with you."

It's true, he thought, and not a bizarre story made up by Jean Baptiste. But Sol Hook was indeed then on foot and John Breen on horseback. Then, looking at Virginia for the first time with seeing eyes, he was taken aback. Her mean little eyes were the same as James Frazier's when he would have to get polishing girls for him. This might just as well be his real daughter, he thought.

The humiliation, the misery of old memories at the loathsome things he had done to appease James Frazier, filled him with despair and hatred. And why had he done them? Because it was unendurable to be without a future and James Frazier had been his only future.

But James Frazier, he always felt, had been most truthful with him—or had he?

"What happened during that ride, Miss Virginia?" he asked, and in spite of his attempt at sternness, his strong voice was gentle and indulgent.

She looked at him fully and boldly. "The same as might happen between us."

Milt was stupefied. He would not betray James Frazier in this manner, although he himself now felt betrayed. More had happened at the pool, he was now sure, than he had been informed. He gazed at her fearfully as another thought forcefully struck him.

"Are you not afraid of such riding after your accident?"

"My accident has nothing to do with it." In spite of herself, her voice faltered, and she said on a rush: "What did my step-father tell you about the accident, anyway?"

Less than you just have, he thought with tremendous regret. He had been played the fool by James Frazier and nearly killed over blind loyalty.

"Don't be uncouth," he said with severity, hoping to shock. "I don't think it is my place to discuss personal relationships within your family. It is time for us to head back."

"If you wish," Virginia replied in the toneless and neutral voice she had often heard James Frazier employ on subordinates. She had given the man too much information, she suddenly realized, and that was a mistake.

She had deceived everyone except Eliza and now Milton, and perhaps a few of the Donner party who wished to believe Sol's story.

Eliza and Milton hardly worried her. They were mere servants, that her step-father could ruin or plunge into despair at her spoken command.

The Donners, especially Sol, were beginning to bore her. Nothing was happening the way she had expected it to happen. Her mother's faint had been a fake and the raid on the Donner men a laugh.

Even though she now considered James Frazier to be a man with a dirty soul, he would handle matters for her upon his return.

Margaret Reed was thinking something near the same.

"Dear Elizabeth," she simpered, although remaining cool and remote, "I feel I must wait for my husband to discuss such a matter."

"But, Margaret," Elizabeth sniffed into a lace handkerchief, "it is the only solution. Solomon will not even speak to me, which determines his guilt. A forced marriage between them is the only answer."

The thought of it had nearly sent Margaret into a real faint. The suggestion that she might be saddled with Elizabeth for life as a near relative was unthinkable.

"It is for the men to discuss and not us, Elizabeth."

"But what if his seed is already within her?"

Margaret pursed her dry and puckered lips into a mechanical smile. "Then I shall gladly strangle the issue at birth."

A rough flush rose under her pallid skin and she tossed her head uneasily. "My son has erred and I came to correct that error. I thought that was how we did things in America, rather than let bastards run around as bastards."

Margaret did not wince. She raised her blond brows. "Don't be odious! I have always found the English bastard system far superior to any other."

"But we are speaking of your daughter and my son!"

Margaret looked at her with bland brutality. "Only if she is with child, my dear," she said, smoothly. "And I pray that such is not the case."

Elizabeth opened her mouth and looked blankly baffled when her ears were suddenly filled with wild cheering. All they could make out of the babble was that a horseman was coming up the canyon.

Even though Margaret couldn't be sure who it was, she gave Elizabeth a furtive malefic glance. "My husband! Please excuse us a private moment of greeting."

She brushed by Elizabeth and posed on the wagon steps. She whined, "Oh, God he looks dreadful! And where is his own magnificent horse?"

She waved, but James Frazier was being mobbed with the selfsame questions and others.

"Where's McCutchen and Stanton?"

"Where's your horse?"

"What took you so long?"

"Easy, easy," he grinned. "They be fine and resting at Hastings camp down on the plains. Hell of a time getting there. All of our horses gave out."

"Where's Hastings? He was to come back to lead us?"

"Now don't fret," he rumbled. He was the center of

attention and he loved it. He also loved the next announcement he would make and felt he had now justly earned it. "He brought me most of the way back and showed me the mountains to lead you over as a deputy captain of his train. We will all meet together as soon as you give me a chance to kiss my wife."

He raced to the steps and inclined his head toward his wife apologetically. "Please forgive me, my dear, but it's important to organize them at once or we shall miss Hastings again."

"Your daughter has been raped," she hissed.

"What? Impossible? Martha Jane is only eight."

"I speak of Virginia. Your pet!"

Her voice, uneven and cracked, made him wince.

"My God! Where is she? Who did it?"

"Sol Hook, and she is off riding with Milt Elliott."

This both amused and angered him. Sol Hook was just a mere boy and a riding Virginia suggested she must not be in too much disrepair. Still, anyone touching her, man or boy, stirred his jealousy.

"All right, my dear, we shall go into the whole matter at length when I have completed this more important duty."

"Is not my daughter *the* more important duty."

For the moment he thought not. His own interests came first over everything else.

As if she sensed his thought, she looked him in the eye with intense coldness, and lifted her head with bitter hauteur. This angered him even more

"I can hardly discuss it, Margaret," he hissed, "without her being here."

"You don't mean to discuss it with her openly, do you?" Margaret was appalled.

At this, a strange flicker passed over James Frazier's face. It was brief and evil. This act had covered up the evidence of his own act. To hear of it might be more amusing than disturbing.

"How else am I to learn the truth?" he said incisively and went down the steps.

Within an hour they had voted unanimously to take the route which James Frazier had explored, and because Doolittle Thornburg had been quick to point out that it sounded most like the one he had found. Reed had never once mentioned seeing an Indian or Indian village, so Doolittle felt safe in the assumption.

Reed's assuming of command without vote riled Jacob, but George took it quite calmly.

"It was Hastings' suggestion," James Frazier explained, "but I strongly suggest that it be the Donner-Reed Party. You handle the train and I shall see to the trail route."

"That's fine," George said blandly.

James Frazier frowned momentarily.

"Now there is this personal matter, George, which I am really in the dark upon. Please allow me time to talk with Virginia before your brother and I discuss it as gentlemen."

At this, Jacob could do nothing but hold his silence. It was put to them in a gentlemanly way and should be handled as such.

"Agreed," said George with a thrust of his hand, but with an uneasy eye on his brother. "I would also suggest you talk with your man Milt Elliott, as well. Took a heap unto himself and might have gotten a man or two killed had we not learned of his scheme. Don't mind telling you that the camp has been most split over this matter. Glad to have you back to shed the light of truth about."

"Truth?" James Frazier snapped. "Are there unanswered questions about the matter?"

George sighed. "James, the whole thing is an unanswered question. One claiming this, one denying that, and one staying silent on all matters."

"My God! Are you saying three were involved?"

"Yep!" George grunted. "But it ain't fair for me to be standing here giving only Sol's version till you talk with Virginia and maybe get a decent word out of John Breen."

James Frazier frowned. Then his face cleared. If the camp was split and he could personally bring it back together, there would be no question in anyone's mind that he was the proper leader.

But as the fires burned themselves low in the camp that night he began to wonder if leading such a group was worth it.

"Heard you had a little run in with the Donner men, Milt."

"Yep!"

James Frazier blinked at him. Milt Elliott previously had always given him some title of respect.

"James Smith still around?"

"Yep!"

"We better forget about him for awhile."

"Have!"

"Now, what do you know about this Virginia and Sol Hook matter?"

"Nothing."

James Frazier pulled out a leather pouch and took out two twenty-dollar gold pieces.

"Here's forty dollars," he said. "I want you to get John Breen over here to talk with me."

"You know about him?"

"Not as much as I want to know, Milt. Say, what is the matter with you, anyway?"

"Nothing!" he grunted, taking the coins. Money could bring his loyalty back to a degree, if not fully.

Then he went off in search of John. He found him fishing for trout down in the rapids.

"Come on!" he said. "Mr. Reed wants to talk to you about your taking care of his daughter."

Milt Elliott was not smart enough to know he had

given his words a double meaning. John preened, as though the words meant he would get a reward for thrashing Sol Hook. Patrick Dolan heard them quite differently and hunched even farther over his fishing pole. Not five minutes before John had finally boasted out the truth to him. He was sick at heart as to what was going to happen, but knew it had to come out sooner or later.

But James Frazier didn't gain as much out of John as Patrick Dolan had.

Respect for elders is something Paddy and Peggy Breen pounded into all of their children. John Breen respected James Frazier enough in this regard to let him speak first and thus learn that the man knew nothing from his step-daughter, so he staunchly stuck with his original story.

Though his desire to end the matter that evening was urgent, James Frazier purposely avoided discussing it with Eliza. Her face could not conceal the fact that she held him in utter contempt.

Virginia was overjoyed at the sight of him, which put him immediately on the defensive.

"You look most lovely, my dear."

"I would look lovelier if I were on a different horse than Billy, don't you think?"

"We will discuss it right after dinner, my dear. Now, I have a million things to do."

That he had effectively put off, even though Margaret continued with her attitude of outrage.

And when he did have to speak with her, he still knew next to nothing.

"Let's take a little walk," he whispered. "It is so good to rest my tired eyes on you. You look so well."

"In spite of what has happened to me?" she snapped. "Isn't that what you meant to say?"

"I know some of what happened," he said sadly. "But we can overcome that, Virginia. Your mother is saying that Elizabeth Donner is trying to force a marriage. I would not wish that for you. I love you too much to see your life ruined in that way. Happiness is too important—"

"Speaking of happiness," she broke in sharply, "what about my new horse?"

"You may have the pick of the lot, of course, but we have got to talk of this, Virginia."

Her hands flew up suddenly and covered her ears.

"I don't want to talk of it!" she pouted. "I just want you to ruin the people who have been so mean to me!"

"Who has been mean to you?" he asked grimly.

"A whole lot of them. Eliza first. Prodding and poking at me after each time and making dire threats about what will happen. She makes me sick, but not as sick as Sol Hook. I hate him. Won't pay a bit of attention to me. Milt, too. Ignored me the whole way back on the ride. Boob! That's all he is!"

"You are confusing me. It sounds as though Eliza was just doing her job and after what happened I can see why Sol might be ashamed enough to hide away and not pay attention to you." He gulped, knowing he had to speak out sooner or later. "I also was so ashamed of my own actions that I ignored you, Virginia."

She looked at him, her small eyes soft and calm, her mouth smiling a little; but he did not like that smile. It was cunning, he thought; like she had the perfect tool for blackmail for the rest of her life.

"Did you?" she asked innocently. "You made me bleed so much that I wasn't aware. I didn't bleed this time. I don't think I would have bled with Milt, either."

"*With Milt?*" he said fiercely.

"That's why he ignored me," she shrugged.

He stopped and looked down at her, seeing her— petite, dainty, rosy-cheeked, full of life, beautiful; and there was pain at the pit of his heart. He groaned inside of himself, thinking: What monster have I created by introducing her to sexual desire? She was to be for me and not every young swain who stepped in front of her.

And then, suddenly, he knew an even more devastating truth. It was so crushing to his ego that he refused to accept it and looked at her strangely.

"James Frazier," she whispered, "you-all don't look right."

"I just realized something," he gasped, his voice deep in his throat. But before he could voice it, he was realizing something else. Their relationship had been altered. He was now "James Frazier" and could no longer be "Daddy!"

"I-you—" he stammered on, "or maybe because I wanted to believe . . . or wasn't here at the time." He just couldn't put into words his belief that she would have only wished him after the first time. Then he added quickly: "But now I see that it wasn't rape."

She stomped her foot and glowered at him. "It is if I say it is, James Frazier!"

"No!" he moaned. "You are playing God with an innocent life and have not the right. I see how you have twisted this now. Should have seen it from the start, knowing how you twist things. But the fault is mine. I made you look like a princess out of a story book. But this time when you kissed the frog he didn't turn into the handsome prince. He was still a freckle-faced Irish lad, so you took it upon yourself to change matters around."

"I did not!" she exploded. "John Breen is the one who spread the rumor all over the camp and I just went along with it!"

"And nearly ruined Sol Hook in the doing?"

"Does it really matter?"

It was said with such cold indifference that it left

him momentarily speechless. It had been Margaret speaking, but he had no one to blame but himself. He had been the one who had imbued in them the feeling that they sat upon the mountain crest and the commoners were far below. The time had suddenly ceased to talk in fairy-tale language.

"It matters to Sol," he said quietly and turned to walk back.

"Where are you going?" she shrieked. "I want him ruined! You will not go over there and change that! If you do, I'm warning you!"

He shook his head sympathetically. "I will take every bit of blame coming to me, Virginia, remember that. Your warning, thus, falls on deaf ears."

"I still demand a new horse!" she got out.

James Frazier sighed. He certainly had created quite a monster.

For a man of James Frazier Reed's sensibilities the rest of the evening was one of discomfiture. A man of gentry and nobility, he tried to handle the whole matter with aristocratic diplomacy.

"I know it is not enough for me to apologize, Solomon," he said, with conciliatory sweetness. "Virginia must speak her own words when the time is right. I do not claim to understand women," he cackled, "especially young ones, but her motive was to make you jealous."

Tamsen's face was a study in near-apoplexy. In her opinion the girl had gone a very, very long way to bring about her revenge.

"I understand," Sol said dully.

James Frazier leaned forward, his eyes bright and eager. He was almost over his first barrier.

"My dear boy, I thank you. But I wish you to understand something else. Your body may have felt the beating you took, but your intentions were that of a

man. Still, it takes an even bigger man to forgive
those who have sinned against him."

"Amen!" Jacob intoned. He was most pleased with
the way that James Frazier had handled the manner
of exonerating Sol.

George was pleased. After all, he had to work with
this man to get them down onto the Mormon plains.

Tamsen was not pleased. She felt that James Frazier
Reed had made Sol look like a coward who had not
spoken out against Virginia's lies before that time.
She was not a hating woman, but this whole pro-
ceeding stuck in her craw.

Ellizabeth Donner was a hateful creature. She had
sat in total disbelief of every word that had been
uttered. It mattered not that her son had been telling
the truth all along. She had been made a fool of
again. He had made her a laughing-stock by allowing
her to suggest a forced marriage. It was unforgivable, and in her twisted way of thinking, it was all
Tamsen's fault.

The oddest reaction, however, was that of the pro-
tagonist in the matter. Solomon Hook, at fourteen,
realized that the tongue of a woman, regardless of
age, was a dangerous weapon. All thoughts of running after the Boggs train had vanished. He had had
time, in the last few days, to determine that the shield
of love and loyalty placed about him by his family
was a treasure that could not be indifferently thrown
away.

James Frazier knew he had one more mission that
night, but forestalled it to stop a moment at his own
wagon. It was still and quiet, whether everyone was
asleep or not. To the side of the amidship room was a
narrow space for his roll-top desk. He lit a candle and
took his diary from a cubicle.

Because he was the sort of man who felt that someday he would enter the pages of history, he felt compelled to note the events of his last five days before the problems of moving on confronted him.

But as he sat the quill shook in his hand and the page blurred before his eyes. Everything so far recorded had been so in a personal first-person tense and the name "Virginia" was dominant.

"My God!" he murmured, "What have I wrought?"

Savagely, he tore the first ten pages out of the diary and tore them to shreds. His pent-up emotions had flowed through his fingers onto the written page. They were not for history but for his private conscience.

For the moment he vowed to change his life utterly, if God would so allow.

Thus, the second interview was conducted in a vastly different manner than the first.

"Well, John," he scowled, "the fat is now in the fire."

The apple cheeks of Peggy Breen turned ashen and Paddy closed his eyes in a silent prayer.

"What the hell you mean?" John demanded, still belligerent.

"I mean," James Frazier said, on a quiet smile, "that I have learned much since last we talked. Or, should I say, since Virginia has talked."

"She-she talked?" John gasped. "What the devil did she say?"

"All there was to say . . . about everything."

"Have you been lying to me, boy?" Paddy growled.

James Frazier raised his hand for peace. "That would be a question hard to answer, Mr. Breen. I like to feel that they each, in their youthful way, were trying to harbor the other from a first time situation."

"Still," Paddy frowned, "if my Johnnie was the one involved, it would be meaning the lad lied about the Hook boy."

"A complicated matter, sir," James Frazier grinned. "A slight triangle between them, with jealousy raising its ugly head. Sol Hook is quite willing to let bygones be bygones."

Peggy turned an amazed face toward her husband. It was fine for men and boys to consider the matter as bygone, but what if the girl happened to be with child.

"Good!" Paddy grunted. "But what if there be trouble?"

James Frazier was well prepared for the question. He did not desire either Sol or John as a son-in-law.

"My maid-girl assures me that it never reached the point," he lied, trying to be delicate in front of Mrs. Breen.

One could almost hear their silent sigh of relief. John Breen's eyes were as round as moons in his freckled face.

Everyone wanted the matter over and done with because the wagons were rolling again. A half mile back up the river they turned up a creek and left Hastings' wheel-tracks behind.

They had to break a road as they went and three-quarters of the day was spent in going three-quarters of a mile. They camped in single file along the creek and ate without the fine tables being set up.

An eighth of a mile to the west was the Indian trail they could have easily climbed, but Doolittle still held his silence.

"In my desire to get us moving," James Frazier candidly admitted to George Donner, "I have been over eager. We could have stayed in camp and come up to do the road work daily. I suggest we do that tomorrow and cut a road up to the rocky higher ridges."

Donner reluctantly nodded. Doolittle had said it

was an easy route. It was rough and tiring, and took the whole next day to cut a path up to the top of the first divide.

"Thought you said the basin was just below?" Jacob scowled.

"Said you could see it," Doolittle lied, "and you can."

It seemed forever in the distance, but Doolittle was breathing easier. A spur in the mountain kept them from seeing the Indian village. It wouldn't have mattered. White Eagle had moved northwestward at dawn.

On the third day they made the climb and eight miles across the divide. Dipping down into the next valley the way was exceedingly rough and crooked and very dangerous on the wagons. They hated this downhill course and the memories it brought back. But down they went and stopped short.

The Bossman (Beauchemin) Creek bottom James Frazier had only seen from the distance and had not blazed. The bottom was an intertwined jungle of willow, alder, and aspen twenty feet tall. The undergrowth was a tangle of serviceberries and thorny wild roses.

The berries and summer roses were welcome on the Donner and Reed tables, but hated by the men. To them it seemed that they grew faster than they could axe and hew them away.

"I be herder, *señor*," Antonio said hesitantly. "Day after day I go with others carrying axes, picks and shovels. Jean Baptiste be hired as ox-driver, but he goes. Why we go and not some?"

George felt guilty. It was easy to grumble at the hard labor and Reed's route through the interlocked alders, but the man was blazing the way south day after day. He, his brother and Hardkoop were just too old for this hard labor.

"James, the dissension grows and the work falls off. I wish Jacob and I could do more, but I must question why the hired people must do more and the Germans do less and less."

"Reasonable question, George," James Frazier muttered. He had never been so tired in his life. "The Germans are not used to this labor and come up more quickly with sore backs and blistered hands. But that is no excuse. Twenty-seven of us to clear a road for twenty wagons . . . it is as much labor as if we were clearing for a hundred. How long since Doolittle left? Oh, I'm sorry, it was just this morning. If he can just find out what is holding up Stanton and McCutchen that would give us three more men." He laughed tiredly. "Double with McCutchen. He was quite a man on our outward-bound journey."

George Donner smiled to himself. It was James Frazier who had fought to keep the McCutchen family from riding with Lavina Murphy.

His surprise at James Frazier's attitude increased the next morning.

"Welcome! Welcome! Who you be?"

The three wagons had rumbled up on them as though on a well travelled road. In their wake was the usual conglomerate of cattle, yapping dogs and a parcel of children that ranged from a married daughter of twenty-two to a nursing infant.

"Franklin Ward Graves, I be," he announced, looking at the line of camped wagons as though he wished to push right on by them. When he stepped down from the wagon perch the fifty-seven-year-old man proved to be nearly as wide as he was tall. "That be my wife Elizabeth and my young'ns. Second wagon be a daughter Sarah and her man Jay Fosdick. Third wagon be a hanger-on named John Snyder. How soon can we be around you and on our way?"

James Frazier fingered the brim of his hat and did

a mental count. There were thirteen, but had among them four fresh men for road-building.

"Unless you wish to do your own blazing and road-building you will not go far going around us. Have you had an easy time tracking us out of Fort Bridger?"

"Most easy."

"Then you can thank these ladies, gentlemen and children. They've been fifteen days out of Bridger building that route."

"Fifteen?" he gasped. "We done made it in four." Then he broke into a yellow-toothed grin. "I'm being Uncle Billy Graves to most who know me, and ain't a Graves, Fosdick or Snyder among us that is feared of work. We be obliged for the effort of your past."

James Frazier laughed. "We welcome you. We have an Uncle George and an Uncle Jake. An Uncle Billy rounds it out. Come. I am James Frazier Reed. I will introduce you around and to our captain, George Donner."

James Frazier could now make that statement without a selfish desire to retain the title for himself. The work of the last several days had proven to him that titles carried with them tiring responsibilities. Work-power out of the Graves addition was his main consideration.

His wife, of course, took a single look at the simply dressed Elizabeth Graves and concluded that one Elizabeth (Donner) was quite enough to entertain in her wagon, although of late Elizabeth had been making only infrequent visits.

The Graves family were not like children at a new school. They were robust, friendly and outgoing. As their father was introduced they marched right along behind and made themselves known.

Tamsen took an immediate shine to Elizabeth Graves. They were women of near the same age, with a similar outlook on life.

For Sol it was the last moment ever that he thought of running away to join the Boggs train. Even though she was six years his senior, he was instantly in love with Mary Ann. The twenty-year-old and her fifteen-year-old sister Eleanor could almost have passed for twins. Petite, small-boned young ladies with flowing brunette hair and laughing dispositions that seemed constantly at the bubble. And when Sarah Graves Fosdick and thirteen-year-old Lavina stood with them it was a real look-alike quartet of glowing beauties.

"My nine peas in a pod," Elizabeth boasted proudly.

It was obvious to all that it was a close-knit, loving family.

It was also obvious to Virginia that eighteen-year-old William was as handsome as his sisters were beautiful. That he rode a breathtaking stallion, with livery he had hand-tooled himself, also captured her attention.

Then all thoughts of William Graves were pushed to the back of her mind.

It was not stature that made John Snyder commanding, for he barely stood five-foot-four, but a quiet manner and overpowering personality.

"This is another member of their party, John Snyder of Virginia." Beside the towering James Frazier he seemed rather small, but quite as dapper in dress with a full head of curling jet-black locks, a narrow mustache and a look of quick intelligence. There was not an ounce of fat on the compact muscular frame.

When Margaret greeted him, John Snyder made a bow, hands stiffly at his sides, almost as if he stood before a commanding officer on inspection. Here was a banty rooster! At once she regretted the ungenerous thought. He, at least, was greeting her as a gentleman should.

The new arrival regarded her fine dress and the

large wagon briefly with an air of disbelief. Suddenly, however, the flesh around the dark eyes crinkled, with a smile that approached a grin, and a voice, surprisingly deep, told her, "Ma'am, the sight of you and this fine home on wheels is like spotting an oasis in the desert. My compliments." John Snyder wanted to be friends, wanted to be liked, for this was the nearest thing to home he had seen in a year.

Within the stocky frame was a most vile temper—a temper which had brought him near to killing one of his father's prized stud slaves and brought about his banishment from the family plantation until he could learn to act his twenty-five years.

Margaret responded immediately.

"How kind of you, sir." It was like music to her ears to hear a Southern gentleman talk again. "May we offer you our hospitality for dinner this evening?"

"I would be charmed, Mrs. Reed."

He would also be charmed to get to know the young beauty who did not hide her delight in his acceptance.

Yet another was being charmed by another young beauty.

Patrick Dolan saw the look in John Breen's eyes as the Graves family met his own.

"One's a mite old for you," he whispered, "and one is a mite young."

John Breen continued to stare at Mary Ann with open-mouthed awe.

"I'm in love," he sighed.

Despite himself, Patrick Dolan chuckled. "You are in lust, not love."

Then he sighed wearily as George Donner rang the silly little dinner bell, which had become the signal for the road gangs to gather. Of late he had been so tired of a night that there had been no clowning or entertainment.

* * *

For a day or two the newcomers gave the emigrants a burst of new energy. They were eight miles up the Bossman and could now begin cutting westward up the discouragingly big mountain.

By James Frazier's blazing marks it was measured as only four to five miles over the big mountain, but here the ground rose steadily and the timber was larger. It was snail-pace work and soon the Graves men were as tired as the rest.

With the dinner linen removed from the table George Donner put on his spectacles and hunched over the roster-ledger. He had not brought it up to date since first started.

"May we have a moment of your time?"

He looked up to see the odd assemblage of James Frazier, Lavina Murphy, Lewis Keseberg and William Eddy. The quartet, for once, were in agreement upon something.

"George, Lavina has come to me with a thought that I think has merit. It's going to take us a good four more days on that road before we can spare the manpower to move the wagons up. The oxen and cattle have nearly eaten this whole area to bare earth and Lewis here is right in asserting that we wear ourselves out going back and forth. Lavina, say your piece."

For once she seemed a little bashful being the center of attention.

"Well, I—weren't much of a thought. Just that the men stay camped at the road site, as Lewis thinks, and we get the food up to them."

"Six days to build the road," George mused, as though he had heard none of the rest.

"I added onto the suggestion," William Eddy boasted.

James Frazier frowned. "And even though Lavina agrees, it still worries me. George, the thought is that with your guidance the women and middle-aged children could start moving up the wagons a bit at a time each day."

George stood up. "You forgot to take into consideration the extra oxen and cattle."

"Did not!" Eddy insisted. "We thought to put them in charge of Antonio and Jean Baptiste. They have to move them almost daily for food now and are thus lost to us for road work."

Jacob came forward. "A hard task, Lavina."

"Not as hard as building a road out of rocks, Uncle Jake." Lavina grinned. Jacob Donner was a man she greatly had come to admire. "We got ourselves fifteen good women, of various ages, and many of them know the feel of reins in their hands. Ten years and upward we got sixteen boys and girls. Same as down on the river, we could let Amanda take care of all the youngsters. We also got you, your brother and Old man Hardkoop."

Jacob and James Frazier could also count. They looked at each other with a twinge of embarrassment. Their wives had been included in on that number and it hadn't worked before.

"Now some of the wagons," Lavina quickly added, as though reading their thoughts, "we shall need some manpower to help move."

"A lot of manpower," Lewis muttered, for he wasn't fully sold on this part of the plan. "I would suggest only the family wagons we move first. The supply wagons and single men wagons can come last."

They all nodded that that seemed a good approach.

George Donner sat back down to complete the work on his roster. Once he had the page finished on the Graves family he carefully blotted it and began to count backward. His enrollment had swelled to eighty-seven. By an odd twist of fate he was off by two. Because he was not really a member of the party,

Doolittle Thornburg had not been recorded; and although James Smith and Charles Stanton were in his original ledger, Mary Florence MacDuff was overlooked.

The names swam before his eyes and blurred. It was a fact he would have to keep from Tamsen. He had always been so prideful of his stamina and physican condition. But now, even recording names in a ledger seemed to tire him.

7

"GEE! HAW!" The long-lashed oxwhips cracked over the yokes of two Donner and three Murphy wagons. They were to be taken to a predetermined new site a mile ahead and then the next group brought up.

In the meantime the other women were preparing food to be sent up to the men who had left long before dawn. To the surprise of all Margaret helped Eliza prepare food for "her" men and Virginia had volunteered to lead the packhorses to the road building terminus.

"Well, if that don't beat all," Phillipine whispered to Eliza, bringing over food for Lewis and Dutch Charley.

Eliza smiled to herself. Margaret had helped only on the special little foods for James and John Snyder, she was left to prepare the rest. And as John Snyder had been almost a nightly guest, Virginia's declaration of help was no great surprise. The girl had been making a near fool of herself over the man, and with Margaret's apparent blessing.

Rather than worry Eliza, it amused her. Virginia might have played games with James Frazier and John Breen, but John Snyder was no lustful stepfather or over-eager teenager. He struck Eliza as a man who played games for keeps, or not at all. Still, she couldn't determine if she liked the man or not. She liked him because he kept Margaret so occupied after dinner that she could sneak away to be with Lewis and Phillipine without being missed. But he was enigmatic, his small black eyes never said anything. As a woman he gave her an uneasy feeling, as though he might explode at any moment over nothing at all.

Then another approach of food turned Eliza's amusement in another direction.

"Good day," Mary Ann Graves said cheerily. "Here is the horse with the food for our men."

Right on her heels, and as fast as he could come, was John Breen.

Margaret stomped up the steps into the wagon as though the devil had just popped from the ground, almost colliding with Virginia as she came out.

"Oh, hello there," Mary Ann called. "I would be most willing to go with you, if you require help."

"Me, too!" John beamed. With Sol helping with the Donner wagons he would not have to keep stumbling over the runt to be with Mary Ann.

"How kind of you both," Virginia said sweetly. Too sweetly, Eliza thought. "But, John Breen, you heard Mr. Donner's order of roll. We wouldn't be back in time for you to help here. Mary Ann and I can handle it quite nicely."

"Oh, oh!" Eliza whispered to Phillipine. "Miss Priss has something up her sleeve."

Mary Ann was delighted. "Give me just a moment to prepare John's horse and I'll be right back."

"Take all the time in the world," Virginia said. "We have to wait for the rest of the food and Skylark is still not quite used to Billy's side-saddle."

Virginia had quickly agreed to gain one tiny bit of information. The night before John Snyder had informed James Frazier that he was leaving his Virginia trotter in the care of Mary Ann. With Mary Ann apparently having permission to use the horse, she now wished to learn how close the young woman was to him in other respects.

John Breen was crushed. He assumed that Mary Ann wanted to go along so she could see Sol Hook along the way. He would just have to thrash the runt again if he got in his way.

Sol had nothing to do with it. Mary Ann had reasons of her own for wanting to go along and get to know Virginia better.

George Donner scolded himself for not having previously inspected the hacked-out road.

"If one can even call it a road," he mumbled, urging the oxen on with another crack of the whip.

It twisted and writhed along the creek-bottom.

"Careful!" Jacob called from horseback.

The overhanging tree branches had not been properly cleared out and the canvas and bows of the first wagon were nearly torn off.

"Whoa! Whoa! Sol, hoist William up for a shimmy and then get him an axe to chop them away."

"They got all our axes up at the cutting."

"What about the pruning saws in the farm tool box?" Tamsen suggested.

"That's back in the supply wagon."

"Well," she laughed, "we do learn each inch of the way. Come on, Sol, I'll walk back with you."

"Let the girls do it, Tamsen," George growled. "It will tire you out."

"Oh, George, you make it sound like a thousand miles. I can still smell the cook fires."

That wasn't the point. He just hated to have her anywhere too far distant to call out to her. Even though they had gone no less than three-tenths of a mile, his arm was already near numb from cracking the bullwhip. He was a little scared of all these little infirmities starting to creep up on him.

She was able to laugh again explaining to the passing girls why they were going back and then grew most serious.

"You like her, don't you?"

Sol didn't have to ask which she had meant, although for once Virginia had kept her tongue under control and been most civil.

"She is beautiful."

"John Breen seems to think the same, from what I have noticed."

This brought a frown to Sol's handsome face. "The next time I shall fight him quite differently, Aunt Tammy."

"Well, I certainly hope there does not have to be a next time, for my needs for you might grow too heavy."

"Needs?"

"Sol, the pruning saw is under the wagon seat already. Lewis Keseberg warned we might need it, but your Uncle George hardly seemed to hear him. I wished to speak to you quite alone. Your step-father and my husband are not young men, Sol, nor are we moving as swiftly as we did over the plains. We can't count on catching up with Lanceford Hastings, and I don't know if I would trust the man after this. But we don't want to tire our two men into a grave, either. Sol, I am not saying don't have an interest in the girl, for she is most charming. But you are the only man I am going to be able to lean upon if anything should happen to Uncle George or Uncle Jake."

He gulped. "Are they sick? I haven't noticed."

"Not sick, in that sense, Sol. It's just little things that a woman would notice about her husband. The groans in the night, the slowness in doing just normal things. All this bickering and grumbling doesn't help. He feels so responsible for all these people."

"And I didn't help much, did I?"

"No," she said honestly, "even though you told the truth."

"But not strong enough, huh?"

"Well," she grinned, "perhaps not strong enough for me, but that's a river we don't have to ford again. Let's just do all we can to keep things off of their shoulders."

He stopped short. "Then don't you think we should start walking back in the other direction—toward the pruning saw."

She tucked her arm into his. "Excellent suggestion."

"Aunt Tammy," he said, on a rush, "did you know I was running away when this other thing happened?"

"Thought as much."

"And you didn't try to stop me?"

"Nope. A man can gain all the advice his ears can stand from kings and fools, but only his heart can tell him if he is going to be a king or a fool."

"Which am I?"

She hugged his arm. It seemed ages since she had been able to do that. "Like your namesake, Solomon, a bit of each. But every man has a bit of king and a bit of fool in him."

Beyond the waiting wagons Virginia was laughing over a quite similar point.

"You must be joking," she laughed, "Baylis Williams is a simple fool and a mere servant."

"I don't find him thus," Mary scowled. "When your father had him help us set up our camp I found him a most pleasant young man."

"But I thought Sol Hook and John Breen were vying for your attention."

Mary Ann laughed, a little ruefully. "Ever since I have been fourteen I have had boys vying for my attention. It doesn't mean I have to give my attention in return, except for being courteous and friendly."

"And men? Like John Snyder?"

"And men, but not John. Ever since he joined up with us, near Fort Laramie, he has been just a good friend."

With Mary Ann thus out of the picture as competition, Virginia could be more honest.

"I like him," she declared, "quite a lot."

"I'm glad. He may get moody at times, but there is a lot there to like."

Virginia sat silent for a long time as the horses bounced along. In her whole life she'd had only female cousins near her own age to be friendly with, and most of them she had never been able to abide. For some reason she felt duty bound to share a thought in reverse.

"I am sorry, Mary Ann, but I don't know that much about Baylis other than he is a servant of my stepfather and suffered an accident that sometimes makes him a little forgetful. But you are right, now that I think of it, he has always been pleasant toward me."

"I don't care if he is a servant, I think he is beautiful."

Virginia laughed. "Don't let my mother hear you say that. She has classed your family, because of John, on her par. Servants, to her, should crawl about like worms."

"Why?" They are people just like us. Look at Baylis's sister, Eliza. Why, she is one of the most strikingly beautiful women I have ever seen in my life. I'm amazed that John Snyder didn't take a fancy to her at once. They are each so dark and romantic looking. But John is very astute, as you shall learn. He probably saw at once that her eyes were only for that golden giant Lewis Keseberg. I feel sorry for her, the man being married already and all."

Virginia looked at her in utter amazement. First, she hardly thought Eliza beautiful or worthy to catch John Snyder's attention; and, secondly, how had utter strangers picked up something between Eliza and Lewis Keseberg that she had missed?

"Don't feel sorry for her," she snapped. "She is vile and hateful."

"Oh, Virginia, how can you say such a thing about her?"

"Easily," she said curtly, and went right on without fully thinking. "She was most crude and rude in examining me each time after—"

She stopped short. Appalled that she had even admitted that much to a total stranger.

"You do not have to say more," Mary Ann said, almost tonelessly. "It would seem that we have both been through that . . . . my sister, Sarah, did the examining . . . we stand a little apart now, too."

Again they rode in silence, broken only by the noise of the horses hooves on the narrow little roadway, crowded by stumps and boulders that still left it little more than a horse path.

"Can I . . . ?"

"Can I . . . ?"

Like twin volcanos wishing to erupt at once, they each wanted to spew forth the burning lava that tormented them and leave the crater free.

* * *

"Damnation, to heaven!" Jacob boiled, "Could they have not told us of these near-impossible hairpin turns and crossing the creek twice to this single mile. Reed is building less than an Indian trail. No more wagons can we bring up today."

Near dusk they sent that message back with the returning girls. Because of their own near-exhaustion no one noticed how quietly Virginia and Mary Ann had accepted their message.

The day had not been what either girl had expected. Sharing dire experiences from the past had been mentally draining, and their individual hopes were dashed upon arrival. John Snyder and Baylis Williams were each a mile further on, cutting away at the big timber. Milt Elliott was the only one they saw before turning back.

"What kept you so long?" Margaret snapped.

"Why, mother," Virginia said sarcastically, "we have been joy-riding." Then she leaned forward confidentially to Eliza. "Now I know why it is so murderous on the men. Could you please help me up to bed?"

Eliza nodded. It was the first "please" she had ever heard from the girl.

She was asleep before Eliza had her fully undressed, but the next morning she was prepared to return to the mountain. Mary Ann was also prepared. And the next group of wagons were ready to be moved up.

For three days the process continued. Family wagons brought food up to the men, family wagons moved another mile, then supplies were brought forward from the left-behind wagons.

Even though the Donner and Murphy wagons took the brunt of being jolted over boulders and big stumps—or were forced to stop to move them aside or chop them lower, the grumbling and carping from the other family wagons grew into a constant din.

Each day took a greater toll on George Donner,

trying to control and cajole a small army of women and children at men's work, but surprisingly, he gained an unexpected ally.

"I will not budge another inch without the men," Johanna Wolfinger wailed. "I have worn out three pairs of very fine gloves on swamps, mountain passes and this horrible path your husband devised. No more! I declare, no more, until the men move us on."

"Shut up!" Margaret scowled. "Did my man, or the men he has hired, come back to help move this monstrous rig? Eliza and I had to figure it out on our own or be left to the supply wagons. And I am frankly amazed we got it this far along."

Frankly, Margaret Reed had amazed herself and everyone else. Fear of being left miles behind with no one but Eliza had spurred her to action. A past, deeply buried since her marriage to James Frazier Reed, surged forward. As a young girl on a Missouri farm she had "mule-skinned" many a plow for her father, and oxen reins were little different.

"But, Margaret," Johanna wailed further.

"Don't 'Margaret' me," she said. "Move that damn wagon, or I'll move it for you!"

Eliza sat back looking at Margaret with interest, but not yet admiration. Virginia, and her daily trips, she could begin to regard with a degree of admiration; but both, she was well aware, could revert to type very, very quickly.

For Margaret it was almost too quick.

"Where are they? They have never been this late before!"

"Don't worry. Mr. Donner is also concerned and has sent his nephew out to make sure that they are safe on the trail."

"Humph!" Margaret scoffed. "After what that young rogue did to Virginia I don't trust him on the trail with her."

Eliza couldn't help but think that after what Virginia did to Sol, he had every right in the world to throttle her on the trail.

But on the trail Sol did not meet her, not even at the summit, where a grand and glorious 'breaking through' party was taking place. The drunkest perhaps, and no one could very well determine where the "booze" had come from, was James Frazier.

"Look, my boy," he said, clasping a fond arm about Sol's shoulder, "that is the Pacific!"

Sol could only see far off over the lower mountains the wide valley of the Great Salt Lake. He was not impressed.

"Where are Mary Ann and Virginia?"

"Around," James Frazier said half in drunkenness and half in utter fatigue. "As we are all going down soon, we told them to wait."

Sol saw neither around and sat down in disgust. His only concern, really, was Mary Ann.

She was not really that far away.

"It's just a serviceberry pie. I baked it myself, just for you."

Bayliss Williams looked at it and at her in wonderment. "Why?"

"Because I thought you would like it," she laughed. "And because I like you."

"You don't even know me."

"But, I would like to."

Virginia had nothing to offer John Snyder but words, and most of those remembered from his many conversations with Mary Ann.

"We have missed you."

"And I have missed your mother's marvelous tables."

"I'm glad."

"You wished me to say that I have missed you as well, didn't you?"

"Not really," she said, and was surprised it was

quite an honest statement. "I have gotten to know Mary Ann quite well while we've been bringing up the food. She was honest with you and has been honest with me."

"So," he murmured, "she told you all?" He sighed. "Poor little lass! Imagine, being so desperately in love with a man that you would throw yourself at him and wake up the next noon to find he was going to marry your eldest sister. The fault, of course, lies with her throwing herself at the man."

"Doesn't Jay Fosdick get some of the blame, sir? From her account he didn't duck or dodge or deny her himself."

"Really, Miss Backenstoe, I find this conversation a trifle embarrassing—first, because of your age and then because I have come to respect Jay and the love that he shows to Sarah. To keep that past alive does him a disservice."

"All right," Virginia said slyly, "we will drop it. But remember: I may be older and more experienced than you think."

James Frazier heard only her last sentence on his approach. His drunken and tired mind gave it all the wrong meaning.

"Get your horse, Virginia," he said sternly. He stood swaying until she was out of earshot. "Keep your grubby hands off her, mister."

Snyder scoffed at the intended insult. "If she were a properly reared young lady she would not go about boasting of experience."

To his amazement, James Frazier flushed a deep red and spun immediately away. A gleam stole into the young man's eye. Mary Ann being honest with Virginia meant that Virginia would have, more than likely, been honest in return. James Frazier's blush gave him quite an insight that he would store away for future use. And if he desired to put his 'grubby hands' on the girl, he would do so. But at the moment he did not desire to do so. He had a cold disregard for young ladies who "chased."

Six solid days of back-breaking work, coupled with their celebration, didn't leave many in the proper mood for moving up the supply wagons—let alone getting the family wagons to the top of the mountain.

During the four days the men had stayed on the mountain, George and Lavina's "women and children" had worked as a team. The return of the men was almost a disrupting element.

"Watch it! Watch it!" James Frazier screamed. "It's tilting, you blundering jackass! You got it too close to the edge!"

Milt Elliott threw his whip down in disgust and just let the supply wagon roll onto its side.

"I've had it with you, Reed," he bellowed. "You've been slaving us for days! We're damn tired of work and of you." Despite his bully manliness he began moaning. "We . . . we're . . . just so damned—"

James Frazier just stared at him in utter stupefaction.

Others came on the run, but it was Lavina who had to take command among the men.

"She went gentle and will come back up gentle. Pike! Foster! Get the team unhitched and to the side. Sol, we'll be needing the ropes we used for the windlass. Noah, you and Sammy Shoemaker go drag up four to six of those cut aspen. You other men can help use them as levers to right her as the oxen pull."

Some of the other men begged off. Wolfinger, Spitzer and Reinhardt claiming they had their own wagons to see after. Keseberg and Dutch Charley already had their supply wagons far ahead on the trail and James Smith was far behind with one of the MacDuff wagons. Some just vanished, because it meant one more bit of work for James Frazier. Nor was he any help. He just sat his horse and watched as though the accident hardly concerned him.

When he saw that no Reed men were helping, Milt got control of himself and bellowed them into work. But a firm decision had been made in his mind. He would continue as a teamster, but never again allow himself to be James Frazier Reed's personal lackey and whipping boy.

There was no joy upon making the summit. Hardly a person looked out at the plains, but down the deep ascent. It was far steeper than the mountainside which had taken a toll of one Reed supply wagon, but Lewis Keseberg couldn't "ski" them down this one; the woods were almost as thick this side as the other. All they could do was securely lock the wheels and brace the oxen back with each downward step.

What men that could be spared by women handling the team moved ahead clearing out the roughest kind of road. To keep out of James Frazier's way, Milt Elliott was one of them, having turned the righted wagon over to Walt Herron.

Partway down the whole train was brought to a dead stop.

"Jesus!" Milt growled, looking down into the little ravine, "Now who is the packass who led us right up to this impossibility?"

The Donner brothers and James Frazier came up on horseback. Rather than admit that he had not been blazing the trail, Reed again reverted to type.

"Where are your eyes? You must have missed my blazing marks a long way back. Any idiot can see that there is no room to get a wagon down into that ravine, let alone up again. Back! Back! Turn everyone back from this stupid mistake."

All that the men who had been axing out the rough road wished to do was form an immediate lynch party. They just stood in silence and looked down at the ground.

"Uncle Jake?" Sol said hesitantly.

Jake Donner looked at him in startled surprise. "What'yah doing here, boy?"

"Noah James got himself some pretty sore blisters and I'm relieving him. But what I was thinking, Uncle Jake, is that this is most like that gulley that kept the wagons from going over to the north pasture and fields."

"Most the same," he agreed, "but we had mounds of field-cleared rocks to fill it with."

"Well, all back along the way we have already felled trees that we can lay in until they are high enough to form a bridge."

"Would never support the weight of my wagon," James Frazier protested.

"Then take it around the way you blazed," Milt said sourly. "Come on, men, we'll get some others to help us start logging them down."

"Wait!" Reed snarled. "I have taken just about as much from you as I can take and still be civil."

Milt eyed him narrowly. "Do you want to fire me?"

"No," James Frazier said, quickly backing down. He could not afford to fire the man, he knew too much. "I just wanted you to know how I felt."

The men quickly moved away, hiding their smirks. For once someone had got the best of the man—and for it to have been Milt Elliott delighted them even more. Previously he had been even more hated than James Frazier, but of late had been the hardest worker about.

To the surprise of all, the Reed wagon rolled quite easily over the log bridge. It was one time, however, that Margaret took the sage advice of John Snyder and walked across the logs.

But overcoming that barrier had an odd effect on

all. The joy they should have felt in surmounting the summit was finally realized. Heartened, they plunged with near reckless speed down the mountain, across the ravine and up an easy slope onto a long meadow grassland.

A shallow, snake-like river ran its length and there was ample pastureland for the lean cattle and oxen.

"I know it has been twenty-one days since we left Bridger," George said, "but I think the men and animals deserve a couple of days' rest."

"Rest?" James Frazier's voice rose as though Donner had uttered something wicked. "Hastings will not wait for us forever."

"If he has waited this long," George sighed.

"He gave me his word," Frazier said firmly.

"He also gave you his word that he would come—" He stopped short and shielded his eyes against the sun. "Aren't those riders coming up the valley?"

James Frazier took a quick glance and drew an equally quick conclusion. "Coming slow and cautious. "Indians!" He spun his horse about and raced back along the train. "Indians! Prepare! Indians!"

The men were riding slowly because two of them were in near starvation condition. Doolittle had only found them that morning, just about ready to eat their horses. For all his knowledge of botany, Charles Stanton did not know how to live off the wilderness and a "friendly" Indian who had offered to guide them out of the trackless mountains had gotten them hopelessly lost and stolen their two rifles.

For the moment Stanton regained his sense of humor. "Always wanted to lose my pot-belly and finally have."

"Did you also lose Glaucus?" Reed demanded.

Mac McCutchen looked up from where he sat cross-legged on the ground, gnawing at left-over breakfast bisquits smeared with bacon drippings.

"Hastings said you gave him a present of the horse for showing us the way."

"That is a damnable lie. Just wait until I get down to his camp."

"Ain't nobody there," Doolittle said drily. "Just another damn note."

"Well," Reed bristled, "we shall still catch up with him."

"Not likely," Doolittle shrugged.

"What do you mean? We saw the plains from the summit. We will be there in a matter of hours, if we don't dally here too long."

Doolittle looked around. These hardly seemed the same people he had left but a few days before. They looked so haggard and wan. Even Eliza's uniform seemed unkept and starchless. He really hated to say what he had to say.

"More like days than hours, Mr. Reed. You've only just come over a divide between the two ridges of the Bossman. Charley and I have been studying it all morning, but Mac thinks the best way is to go back upstream and over a saddleback."

"Studying?" James Frazier flared. "*I* was the one who found my way directly back from Hastings and know of what I speak. At the end of this valley is a gentle sloping down to the plain."

"Bullcrap!" Mac snarled. "A slope ten times worse than Weber's Canyon. So damn bad we couldn't find an Indian or animal trail on it."

"But I know that is the way that I came!" Reed insisted. Then he had an instant thought. "The ravine! Damn it, we should have gone down the ravine."

"Which is it?" Jacob demanded. "Do you have us lost as well? Hastings sure as hell never set foot on this land, nor did he guide you back too damn well."

"But can we even be sure of this other way?" Hans

Wolfinger exploded. "Another piece of doomed madness!"

"Nightmare!" Augustus Spitzer hissed. "Are we to work ourselves to nothing, wandering about cutting blindly through every canyon and divide our hapless leader stumbles upon?"

Because of the mood of panic that was growing, nobody thought to point out that he had done the least cutting of all.

"Now let us all just calm down," George said quietly.

"Calm down?" William Eddy sniffed. "This whole train has been mismanaged from the first."

"Seems to me," Lavina chuckled, "that the man you wanted most for captain is the very one who stuck his nose in and got us into this pickle."

"You all agreed to follow me!" James Frazier declared, haughtily.

"But not blindly," James Smith sneered.

"Now listen here, you little—"

"No!" The shout was forceful and yet almost quietly uttered. "You all listen and listen good!"

They all turned on little Tamsen and shrank back as though she towered above them.

"There is no use going back, and to go ahead we had best have a bit of sense about us. It has been just as rough of a time for the women and children, and don't you forget it. But if it means more cutting, we will cut. If it means more road-building, we will build. If it means our manning the teams, we will man. But I am sick up to my gills of blame-laying. If James Frazier made a mistake in blazing, I can understand it. Look! Look about! We be plains farmers used to seeing from horizon to horizon. That damn mountain looks the same to me as did its other side and the one just behind it. If we didn't see the sun high above them for a while each day I wouldn't even be able to tell you east from west. North and south I've given up on altogether. But after supper and a good night's rest, I'm going to be looking at another mountain ridge and, with or without you, I'm climbing over it and the next and the next."

For the rest of the day and night, Tamsen's words quieted them. The route would be laid out by Thornburg, Stanton and McCutchen. James Frazier felt slighted and gave a lavish dinner party that night for John Snyder and the Wolfingers, despite what Hans had said.

George Donner gave the planners carte blanche approval of whatever they decided and went to bed without supper. It was the first time he admitted how drained he really was. The Donner meal was thus simple, quiet and subdued.

Lavina put on quite a feast for the Breens, McCutchens, old man Hardkoop and the MacDuff parties. Ample, but not lavish. Ample because she knew full well the larder conditions of the others. Wasn't a family that hadn't left Fort Bridger well stocked for the twenty to thirty day trek as suggested in Lanceford Hastings' guide. Twenty-one days' worth of supplies had been used up and they had come only thirty-eight miles from Weber Canyon.

William Eddy was too proud to admit that he and his family ate flour-water pancakes and molasses for dinner. After the way Lavina Murphy had insulted him that day, in front of all the men, he was not willing to accept her charity.

To show his gratitude for the "rib-sticking" supper, Patrick Dolan put down his tail-gate and gave a performance in honor of Lavina.

"He is trying to sound so happy," Mary Florence said, "but his voice is sad."

Doolittle grunted.

Impulsively, she stole her hand into his.

"Been lonely around here without you."

He grunted again.

"Doo," she whispered, "I'm going to be brazen. The other side of my bed is right cold with no one in it. I'll leave the back flaps of the wagon loose, if you have a mind."

His eyes wandered to another campfire where Eliza sat in huddled conversation with the Kesebergs. It was just next to impossible for him to get near that dark-haired beauty.

"I've a mind," he sighed.

Mary Florence rose with regal grace. Never had she thought she would play second fiddle to a serving girl. Never had she thought she would fall in love with a man like Doolittle Thornburg. During the days he had been gone she had scolded herself over such a foolish notion. But seeing him ride across the grasslands had brought pleasure to her heart and tears to her eyes. She had felt giddy and excited and foolish. Like a mother greeting her first-grader on the opening day of school, she had been hesitant to show too much love and affection and concern.

Then during the Murphy dinner, as she saw his eyes steal to the Reed camp and later to the Keseberg camp, it came to her that she would have to approach Doolittle in a language he would understand.

It would debase her, but did that matter? She was manless in a godforsaken wilderness. If she did not grab onto a piece of life now, it might to too late. For a long while, her nightmares had been filled with what she laughingly called the "Selkirk women's curse." The highland women of the Selkirk clan had always claimed they could smell death in a person. For six nights running she had come awake gasping for air, her nostrils filled with the scent of death. She had put it all down to the fact that she could still smell Harlan in the wagon.

But that night, debasing or not, she was determined

not to have a nightmare or scent a single thing in her nostrils except Doolittle Thornburg.

They were, perhaps, the only two happy people in camp the next morning.

Barely able to stand, even after his long sleep, George Donner rang the silver dinner bell.

Road work commenced again!

It was like a recurring nightmare. For five days they seemed to be felling the same trees, hacking at the same brush, rolling aside boulders that had been rolled aside before. Yet in this six miles was a degree of difference. Side hills had to be dug down for the semblance of a roadbed and the creek-crossings on the watershed side had to be leveled going into and coming out of.

There was also a marked degree of difference in the people. Tamsen's words had stirred them only for the moment. The men did not want to stay on the mountain with the food brought to them. The morning and evening trek meant a little bit of a respite from the work. The teamsters raised the cry again that they had been hired for rolling oxen and not rolling boulders. The ways of shirking on labor became ingenious.

On the sixth day they moved over their six miles of road, but as individual units. There was a great lack of cooperation. George Donner was too weak to rise from his wagon-bed that day, Jacob felt his first responsibility was to the Donner wagons, and James Frazier Reed still sulked that this was not his route.

Again they were in a meadow. Again a narrow canyon faced them on the south and the steep ridge wall of the canyon kept them from seeing westward.

"No more!" Johanna Wolfinger wailed. "I can stand no more of this! I will just die here rather than face another canyon!"

Although they all felt the same, they also felt she had the least to complain about. She and her husband had done no work whatsoever on this stretch of road and now ate nightly from the Reed supplies, that somehow didn't seem to dwindle.

Now the three new trailblazing masters were being accused of dragging them further into hell.

Over the strong objections of Tamsen, George pulled himself from bed and dressed. When he insisted upon a horse, Jacob quietly told Sol to also saddle and ride with his uncle.

George didn't object. He was calling up every bit of his reserve energy to act as a leader.

Within the hour they were deep enough into the canyon that it seemed like night. The trees were so closely spaced that a horse could hardly squeeze through, and towered thirty to forty feet.

"It certainly is a jungle."

"I was not questioning the word of Mac Mc-Cutchen," George growled in mock wrath. "But some of those fools would have questioned me if I had not come for a look-see. Come on."

"Yes, sir."

Sol had always stood in awe and fear of the man. As a step-nephew he had never felt fully accepted by the man as family.

"We will cross to the north side of the creek here, Sol. Best we keep to the trees and not let the camp see that we are going up the ridge for a look-see of it, as well.

"Why is that, sir?"

"Man and boy, Sol, I have dealt with people of all sorts. When they trust your word they will follow you to the brink of hell, and sometimes over. Our folk have lost confidence. That makes them near to being a mob. Son, you handle a mob in the only way, because they wouldn't be in the mob if they still had some confidence in themselves and their leaders. No, you and I have to figure the best way out of this meadow and flat-out tell them that's the only way. Democracy is a fine thing, my boy. I was born the year the war ended to bring it about. But my father always maintained that monarchy was also a good thing when you needed a strong hand at the helm. You would have liked my father, Sol. He could fiddle a dance in the barn until dawn and go right out to shoulder a plow for the day. You've been doing the same. A full-grown man you'll be before this is over."

Sol looked at him in gratitude. It was the most the man had ever talked with him since his mother had married Jacob.

George Donner had a dual purpose in keeping his speech quite long. This wooded section was steep and even on horseback he could feel his heart pounding. To talk kept his mind off that and on a subject that had begun to worry him of late. If anything did happen to Jacob and himself, Sol would be the man of the family. At fourteen, he had to start preparing himself. At fourteen, George Donner was preparing to take his first bride. At fifteen, he was a father and farming eighty acres.

"Look!"

The trees just seemed to part for them as they came to the summit. The sun was hot on their faces after the cool shade. George's heart eased. All of the answers were before him, but he didn't need to learn.

"What do you think, boy?"

"Must be the canyon Hastings meant all along. Hardly any slope from here down into it, and no more need for tree cutting. Would you look at that! Open and easy all the way out of the expanse of the valley."

Then he turned to look back along the ridge and down the steep canyon wall to where the wagons were huddled like toys.

"Getting here is the problem," he frowned.

"I agree," George shrugged, but added no more as they rode along the ridge examining every bit of it from top down.

"Uncle George," he said hesitantly, "look at this spot. It may sound foolhardy, but if we worked together and double-teamed each wagon, couldn't we make it straight up this grade?"

George chuckled. "I guess we are damned if we do and damned if we don't."

Sol grinned. "I wonder how James Frazier Reed will feel, bringing his big wagon up this way?"

"Ain't going to get a chance to feel or comment. I suspect that we have been spotted up here by now, Sol, so let's ride right down this slope like our minds are already made up—and by damned they are! My, don't that sun feel good! I guess all I needed was a bit of exercise."

All George Donner had needed was to regain his own confidence. James Frazier Reed had made him feel old and useless. By this action he would be asserting his leadership again.

He had read the emigrants quite well. Because he made it a resounding declaration of fact, there was not even a murmur of protest from James Frazier.

The man, actually, wanted to scream out more in pain than protest. The moment he had started to step forward after the announcement Margaret had clutched him by the forearm, digging her nails right through the silk of his sleeve and nearly drawing blood.

"James," she hissed, "even if it means leaving this monster behind and me walking the rest of the way, that's how it shall be!"

A night to sleep on it and another look at the steep north wall in full morning light made a few hesitate, but not enough to speak up.

"Damned dangerous," Jacob said on a worried note. "Don't blame me."

Jacob turned wonderingly to his brother. But George simply stood there, his square beard half-hiding a huge grin. "Sol," he called, "take my family wagon up first, so the next will have a path to follow. Do it just the way you planned it out on our ride down yesterday."

"George Donner," Elizabeth scolded, "I forbid this! He is just a mere boy!"

"Elizabeth, why don't you just shut up and start walking up with the other women and children. That *man* has work to do."

Jacob mouthed a silent "Amen!"

It was work, but nothing like felling trees and moving boulders.

With Sol on one side and Noah James on the other, they whipped and led the four oxen sheer up the north wall. Before them, Milt Elliott and a crew levered rocks and fallen trees out of their path. Behind, Mac McCutchen and Lewis Keseberg strolled with tree-trunk sized poles, ready to jam them under the back wheels if they gave the slightest sign of starting to roll backwards.

Running from side to side, keeping the wheels well greased for easy rolling, was an unlikely volunteer. It was to have been Jean Baptiste's job until John Breen heard that Sol Hook would lead the way in the first wagon. He was not about to be outshone in front of Mary Ann Graves.

Feeling himself made a fool of again, James Frazier sat the steps of his wagon and silently prayed for a disaster. He was also rankled that assisting Milt were James Smith and John Snyder.

But no disaster happened, although it could have very easily. The wagon and teams were at such a sheer angle that one slipping animal could have thrown the others off-stride and rolled wagon and teams together three hundred feet back down the slope.

When the wagon came to a stop on the summit the women and children let out a joyous shout and came running. It had taken the wagon a half hour to make the same climb they had made in fifteen minutes. But none had minded, if this way proved to save them another week down in the other canyon.

In their happiness they hugged and kissed Sol. Mary Ann's kiss was one of congratulation, not love, but Sol blushed scarlet. Not to be outdone, Virginia rushed over to plant her kiss as well.

John Breen glowered from one to the other. "Well, I helped too, you know!"

The girls looked at him and both began to giggle at once.

"Oh, John," Mary Ann laughed, "you should just see yourself. Grease from head to foot!"

"Well," he pouted, "someone had to do it."

"And a damn good job it was," Sol said, slapping him on the back. "We were all a team, and best get back down to help guide the others."

"Then the team must be rewarded," Mary Ann grinned, putting her fingers to her lips and then touching them to a clean spot on John's forehead.

John floated down the slope, as though her gesture was a promise of better things to come. Sol walked proudly with the other men, discussing a few places where they all agreed a slight route change could make the going easier. He had thought they would rib him about all the kissing and hugging. They thought it was justly deserved.

After the second and third Donner wagons were safely up, and two more teams trained, they experimented having three wagons toiling up the slope at hundred-foot intervals.

For men who had been completely wearied and simply could not face any more labor, this was child's play.

Nor did George Donner let up on herding his mob. When six wagons were on the summit he put them in Lavina's charge, to take the women and children down the opposite slope and through the canyon toward the valley.

"Yoohoo! Margaret!" Johanna called. "Hans has our wagon up, come ride with me, for a change."

She was on her way to have a word with Tamsen and Elizabeth and waved her away for the moment.

"I just wanted to tell you," she said, looking directly at Tamsen, "how proud I am of the way Sol has handled this operation."

Tamsen was taken aback. It wasn't too long ago the woman was calling Sol a rapist.

"Really, Margaret," Elizabeth clucked, "are you forgetting that he is *my* son?"

"One can hardly forget that," she said a little snidely, "but it was Mr. Donner who found this route with the young man, and I wanted him to know my feelings directly through Tamsen."

"I shall be happy to pass it along," Tamsen said quietly.

"Oh, and another favor, if I might. Would you have room for me to ride with you?"

"All the room in the world," Elizabeth chortled with glee. To get the advantage over Johanna Wolfinger almost sent her into the vapors.

Tamsen knew the question had been directed solely at her, but saw no reason to spoil Elizabeth's pleasure. If this was a way for Margaret Reed to offer an apology, she could accept it. Others might be rejoicing, but she feared they would all have to work harder together against another enemy—time. Even an ex-schoolteacher could see that the sun had swung farther to the south. It was the twenty-seventh of August and from this vantage point she could look back at the higher peaks and see that they were already snow-capped.

Twenty-eight days from Fort Bridger and the journey had hardly begun.

8

IT WAS like starting over again. George Donner felt alive and in command again. James Frazier and Virginia rode off across the open country, although he missed Glaucus sorely. Elizabeth and a pouting Johanna returned to riding with Margaret, and Lavina Murphy could be heard bullwhacking, her voice drowning all others.

Within a few hours they came upon the Hastings trail and made more mileage that day than in the preceding ten.

That night, a mile from the Great Salt Lake, Patrick Dolan put on one of the funniest shows of his career. Mary Ann sat most ladylike, between Sol and John Breen, with wistful glances at Baylis Williams. Virginia just sat wistfully. For once she was being quite her own age with her thoughts. John Snyder was paying her no attention and she knew Mary Ann didn't want that much attention from the other two. She wasn't quite sure what she wanted.

Mary Florence sat openly holding Doolittle's hand. She no longer cared who might think anything of it.

Eliza's handholding with Lewis was supposed to be secret, but from behind it was noted by Johanna and she could hardly wait to gossip over the point the next day.

She could not that night, because Margaret had taken to her bed finally exhausted from her ordeal. James Frazier sat on the wagon steps puffing his pipe and knowing full well that Margaret had taken to her bed because he had made sly amorous suggestions at the dinner table. His guilt rose anew that Margaret knew something and he was being punished. He was forgetting that Margaret had pulled the act many times since Thomas was born three years before.

Tamsen did not go to the show, but not because she wouldn't have fully enjoyed a night of relaxation. The long passage through the mountains had turned Luke Halloran's cough worse.

Even after the music and dancing had ceased she nursed him through the night like he was one of her own children.

"The paroxysm is upon him," she whispered to George the next morning. "Say nothing."

The mood of the wagon was such that they considered their luck had changed. She did not want to dampen it with bad news.

It was like the crack of a rifle report. The large wheels made another quarter turn and queerly began to spread outward as the axle assembly split and began to plow.

Rolling down the mountainside and being toppled had finally taken its toll on the Reed supply wagon.

James Frazier elected to keep his unit intact and

send some of his men back to find a timber to replace the broken axle.

Johanna Wolfinger wouldn't get her gossip in that day.

By noon the going was getting rougher as they rounded the point of a mountain near the lake. Once a massive lake bed or even an ocean, it was strewn with rocks they had to jolt over.

The Donner wagon pulled out of the line and stopped.

"Luke can't take this, George," said Tamsen. "Leave me Sol as teamster and we'll catch up when the Reeds come along."

He patted her cheek tenderly. He had no fear of her not being able to take care of herself.

It was dusk by the time Sol spotted the oncoming Reed wagons. Milt and Walt Herron had had to go fifteen miles to find a timber to cut and haul back to splice across the broken axle. Then, until they could camp and properly repair it, the going had been very slow.

Luke Halloran had breathed his last during the late afternoon, but Tamsen would not let Sol take them on until she had talked with James Frazier. Going through Luke's personal trunk she had come across something that she knew Reed would understand and know how to handle.

James Frazier peered into the old trunk in utter disbelief. "We all thought him nothing but an orphan, a waif." He lifted out the emblems of a Master Mason with great respect. "This I never would have suspected. Just shows how little we knew about him."

Tamsen nodded silently. There were many statements she could have made to that point, but knew they would no longer help Luke.

"On top was a letter leaving us his all for caring for

him. But the emblem I thought you would know how to handle."

"But of course. It must be buried with him and with a Masonic service that I shall conduct. We will see to it all when we get to camp."

Tamsen nodded again and closed the trunk. Besides his horse, bridle and saddle, Luke had left her fifteen hundred dollars in coin. Hardly a poor waif.

As Sol bullwhacked the team along, Virginia jumped from her horse and walked beside him.

"It's kind of eerie," she whispered.

"What is?"

"Our first dead person," she shuddered.

"You forget Mr. MacDuff."

"Didn't know him and we were up on the mountain when they buried him."

"You really can't say that you knew Luke, either," he said, not unkindly.

"Why don't you like me, Sol Hook?" she snapped.

"Why don't I like you?" he mimicked her. "That's a fine question. You, at least, have stopped sticking out your ugly little tongue, but am I supposed to fully forget what you and John Breen said against me?"

"You certainly seem to have forgiven John Breen, letting him grease your wheels and all."

"That has nothing to do with it," he snorted. "That was out of necessity for the good of all."

She was silent for a long while. "I suppose I should say that I am sorry."

"Suppose?" he chuckled sarcastically. "If you put it that way, then you really don't mean it. I 'suppose' I should forget that it still hurt like hell when I sneeze through a broken nose."

"That was gallant of you to come to my rescue," she cooed.

"Don't try to sweetmouth me, Virginia. Seems to me now that you were enjoying it quite a bit until you knew you were caught. Seems to me now that you were using me to keep blame from yourself."

"I'm sorry, Sol. I was using John just to make you jealous."

"Seems like pretty extreme using, if you ask me."

"I said I was sorry," she sniffled.

"You're sorry!" he exploded. "That's something you are supposed to save for love and your husband. You don't even know what love is."

"Well, I suppose that you do?" she sniffled louder.

"Nope! Thought that I did. When we split trains I was sick inside, miserable and I thought heartbroken. I was running away that day to join the Boggs train. That would have been a mistake. Then, if you want to know the truth, I thought I was madly in love with Mary Ann. I'm not, really."

Virginia snuffed back her nose. "Then who are you in love with?"

"Nobody!"

"Then you have permission to fall in love with me!"

She quickly turned his head, without losing a step, kissed him fully on the mouth, slowly, with so much tenderness that Sol was momentarily stunned and nearly tripped. Then, before he fully realized it, she pulled away and jumped back upon her horse. Without a word she spurred the horse into a full gallop.

"Of all the damnable tomfoolery. . . ."

Then he grinned. It wasn't love that he felt, but a bit of growing manly pride. He had been able to get Virginia to admit the truth.

Uncle Billy Graves donated boards he had carried all the way west and Lewis a handful of brass nails. In full regalia James Frazier conducted a most impressive service. Out of deference to the dead man they could not travel that day.

And Johanna could not gossip.

It was after eight when they rolled in and the news spread quickly.

The camp had been made at the black rock where Reed had found Hastings three weeks before. There was no note because Doolittle had already found it.

Mary Florence came to help Tamsen prepare the body.

"Am I doing wrong?" she asked, unexpectedly.

"Ain't my place to say," Tamsen said, knowing full well what she meant.

"Ain't?" Mary Florence laughed lightly.

Tamsen laughed. The schoolmarm stood corrected. "I guess all rules are a little different out here."

Except one, Mary Florence thought. It was still just a one-sided love, and she knew it well.

Those who used logic did not look upon the two events as bad signs: the wagon was overdue for the break and Luke had been sick when he came to them.

The logic held for two more days of good travel. The arid plain of sagebrush was almost better than an Illinois road. Then, as though a knife had slit the landscape, they rolled onto a meadow with spring-wells so deep that a seventy-five foot roped bucket would not touch the bottom.

"Think you'd best see this, Mr. Donner," Doolittle said, taking him to a standing board near one of the wells. In such a place it was obvious that the board was from the side of a wagon. But the scraps of paper that still clung to the board, and were scattered about the ground, were of little use to them now.

"Pecked off by birds?"

"Or destroyed by wanton Indians."

Others strolled up.

James Frazier cursed. "Not enough left to see if it is a message or a warning."

"Warning," Doolittle said, "most likely. The desert is ahead of us."

"How far across?"

"Ain't ever been over it," he said, truthfully for a change.

Tamsen had been looking closely at the board and knelt down to pick up some of the scattered tatters. She turned them about to gain a clue.

"It's Hastings's hand," she murmured. "Sol, you and the girls find me more of these pieces."

She took the board from the ground and sat down with it across her lap.

"What you about?" Lavina asked.

"What I used to do with the children in the schoolroom. Tear a picture into pieces and make them put it back into a whole."

Lavina chuckled. "Always said it was good to have a schoolma'am along. Everyone, search up every last scrap for Tamsen!"

Even though they couldn't find all, Tamsen pieced the puzzle together, but it wasn't much.

"Two days and two nights of hard driving before the next grass and water."

"Does he mean steady travel?"

"That's all it says."

"Don't say enough," George frowned. "His guide said about thirty-five to forty most across the dry drive."

Wolfinger scoffed. "It has hardly been correct to date. Two days and two nights now stretch it out to fifty miles or more."

"If it be a truthful report," Jacob said sourly.

"Why do you say that, Uncle Jake?"

"Old-fashioned logic. Did the man write the note before he left here or make a four day and four night round trip because he loves us all so dearly? If ladies and children weren't present I'd give my honest opinion on—"

James Frazier's screech was enough to stop him

short and send hair ends rising. He raced away, skipping and shouting like a ten year old. On the far side of the meadow Glaucus stood grazing. Was it another omen.

"All right," George said suddenly, before Jacob could go on with his opinion of Hastings, "I say we take his message as a warning and plan even better. We will camp for thirty-six hours, for it will be a long, hard march with only a short rest each night. I want everything available filled with water, including all the animals. Men, cut every blade of grass you can find. It's obvious now that we will be the last train through here this year. Women, there will be no fuel out on the desert. Cook your food now and we will just have to eat it cold. John Breen, I want you to train all the boys near your age about axles and grease up every wheel good. That desert will melt it out like a candle thrown into a fireplace. Sol, I want every iron tire pounded firmly onto each rim. While we have water, soak the rims and spokes good so that they swell. The younger children can sit with bacon drippings and rub it onto every bridle and oxen line. But, also everyone must rest."

Glaucus was a mystery and a blessing. Although fully saddled and bridled, he had been tethered to a long rope. But nowhere on the horse was a note or clue as to why he was left behind. Still, during the thirty-six hours James Frazier had no time but for the horse.

Margaret was just as glad. Johanna had finally found a moment to spread her gossip. Margaret was in doubt as to what her reaction should be. Avoid it, she could not. Johanna was so thick-skinned when it came to the feelings of others that she had told Margaret while Eliza stood right there at the tent stove.

"Have you no food to prepare, Johanna?"

"Is not Eliza preparing it?"

Margaret rose from the chaise longue and faltered. Eliza thought she was going to pull another of her fake faints and ignored it. She dreaded what Margaret Reed would have to say.

"Eliza," Margaret said, catching her breath, "has her hands quite full preparing two whole days of food for this family and our teamsters. We shall not be entertaining."

Johanna rose, confused and baffled. Fiddling with a heavy gold necklace she departed. That she was going to miss out on Eliza's tongue-lashing upset her more than missing out on two days of Eliza's fine cooking. Then that began to anger her. For the Reeds to share from their bounty, she had come to expect as her due, although she and her husband had not been wholly truthful. Beneath the false floorboards of their wagon were enough hoarded supplies to keep fat upon their flesh for some little time.

"Oh, Tamsen," she called, "I was just coming to see you. I don't think Margaret is well and poor Eliza has her hands full cooking for so many. I told the poor dear that Hans and I could not feel right eating with them. Would you have a few things in your stores that you might be willing to sell me?"

The last thing in the world that Tamsen needed on the edge of a salt desert was cash money. "I will be happy to share until you can replace, Mrs. Wolfinger."

It was exactly what Johanna had hoped the foolish woman would say. She began to make a mental list that would leave her secret hoard quite intact.

"Eliza," Margaret said quietly.

Eliza spun, ready to do battle and get in the first word. "I know what that gossip said and it's true. I was holding his hand. I love him."

"Eliza," she repeated, even more quietly.

"No, I will have my say. I could have run off with him to become a Mormon, but I knew that was no good for him. But I am not being bad, as that witch would like to think. I wouldn't hurt Phillipine for anything in the world."

"Hurt . . ." Margaret murmured, lowering herself back to the chaise, but it had nothing to do with the conversation.

"Yes, hurt. She's become a dear friend and would laugh at the way Mrs. Wolfinger put the whole matter."

Margaret's senses cleared for a moment and the dizzy sensation ceased. The pain that had shot flaming arrows up her right side was now dull.

"For the moment, Eliza, I will say that I have been most aware of you spending your evenings with the Kesebergs. In front of my husband and Mr. Snyder I have not wished to raise the issue."

"But it is now raised, by gossip," Eliza said stiffly.

"And dropped," Margaret whispered, suddenly unable to feel her left foot and leg as she sat on the edge of the chaise. "Because . . . because . . ." Her tongue grew thick and the word slurred.

As though through a fog she saw the expression of doubt on Eliza's face.

Someone came up the wagon steps and Eliza turned.

"Mrs. Wolfinger says that Margaret is not feeling—" Tamsen started and stopped. Margaret's whole left arm began to shake violently and she seemed utterly unaware of it.

"No tell . . . no tell . . ." she stammered.

Eliza frowned. Even before Margaret began to crumple like a rag doll she knew this was no fake.

"Lay her down flat!" Tamsen barked, rushing to grab Margaret's head before it dropped. The jaw was already starting to lock and she had to pry it open to pull out the tongue before the woman swallowed it.

"What is it?"

Tamsen didn't have time to answer, even if she had been fully sure. She prayed it was nothing more than just a seizure like her eldest sister used to experience.

"Knife! Got to cut this stupid corset away. Then blankets to keep her warm! Doesn't this damn thing lie down flat?"

"No, Tamsen!"

"Then help me twist her around in the other direction."

Without knowing it they were doing the most proper thing. By elevating her feet it was causing the blood to be pumped back to the portion of the brain that had suffered the slight stroke.

James Frazier was angry. With a muffled "damn!" he brushed Glaucus faster, his face heavy with frowning.

"Will she be all right?" Virginia gulped.

"Hell, look at the attention she is getting. Her bed moved down and clucking human hens everywhere."

"Tamsen and Eliza sent them all away."

"Eliza should be getting our dinner ready."

"I'll see to it."

"You'll see to it?" he echoed blankly. "That's a laugh. You've never cooked a thing in your life."

"I've been offered help."

"Well, about time some of those people did more than just come and eat up my food."

"Not those people," she said patiently, "but ones who owe us nothing. Phillipine Keseberg and Peggy Breen."

"Probably want to take the leftovers back to their camps," he said callously.

"How cruel!" she quavered. "They are doing it for mother, even though she has never done anything for them."

"And do you know what she is doing for us?" he snorted. "She is making it a great possibility that they will have to move on without us. I will never forgive her if that should come about."

"Did you ever love her?" Virginia said quietly.

"But, of course," he lied.

"You don't act like it. I sometimes think that the only being you love is yourself and that damn horse!"

"Tommyrot!" he snorted. "You know that I love you!"

"That's not love," she said, with a show of calm, but he could see the fires dancing in her eyes, "but only the using of me to fulfill your own desires."

"Which," he snarled, "you had to retry on every young buck that came along."

"Only one," she said with chilling clarity, "Whether you believe it or not. I am thankful that the other two were more gentlemanly than you and John Breen."

All the inherent snobbishness in his upper-class soul came to the surface.

"Without me, you and your mother would be nothing, and don't you forget it!"

"That is positively idiotic! Mother had a small fortune when she married you!"

"Virginia," he said sternly, "I am not about to argue financial matters with a mere child, who could not possibly understand their many ramifications."

"Glad you recognize me again as a mere child," she pointed out coldly. "Now, I have work to do and you *must* see to Glaucus. Mother will move, sir, even if she has to lie abed like Luke Halloran."

"—And he died," he retorted snidely.

"As we all must some day," she said firmly.

As Margaret had ridden mostly in the wagon, this was hardly a change for her. She fought to be a good patient. After so much fake illness, to really be sick was not to her liking.

"You . . . gawon . . ." she slurred to Tamsen. "They see . . . tah me."

Eliza's constant care of the woman was not to the liking of Lewis Keseberg.

"You wear yourself out. Come sit with us for awhile."

"I wish I could, Lewis, but there is so much to do."

"Bah!" he gruffed. "Let her daughter do it! You owe her nothing."

"Virginia is already doing all one can expect. Oh, let me see later if I can break away for a few moments."

Later she was so tired that she fell asleep sitting beside Margaret and the bedridden women had signalled her daughter not to disturb her needed slumber.

Lewis Keseberg was furious at Eliza's non-arrival. For the first time in over a month he took his fury out on Phillipine. For once she hardly felt the pain and did not cry out. But it set a determination in her brain. The next day on the trail she would confess her husband's sadistic nature in full to Eliza.

On September 3, 1846 she didn't have a chance to see or talk with Eliza. The pain she had not felt the night before she felt greatly in the morning. She could hardly breathe from cracked ribs and her left arm was broken in two places. Lewis paid her ailments no mind and Dutch Charley silently made a splint for her arm. For a month his mind had been free of worrying about the woman and her domestic troubles. He shuddered to think that it was starting all over again.

They moved out while the sky was still pearly gray, following the wagon tracks that seemed to converge together far out on the great open valley. This optical illusion led them to think that the rough high hills to the west would be the end of the dry drive. For hours they didn't seem to change in shape or form or draw any nearer. They just seemed to sit there as a challenge to be skirted or crossed.

Then, as the desert sun can do to weary eyes, they were suddenly upon the foot of the hills and the trail rose to the north and a pass that went through the formations that looked like deserted castles.

"Slow 'em down!" George warned each of the teamsters. "This sun is mighty rough on them."

Having crossed the dry drive in three-quarters of a day he could not help but feel that Hastings had erred again. His caution had nothing to do with the good time they had made, but the climb up into the pass. It was steady but steep. Every few hundred yards the oxen had to be rested as they toiled to pull the wagons more than a thousand feet above the valley. A handful of water or a bit of cut grass was used to coax them on.

Near the top of the pass, Doolittle stopped to listen. James Frazier also heard the sound and turned Glaucus toward the caravan with a shout:

"That damn lying Hastings! I can hear a waterfall and stream up in the pass!"

Doolittle rode on to find it, and what lay beyond the pass. Both findings so stunned him that he just sat his horse, watching the sun begin to set, and waited for the train to top the pass.

High up, a spring flowed down a cascade face to become a roaring stream that plunged to the valley and literally disappeared. Oddly, not a single green thing grew along its banks.

"Salt? That damn water is saltier than the ocean!"

Jacob Donner hardly heard his brother. He was near tears as he looked down and out.

"Lord God, the man most grievously lied! Another plain and another ridge of volcanic hills? He said nothing of this!"

But it was the plain beyond the ridge that was really shaking him. Only the setting sun showed them the distance to the mountains as it sank behind them. No man wished to utter aloud what Jacob Donner was thinking.

A great deal more than forty miles of desert lay ahead and it was nothing like the sage plain just come through. It was perfectly flat, dazzling white, like the first heavy frost on their Illinois farm fields, but it had an ominous glitter to it. Salt! Everywhere they looked the world was salt encrusted.

No one uttered a single word as George motioned for them to roll down the mountain and into the valley before full nightfall. They were too sick at heart to even discuss the awesome sight within their own family group. No one wished to remind the other that they had used up too many water-buckets in coaxing the oxen up the steep grade.

Hastings's brief note was becoming like a gravestone epitaph—telling so little, when it could tell so much.

The Hastings wagons also had another advantage, besides being sixty-seven strong: they had the man with them who had written the guide. Every empty flour, corn meal and bean barrel had been saved and filled with water. The Donner party had been burning or discarding them.

"A quart of water and three hours rest for each animal? George, that is hardly enough of either. Don't you realize I have a very sick wife?"

"I do! Also realize it will be easier on her to get across this little stretch and the volcanic ridge in the coolness of night."

It wasn't cool, it was downright marrow-chilling cold and eerie. A great white moon floated along with them and made the salty sand glitter like the starry sky above. By midnight women were digging into trunks and extracting long unused winter clothing.

Again they made good time on the hard-pack, but the volcanic ridge was even steeper than the last. Only the piercing chill of the desert kept the oxen from realizing their great thirst.

But dropping down again to the great plain in the awesome moonlight was almost sheer madness.

Plunging over the volcanic rocks the wagons were so jolted and jarred that Eliza and Virginia had to tie sheets around Margaret Reed to keep her from falling out of bed. James Frazier's concern was more for his wagon than his wife.

"Damn bastard must have lost the trail in the night!"

Doolittle and George had not lost it. Hastings's men, working in a hundred degree temperatures, had just done a dreadful job of building it.

The order for the women and children to sleep could not be kept. Everytime they would snuggle down on the wagon floor to get warm and asleep, they would be jostled awake and have to start over again. Somewhere on the ridge a pack of coyotes began to bark and bay at the moon, causing the train dogs to bark back, babies to cry and the younger children to whimper in fear.

The ridge was not conquered in a single night. They were well into their second day before all the wagons were down onto the next plain and facing a new threat.

"They are called dunes," Tamsen advised. "The wind shifts them and packs them tight."

"They are not too bad to lurch over. It's the level spots in between that make it terrible work for the oxen. We sink inches deep in this light, ash-like sand. It slows our progress more than the steep climbs and descents."

"And I, for one, am going to slow you down, too,

George Donner. Climb up into that wagon and get some sleep. Sol and I can handle this for awhile. That goes for you, too, Doolittle Thornburg. You might pass the word along to the other men that they can't be expected to go forever without rest." Then she laughed. "And how can one possibly get lost out here?"

The intention was well meaning, but the results were fatal.

As the temperature began to climb toward a hundred, the supply wagons, near voided of supplies, were less of a burden on their teams. They just seemed to float along, while the heavily laden wagons plodded.

Inch by inch, yard by yard, a slow, go-as-you-can march took place until they were stretched out over a mile or two. There was no wagon captain or guide about to stop the action. Nor did anyone really worry about it. The mountain got no nearer and the plain was so flat that they could see the Eddy and Graves wagons in the front and Reed's great wagon at the tail end.

They didn't worry because their brains were being baked to a non-thinking stage and their eyes blinded by the white surface below.

"Well, I'll be damned!" William Eddy gasped, astounded, plodding along beside his wagon. "What damn idiot is making you guys march across this wasteland?"

None of the twenty men marching in single file at a distance from him answered, although they all looked his way.

"Hey!" he hollered, waving at them. "Didn't you hear me?"

They all waved back in unison, but still did not answer.

He stopped short. The men stopped with him. He shrugged and moved on and they followed his lead.

Eleanor Eddy crawled through the front bow flap and out onto the driver's perch. "Who you talking at, Bill?"

He pointed, started to answer, and stopped himself short. As the twenty men pointed back at him he suddenly realized that they all possessed his face, his clothing and his pointed hand and finger.

"The oxen," he said weakly and plodded on.

It was not the only mirage to trick them on that seemingly never-ending Friday.

Johanna jumped agilely down from the Wolfinger wagon and began to run to a point that only she saw.

"*Fraul*" Hans shouted. "Where you go?"

"I cannot stand the itch of my scalp another minute, Hans. At long last I can wash my hair."

She knelt on a rock, which was only a wind-whipped sand dune ledge, and joyously began wetting her hair with scooped up handfuls of lake water.

By the time Hans reached her and got her back to the wagon, her hair was covered with the gritty sand. Coming out of the vision she began to wail so miserably over the sand in her hair that Hans took her inside the wagon and poured her a basin of water and soothingly washed her hair. She was not fully satisfied until it had been rinsed three times.

Neither of them fully thought as each basin of water was tossed from the tail-gate of the wagon to be quickly absorbed and evaporate on the burning sands. Their oxen would have absorbed it just as quickly. By the next day Johanna would have drank it herself.

"Hastings?" James Frazier asked, on a quizzical note. "Have we at last caught you, you horse-stealing bastard?"

He rose from where he had been seated on the wagon steps and jumped to the ground. The heat within the wagon was almost as intolerable as the cold had been the night before. There was no way that he was inhumane enough to ride Glaucus in such heat, but he wished at that moment the beast was saddled.

The train, now stretched out for nearly three miles, was overtaking the Hastings party, on a parallel course a tenth of a mile north. They were also stretched out, but he could see even the dogs trotting along beside the wagons.

At last he could have a showdown with Lanceford Hastings and become the real captain of this train. That it was being allowed to falter into family units he thought a disgrace.

He trudged toward the train and walked through it before realizing it was just a reflected mirage of the Donner train.

Night came as quickly as a mirage, and with it a feeling inside as chilling as the air was outside the body.

"Thank you, Tamsen. That was a good sleep I had and a good supper. As soon as fresh oxen are yoked, I feel we should keep pushing right along. Doolittle has gone ahead to see what progress Eddy and Graves have made."

She knew that was not what he was thinking. Hastings's note had said two days and two nights. They were already into their second night. He wanted to know if a third day would be required to get them across the salt plains.

By the third morning he had an answer he did not like. There was no longer a single trail, even from his own advanced wagons. The plains had turned into a salt marsh, the wagons breaking through the thin crust and sinking several inches into sandy slush that oozed with salt water. The wagons had been forced to fan out to make their own trail or be mired in the tracks of the one before.

But a greater danger lurked. Whether it felt horrible on their feet or not, the teamsters, women and

older children had to plod through the oozing salt
water and keep oxen, cattle and horses from dipping
their thirst-crazed heads for a drink that would sicken
and kill them.

The third night posed another problem—the prepared food was exhausted, and no end in sight.

"Here, my loves," Tamsen encouraged, "this will
help to solve both problems."

She gave all of the Donner children sugar lumps
moistened with peppermint.

Elizabeth sat unaiding. "I wonder how Margaret is
faring?"

"I wonder too," Tamsen said quietly, "but for the
moment my concern is with our own children."

As long as Tamsen was there it was no concern for
Elizabeth. "I think I shall walk back and check on the
poor dear. She is, after all, my best friend in the
world."

Tamsen didn't comment. Her throat was too dry.
She had deprived herself of her water ration for the
children. Elizabeth had complained that an eighth of
a cup was hardly a swallow.

Happenstance kept her from getting her feet into
the salty marsh water. Just as she stuck her head out
of the wagon, James Frazier came riding along on
Glaucus.

"Oh, James Frazier," she called, in a cooing tone,
"how well timed. I was just on my way back to check
on Margaret. It has been years, but could you give me
a ride behind you?"

He looked at her as though she were deranged.

"Elizabeth, because your brother-in-law is so inept
I must go myself in search of water. I hardly have the
time to take you back for a social visit."

Tamsen pushed her head out beside Elizabeth. Her
sweet smile was laced with acid.

"Mr. Reed, how nice of you to volunteer in this way.

As the men have just started a short nap, after so many hours of work, I shall inform them of your whereabouts."

It didn't phase James Frazier. Being the last wagon in the train he had come to the strange notion that they were leaving him behind as punishment for having brought them this way. As always, he felt that they needed him more than he needed them. He had left orders for his teamsters to get his wagons out of the slush and then take the oxen on ahead for water.

A mile ahead he found that the MacDuff wagons were already on hard-pack and still moving ahead. He gave a casual wave of his hand and rode on.

Only moments before Doolittle had dropped down onto the mattress bed.

"Who was that?"

Mary Florence sat down on the floor beside him. "Reed."

"Is that all the damn fool can do is joyride?"

"Perhaps he is going in search of water."

"Humph!" he snorted. "Then let him find the same heartache I have found throughout the night."

Mary Florence began unbuttoning the bone buttons of his buckskin jacket.

"What in the hell are you doing, woman?"

"It's near noon, Doo. I thought it would be cooler for you to sleep with this off."

"Like hell!" he roared. "I know how you think. I am too damn tired and thirsty to play games."

"That was not my—"

"Don't give me that crap! That's all you ever think about."

Mary Florence rose as though she had been slapped. She turned away, biting her lip so she wouldn't cry. She was tired and thirsty, too. Her nerves were also raw with worry, but she would not give in to them. He had taken her intent all wrong, because he did not understand simple little acts of love. Someday, she prayed, he would be different.

She was not aware that raw nerves and worry was bringing about most similar spats in almost every family unit. The salt plains were too vast to scream against so frustrations were taken out on each other.

James Frazier's frustrations were directed mentally against the guide and train captain.

The trail swung off to the left. Aha, he thought, a sure sign that Hastings was turning off course toward water. A good guide would have come back along the line to so inform.

It wound around an isolated volcanic crag that thrust up out of the salt crust like a beached ship after a tropical storm. Beyond the crag he stopped short and looked into the distance.

"Damn Donner for sleeping and not letting us know this fact. Come, Glaucus, you will have water shortly."

He urged the near jaded horse on toward a mountainous ridge that showed a grass-like green. He began to pass the other sections of the train, and although they were in various stages of disaster, he could not understand why they were not taking heart in knowing there was water ahead. He could only surmise that Donner and Doolittle had not informed them and felt no such obligation himself.

Now he didn't even wave at those who still pushed their wagons ahead, but did give some credit to those who had unyoked their oxen and were driving them wagonless toward water.

The deserted wagons tended to depress him. From some not so deserted faces peered out but called no greeting. He felt they should have used the last ounce of walking strength to get to the water. He felt more sorry for the exhausted cattle that lay about nearly every wagon.

"What's this? Why aren't there cattle and oxen grazing and drinking?"

He rode up the mountain trail, Glaucus beginning to stumble and tire. James Frazier's mind began to stumble and nearly weep. All over the mountainous promontory was a treacherously alluring green.

"Greasewood," he said sadly, "and not a drop of water in all of its green. To the top, my gallant friend. The oxen have gone somewhere."

A half hour later he was more disheartened than ever. The oxen were below, stretched out over still another salt plain for twelve miles to the foot of another set of mountains.

"But will they have water or be as devious as all of these? Sorry, but we have to go on. You would never get me back without water."

The afternoon desert sun baked down on him. Glaucus began to stumble with most every step, but James Frazier was hardly aware. His mind was beginning to wander and constantly see visions. The real became the unreal. The Graves wagons seemed to roll along with him for hours. They had been deserted the day before with Uncle Billy and John Snyder taking the family and every animal toward the mountains. A few miles beyond he passed the Eddy wagon and didn't even see it.

Near sundown he totally refused to accept the next mirage. The willow thicket around a spring was right on the edge of the sand. Behind it the mountains were just as volcanic as the last. It just had to be a mirage because his mind could not accept another disappointment.

He so steeled his mind to the thought that he did not see the people and oxen scattered throughout the thicket at various watering holes. Glaucus kept moving forward and he sat ramrod stiff.

Then everything became deathly still. The emigrants knew what he had been through, for they had been through the same. It was best to say nothing until his own mind could accept this as fact. Some, like Bill Eddy, who had been there since ten that morning, could still hardly believe that he was not dreaming.

A sound made James Frazier look down. Glaucus was nuzzling water. This was the wildest mirage of all—it had sound to it.

Bill Eddy came and gently helped him down from the saddle.

"Easy on, Mr. Reed. It's for real. But just wash your mouth out a few times before you swallow. Some of the children made themselves right sick drinking too much too fast."

He sprawled face down by a pool and slowly dropped his whole head into the water. It was so cool and refreshing and life-giving that he stayed that way for a long time. But as his mind came back to normal it was visited with another horrible thought.

"I must have come almost thirty miles."

He was not aware he had spoken aloud until Eddy answered him.

"You that far back?"

"I left my wagons at noon."

"With luck they should be in then by morning."

"Luck?" he said wearily. "I told my men to bring the oxen on. I must go back for my family. May I borrow a horse and some waterskins?"

"Anything you desire, Mr. Reed. I'll go part way with you. I have an oxen down out there that I would like to revive."

Under the full moon the return was like seeing a different manner of mirage. Women and children struggling along wide-eyed with thirst. Cattle dotting the plain like strewn rocks. Men grumbling that Hastings could have so lied to them.

Bill Eddy found his ox, but it was already dead.

"Forty miles," he carped. "Been more like eighty, Mr. Reed. Here, you take this covered bucket of water. My ox don't need it no more."

He turned back alone, never once taking into consideration that he could have given the other emigrants heart and led them faster to the springs.

James Frazier kept on in the opposite direction. He, too, could have given some heart by telling them of the water ahead. The MacDuff wagons he purposely did not want to tell, because he felt Doolittle should have found the springs rather than sleep the trip away.

After crossing back over the greasewood mountains he came upon his own oxen, cattle and horses.

"Milt, where is my family?"

"Left them with Walt Herron. You just said get the animals to water."

"Idiot!" he scowled, not remembering that was his exact order. "Water is a good twelve miles beyond this mountain. Get them there and a team back as fast as you can. We can come back for the supply wagon tomorrow."

An hour later he came across the Donners driving their own animals, Tamsen allowing the younger children to ride bareback.

"Well," George grinned, "I see by the bucket and skins that it is water at last."

"Is," he said curtly, "just beyond that mountain."

But his ego would not allow him to say how far beyond the mountain.

"Reed," Jacob said, "your men passed our wagons over an hour ago, meaning they'll be getting back before us. My Elizabeth took sickly all of a sudden and I had to leave Sol with her and the children. Be most obliged if you could stop and give them some good news and a skin of water to hold them until our return."

James Frazier nodded, but didn't say if he would or wouldn't.

He wouldn't. His constantly changing moods still smarted over the hero worship given to Solomon Hook over getting them up out of the canyon. He still felt wronged for having gotten them into that mess.

"If Sol is such a genius, let him wring water out of the sand."

It was near daylight when his wagons loomed gigantically against the stark horizon. The sound of the five family dogs greeting him was a wonderful welcoming home note.

He whooped and hollered back at them, awakening all.

"Water! Beautiful, glorious water that tastes like heaven. Walt, here, quench your thirst and then take this beast back to Bill Eddy. You may return with the men and my Glaucus. Baylis, take these skins into my wife and children. We have ample until the men return with the teams and more. Oh, Eliza, take this bucket and give Mrs. Reed a refreshing sponge bath. That should lift her spirits. Now, forgive me if I retire until their return. I am a little bone-weary."

He was asleep almost before he could stretch out fully clothed on his own bed. He had been going nearly non-stop for twenty-four hours.

They thought they were doing right in letting him sleep for twelve. He came awake in a state of confusion and stumbled down to the amidship room. Beyond the folded back flaps the sky was the same hue as when he had retired.

"Oh," he giggled, inanely, "I must have just dozed for a little while."

"Sundown," Eliza whispered, looking anxiously at the three younger Reed children seated at the table eating bread and jelly.

"Impossible," he snorted, "and what manner of food is that for them? Send Baylis over to the supply wagon for something more nourishing."

"Baylis is gone," she said quietly. "When they weren't here by mid-afternoon I gave him a water skin and sent him looking for them."

He started to protest and then saw the wisdom of her action. He also saw a culprit behind why the oxen were not back to get them—Milt Elliott. The man was getting revenge in a most dastardly way and he would kill him when next they met.

"But that doesn't solve our immediate problem," he said, as though he had spoken his mind on Milt. "I only brought back enough water for a few hours and now a skin is gone with Baylis."

"We still have the bucket," Eliza said hesitantly. "I've held back bathing Mrs. Reed with it."

She had expected him to flare out because his order had not been fulfilled. Instead he looked at her with gratitude.

"Thank you. It might just see us through the decision that must now be made. We must set out on foot, Eliza, as best we can. Jacob Donner's wagon isn't too far, and if I have slept this long, he should be back within a couple of hours."

"But what of our own men and teams?"

"Frankly, Eliza," he said honestly, "I really don't know. I pray that we come across them, but in the meantime we must do as you did with Baylis—take the next best action possible."

"Mrs. Reed?"

"Yes," he sighed, "I have thought of that."

"Then stop thinking."

They both spun. Margaret stood on the ladder steps,

with Virginia just behind her. They were both dressed in winter woolens.

"This slight infirmity has not affected my ears or thinking, James. Eliza, Virginia has laid out some warmer clothing for the children, please help her dress them quickly."

"Margaret," he protested, "are you sure that you are strong enough?"

"Why?" she asked coolly, "Had you planned on leaving me behind? I hear the Indians do that with deformed children and the elderly. Well, I am not Indian, elderly or deformed. I will make it, thank you."

She was plucky, although still in weak health and not strong enough yet in the stricken limb to do more than draw it along like an unwanted anchor. Eliza and Virginia kept a close eye on her, although she waved aside their assistance. She knew that every dragging step that she took was a challenge for Patty and little Jim, even though Tommy had to be carried in his father's arms.

Or is that my real challenge, she thought? Eliza and Virginia could fend for themselves, but what of her husband? Without a horse under him and a wagon under her, would either make it?

She owed her life to strangers. What did James Frazier owe? She plodded along until her good leg was nearly as numb as her lame one, but no whimper or request for rest passed her lips.

"Margaret," he finally said, as an excuse, "I think we should let the children rest for awhile."

"I am quite fine," she insisted.

"But *they* are not," he said, laying down a blanket for them to huddle upon. "They are cold and tired."

"All right," she agreed, sitting down where she had stopped. It really was the last step she could have taken, but she was not about to admit it.

Even huddled into the blanket the children were

whimpering from the cold night. The wind was rising and piercing them fiercely.

"Hey, you! Bedtime!"

The family dogs had been following along silently and now hung back hesitantly. They sat, tails wagging, but little Cash, the children's pet, boldly darted for the blanket and snuggled next to little Jim.

"All right, you varmints," James Frazier chuckled. "I am most aware that you are smuggled into the wagon each night. Tyler, Barney, Trailer, Tracker! To bed!"

To squealing delight the dogs bounded to the children with licking tongues and quivering bodies.

"Keep them away from me," Virginia protested. "I don't want their fleas and lice."

"One night won't hurt you," James Frazier said sternly, motioning for Eliza to sit down with Margaret. He immediately did likewise, so that their backs in a triangle gave them some warmth and created a wind-break for the children.

The dogs were the quickest to accept this new adventure and curled close to youthful bodies. There was no more whimpering.

There was no sound except the howling desert wind and the beating of Eliza's heart. She could scarcely believe what was happening. Despite the situation that they were in and the closeness of his wife, James Frazier had almost at once tried to move his hand onto her thigh. She had placed her arms down along the inside of her legs, but his demanding fingers were trying to crawl beneath her arm and ever higher. Any movement or statement she made would be detected by Margaret. She steeled herself to silence, even when the hand thrust under her elbow and the fingers found a most sensitive area to wantonly explore and caress.

"Are you warm, Margaret?" he whispered.

"Fairly so."

"Eliza?"

Even though there was uniform cloth between, she closed her mind to the fact that the finger was trying to penetrate anyhow. She was not warm, she was on fire. Nightly, she had thought of the experience with Lewis Keseberg, but no opportunity had presented itself for a renewal. Despite the sensation he was building within her, she did not want the renewal to be with James Frazier and hardly at this time, under any circumstance. But she was stymied as to what to do.

Rescue came before she had to answer. Tyler suddenly jumped up from beside Paddy and began snarling and barking out at the darkness. Like a fire alarm set off the others followed suit.

"What is it?" James Frazier inquired, snatching his hand away to feel for his pistol.

As though in answer the dogs charged into the night barking and yelping.

"Huddle!" James Frazier barked, as something huge loomed directly at them. The dogs came yelping back, biting at the beast's ankles and swerved it off.

The curved horn of the ox passed within inches of James Frazier. Although he suspected it to be one of his own beasts, he had never seen anything quite to equal it. Its eyes were fiercely red and a beard of white foam dangled from its mouth.

"Mad," he called out unguardedly, "the beast has gone mad and is a killer!"

His words brought forth instant panic. The children scattered as though the ox were breathing down each individual neck. The dogs lost interest in the ox and began chasing the children as though in play.

"Come back!" James Frazier bellowed, and then turned angrily on his wife and Eliza, who stood a little stunned by the speed of the event.

"Well, what are you doing just standing there like two nincompoops? The children are in danger. Eliza, go fetch them back!"

Eliza turned and looked at Margaret, seeing her face pale, her lips trembling visibly. She knew that she could not afford to make a scene—that, indeed, she must appear utterly calm while that lecherous man was losing his head. This she felt she owed Margaret for having said nothing to him about Lewis Keseberg. But his finger had made an impression on more than just her flesh. It had seared into her memory and would never be forgotten.

She put two fingers between her teeth and let out a shrill whistle. The dogs responded instantly and began herding the children back. Once they were spotted, James Frazier began to rail at them so that they could scarcely be calmed.

"Enough!" Eliza growled. "I will not tolerate this! You are not allowed to act this way around the wagon and it will not be allowed here! Tommy, let your father pick you up! Virginia, help your mother. Patty, Jim, take each of my hands. The dogs seem calm, so should we. Let's go!"

"No!" Margaret protested. "Virginia, you see to the children. I want Eliza to assist me."

James Frazier didn't protest over anything. He had been just as frightened as the children. That Eliza had taken command away from him he did not see as unusual—after all, she was a servant who should be seeing after the children. That was her responsibility and duty.

"You handled the beasts well," Margaret whispered, leaning heavily on Eliza.

"Beasts?"

"My blindness is self-imposed, Eliza. I see and hear all and brush it aside. I was hurt deeply by Virginia's father. I vowed with James never to be hurt.

Certain aspects of his character I just lock out of my mind."

"Even though others may be hurt?"

Margaret scoffed. "You have a knack, Eliza, of twisting the knife as you plunge it. We are quite in the same boat, yet different. You go about in search of a man for your future; I have a man for the present that I must cling to for a future out of this wild madness. I don't think either of us have a great bargain in the deal, but what woman really has?"

Eliza let her keep talking, because it kept her moving. She had always considered Margaret a very selfish person; she could now see that a lot of that was brought about by frustration and loneliness. All of the Reed money couldn't buy her out of this situation.

Another daylight was dawning when they stumbled up to the Jacob Donner wagon. Surprisingly, it still stood teamless.

To their greater surprise, as the family began to wake up, they found Baylis among them.

"What is this?" James Frazier exploded. "You were sent to find the oxen!"

"Found them," he said wearily, "most after dark. One of the horses laid down and while they were trying to get him up the oxen stampeded back toward the water in the dark. Milt sent me back with water and that report."

"And I find you sleeping?" James Frazier was incredulous. "Sleeping, while my poor children have been forced to suffer—"

"You'd best learn all the facts," Sol Hook said acidly. "He sprained his ankle in the dark and barely made it back to us."

James Frazier did not want to hear such a petty excuse, especially from Sol. He turned to his wife.

"Margaret, my dear, I shall leave you and the children here. It should not be long before I find the oxen and return."

Again he found himself heading for the spring, but this time on foot. In his anger at Milt Elliott and Baylis Williams he totally forgot to take any water with him.

After trudging along all night he was near exhaustion when he came to the last salt plain. It was quite a scene change from the day before. Men rode its vast expanse in search of cattle, while others with watered teams were driving back their wagons.

A mile onto the plain he gave out and sat to allow a herd of oxen and horsemen to come to him.

9

FOR THE SECOND TIME in as many days he was brought to the spring in a near mindless state. This time the recovery was not as rapid. He lay in the willow shade shivering from heat exhaustion, not even knowing that it was the Donners who had found him and that Noah James had brought him in.

Late that day his family was brought in on the Jacob Donner wagon. After six full days everyone was off the salt plains—except for a quarter of their oxen, cattle and horses.

Although they had been seen from time to time that day, the Reed men were still out on jaded horses scouring the country for their oxen.

To the chagrin of James Frazier, Tamsen saw to it that the Reed party had food and blankets for the night.

"Everything that I own," James Frazier moaned,

"except for an ox, and Glaucus is still out there. Unless they find the oxen before the Indians we will be at the end of our rope."

Others had also suffered losses, but he wasn't thinking of them.

"It's no good, Maw," Pike said, as Foster nodded in agreement. "It was an old wagon to begin with, but the desert air has so dried it out that it is just falling to pieces."

"A case of tit for tat," Lavina Murphy sighed.

"How's that, Maw?"

"Ain't got enough oxen to pull it anyway." Then she brightened. "But we should count our blessings that not a single life was lost."

One wagon, however, did lose a sleeping passenger. That night Doolittle Thornburg went back to his own bedroll. It had not been asked for, it was just something he felt he should do before Mary Florence got her clutches in too deep.

He had another reason for wanting to keep a low profile. There were too many signs that Indians also used these springs. Although the possibility was remote they would have word of him this far west, he wanted no Indian to know his whereabouts.

The next morning he rode out south along the ridge, under the pretext of looking for cattle in the canyons of the mountain. He had seen them coming from the north and was long gone before the two Indians rode in.

He had been the last man to leave camp and the women stood about in fear and awe, except for a couple.

"What in the hell does he want?" Lavina scowled, keeping her hands tight on a rifle.

"I think he is trying to tell us they have seen some of the cattle," Tamsen replied.

"I just wish they would go away," Elizabeth whimpered. "They are frightening the children."

Tamsen ignored the weak excuse, although she was not comfortable with them in camp either. Boldly, she started walking toward them. When she had seen them coming she had quickly gotten into one of her trunks. Now she dug into her apron pockets and brought out two handsful of brightly colored glass beads.

"Thank you! Thank you!" she said very slowly, holding a gift up to each.

They accepted the beads with broad grins and rode off waving them over their heads.

Johanna Wolfinger did not mind expressing the opinion that Tamsen had made a grave error. Stupidly, for all the children to hear, she declared that they would bring back now a thieving, scalping, murdering horde.

Upon his fruitless return James Frazier did not mind expressing the opinion that the absence of Doolittle kept them from gaining a clue to the lost animals.

He softened his attack when Doolittle came back with one of Reed's oxen. Milt Elliott and the men were coming in empty-handed each day.

"This is becoming a waste of time," Hans Wolfinger insisted, mainly because he had already retrieved his oxen and horses. Spitzer and Reinhardt fully agreed, for they had lost nothing either.

Tempers were terribly short and many were quick to point out those facts to them.

"I want to get started just as quick as the next man," George barked, "but we still have supply wagons out on the salts."

"And all of mine," James Frazier corrected.

"Now," George said, ignoring him, "Hastings's word hasn't been too accurate to date."

"That is certainly an understatement!" Keseberg scoffed.

George ignored him, as well. "So those supplies might mean a great deal to us. The oxen need a good twenty-hour rest."

"More like twenty-four days," Paddy Breen huffed.

"So," George went right on, "in the morning we will let two teams, of a man and a boy, keep searching for the lost animals. The rest of us, with just horses and mules, will go after the wagons. Now, just a minute Wolfinger, before you open that loud yap of yours. The horses and mules can get them back faster and don't seem to thirst as much. I know that these are not plow horses, but damnit we have all done work we never expected to do either. That's the way it is going to be."

They didn't like it but that's the way it was for the next five days.

Five days in which Milt Elliott and Billy Graves teamed to the north and west, while Noah James and John Breen rode to the south and east.

Milt's luck was not holding. He found Murphy and Keseberg stock, but not Reed. Noah James found Virginia's horse but not her pony Billy.

James Frazier's luck was not to his liking either.

"I don't give a damn if you don't like it," John Snyder glowered. "We are doing you a favor by bringing in one wagon and that is it."

"But think of the supplies and family necessities I shall be leaving behind."

"Transfer what you can to the family wagon," George said, being the peacemaker, "and cache the rest. When we come back for my supply wagons tomorrow we will pick it up."

To cache it proved an impossibility. Every time a spade would scoop out a shovelful it would immediately fill with salt water.

"Wagon ain't going anywhere," Walt Herron said drily. "Chop off its wheels, take down the bows and cover the canvas with sand."

"Helluva lot of work if we're coming back tomorrow," Snyder fumed.

"Perhaps not," Doolittle said, as though not concerned. "Those beads will turn the rest of the Indians about here into vultures."

"Vultures!" Jean Baptiste said suddenly. "There have been none except over the animals we already know are dead. They must still be alive in all of these canyons."

"Unless the Indians have them already," Doolittle shrugged.

The very thought of Indians made them drop the wagon down for a platform and cover it with sand. No one took into consideration how conspicuous was the mound on the flat plain.

The next day they knew how conspicuous. It had been like a beacon in the night for the roving Indians. They wished no fight with these people, as long as they continued to roll through their arid land and did not ruin their springs. But what was left behind on their land they felt was theirs. But what was left behind was hardly of use to them.

The cherrywood furniture had been splintered by tomahawks, Margaret and Virginia's fine clothing shredded into tatters, James Frazier's fine volumes of literary work ripped from their bindings and the pages tossed to the wind. Boxes of crystal and china had been smashed and the rainbow prisms taken from a brass chandelier. It was about the only retrievable object.

Oddly, the Donner supply wagon was not even touched. It helped to increase James Frazier's feeling that he was the only one being made to suffer.

That feeling was intensified back at the camp. Everyone was near to the point of panic. Noah and John had sighted a war party of twelve braves on the south ridge. No one wished to learn if they were going to or coming from the raid on the Reed wagon. They just knew that the willow thicket was not defendable against an attack.

The Germans had already yoked up for departure, even though Lewis would have to abandon one of his wagons. Mary Florence had also come to the conclusion that one wagon and a lot of Selkirk treasures would have to be left for the Indians to lighten her load.

"But I can't depart with just two oxen," James Frazier tried to reason with George. "It takes four at a minimum and six at best to pull that wagon."

"Then you should have brought the smaller wagon, James. I'm sorry, but my oxen are such that I will have to leave a supply wagon behind as well. Why don't you talk with Graves and Breen."

The men were willing to help, but with a strange proviso: they would each loan him a single ox, but if they ran into trouble then they would take the ox back and he would be on his own again.

James Frazier had no choice, unless he wanted to stay behind and pray that Milt would find some of his herd. He still could hardly believe that sixteen head of oxen could stay so utterly hidden.

Then his feeling of suffering turned to near despair. It had taken eight horses to pull the wagon to the spring, and the four weakened oxen could not even make the wheels turn an inch because the great wagon was so heavily loaded with the supplies taken from his abandoned wagons.

Everyone had a solution, but no one dared voice it.

"Some of you," he said, "now have fairly light loads. Will you help lighten my load by carting some of my goods?"

They could now voice their solution.

"Be reasonable, James," Hans Wolfinger said. "If we carry your food in our wagons, then we should be allowed the use of it."

Spitzer and Reinhardt were quick to agree that was the only fair way.

Paddy Breen hung back hesitantly, until Peggy dug her elbow into his ribs and shoved him forward.

"Well, I could sure use some supplies for the carting of it and the loan of the ox, Mr. Reed."

Again, James Frazier had no choice, and was forced to distribute some of his supplies or leave them behind.

Ironically, the wagons of Wolfinger, Spitzer and Reinhardt were loaded with the majority of his excessive and needed it the least. Paddy Breen didn't have much extra room but had a distinct need for the food. Over the strong objections of John Snyder, Uncle Billy Graves took some of the supplies and put them in John's wagon for carting.

"Now look, son," Uncle Billy said gravely, "you ate at the man's table for quite a spell and at my table the rest of the time. You'll cart the food or find yourself another grub trough. The man has enough miseries without you adding to them."

Moving along the base of the mountain range James Frazier also wondered if there was a misery left in the world that had not befallen him.

Weary and shaken, he was again the tail end of the slow moving caravan. Even the watching Indians knew it was a woebegone and spiritless outfit. The pulling oxen were gaunt, and to keep all of her wagons moving Lavina Murphy had put cattle in yoke with oxen. Their udders had gone dry so she might as well use them for something.

The wagons creaked from their dryness. Although it had been necessary at the time, some now ques-

tioned if John Breen had not over-used the axle grease
to climb the steep mountain.

They followed Doolittle, and Doolittle did little
more than follow the Hastings wagon tracks.

The tracks swung right and up another pass through
the mountains. At first the cool breeze felt good after
all those days of hot, arid, baking desert. The clouds
gathered quickly and as farmers they could smell the
moisture they held.

The rain was joyous falling on parched skins and
long unchanged and dusty clothing. It fell softly and
the animals seemed to rejoice in it even more than
the humans. Their steps became stronger, springier
and they climbed higher and higher through the pass.
Even James Frazier marvelled that his great wagon
was keeping up with the rest.

But, as though God wanted to show them how
strange was this different world of His, the wind
turned as bone chilling as it had been each night.
The clouds darkened and the rain increased.

"Damn! I don't believe this! Has the rain turned
to snow or is this another damn mirage?"

It was snow. Heavy and wet. The rain had been
refreshing. The first rain, someone had recalled, they
had had since before Fort Bridger. But snow on the
15th of September? Snow that was sodden and cold.

Children were bustled back into the wagons for a
change and drying off. No use taking a chance on
a cold if winter came this early in this unpredictable
land.

"Odd," Jacob said, riding up along side his brother.
"These ain't even the Sierras that Hastings talked
about in his guide. Wonder if they are getting snow
this early in the season?"

George was dispirited. "Our children," he said
strangely, "are probably just getting ready to harvest
the field corn and more than likely still soaking sheets

at night to ward off the thick heat. Do you know what I had a hankering for just before it started to snow? An ear of that sweet corn dripping with golden butter. Almost was tempted to make Tamsen break out some of that seed corn she's got stashed away for our first planting."

"Jacob," he suddenly broke out of his reverie, "did I see something moving ahead of us in this swirl?"

Jacob stared, but at first saw nothing. Then two slow-moving figures on horseback appeared. They were so laden with sodden snow that they were at first not recognizable.

That Milt and Billy Graves had gotten by Doolittle undetected coming up the pass was no surprise to Doolittle. He sat snug and warm within a cave on the lower, western side of the range.

Milt and Billy, who had been wearing the least amount of clothing against the desert heat, were near frozen to the bone.

"My wagon is first," George ordered. "Get in there to dry and warm."

It was horribly crowded. Tamsen had all of the younger Donner children because Elizabeth still claimed an illness that could not stand noise. Her illness was mostly hurt pride. Margaret had issued no invitation to ride in the great wagon. Margaret had no way of issuing such an invitation. The amidship room was now more storage area than living quarters.

Fourteen-year-old Elitha Cumi Donner was quick to get a towel for Billy's dripping locks and a blanket to wrap around his shivering shoulders. The smile of gratitude she received from the eighteen-year-old youth was more warming to her than the desert sun. She then hung back as the men talked, but their eyes kept shyly meeting.

"We tracked two horses to a spring in this valley," Milt was able to say at last. "One was Virginia's pony.

We shackled them, rather than bring them back, because we thought you'd want this other news first. Hastings has left another note. Beyond this spring is another waterless stretch of forty miles."

"More fiction from the man?" Jacob snorted. "I say we forget that Milt even found this note."

"Can't," George said wearily. "They have a right to know, even if it is bad news. We will just have to prepare for eighty and pray that it is forty."

What with the snowstorm and this news they made only five miles to the spring that day.

"Not far for the Indians to catch up," Eleanor Eddy quavered.

Everyone else had been trying to ignore that thought. Badly needed sleep was restless, with people jumping at the least little sound and nerves drawing tighter.

"Seems like I have been putting these critters in and out of the yoke my whole life," Lewis said.

Eliza only nodded as she watched him prepare for yet another day's march. Her time with Lewis and Phillipine had been short-lived the night before. The broken arm and ribs had been a shock to her. She couldn't fully accept the story that Philippine had fallen off the tailgate of the wagon, but with Lewis present, Phillipine had remained silent.

"After we get rolling," Lewis went on, "you come back to see us. Phillipine should be awake by then."

Eliza nodded again. She was almost sure she had seen Phillipine cooking breakfast by firelight a short time before. Because the woman had an arm in a splint and sling, Margaret had sent her to see if she could be of help. For the moment she would not press the issue, although it was beginning to trouble her as much as the Hastings message was troubling the men.

"If that man has lied to us again I'm going to boot his bottom!"

"If he lied, you won't live to get the chance!"

The day and night were like a relived nightmare, except it was now the dark of the moon. Thus slowed it made the forty miles seem like a hundred and forty.

At dawn, when green meadowland and springs appeared in the distance, they just silently rolled toward them.

"But, George," Tamsen said with gentle insistence, "you can't push yourself any harder than the animals. They are near skeletons and so are you. If Wolfinger wants to be a fool, let him go right on with whomever wishes to follow him. We can see the Indians coming from all sides here, so why not a twenty-four hour rest?"

"Food and winter," he said ominously. "We are to meet on those points now."

Rest was not the only point they wished to raise at the council meeting.

"As a late-comer," Uncle Billy said gravely, "I don't wish to stick my nose in, but from what I gather we ain't got enough food to last this many unless we get help from the other direction. It's time, I say, to send a couple of men on to the fort and see if we can't persuade Cap'n Sutter for a loan of supplies."

"What about sending back to Bridger?"

"Too damn far!"

"And who do we send?"

"The guide and one other," James Frazier suggested.

"We'll need Doolittle in case Hastings has lied again along the way," George said, but that wasn't his real reason. He felt sure that once Doolittle got to Sutter's that was the last any would see of him.

"What about Stanton and me?" Mac McCutchen volunteered. "We are used to travelling together in the Wasatch, and this time we won't take any directions from Indians."

It didn't produce the laugh he had expected, but was quickly agreed upon. The twenty-four hour rest was also quickly agreed upon, but the other points were almost personal.

Two more oxen had died during that pull, one of Uncle Billy's on the Snyder wagon and the one loaned to James Frazier by Paddy Breen.

Uncle Billy Graves had wanted to raise the point quietly with James Frazier and was taken aback when George Donner brought it right out in the meeting.

"With just three pulling we had to slow for you, James. Reduced to two, you will just have to lighten your load again. I don't mean to sound harsh, but we learned a most bitter lesson by getting stretched out before."

"Well . . . I . . ." For once James Frazier was at a total loss for words. He looked helplessly at Graves. It made the older man feel mean and ruthless, but one ox would not pull the Snyder wagon—and that ox was on loan, too.

"Perhaps I could make a suggestion," William Eddy said slyly, sidling up to James Frazier. "My team would bring you back to four. I have few possessions, except for a wife and two children."

"What will you do with your wagon?" Pike asked before James Frazier could agree.

"Leave it! What else?"

"I'll take it!" Pike barked, as though it were an auction.

"Well, Mr. Reed?" Eddy asked hesitantly.

Again James Frazier had no choice and reluctantly nodded agreement.

There was nothing wrong with Eddy's wagon—it was far superior to the one Pike would leave behind. But the opportunity to put James Frazier into obligation seemed too golden an opportunity. Besides, Margaret could not disallow Eleanor an opportunity to ride in the great wagon.

But the great wagon was still too heavily loaded, even though Eddy's possessions were few.

"What can we possibly discard?" he moaned pitifully.

"The two chaise longues," Margaret answered crisply, "and the desk and chair out of your office area. We will need it for storage. The weight of that stove is probably equal to Eleanor and her children."

"Why?" he cried. "Why must I tear apart this beautiful thing?"

"For their oxen," she said simply and pointedly.

With Charles Stanton going off again and no expected help from Doolittle, Mary Florence again reduced her Selkirk past into a single wagon.

"It will be easier for you and me to handle, Jim."

"What about the other oxen?"

"Tie them to the tail-gate. They are worth more for barter right now than all the gold in the world."

Oddly, James Frazier never thought to barter for them at the time. Most of what he left behind could have been easily pulled by six oxen.

Now they were only eighteen canvas-tops stretching out in a line. Now the days became near the same, but in a different degree. The land was not as arid. They would leave a spring, climb through hills and mountains, cross another plain to the next set of springs. Then came mountains higher than any since the Rockies—and a southward trail!

Anxiety grew as the trail continued southward for three days. Two things kept them from thinking Hastings totally crazy. To the west their eyes could not spot a single pass through the peaks and each day Doolittle and Bill Eddy came back from those mountains with an antelope or mountain sheep kill. A fresh steak each night soothed their hunger and their worry.

"Your turn today," George ordered.

James Frazier didn't complain. It was the one thing that eased the monotony. To keep the oxen as fresh as possible a different wagon now broke trail each day and the next would fall to the back of the line.

A mile later the trail bore off to the right and into the mountains. Even the greatest Hastings-haters among them had to agree that for once he had done something quite correctly. The gap through the mountains was so steady and easy that even Reed's great wagon was able to maintain the lead and get them into the next valley.

It was the twenty-fourth of September and mountains still loomed to the west.

The Hastings-haters were quick to forget their kind thoughts.

"North! Impossible!"

For three days they reversed the route they had taken on the other side of the mountain.

Even though they were rolling along accident-free for fifteen or more miles a day a new petty weariness began to set in. Even the sighting of Indians would now bring a yawn.

Doolittle, accomplishing something for a change, had determined that the valley was home for a small tribe of Modoc, who were rifleless and terrified of the white man's village that moved on wheels.

Boredom was also evident in the changes in their social habits. Formal dining was no more a ritual in the Donner and Reed camps. Because Margaret's finery was scattered back along the desert. Tamsen put out simple everyday earthenware on the plank boards.

Because their food supplies were also vanishing, it was a topic heard less often in Uncle Jake's nightly prayer. Many topics vanished from his prayer as they got shorter and shorter, and sometimes so quietly spoken that the family had to strain to hear. Most of the time he just complained about his constant indigestion.

Patrick Dolan stayed away from his tail-gate stage, Doolittle stayed away from Mary Florence, and Eliza began staying away from Lewis and Phillipine more and more.

Their evenings had become tense, uneasy. The conversations, once so light and spirited, were strained and forced. Phillipine was turning into a gaunt skeleton, her words barely whispered, and in constant pain from the broken arm that refused to heal. She would not discuss it, she would not discuss anything with Eliza. Everytime Eliza tried to see her alone she would make wild excuses and work at being too busy to talk.

She was a woman living in mortal fear. Times had been bad for her before Eliza Williams came into their lives, but now Lewis meanly and savagely warned her to keep quiet about the past with Eliza or he would keep that arm broken forever. For the moment he controlled his lustful thoughts about Eliza, but the irritation of these added days to California were nearly driving him insane.

The younger generation were not without their problems and boredom.

Although Sol could now be quite friendly with Virginia, to her chagrin that was all it had become.

Mary Ann Graves was learning that Baylis Williams was growing more and more childish. At times she felt more like a mother than a would-be lover.

John Breen was too weary each night to even worry about romance. His father had developed a boil in his groin, which kept him from walking, and John had become the family bullwhacker.

Life around the Reed wagon was probably the greatest change. Now that William Eddy had James Frazier's ear he never seemed to stop talking. Margaret tried to communicate with Eleanor, but it was like talking to a piece of petrified wood. They felt almost strangers in their own wagon.

James Frazier felt even more. He had once been the wealthiest and now felt the most ruined and put upon.

"Useless! I had five hired servants and now all they do is eat up my food. I should yoke them instead of the oxen, that's what I should do." He sniffed, which was becoming an unconscious habit. "Six days and we are camped just across the same mountain range. Well, tomorrow we shall go through that canyon and then it will be California. There is not a thing that I have lost that I cannot buy back again with my wealth. Then let's see if they remain complacent toward my present ill fortune."

Not everyone was wholly unhappy over the roundabout journey.

"Look at that rock formation," Billy Graves chuckled. "It looks just like the square of your father's beard."

Elitha studied the canyon rocks but could not see what he described. Billy slyly took her hand and she froze in place. He hesitated a moment and dropped it.

"I'm sorry," he gulped. "I didn't mean to offend you."

He was surprised, when he looked at her, to see that she was crying.

"Who are they?" she said suddenly, fiercely. "And why are they . . ."

Before she could finish he grabbed her into his arms and shielded her eyes from the view. The rocks had come alive with stark-naked brown figures scurrying down toward them and the camp. They were all grinning broadly and gesturing with their hands.

"How crude," he said, hurrying her back to the safety of the wagons.

"I've never seen a naked man before," she panted, as they rounded the first Donner wagon. "Are you all like that?"

Even at eighteen Billy Graves flushed scarlet. "I didn't take that good a look at them. Now, get with the women. I'll go for Doolittle."

In this instance Jean Baptiste proved more of a help than Doolittle.

"Don't be embarrassed, for they are not." It was like telling the wind to stop blowing. "They are most like an Apache tribe of my own arid lands. It is still the warm season and they await the fall for a new kill and new clothing."

He attempted what sign language he knew and Doolittle stood silently impressed.

"These are their mountains to the westward flowing river," Jean Baptiste said.

"The Humboldt!" James Frazier sighed. "How far?"

Jean Baptiste grinned after several attempts to get the question across and determine the answer. "They have heard, from across the mountains, that these moving tepees drop gifts like the cow-deer in her season. The last tepees through did not drop such gifts. They wish to know if these shall?"

"Hell no!" James Frazier bellowed. "Their damn heathen friends have everything I own now. How far?"

"Be still!" Doolittle hissed, stepping forward and giving a sign of welcome. "They are not stupid, you know. They can read the tone of a voice very well."

"That is not answering my qeustion," James Frazier said, through clenched teeth.

"I make it out to be two rough days," Jean Baptiste

said, and looked hesitantly to Doolittle for confirmation.

Doolittle ignored both the Frenchman and James Frazier. "Mrs. Donner," he said quietly, as his hands tried to get a clarification of the "two days" from the Modoc leader, "I think that it is time for more of your gifts."

It was a long, strange silence, while Tamsen went into the wagon. The Modoc and Doolittle kept making signs back and forth without a spoken word. The tribesmen looked the emigrants over most carefully, but the Donner party kept their eyes glued to the ground.

"I think I have enough," Tamsen whispered.

Doolittle looked down at her. She seemed so small beside him.

"I hate to ask this of you," he whispered back, "but if they accept a gift from your hand, then they have to be obligated to give us safe passage through their land."

"I can do that," she answered firmly.

"And with pride?"

She looked up at him and her face broke into a knowing grin. He had put what would be expected of her in the softest request he could muster.

Tamsen walked forward, her apron pockets full bulging. To be proud, she did not have to look upon their handsomely muscular bodies. One quick glance upon their arrival had told her that they were all most youthful and in the prime of physical condition. She concentrated on faces. Too many years as a school teacher had taught her that if she maintained eye-contact, the student thought she was seeing everything. And from Jean Baptiste's words she had already determined that they did not appear this way for carnal reasons. She was on their home ground and would have to accept their natural ways.

One by one she presented with a strand of the glass beads. They stood staring at her rather than the beads.

"They are too quiet," George whispered to Doolittle. "Is she safe?"

"Just look at them," he chuckled softly. "I tested them by saying our woman-chief bore all our gifts. It must be a matriarchal tribe. They are honored that she is the presenter."

"Which still teaches us nothing," James Frazier sniffed.

"Learns us everything," Doolittle said calmly. "Beyond their river is the land of the Diggers and the marked trail of the moving tepee."

"Well," James Frazier snorted, "you might have told us right from the first that we were that close to the main California trail. It means that Stanton and Mc-Cutchen will be back with us in a couple of days."

"Doubt it," Doolittle said sourly. "The Diggers are their common enemy. The land of their enemy runs for two hundred miles before the river flows into its sink."

It was just one more bad piece of news.

It was the second of October when they got down out of the rough canyon. More bad news was to follow.

The grass was growing scarce along the river and its flow was such that they had to start looking for alkaline pools again to water the animals.

It was one time Doolittle had a suggestion of merit. James Frazier, of course, saw no merit in it.

"Look, Mr. Reed, if we split into two camps at night it gives all the herd a better chance to graze. It also makes it harder for the Diggers to steal horses. Mr. Donner has said that he will be glad to pay and feed all your teamsters, except Milt, for being herders in the front group. That helps even things out."

The Donner and MacDuff wagons took the lead. Because there were no squabbles they were soon a day ahead. Petty disagreements were the rule of the day in the following twelve wagons.

The Donner party began leaving notes for the Reed party. For James Frazier they became as despised as the Hastings notes. He felt he was being treated like a child who could not "captain" the second group. A group that he despised as much as the notes.

"They advise that we double team for this hill."

James Frazier looked at the unusually high and long sand-hill, covered with rocks at the top, and thought it no worse than countless others they had ascended. But the day had been filled with so many vicious arguments that he merely shrugged.

"You do as you see fit, Milt."

Everyone else, except John Snyder, saw merit in taking the advice. Graves would use all his oxen to take up two of his wagons and then send a team back to bring up Snyder. Behind Snyder Milt would add on Pike's animals. Then all the oxen would be brought back down to start up another group.

John Snyder, thinking that his oxen could make it without assistance, began to follow right along behind Graves. Because he was keeping up on the lower portion of the hill, Milt followed suit.

But the grade began to slow him and Uncle Billy's wagons pulled farther and farther ahead. Snyder slowed even more and then began to take frequent stops to rest and cool the oxen.

These stops were beginning to irritate Milt. It was putting a needless drain on his own oxen to start and stop and start over again.

"Hey Snyder," he called, "stop being a damn fool and pull them to the side until you get another team yoked. It's too much of a burden if I can't keep this wagon constantly rolling."

Snyder ignored him. He cracked the whip over the heads of his oxen and they jerked a little forward and to the right. He was not about to be called a damn fool and intended on moving them forward. Milt took it as a sign that he was moving them to the right and swung the great wagon aside to make a pass.

The way was narrow and John Snyder made it more so by moving his team a little more to the left. His two against Milt's six could not keep ahead. The lead-yoke started to pull abreast. His anger growing at being passed, Snyder urged his oxen into more of a left swing.

Milt was to the right rear of the last yoke and couldn't see the maneuver, but the two lead oxen were not happy with having Snyder's so close and became unruly.

"Get back!" Snyder yelled.

It was Milt's turn to ignore him and cracked the bulls forward. There was a crunching of wood and snorting of beasts as the oxen became entangled.

"You jackass!" Snyder screeched, running to the front of the teams. "I told you to get back!"

"And I told you to move aside, idiot!" Milt responded, running up.

"Listen, ass-kisser, I'll give you one second to untangle them and fall back!"

"Eat shit, you fool! I'm going around even if I have to drag those skinny critters with me!"

Their words echoed back down to the valley. James Frazier came at a gallop, William Eddy on a sprinting run. Margaret and Eliza came out onto the side steps to see what the ruckus was all about.

"Fool, am I?" Snyder snarled enraged. "Well, stand back while I untangle them."

His manner of untangling was as vicious as his temper had grown. He began beating the Pike oxen violently over the head, making them snort wildly and try to rear up out of their yoke.

Milt moved around to stop him and was rewarded with a swift blow to his jaw that sent him reeling into the sand, out cold.

James Frazier jumped from the saddle right in front of the still flailing and cursing Snyder.

"Stop!" he roared like an angry bull. "What manner of man are you?"

"Not the same manner as you," Snyder snarled, his rage shifting. "You filthy swine."

"I hardly beat animals or men doing their duty," James Frazier retorted arrogantly.

"Duty, hell! Get your damn wagon back or I'll give you the same kind of cowhiding."

"It would seem," James Frazier said quietly, trying to calm Snyder down, "that it is your wagon that needs the assistance of another team and not my own."

"You arrogant bastard!" Snyder hissed, curling the bull whip right in James Frazier's face. "You think you own the whole world and can push people aside. I don't push easily for the likes of you. God, any man who would seduce one of his own should be bullwhacked."

The words James Frazier had long dreaded becoming knowledge had been spoken. His fiery mind exploded in rage and without fully thinking about it he instantly drew his hunting-knife.

Snyder took a step backward, glancing warily at the Bowie-bladed length of metal, knowing he was too close to ward it off with the bull whip.

Also knowing this, James Frazier stepped forward. "Take back those words!" he threatened.

Snyder smiled wickedly. He had not been asked to take back a lie—just words. Suddenly he reversed the whip and smashed the butt viciously with all his force across Reed's head. James Frazier's scalp broke open in a long gash from the impact, the blood running down over his chin and neck, but his hands were quick to strike back with the knife.

It sank into the hilt just below the collar-bone. On a piercing scream Margaret ran to get between them as her husband pulled the knife forth.

Snyder pivoted away, whipping the whip butt about. It caught Margaret right across the mouth, crashing her into the oxen. Stunned, she began to spit up blood and broken teeth. Now, the scream was taken up by Eliza as she came to aid Margaret.

"You'll die for that," James Frazier wept, his face a twisted mask.

But Snyder was not about to let him get close again with the knife. He charged with the butt swinging, putting his weight behind each blow he was able to land upon James Frazier's shoulder and knife arm. The blows felled James Frazier to his knees.

Staggering, he started up the hill, to where Billy Graves was bringing back a team of oxen for him.

Paddy Breen's long legs had overtaken Eddy. As Virginia was right behind him on Skylark he didn't bother to stop. Billy Graves was easing John Snyder to the ground when he came hurrying up.

"Uncle Patrick, I am dead," Snyder gasped weakly, motioning the man to lean down closer. "I am to blame."

"What did he say?" Billy asked.

Paddy Breen was silent for a long moment, watching the man die. What seemed a hundred years past he had respected the manner in which James Frazier had handled the affair over his son. But since the splitting of the train the man had been rude and nasty to the boy, even threatening him once when he caught him just casually talking with Mary Ann Graves and Virginia.

"I couldn't quite make out his last words," he finally answered.

Virginia tried to see to James Frazier's wounds, but he rudely pushed her aside and ran back down the hill to the river. As though it would take away his anguish he threw the knife into the water and watched it sink.

Everyone left him quite alone while they got the rest of the wagons up the hill and a camp made. Judging their mood correctly, Milt Elliott kept the great wagon a little distance from the others. Then he took Glaucus down to the river and brought a mute James Frazier back. Still not speaking he allowed Virginia and Eliza to now clip back his hair and dress the scalp wounds, which proved to be three, rather than one long gash.

Margaret was prostrate, her lips and gums so swollen she couldn't speak. The younger children huddled together, whimpering and crying.

Eliza didn't ignore them because she was busy with Margaret and then James Frazier. Her stunned mind just didn't hear them. Stunned not so much over the battle and the death, but over the "I-am-not-a-part-of-this" attitude taken by Virginia.

For the moment Milt Elliott and William Eddy were the only two men to take James Frazier's side on the matter. Milt, because he knew how the whole thing had started, and Eddy because it put Reed that much more under obligation to him.

Eleanor Eddy was terrified. It was a nightmare relived. Her Bill was siding with the wrong faction again—and again over a murder. The last time had cost them a burned-out carriage factory, a burned down home, and a threat to get out of town if they wanted to see their children grow up. Bill Eddy had stubbornly stuck with his conviction that the wrong man was being accused of murder. The people with power quickly hung the man without a trial and got many to believing that Eddy's only reason for sticking up for the man was that he was an accomplice. The sheriff gave them warning that another lynch party was afoot.

In the dead of night, with what little they had left, they had departed.

She now feared this dead of night.

The group were in agreement that murder had been done, but in disagreement over the action to be taken.

Overcome with grief at the loss of their friend, the Graves family demanded full vengeance.

Pike and Foster disagreed and Lavina strangely sulked. She had little use for either man. James Frazier on general principles, and John Snyder because she had come to look upon him as the same ilk of her late husband.

The first time she had caught Amanda McCutchen sneaking off in the dead of night to be with John Snyder she had severely scolded the young wife and mother. In blunt terms she had been told to mind her own business.

Now, looking at the ashen and shocked face of Amanda, Lavina would mind her own business. Amanda was paying heavily for the adultery.

Paddy Breen did not have to remind his family why they should make it none of their business.

The German wagons, except one, stood calmly aloof.

"I need to know their thoughts," James Frazier said, breaking his silence.

"I'll go," Eddy volunteered, and his wife stifled a moan.

"No," Reed said, every ounce of emotion drained from his voice. "I wish for Eliza. She heard all." He stopped and then strangely added: "I wish to donate boards from this wagon for a coffin."

Eliza went, but felt odd in the going. She could not fathom how John Snyder had picked up the germ of truth which had set James Frazier off. Because of Virginia's reaction she could only guess that it had come directly from her. That perplexed her even more. Both men had been wrong in what they had done, but that would not bring John Snyder back to life.

James Frazier's suggestion was also taken wrong. It raised the indignation around the Graves campfire to a fever pitch. Mistakenly, they abused Eliza with words for having brought such a dastardly offer.

Her cheeks burning, and having learned nothing, she thought a few minutes with Phillipine and Lewis might make her forget these last several hours.

"What are you about?"

Lewis turned from his work, a cunningly sadistic leer on his face. "Propping up my wagon-tongue for the morning. It is the only thing available on this treeless mountaintop."

Eliza looked but didn't understand. Then she shivered as the understanding came. An ox-yoke held the tongue skyward, from which dangled a knotted noose.

"Has it gone this far?" she gasped.

"As far as I am concerned. I shall cherish listening to that bastard beg for mercy before I personally kick that barrel out from underneath his feet."

"But, Lewis," she protested weakly, "all he did was have you banished."

"Wasn't that enough," he growled. "That low-grade Polish swine made a decent German like me crawl back for forgiveness. If we were not so far out in the middle of nowhere I would love the pleasure of letting the Russians get their hands on his thieving throat."

"I'm sorry I told you that was one of the reasons we left Springfield. It has nothing to do with this, Lewis. It was his family and not him personally."

"It matters not," he said huskily. "You no longer will have to put up with the man."

"Lewis," she pleaded, "be reasonable. Give him banishment the same way he gave it to you."

He looked at her strangely. "That is not what I meant, *Elisa*. Whether we hang him or banish him, you will no longer have to put up with him. You are, as of this moment, coming with Phillipine and me."

"I—I cannot," she muttered. "I still have Margaret and the children to consider."

"You have nothing to consider," he said sternly, "but *me!*"

"Oh, Lewis," she started to weep, "You just don't—"

The backhanded slap caught her directly across the cheek and snapped her head to the side.

"Don't talk back to me," he growled. "I gave you an order to leave them and come with me."

The slap had cleared her befuddled mind. She took a step back, her Irish temper tindered.

"You keep your hands off me. You have no right to do that!"

"I have the right," he insisted coldly. "You yourself said that you are my woman."

"Woman, yes," she said, with the same amount of ice in her voice. "A woman who would love, who would cook, who would sew, who would rear children. But not another Phillipine! I am not blind to her reason for silence. No man has the right to treat a woman as you treat her. And no man is going to treat me in that same fashion."

"I will treat you," he said, through clenched teeth, "any way that I so desire."

"Afraid you won't," a quiet voice said behind them.

Lewis spun. Old man Hardkoop stood with a cutlery knife in each hand. Lewis struggled furiously with his emotions, his eyes blinded by a new hatred. The old man looked at Eliza's rapidly swelling face:

"You run along, miss. He'll see reason after you've gone."

Wearily, Eliza nodded agreement.

"No," Lewis muttered. "You keep out of this. She is the one who has to be made to see reason. I will take her in, just as I took her in within the wagon and just as I took you in, old man."

Eliza turned and did not listen. It was starting to rain. The campfires were beginning to pop and hiss as the Graves prepared to hold a wake over the shrouded body. She didn't see or hear. She walked through the rain toward the great wagon, her head bowed, her footsteps dragging. She had just banished her own future.

William Eddy stood on the sidesteps with Milt at his side.

"We cannot help but guess that you have failed," he said, quietly.

"What was there to win?" she mumbled through her swollen jaw.

Eddy sniffed and went off to handle things as he thought they should have been handled in the first place.

"Will they hang him?" Milt asked, almost indifferently.

"Whatever happens, we are stuck with the rest."

Then she climbed into the wagon. Milt stood there for a long time with the rain dampening his hair. Then he sat down and let it drench him.

Some loyalties, he thought slowly, bitterly, are hard

to walk out on . . . And he was stuck with the great wagon if it became masterless.

Ever after William Eddy considered himself a great diplomat in securing banishment for James Frazier. He started his vote gathering with a still hostile Lewis Keseberg. Lewis finally determined that banishment would win him back Eliza faster than a hanging. Paddy Breen refused to say, so Eddy took it upon himself to hint that the Breens leaned toward banishment. For the sake of Margaret, the Germans leaned that way or faced the wrath of Johanna. Pike and Foster split. When Amanda McCutchen angrily declared that the "man's neck should be stretched," Lavina voted for banishment. The Graves wanted him buried alive up to the neck so that the ants could come and gnaw on him.

James Frazier Reed, weaponless and on a horse almost as tired as himself, left behind more than a buried corpse and distraught family.

The second string of the train was now totally leaderless, although Eddy thought the mantle had automatically fallen on his shoulders as the "man" of the great wagon.

The wagon became almost as much a symbol of hatred as James Frazier himself. It was even shunned now by Johanna Wolfinger. Family groups seemed to pull into themselves for secret little conclaves. Perhaps the Graves were the worst on this score. They had not really been part of the original party and now by choice separated themselves and flatly refused to cooperate on any matter that didn't mean gain for themselves.

"Come on, Uncle Billy," Eddy pleaded. "For reasons Keseberg says he knows nothing about, Hardkoop has fallen behind. I just want to borrow Snyder's unused horse to go back for him."

Graves locked his lips tight and shook his head. He had heard how the old man had held knives to Lewis to keep him from finishing the homemade scaffold.

Eddy went five miles back on foot. All Hardkoop would say was that Keseberg put him out.

Keseberg again left without him the next morning, but Eddy faced a more serious problem.

"It's not a question of it being too big and lumbering, Milt. Sand has gotten into the rear wheels and nearly ground them away from the axle. It's best to change now, rather than have it collapse on the trail."

It was ironic that for the Reed family to continue on he had to negotiate for the purchase of John Snyder's wagon. Graves made the sale price steep—the major portion of the Reed food supply.

Margaret took this newest defeat calmly.

"Reduce us to one change of clothing each, Eliza. It will have to be bedrolls instead of mattresses from now on. I ask only to keep one personal possession—the last of the gold dinner service."

"Mother," Virginia protested, "won't that make us look a little silly?"

Wearily, she shook her head.

"No," she muttered, "I am not thinking of it to eat upon, Virginia, but for barter."

In a roundabout way, Eddy told Hardkoop that they would take him along to catch up with Keseberg. He did not count on the time it would take him to change the wagons about. Eleanor grew to near panic being left so alone. The last Donner note had told of an Indian raid which had killed many cattle.

To ease her fear Eddy and Milt hurried up their departure. The toil of catching up took every other thought from their minds.

It was well after dark when they came into camp. When they passed the Keseberg wagon Eddy grew conscience-stricken.

"My God, Milt! The old man!"

"He left with the Breen cattle while we were changing wagons."

All that John Breen could recall of him was that after several miles of walking he had totally played out and sat to rest his swollen feet until the Reed wagon came along. But John Breen couldn't remember how far back it actually had been.

"How could we have missed him?" Eddy moaned.

Milt Elliott thought it most easy. The cattle ran a parallel course to the trail and a sitting old man could be passed unnoticed. He did not want to think on why the old Dutchman had not seen them and agreed to stand half the night with Eddy to keep a signal fire going.

At dawn the sky was leaden and storm clouds hung low over the next mountain range.

Margaret limped over to Lewis Keseberg.

"Do you feel no human obligation to go back for him?"

"None whatsoever," he said curtly and turned back to yoking his oxen.

Paddy Breen and Uncle Billy Graves were the only ones left with saddle horses.

"Milt," Paddy said coldly, "you stood the night over the fire and he didn't come in. Why? Because the man is already dead in my opinion."

Uncle Billy would make Hardkoop suffer for another cancer on his mind.

"Look, Eddy, you would be able to go after him if that damn girl hadn't broken our rule. We said no weapon for Reed, and his step-daughter not only sneaks him out a weapon with ammunition but lets him take along her horse as well."

"Graves, that has nothing to do with Hardkoop."

"And he has nothing to do with me," he said indifferently.

"He is a human being!"

"So are my family," he shot back angrily. "The day may be coming that I have to replace oxen with horses. I will not allow them to be killed off now galloping back on some damn wild goose chase."

"All right," Eddy sighed. "Milt and I will just go back on foot."

"I'll go with you," Pike quickly volunteered.

"Do as you wish," Uncle Billy returned to his indifferent tone, "but we'll not be waiting for you."

Lavina was proud of Pike stepping forward, but quietly had to think of family also.

"Pike, we're looking starvation right in the face if we don't meet up with Amanda's husband soon. Even a half a day's delay here would be more than we could afford. May God forgive me, but we got our young'uns to think of first."

But it was another woman who may have had the final say. Eleanor Eddy went into such a screaming fit of fearful rage at her husband's plan that to calm her he had to depart with the rest of the wagons.

Hardkoop was left behind, but hardly forgotten.

10

"THESE ARE PARLOUS times."

Tamsen nodded at her husband's sorrowful words. Since the rejoining of the wagons all had been disaster and disagreement.

George Donner had come under attack from Uncle Billy for allowing a "murderer" to exchange Skylark for food and rifle; then depart with Walt Herron on foot. He was so set in his vengeful mind that he could not see that Reed might be their only salvation. George feared that Stanton and McCutchen were dead or would have long since returned.

Uncle Jake's prayer was silent that night, but dealt at length with Uncle Billy Graves.

As though God had answered in a mysterious way, Indians, that night, ran off all the Graves' horses and killed four oxen. Uncle Billy was forced to abandon a wagon.

For the day, Uncle Jake wore a knowing little smile. The next morning he wasn't smiling. The Diggers had struck again and ran off eighteen oxen and a milch cow.

The Donners and Wolfinger were reduced to cattle for pulling power.

The train was further slowed, but stayed together out of fear of further Indian attacks, attacks that came nightly until the Diggers had taken a toll of over a hundred cattle.

Uncle Jake thought it a most unholy waste—which it was.

The emigrants could only cut off a few steaks to be cooked and eaten before they spoiled and leave all the rest for the Diggers and buzzards.

When they got to the sink of the Humboldt they had one last desert and one last mountain range to cross for California.

"These are parlous times," George repeated.

"Get some sleep," Tamsen murmured. "The animals are corralled and guarded tonight. It's only a day's march to this Truckee lake. Rest."

It was at first a decent night's rest for all, quiet and peaceful, with no Digger's arrows twanging into the cattle. Then the night turned bitter cold. The guards shivered miserably but kept up their vigil.

Doolittle curled further into his sleeping roll. He could have saved the guards their freezing. The naked, squat Indians were not about to attack with the mid-October temperature hovering down near the point where he expected to see the river iced over by morning.

He could have saved the whole train loss to the Indians, but his suggestion had fallen on deaf ears as too brutal. As a mountain man he would have handled it in a mountain man's way—captured two of the Diggers and staked them out on the desert to die as an example to the others. Because no human life was being lost, George Donner would not allow him to take human life as an example.

But as he started to grow warm again he put it out of his mind. The next day they would cross the last desert and he would then be free and have money in his saddle bag. He had only agreed to get them to the Truckee. It was just a day away.

It was going to be a very long day.

At dawn the animals were taken out of the makeshift corral and driven out under guard for grass and water. A thin sheet of ice had to be broken for them to drink and the grass was white with hoar-frost. The far mountains were shrouded in puffy white clouds and the sun seemed unable to penetrate the leftover night cold.

"Ain't no damn Indian going to be out in this weather," Paddy Breen said. "Let's all go in for some hot coffee."

They trudged back on near frozen feet, resentful that Paddy was the only one ahorse. Because the ground had frozen a little solid during the night he was paying no attention to sinkholes.

Suddenly the horse began to rear and paw the air in utter fright.

"What the hell!"

Almost before he could scramble off the beast the mare sank and bogged down in the hole and continued to rapidly sink.

"Eddy," he called to the nearest man, "come and give me some aid here!"

Eddy didn't even turn. "Go ask Old man Hardkoop to help you, Breen!"

Breen would have run after him to give him a

thrashing but the air was suddenly filled with whistling arrows.

All of the men began running back toward the grazing animals, watching them drop as though the arrows were coming from nowhere. The poor mare was left to smother in the mud.

The men fired, but they fired at phantoms. The Diggers were the same color as the earth and slipped unharmed away in the dawn shadows.

The Diggers were maddened that they still had not done any harm to the hated white men, and the sink was about the end of their land. They could not know that they had just dealt almost the final stroke to the emigrants.

Margaret sat stunned, Eddy ready to cry. All their oxen were dead, except for one that was too badly hurt to pull the wagon alone. They were stranded.

They were not alone.

Spitzer and Reinhardt would have to share their oxen on a single wagon. Hans Wolfinger had not a single animal left whatsoever.

"You will walk ahead with the other women, Johanna," he whispered to his wife.

"I will do *what*?" she exploded.

"Keep your voice down!" he snarled. "Augustus and Joseph and I shall stay behind as though we are caching our goods and putting some on their wagon."

"Can you not do that right now?"

"Sometimes, Johanna, your thick brain gets in the way of sound reasoning. The moment these half-starved people would see what we carry beneath our floor-boards they would turn into an unruly mob and rob us clean. I am reluctant to even let Spitzer and Reinhardt know of our foodstuffs, but we cannot carry it all on foot."

"You are making me go on foot," she pouted.

"You will not be alone. Donner has decreed that to save the strength of the animals left only the smallest children will ride across the desert."

"I will starve," she sniffled.

The chuckle was only in his mind. The woman had been eating regularly and had ample fat to see her across several deserts.

"Don't fret, my dear. I wish you to wear your bulkiest dress, for I have been tying foodstuffs onto the wire hoops of one of your petticoats, and you can take more in a cloth satchel."

"I shall need it for my jewelry."

He pondered it a moment, as though reading the future. "Don't weigh yourself down, my dear. I shall be bringing all your trinkets in the chest. You just take food."

"Really, Hans, it is said to be only a day's journey."

"We have heard that too many times before, Johanna. I am giving you enough for two to three days."

"And where shall you be all that time?"

"Johanna," he sighed, as though tired of explaining, "I can do nothing until everyone departs. Then it shall be barter time with those two. Three wagons into one will mean much left behind. They will see reason when their eyes land on enough food to last the four of us for another week or so."

Except that they were walking, it might have been a reunion for Johanna, Margaret and Elizabeth.

Tamsen had made arrangements for the younger Reed children to ride with her own, although Elizabeth was quick to take credit for the suggestion.

But it was not a reunion. After a little while, Elizabeth and Johanna ran out of things to say. Margaret had said very little since learning they must walk.

What little foodstuff was now left was more precious than carrying along the gold plates. When that was gone she would be really destitute. It had never crossed her mind to ask what James Frazier had done with his hidden cache money. As far as she knew it still sat back within the great wagon.

Despite her illness, she was able to withstand the horror of that day better than the other two. Because of their bulk, and constant riding, they felt the thirst, the rapid rise of the temperature up to over eighty degrees, cringed at the dust that soon made everyone a powdery white. It became more torture to get up from the rest stops than to plod on into sheer exhaustion.

Nor were the rest stops for the humans. They were for the scrawny mixed teams of cows and oxen that pulled the remaining dozen wagons.

Kindness seemed something left only for the younger generation, and then it wasn't always appreciated.

"Would you care to ride with me?"

Had John Breen not been riding bareback, Virginia might have gladly accepted. But Paddy Breen curtly gave his son an order to get back to tending the cattle, of which the Breens' had been the least affected, and glowered so at Virginia that she kept walking.

When no one was looking Billy lifted Elitha up onto the tailgate of one of the Graveses wagons.

"You look most tuckered."

"You could have added, frightened."

"You don't have to fear when I'm around."

"I know," she said, dropping her eyes. "I'm most glad we are travelling together again, Billy. I don't fear when I know you are about."

"We won't be separated again," he boasted. "The train is a unit again."

It was a boast he could not keep. The train was already getting spread out over the desert and up through the ridges of jagged volcanic rock.

Those still possessing oxen pulled farther and farther ahead of those with yoked cattle.

Those walking struggled to keep up. For Bill Eddy it was near an impossibility. No one would take his two children up to ride in a wagon. Eleanor struggled along with the baby and Bill carried his young son on his shoulders. Under his arm he carried his last prized possession for barter—a three pound sack of sugar.

The rain came fiercely and blindingly. They were too far back to see that George Donner had relented and let everyone ride during the storm.

The Eddys toiled against it, Bill keeping his eyes constantly downward on the wheel tracks. A few times he came near panic, thinking he had lost the way. But it was not the rain washing out the track but the change in terrain. The rocky trail barely showed the wheel marks and were sharp enough to cut through boot leather.

The storm passed as quickly as it had come. It had been little relief—a hot rain with a strange taste. Behind the scudding clouds, an old moon rose. Eddy allowed the near prostrate child a short rest and a little sugar to suck upon. He and his wife ate none before they pushed on.

Hours later, hours which he had stopped counting, they rounded a bend and came upon an infernal sight. The wagons were parked in a little basin where over a hundred holes oozed up boiling hot water and steam jets that without warning spurted high into the air.

"It is hell," Eleanor moaned, "and we have all been banished there together for our deeds."

It certainly seemed like hell. The water was bitter

and too hot for drinking. But the early arrivers had learned that if left to stand in a bucket until luke-warm it would overcome thirst despite its bitterness.

No one seemed to even notice Eddy until he got to the Donner wagon.

"It will still be another day, Eddy. Can you make it?"

He nodded wearily.

Tamsen's heart sank at the sight of the children. She took the coffee pot they had just emptied and added another handful of grounds. Two more hand-fuls and that would be the last.

"We found, Mr. Eddy," she said, thrusting it for-ward, "that if you hold the pot right over one of these holes that it brews the coffee right up and takes away some of the bitter water taste."

Then she motioned George away.

"I've a thought as to lightening the load so that those poor children can ride. We will have to cache the two bureaus, except for the quilt."

"Clothing don't weigh that much, Tamsen, unless you are thinking of leaving behind something heavier."

"You know?"

"My dear," he said gently, "I've known of your books and school supplies all along. You did that for the future of our girls and would now leave them behind for the future of these children. It is a most loving thing and I shall gladly help."

Later, it seemed to many that several events were crowded together—although they were spread out over a week.

"Smell! Would you just smell that! Wild peas at this time of year."

"And trees," James Smith, grinned back at Mary Florence. "I didn't think I would ever see cotton-woods again. That Truckee river may be fifty feet wide, but it will be a dry hole by the time I finish drinking."

"Then drink quick," Doolittle snarled, riding by. "Only one day to rest here."

"My," Mary Florence said archly, "aren't we in a good mood today?"

"Matter of business," he said curtly. "This be the Truckee, but Donner won't pay me until I get you to the lake and foot of the pass."

To quickly gain his money Doolittle finally became the guide. Up the Truckee he found a better pass than that taken by Hastings. It was still hard going for the worn-down oxen, but it saved a day.

That night Spitzer and Reinhardt caught up with them. Claiming little English, they avoided Johanna until they could get Keseberg to speak for them.

"While they were loading the wagon," he repeated their story, without a trace of emotion, "the Diggers attacked again and killed Wolfinger. They barely got away with the wagon and their lives."

For three days, as Doolittle plotted their course, he pondered this. Among mountain men to come back without your companion and such a skimpy tale would have raised many doubts. The Diggers had only been successful before against the animals. How did they get close enough for this attack with their weak bows and puny arrows? And why were the Germans so doubtful as to the number of Diggers they had shot during the attack?

Normally, Doolittle would not have worried over the matter, but when Johanna Wolfinger almost collapsed at the news, it was Tamsen Donner who took her in. It didn't set right that the Germans didn't offer to take her into the wagon or report on what of the Wolfinger goods they may be carrying for her. Was it just that they were all as cold-hearted a people as Lewis Keseberg?

The next day, scouting, all of these thoughts were washed from his brain. For a few minutes he was king and hero for leading back to the wagon train three riders and seven pack-mules.

The train was suddenly a place of celebration and myriad questions.

Charles Stanton nearly went hoarse explaining that Mac McCutchen had taken ill and was with the Hastings party. That Hastings had gone through the pass on October the seventh in a light snowstorm. That Reed and Herron were on their way to Sutter and that the good captain had gladly given the food, the mules and two Indian guides to help bring it back.

For a while they were a reunited group.

No one even complained at the manner that Uncle Jake Donner carefully doled out the supplies according to family size.

But bad news seemed to walk hand in hand with every bit of good news that came their way.

Having just come over the route, Stanton was able to help Doolittle get them back to the Truckee Meadows in under three days. The weather had been cloudy and threatening the whole time, and some, their bellies again full, seemed content to go slower. They were again stretched out when the Donner and Murphy wagons got to the grasslands.

"You really don't need me any further, Mr. Donner."

"Will until we get to the lake and pass," George stubbornly insisted.

"You've got Stanton and his Indians."

"Amazed he trusted them after the Wasatch!"

Stanton grinned. "They be Catholic Christians who speak only Spanish, Mr. Donner. Besides, Captain Sutter said that he would hang them if they lost his mules and all his Indians take that man at his word. But Doolittle didn't bring out another point, sir. I recommend rest here for awhile."

"But what of the snows, Stanton?"

"Snow is one thing, Mr. Donner, but you would be inviting catastrophe with these animals even if it were the middle of summer. This trail goes right up broken domes of granite and makes the Wasatch look like land good for farming. It was a struggle for the Hastings oxen. They had to double and triple team, sometimes using every man available for the windlass."

Stanton looked around at the stragglers coming in the second section. They were like people he had never seen before. They, too, needed to be fattened up as much as the cattle.

"All right, Doolittle," George said sourly, still with misgivings on Stanton's advice, "come along, I'll be paying you off."

Before they could move there was an explosion. It was too close to be a hunter and they all turned toward the sound.

Before the Murphy campfire Foster sat looking a little stunned. Before him Pike stood with his back half turned. A foolish grin crossed his lips before he started to collapse and Sarah and Harriet scream.

For an hour Lavina and Tamsen worked to save Pike's life. Foster continued to sit stunned and Doolittle to grow curious over the pepper-box pistol that lay at his feet.

Doolittle squatted down beside him. "Best you talk it out."

"Yah," he said dully, "but it don't seem like it happened, Doolittle. We was sitting here jawing the fat while Pike was cleaning the pistol. My wife barked for more firewood and Pike said he's get it. As he rose he handed it back to me butt first and the damn thing went right off. I didn't even know he had taken a bullet to the back until he went down. Oh, damn, what luck!"

"Interesting piece," Doolittle mused. "Where'd he get it?"

"Traded. He was always trading things. Spitzer is afraid of guns and traded him a brace of geese he shot a day or two back."

And many, many days before that Doolittle had seen the pistol in the hands of Hans Wolfinger. Now how could Spitzer have gotten his hands on the man's pepper-box pistol when they were running so fast from the Indians?

It was a question Doolittle would have loved to ask of the man, but to get an answer he would have to go through Keseberg or Johanna Wolfinger. Because of Keseberg's interest in Eliza he was not about to approach him, and even after so many years in the wild, he still had enough social graces left not to approach the widow on a matter that was only a question mark in his mind.

He waited for Pike's burial and his pay.

"Time to say good-bye!"

Mary Florence looked up. It was hardly like the first time she had seen Doolittle Thornburg. Three months? Could it really be nearly three months? Or had it been almost a whole lifetime.

"Well, Doo," she smiled, "there were parts of it that were fun."

"You'll be all right. You have Stanton and Smith to look after you again."

"Comforting," she said sweetly, starting to turn. "Take care."

Eliza and Tamsen had near the same reaction as Mary Florence. It was hardly the same man that they had first seen. The buckskins had taken on a much darker hue from constant wear and the moccasins were developing tiny holes in the soles. He was still golden and handsome, but the short rations had sunk his eyes into hollows and made his cheekbones more pronounced. And there was no more gaiety in his eyes. Like the whole camp, he was feeling the sorrow of Pike's death. Of this whole variety of human nature he had always felt more akin to Pike and Foster. Now Foster was as good as dead, too. He just sat and brooded, the gumption burned right out of him because Pike was no longer there to share it.

"We shall miss you, Doolittle," Tamsen said sadly.

"And I shall miss you both," he said honestly, looking from one to the other. But no longer was there a wink for Eliza.

"A fine man," Tamsen said, as he rode away.

"Do you really think so?"

"Said so, didn't I? Oh, I'm not saying that there isn't some fault there, but that's because he is a free-spirited man. He just hasn't found the right woman to tame that spirt."

"Will he go back to being a mountain man?"

"He didn't say." Then she laughed. "I don't think he really knows what he is going to do from one day to the next."

This time she was wrong. Doolittle knew exactly what he wished to do next, but didn't quite understand the unusual urge in him that made him head back toward the east and the desert of the Diggers.

11

THE SORROW which had brought them together for a day also separated them.

With the departure of Doolittle, everyone seemed to become an expert guide, or latched onto one.

Oddly, Paddy Breen put aside all of his petty differences with Bill Eddy, because Eddy was the best hunter in the group and the mountains would afford game to supplement the Sutter supplies. He had lost the fewest cattle to the Indians and wanted to keep it that way. It was not odd that Patrick Dolan would depart with him, carrying Eleanor Eddy and her children, but most odd that Lewis Keseberg would ask to join the first party out.

Keseberg had added another hatred to that of church and family. Again he had demanded that Eliza divorce herself from the down-and-out Margaret Reed and go with him. Again Eliza was firm in her own conviction and Lewis knew that if he did not get away from her he might be prone to commit murder.

Margaret Reed was not so down and out. With James Smith handling the MacDuff wagon Stanton was free to take the Reeds in tow and let them ride the pack saddle mules. Margaret was most indebted to the man for an even greater reason—he had brought her word that James Frazier was still alive.

With the pack mules ahead, the Graveses and Murphys followed in the second group to depart.

George Donner's misgivings made him stubbornly hold back. Only after six days of rest, did he become his own guide again.

Margaret Reed was gone, but Elizabeth and Johanna were still together. Elizabeth could not help but lord it over the new widow, who looked almost naked without all her heavy jewelry.

Possibly only because of Tamsen, Mary Florence stayed in the last group.

No one had really asked Spitzer and Reinhardt to join any group, but as though they felt they still owed some answers to Johanna they hung back as the tail end.

Every group, at least, knew they could now count on Stanton's word. It was a two day journey, across an easy range and large valley, to a cabin built two years before by winter-bound emigrants. Then, even though the great pass seemed to loom high above, it was still fifty miles from the lake.

"Damn, Stanton, it rained for a full day before you got here. What do you mean, wait for the Donners? How in the hell can anyone tell when that bullheaded old farmer might have decided to move out."

Everyone except Stanton agreed with Paddy Breen. A little rain wasn't going to hurt them. They had had their rest by the Truckee and, besides, the cabin roof leaked so that they wouldn't even stable animals in it.

As men of the plains, they were not taking into consideration that rain which fell in torrents in the valley. would be fluffy whiteness another thousand feet up.

Perhaps it was kindness in return that made them leave the Donner brothers a note at the cabin.

It was a note they would never get to read.

"Whoa! Brake them! The downward pitch is too great!"

Tamsen Donner had the sick feeling she had heard that warning before. She shouted for the children to jump out the tailgate and crawled forward to the perch. Just as she got over the front axle she heard it crack and splinter beneath the boards. She was pitched forward as the wheels collapsed and the tongue snapped in two, bouncing back up to disembowel one of the oxen with its jagged end.

The front of the wagon hit the downward slope with a jarring crash, sending the jockey box back over her head and out the canvas roof. The tongue end caught the ground and spun the wagon over into a roll. Tamsen's ears were filled with two horrible sounds: the death cry of the ox and the frantic wails of two of her daughters who had not heeded her warning.

She, too, thought she looked death in the face, but after a complete roll, which shattered all the bows, a tall pine tree kept the wagon from rolling again.

Shaken and bruised, she crawled out over the perch where the jockey box had once been affixed. Unmindful of her own hurt, she raced back to begin pulling away the wagon-sheets. Before a single man had arrived, she had found Georgia more frightened than hurt. But the baby was still missing.

"Eliza! Little Eliza! Answer Mommy, darling!"

There was no answer. Tamsen began to dig frantically through the shattered tumble of household goods.

Elizabeth and Johanna came stumbling down the hill, Elizabeth fluttering her arms and causing further panic with her screams. She had nothing to fear— her children had, at least, minded Tamsen and instantly jumped.

"*Bitte!*" Johanna said, moving Tamsen aside by the shoulders. "You might do the little one more harm by pawing that way. Carefully."

With an agility never before shown, she began to sort through the rubble and hand it out. Elizabeth stood as a spectator, Tamsen having to inspect each piece until Sol and Uncle Jake were on the scene to help.

For Tamsen it seemed an eternity before the large German woman came across the limp but still-breathing little body. She was breathing shallowly, but there was no blood or broken bones. Within moments she was crying out her fright in Tamsen's arms.

In their panic no one but Elizabeth saw the secret that was housed beneath Johanna's skirt. The woman had been most careful with the final little gifts from her husband. Elizabeth selfishly stored the knowledge away for future reference.

The future was now on every mind. Jacob was quick to suggest they abandon the broken wagon. Because the MacDuff wagon was falling so into disrepair, James Smith thought it too would soon have to be left behind. George Donner was still stubborn. They would just have to chop a timber to splice up the axle.

The best wagon of the last group came lumbering down the slope as though no accident had taken place. Spitzer and Reinhardt didn't even cast their eyes in its direction.

In German Johanna called out to them that help would be needed to fell a timber and hoist up the wagon. They rode right by without a muttered answer.

Even without knowing the language no one had to guess at the meaning of her guttural Germanic tirade at their departing.

Perhaps George Donner was being too stubborn. Just as the shaping of the axle was almost completed his chisel slipped and cut a long, deep gash in the back of his hand. To the men he made light of it, and bound it up with a well-used handkerchief.

Men? To hoist up the wagon and attach the axle slice, they were reduced to the two sixty-year-old men, the two teenage Hook brothers and James Smith —who still suffered pain lifting anything with his gunshot shoulder. Tamsen and Mary Florence did what they could to help, aided by a new recruit. Johanna proved to be nearly as strong as the men. Elizabeth, who at least held a torch for them to see by after dark, thought it most logical. After all, the woman had eaten better in the last three months than any of the rest.

But the fatigue felt by all of them required another day of rest, especially for George Donner. Tamsen fretted over the hand wound and the blood that he had lost, but he still made light of the matter.

His fear was more in what he smelled with his nose than the pain in his hand.

As nature will sometimes do in its odd course, snow can skip from mountain range to mountain range and leave rain to shower down on the valley in between.

An hour after the axle was finished his nostrils proved him correct. The snow came soft and fluttering and fleecy—the kind that thrills children in the fall and makes them dream of toboggans.

It was not to George Donner's liking and he turned and fretted throughout the night.

For a long time, Mary Florence had watched it out of the tailgate of her wagon. She tried to determine if she felt wistful, sad or lonely. It was true Manitoba weather. Before, she had always loved snow. But that had been home, within a warm room that gave her a safe window view of the raging snowstorm.

She shivered, but not from the cold. As warm as the room had been in Canada, it had always been just as cold with lonesomeness as she was now.

"Cold?"

She spun. Although he had never done it before, the only logical person to climb into the front of the wagon would be James Smith. But the voice she had come to know too well.

"What in the hell brings you back?"

"Some welcome," Doolittle chuckled, crawling forward.

"Equal to your departure," she said coolly.

"I'm wet to the bone."

"Your problem."

"I didn't mean to barge in on you."

"Equally your problem." But though she was sorely puzzled at his quick return and the quiet manner in which he spoke, she was not about to let down her guard against him.

"I seem to have stumbled into a heap of problems, perhaps for all of us."

"All?" she said unkindly. "I thought you had said good-bye to *all* of us?"

"Where is everyone—especially the Germans?"

The last caused her to lift her head and stare at him wonderingly.

"Mrs. Wolfinger is with the Donners. Keseberg is a day or two ahead and the other two, as usual, took off just before sundown because there was work to be done."

"Good," he sighed with relief.

"And what does that mean?"

"I could explain better if I were dry and warm—and I promise to be a gentleman about it."

"Really?" she smirked, remembering that she had been the one accused of trying to denude him the last time. But something about his quiet, mysterious manner got her curiosity. "Oh, damn you, to hell! You know where I keep the extra blankets."

"I'm sorry to put this on you," he said, starting to pull out of the soaked buckskins, "but I couldn't put this on Tamsen until I knew the lay of the land."

"Oh?" Now her curiosity was pricked.

"I rode back to where the Diggers were supposed to have attacked and killed Wolfinger."

"Oh?" she repeated. "Why?"

"Oh, damn-it-all, Mary Florence, don't ask me a question I can't even answer in my own mind. The whole thing smelled to me . . . then Bill Pike. I liked that rascal. But I think I might have gone after some answers even if he hadn't been killed."

"Answers?"

He came and sat with a quilt wrapped about his big frame. "Best I just tell you what I found, for it answers all. Wagons right where they had been left, but the Wolfinger wagon gone through carefully. White-man carefully, Mary Florence. Those two had a false floorboard and under it, from the scraps I found, quite a cache of food and probably valuables."

"Why not the Diggers?"

"Wolfinger himself. He was still there, although buzzards had been at him plenty. Buzzards don't make that kind of a hole in a skull and we know the Diggers didn't have any more firepower than arrows. Oh, I'm not saying that they didn't watch. As a mat-

ter of fact I'm damn sure that they did. Ain't like
them to leave so much lying about. First time they
probably ever saw one white kill another white and
their poor minds are probably still wondering over it."

Mary Florence was looking at him with wide-eyed
disbelief.

"Murder?"

"I doubt," he said acidly, "that they would call it
that. They probably hung around Mrs. Wolfinger to
learn if she had anymore of her jewelry with her. I
found none at the wagon."

"What will we do?"

"You will do nothing, nor say anything. When I am
warmer and drier I will go after them, or at least
get ahead of them and warn the others."

She was silent for a long time. "Again, I ask, why?"

"Let's just say for Pike. It was Wolfinger's stolen
pistol that killed him."

She sighed. "This isn't like you."

"Do you know the real me? Do I know the real
me? Hell, I've never championed a cause in my life."

"Perhaps it's time," she said quietly and then
stopped herself from adding that she liked what she
saw.

"You had best get to bed."

It took her a long time to muster up the courage
to gulp: "Alone?"

"I can't make any promises."

"I've stopped asking for them."

He was gone when she awoke. Outside the world
was bleak and white. She didn't know if she should
feel just as bleak.

Even for Doolittle, the day was cold, the clouds
still hovering over the mountains. At the lake he
found where they had skirted the north shore, some
going so close he could not help but wonder why they

hadn't toppled in. Beyond the lake the snow was already three feet deep and it was easy to follow the path where they had laboriously dug a path through for the wagons.

"Oh, the fools," he thought a few hours later. The wagons were deserted in drifts over their axles. The plowed-up snow was evidence enough that the oxen had not taken kindly to being converted into pack animals.

Because one phase of the storm had passed over, it was hard to tell how long before they had started their floundering way. Almost in mockery the storm clouds momentarily parted and he could see the towering peaks and the formidable pass. The pine boughs below were marshmallowed in snowy frosting and not a speck of granite gray showed through the solid mantle of white on the peaks. It was the second day of November and winter had come to stay.

But the second wave of the storm dropped the clouds low again before he could sight them on their march.

The day was growing late. After a few more miles, even Doolittle was forced to get down to plow through the waist deep snow and pull his horse along behind. The snow kept falling but their path was easy to follow. Every so often there was a packed-down area where an ox had decided to wallow and rid itself of its pack. Here and there, also, was evidence of a pack that had been too heavily loaded and now lightened—a bolt of calico, a small trunk of clothing, and even an oak rocking chair eerily swaying back and forth in the midst of the raging storm.

The road did some very odd turning and twisting, if the so-called road was even beneath the deep snow. Logic told him that its buried condition was forcing

Stanton to follow it out of general memory and not by sighted landmarks.

"Landmarks, hell," he grumbled. "If they weren't such a large group, with so many children, I might wallow right on by them."

Night fell and so did the storm. Two figures did wallow by him unseen in the darkness and swirling vortex. Spitzer and Reinhardt had also been tracking the party to catch up. They were men who knew snow from European experience and rightly guessed that the storm would not be of short duration. They weren't intending to freeze to death with their new-found wealth.

Spitzer and Reinhardt had come within an eighth of a mile of the halted and demoralized emigrants. Stanton and the Indians had gone ahead to find the proper route again.

"Lewis," Uncle Billy barked, "I thought you said that the rain usually washed away the first snow of the season."

Keseberg sat gritting his teeth upon a horse. It was not because of Graves's words, but due to the most intense pain he had ever suffered in his life. After leaving the lake he had stumbled headlong into a snow-filled gully and badly sprained his leg. His horse had then had to pack him rather than his goods.

"And what in the hell are you about?" Graves then snapped at his son, when getting no answer from Keseberg.

Eighteen-year-old Billy Graves was doing a most logical thing. He was setting fire to a dead pine that was full of pitch. The outer bark was damp but the pitch soon turned the whole tree into flame. For thirty feet around it gave off a most comforting warmth.

"I don't think I have ever been so tired," Eliza sighed.

"Because you have been carrying Tommy most of

the way," Margaret answered guiltily. "I wish I could be doing more."

"You are doing fine taking care of yourself."

And Eliza knew she was not alone in her weariness. Everyone was worn out from having to take turns carrying the younger children. The pack-mules were too few for carrying them all.

"Eliza," Margaret whispered, "if we bed the children down now, might they not sleep through and never question missing supper?"

Others were having the same thought and rolling their children into blankets on the snow. Then they huddled by the burning tree and ate sparingly of the rations that were to get them through the pass in that single day.

The children thus slept through the argument that arose on Stanton's return. Again he had reached the summit and again returned for them.

"We can get through, if it doesn't snow anymore."

"That's a mighty big 'if,' Charles," Lavina mused. "While you have been gone the temperature has dropped, the wind has risen and the snow turned to sleet off and on. I don't think these old bones wish to move until morning."

"We have got to push forward," Lewis insisted.

"That's easy for you to say from horseback," Eddy countered, "but the rest of us have to carry children."

"My wife is doing the same!" Lewis huffed.

It was a statement everyone knew for fact, but dared not cross the man by asking why he didn't take the children up on his horse.

As much as they desired to get through the pass, the majority vote was for spending the night where they were.

Doolittle had no one to vote with but his horse. It would have been a split decision. But winter in the wilds was nothing new to him. He knew how

to conserve himself and the animal. He would find
a fairly windless gully or heavy growth of trees to
force the horse down on its side in the snow. He
would snuggle up to the warm belly and blanket
himself from head to foot.

For an hour or two he would let his body totally
relax as the wind hissed through the swaying pines
and the snow fell steadily.

Rested, he didn't spring right up, but cautiously
rolled the blanket from his side and studied the de-
posit left on horse and blanket. Each time it was an
inch or so.

Trudging on, he would calculate the hour of the
night and the accumulated snowfall. It was piling
up fast. To keep his mind alert he tried to discount
his own reasoning, but it came out near the same
each time: if the drifts had been three feet down by
the lake, then they would have to be over ten feet
in the pass by morning. Easily a full foot or more
of new snow would have fallen on the area between
dusk and dawn—unless it let up.

And he measured another matter to keep his mind
from freezing. What was he to do if the emigrants
had made it through the pass before he stumbled
upon them? Warn them about the Germans and keep
on heading for California? He, too, had waited for
over three months to get through this pass in the
Sierras. Or would he turn back to see that Mary
Florence and Tamsen got through safely?

He scolded himself and scolded the horse and
scolded the falling snow. Then he scolded Mary Florence for once again getting him into her bed. Damn
that woman for making him feel like a man! He
told himself that it wasn't love but just lust. But
what lust!

Then he scolded Tamsen Donner. Why did she
have to be such a sweet, loving, caring person who

made him feel obligated to go back for her safety?

Doolittle Thornburg took care of Doolittle Thornburg! Three months before he would have just taken Donner's money and let them find out the hard way about the Germans.

"No you wouldn't," he said aloud into the wind. "You're not half as mean as you make out to be. You may say that you are doing it for two women— three, really. But every damn one of them knows you, Doolittle. Ain't lust, either. You're a damn lonely coot. You go out for Eliza, because you know damn well you can't have her. You found out you could have the widow whenever you wanted her, so you didn't want her anymore. And while you are being honest, you bastard, admit that Tamsen treats you like a son and that's something you've missed for a hell of a number of years."

He stopped short and sniffed. He grinned and let his nose be his guide. Pitch smoke meant a campfire because no forest would burn in all this dampness.

The pine tree was now little more than a smoking stump, the clouds keeping the smoke down around the campsite. Like witches in a coven, some of the men kept circling the tree trying to set it back ablaze. And as Doolittle approached it looked like the spell they were trying to cast was being conducted in a graveyard. The smooth snowbanks began to erupt like ghosts being risen from their graves. With forty-one women and children thus emerging from beneath blankets it would have greatly startled a stranger.

"Doolittle?" Stanton gaped, as though he were the one seeing a ghost. "Thought you'd be long gone over the pass."

"Lost my way," he lied. "Smelled your smoke."

"How is it above?" Eddy asked.

"Worse than here," he said, looking around. It

really wasn't a total lie. The drifts around the camp were ten feet deep and the children were crawling out from beneath a foot of new-fallen snow. It was only reasonable that higher into the peaks and pass it was not going to be better. But his looking around was for another reason. Puzzled, he looked around again for the faces of the Germans, but they were not there.

Lewis Keseberg limped up, his face wracked by pain. "Are you saying we can't go on?"

"Ain't your guide to say one way or another. I ain't going on, if that is worth anything."

"It is worth something to me," Stanton sighed. "We had best turn back to the wagons and shelter."

Not even Lewis Keseberg uttered a protest. The ligaments in his leg had been so badly torn that even on the horse he knew he would never make it farther upward. Downward would be hard enough, but at least a dry wagon and bed awaited him in that direction.

Throughout the morning and afternoon Doolittle continued to puzzle over the missing Germans. He was positive that he had seen their wagon with the rest. For the moment he thought it best to keep what knowledge he possessed even from Stanton.

But once the wagons were reached in mid-afternoon, he knew Stanton had to be approached.

Everyone thought that Indians had rifled through the wagons, although there was nothing of real value to be taken. The snow had cunningly covered up the Germans' departing wheel tracks.

"What do you think?"

Doolittle knew exactly what Stanton meant by the question. He had been watching the Sutter Indians. They knew just enough English to know that Indians were being blamed. They looked doubtful and Doolittle knew for good reason.

"I don't think you'll get all the wagons back to the cabin by dark," he said, avoiding Stanton's real question. "Tell them to double-team the oxen and mules on the most important wagons for tonight's shelter."

Knowing his words had been heard and would not need to be repeated, he gently took Stanton by the arm and nudged him out of earshot.

"Seen Spitzer and Reinhardt?"

"They're with the Donners."

"Nope. Left them stranded after George Donner broke an axle. Saw their wagon with the rest when I came by here."

"How the hell—"

Doolittle gently put his hand over Stanton's mouth. "Keep it down, Charley. We don't want a panic on our hands but I went back into the desert and found they had killed and robbed Wolfinger."

"Then they . . . ?"

"What else? Leaves two questions. Where are they and where are the Donners? From that last ridge I didn't see a trace of smoke coming from the cabin."

"What shall we do?" He gulped. "Murder?"

"For the moment, Charley, we do and say nothing about it to these people. I will work my way back to check on the Donner train. If those two show back here, you do or say nothing to them, but keep a close eye on them. They know that they are not suspected, so they won't be wary of being watched."

"Donner knows, doesn't he?"

"Nope."

"Then what made you go back to check on it?"

Doolittle grinned. "Charley, we are both bachelors. What made you come back from California over that pass? We are both just damn fools, that's all."

Charles Stanton, because of Mary Florence Mac-Duff, had never really liked Doolittle Thornburg. He had thought the regal lady had really lowered herself taking up with the lazy, worthless, "do little" bum. He had done what he had done for the whole party—the good, the worthless and the arrogant. He had done it to save their lives with food. Doolittle had done it to save their lives from another murder. The man couldn't be all bad.

The storm lasted, with a few hours respite now and then, for two solid weeks.

It was the longest rest period that they had ever had. But it was hardly a rest period.

The cabin needed a new pine bough roof and two additional cabins constructed when it became impossible to get back all of the wagons through the ever-deepening snow.

Because the hope was daily present that the storm would pass, the cabins were not built for a long duration of stay. They were squat, windowless, with green poles laid across for a flat roof covered with wagon canvas, hides and boughs. The "new" cabins were double in size to the one already standing. Each, oddly, stood at least one hundred and fifty feet apart.

Not so queer in light of the new social structure. The Breens, once the poorest of the lot were now the wealthiest in beef cattle and oxen. They had been the first to the cabin in the driving rain and the first back to the cabin on the return trip. Even before Charles Stanton had led the last of the people from the lake, Paddy, Patrick Dolan and John were repairing the leaking roof.

The social structure did not dictate the building of the cabins at such odd distances. They were built hurriedly and primitively along a little creek and as close to where the trees had been felled to make their square.

The only thought was to get sixty people in out of the storm. Upstream the Eddys, Murphy clan and

Amanda McCutchen shared. Downstream was the unusual coupling of the Graves and Reed contingents.

Because of his bad leg Lewis had not helped on either cabin. He stayed within his wagon for a week until forced to move it next to the Breen's cabin and build a lean-to between.

As each day came and went, so did the dying of the remaining oxen and cattle. Because of the constantly freezing temperatures, they were stacked up like cord-wood by the cabins, but as yet not eaten. The hunters were still having luck because the storm had driven deer and antelope down out of the high country and geese to the lake on their southward winter flight.

The two weeks were not easy on Doolittle or the Donners. On the very day that he had left the others at the lake he had found them five miles down the creek. They had not seen the Germans, so he let that matter rest and again pretended that he had been forced back by the storm and was doing Stanton a favor by checking on them.

His story didn't fool Mary Florence, but she kept his secret. Shelter was also of prime concern here. Even though just five miles away, Doolittle advised against pushing the wagons through the storm and drifts.

The five miles also made them consider putting up even more temporary and cruder structures. Tents, really, covered with boughs and inner lined with quilts. From green pole aspen and wagon canvas, the Donner and Reed teamsters erected a wigwam-like structure. Again there was a strange coupling as Johanna Wolfinger went into the tented hovel of George Donner and Mary Florence was given a damp corner of the Jacob Donner tent—James Smith, of course, stayed with the teamsters.

That Doolittle could not have privacy with Mary

Florence he didn't even think about, for he was hardly ever there. As a mountain man he claimed to be out in the storm each day hunting, and each day he did bring back some form of game. But he was luckier with game than his real quarry. The Germans just seemed to have vanished. He was not sure how far north or south they would have to go for another pass through the mountains, and he was sure they would not have headed back east through Digger country.

His treks were really too far afield.

No less than a mile from the Breen cabin the Germans's wagon had floundered into a gully and become snowbound and covered. Their oxen had died of exhaustion trying to pull it free and they had left them yoked to freeze in place. Because they had ample stolen blankets, a snow covering in the almost windless gulley, and sufficient dried foods to eat upon, they did not bestir themselves to gather wood for a fire. They could sit out the storm in more or less comfort.

Because of his search for them—known only to Stanton and Mary Florence—Doolittle became a communications link between the two camps.

He found he was more of a gossip carrier than anything, because there wasn't that much encouraging news to carry back and forth.

Sol Hook, surprisingly, was concerned about the well being of Virginia. Billy Graves wanted to know everything there was to know about Elitha Donner. Mary Ann Graves had all but given up on the childlike Baylis Williams. John Breen, at the moment, wasn't thinking about girls. Suddenly, and without warning, Paddy Breen was struck down by what he called "gravel in his lungs." Had Tamsen or George Donner been within their camp they could have told him the "rattle" was consumption.

But there were also some non-communicative links within the individual camps themselves.

The half mile that separated Eliza and Lewis was much to her liking. Although the duties were now limited, she played "maid" to Margaret and the children. Her absence, and Lewis's near inability to get about on his bad leg, forced Phillipine into becoming what she had always been as a young woman— a strong and resourceful individual. If wood was to be cut, she and Dutch Charley cut it. If food was to be gathered, she and Dutch Charley hunted or fished for it. If decisions were to be made, she and Dutch Charley made them together, while Lewis lay on his mattress moaning.

While some others grew weak and pale from a meat-only diet, she grew stronger and rosier. While her ribs and broken arm healed, the ligaments stayed swollen in her hapless husband's leg.

Dutch Charley Burger could not have been happier. He believed in a just God, and this was surely justice being served.

"Trout from the lake," she exulted, swinging into the lean-to.

Lewis cursed in German. "Meat and fish! Fish and meat! I am sick to death of them both."

"Be thankful it is not just meat," she amazingly snapped right back. "The others are only used to mud-stream fishing and Dutch Charley knows how to bait and cast for these fish."

"Or is he just baiting and casting for you?" Lewis asked snidely.

"Does it matter?" she asked, without fear of him. "Your desire for a trio served only your personal pleasure. My desire for the same puts fish and venison before you."

"At the cost of your body?" he demanded.

Phillipine laughed. It was not a kind sound. "He

has not put such a price on his service to us, Lewis. But should he, to keep *my* children alive, I would willingly pay him back twenty-fold."

At the other camp the communication stoppage was between Johanna and Elizabeth. The big, raw-boned, Johanna had been doing a man's work. To pay for her keep she chopped wood, cleaned snow daily from the pine bough roof covering, helped with the children, but never once reached into her petticoats for an added morsel of food.

It was this point that kept Elizabeth fuming, although she shirked on the work and still kept eating her daily ration.

Several times, Tamsen came near to pressing for a merger of the camps. The first was the day after the storm, November twelfth.

"I think," George said wisely, "we'd best wait for a bit of melting."

It was healing, not melting, he was waiting for. The chisel wound was deep and painful.

On that day, some from the other camp made another attempt on foot to get through the pass. They were back before nightfall, never having made it beyond the lake.

Nature now played two horrible tricks. For nine days the sky was azure blue and cloudless, but the daytime temperature never rose above freezing and the nighttime cold was always below zero. The lake and creek froze, cutting them off from what little fish it had given up; and the game animals were now down around the Truckee where they didn't have to burrow so deeply through the snow for food.

Weak and listless, on near starvation rations, nothing much happened from day to day, except Paddy Breen's bartering business.

As sick as he was he took relish in being propped

up by a log to personally see to every transaction. He was heartless and ruthless in extracting prices for a quarter beef that would have made Jim Bridger balk.

Perhaps to escape Breen's ever increasing price demands an even larger party attempted another scaling of the wintry pass. It lasted a day and a half before having to turn back to the cabin.

It was during this time Tamsen pressed again.

"He has got to be moved up, Doolittle. He does not complain but this dampness is not good for him or that wound."

"Nor would the starvation there be good for the twenty odd people you've got here, Mrs. Reed. Breen is a fool. They eat up what he sells almost as fast as he sells it. You are still a family unit and ration out your meat."

"You?" she asked curiously. "Doolittle, you make it sound as though I were the voice of authority around here."

"Aren't you, Mrs. Reed?" he chuckled.

Tamsen blushed at the compliment. Later she felt humble when Doolittle came in with a woven birch frame that would keep George Donner's mattress up off the damp ground.

Mary Florence, who was quietly trying to help nurse George Donner without his knowing it, felt pride rather than jealousy over Doolittle's words and actions. She liked the feeling.

Stanton was discouraged by the futile attempts. He also began to worry about Sutter's Indians. They jabbered constantly at each other in Spanish. He wished that Antonio or Jean Baptiste were in this camp to help him understand them.

Their fear was not lack of food, but the hanging they would experience from Captain Sutter if these people became so desperate that they slaughtered and ate his mules.

Nature took care of that fear for them.

"I have devised another mountain-party plan," Bill Eddy exalted, taking over from Stanton without consultation.

"Weather is changing," Billy Graves advised.

"Just a little rain."

The next day he said: "Just a little snow that is melting as quick as it hits the ground."

And the next: "It will break any moment now."

Instead of breaking, it put down three feet in twenty-four hours and still kept falling in a strangely languid fashion. Even the nearer cabins lost contact and it grew more difficult by the hour to secure firewood.

Windowless they did not notice that it rose to the cabin roof tops and above. They lost track of days, as November changed into December.

A few days of such close confinement was near impossible. Eight to ten days was near impossible.

"What manner of weather is this?" Lavina snarled, even her nerves finally getting on edge.

Two men, on either side of the mountain were wondering the same question.

Paddy Breen looked at his son John in horrible disbelief. "They *what*?"

"I plowed through the snow until it almost collapsed and smothered me, but they are all gone. Our last four cattle, the horses and even Sutter's mules. They have frozen and the drifts covered them over."

Paddy Breen lay motionless and unthinking. Like James Frazier Reed, and Midas before him, he was soon to find that all of his new-found wealth would buy him really nothing because there were no foodstuffs to purchase back.

James Frazier had the foodstuffs and no one to

purchase. His differences solved with Lanceford Hastings over Glaucus, he had been given a line of credit with Captain Sutter and sent back out with an again-healthy Mac McCutchen and Walt Herron. But the Sierras from the west were just as storm laden as the Sierra from the east.

At Fort Sutter, a few days before, James Frazier had chided Hastings about a passage in his *Guide*. The man's answer was now almost heart-sickening:

"My dear Reed, I penned those words after a single venture through the land. Yes, I made reference to the mildness and uniformity of the climate. But reread to note that I stated this was applicable only to the valleys and the plains. The wary emigrant would have noted that I stated that the mountains present but one eternal winter. Sutter can tell you that he has seen snow fall in those mountains on the nation's birthday. But take heart! My vast party is through and the Stanton supplies will see your party through. You take your supplies back in vain, but then you are a caring father. The Hastings route is well established for thousands to now follow."

Doolittle might have choked had he heard such words spoken. He was almost beyond choking. Even mountain men get lost in such a storm and he had been out in its fierceness for over eight days. Somewhere back on the routeless trek his only real possession in life had turned cold on him and had not risen the next morning. Doolittle had cried over the nameless beast that he just called "horse" until the tears froze on his cheeks. The saddle was too much for him to shoulder through the wet drifts, so he finally just took his bedroll and a single saddlebag.

It had to cross his mind, as he plowed back toward somewhere, if this had all been worth it. He had not found the Germans, he had supplied a bit of fresh game until it ran out, but other than that, little else.

He stumbled into the Donner camp, never fully realizing that his words and deeds had been keeping two women strong enough to make this camp far more death-proof than the other.

Tamsen and Mary Florence wrapped him in the last available quilt and built the fire high.

"He is not going to make it."

"Nonsense," Tamsen scolded, "his breed always makes it."

"What do you mean by 'his breed'?" Mary Florence asked, a little snottily.

"Exactly that," Tamsen answered, without taking offense. "He is set apart from the rest of us. Have you noticed that we women seem to be standing up under all this strain and lack of food better than the men? I am sure that is true in the other camp, as well. Not Doolittle! This is the first time he has let anything get him down. Tomorrow, I hope he realizes the Germans weren't worth all of this bother."

"You know? He told you?"

"No one had to tell her anything," George Donner said quietly from his raised bed behind them. "I questioned his return and Tamsen pieced together its reason. Young buck has been trying to keep us all from murder, but keeping us in food at the same time. Tamsen, is *my* guide warm enough?"

Tamsen smiled. Doolittle was under the ten thousand dollar quilt.

Two other men had struggled through the last days of that storm and collapsed at the other camp.

The first was Baylis Williams. The shy, sensitive young man was a lost soul without his sister. Although always a good worker, the other teamsters oft times made fun of his childlike ways. Cooped up with them in the wigwam for so long he could no longer take being the brunt of their unintended mean and sadistic jokes. It took him two days to make the five miles.

Communication were such between the three cabins that as Eliza and Mary Ann began caring for the failing Baylis, they were not aware that Patrick Dolan, while searching for wood, had found the near-frozen body of Augustus Spitzer near the Breen cabin. He was too weak to rise by himself and the gangling clown had to carry him.

Spitzer was failing more from exposure than hunger, and a mentally sapping case of fear.

On the first day of the storm, a power struggle had developed between the Germans over the remaining food and how it should be rationed, should the storm prove to be of the lasting duration of the first storm.

The verbal battle turned into a bodily struggle during the night. Reinhardt, being the stronger, soundly thrashed Spitzer and threw him out of the wagon with only the clothes he wore. Then he sadistically threatened Spitzer with rifle shots into the snow drift around him. As Reinhardt had been the one to fire the shot that killed Hans Wolfinger, Spitzer had fled for his life.

That he was alive, after a week in the storm, was amazing. His hands and feet were frost-bitten all the way to the bone. His eyes had sunken into deep hollows and were staring points of nothingness.

His clothing was like stiff boards that Dolan and John Breen had to cut away from his body. His skin was a strange blue from the exposure.

"I cannot keep him as a patient," Paddy said meanly, from his own sickbed, "unless he has some way to pay for his keep."

As John Breen took away the frozen woolen trousers he noticed the bulge in the right pocket. He

reached in, half extracted the object causing the
bulge, and quickly turned his body to hide his action
from Patrick Dolan.

As though going to place the trousers by the fire
to thaw, he hesitated just long enough by his father's
bed to secretly drop the object into Paddy's hand
and warn him to silence with his eyes.

Paddy looked down at the sparkling emeralds
housed in the heavy gold link chain. He tucked it
quickly under the covers, knowing full well where
he had seen it before. Until Spitzer could account for
having it, he would keep it for "patient" payment.

Later, when it was shown to Peggy Breen, the
Irishwoman sensed the worst.

"Ill-found gain ain't ours to keep, Paddy."

"She's with the Donners," he said savagely. "Do
you want to trot right on down to them and return
it to her?"

"Didn't say that," she said, on a worried note.
"I'm just fearing the other one coming about looking
for him and what they must have stolen."

"Then stop fearing. Just warn the family that no
one is to know that Spitzer is here."

Thus Charles Stanton did not learn of it, although
in the cabin a hundred and fifty feet away.

Besides, he was too busy with a scheme with Uncle
Billy Graves and had spent most of his time down
at that cabin.

"Well, what do you think of the oxbows now?"

Uncle Billy had been raised in the heavy snow
country of the Green Mountains, Stanton in northern
New York. They were used to "eternal winter" and
how to transport oneself about in it.

Uncle Billy grinned as he flexed the oxbow that
Stanton had managed to saw into strips.

"It's good hickory, Charley, and the U-shape is
near enough the size of a snowshoe frame. They won't

have the turned-up toe and tapering heel, but except for you and me the others will have to be taught to use them anyway. Now, what about webbing?"

"I've been collecting all the reins, whips, anything that is rawhide. I figure that if we soak them in water they will be soft enough to weave back and forth. Then we'll let them sit in the cold to dry and harden."

"Gonna take a heap of material, Charley."

"Now that the weather is clearing I can go get all the oxbows and rawhide off the wagons at the lake. Thornburg should be along soon and we can send him back to do the same at the Donner camp. Oh, Breen's a problem. Wouldn't even let me in the cabin to talk with him. Won't give up any of his oxbows or rawhide because he still holds out hope that his son will be able to find the missing cattle and mules."

"Fool!" Uncle Billy spat. "Getting hard enough to find wood that ain't green under these damnable drifts. Cold or no, last night, I told the women they would have to cuddle up closer because I wasn't going to waste wood keeping the fire up all night."

"That's hard on your patient, isn't it."

"Ain't cold or hunger ailing Baylis, Charley. It's lack of salt on all this damn lean meat we have been eating. Salt and some vegetables would take away some of the fatigue we feel when doing hardly nothing."

Unexpectedly Charles Stanton laughed. "Never thought I would see the day when I would hanker for a plate of beans. Got so sick of them on the salt desert I thought I would puke."

Uncle Billy didn't laugh. "We cursed the damn salt then and now crave just a little pinch of it."

It was curious that even with this thought they kept their hopes and planning centered on the white wall of the pass. No one ever thought of going back eastward to better climes for hunting, or while they still had mules to make it back out to the desert for salt.

They kept their eyes westward, their fingers busy on the snowshoes and their bodies fatigued as it became more difficult each day to go farther and farther afield to cut and drag firewood through the deep snow.

Each day saw more and more snowshoes constructed, because each day the number grew who felt themselves strong enough to make the journey.

Noah James made it up from the Donner camp to check on Baylis and give them bad news on Doolittle. His exposure had resulted in a deep chest cold and he was starting to spit up blood with each wracking cough.

It was bad news for Charles Stanton. He needed a man like Doolittle to help him get the snowshoe party through. It was thirty miles through the pass to Bear Valley. Even at five miles a day—that was six days. He also needed more supplies from the Donner party for the shoes, for food and for manpower. Oddly, he thought the Donner camp far better off than the ones at the cabins.

"The weather is threatening to change," he told Noah. "I want you to get back with one of these shoes as an example and get the teamsters to making them. I'll need them all and all the food they can bring along."

"I'll go with him," Milt Elliott said. "I've been helping to make them and can show them how faster."

"Don't you need to stay to help with Baylis?"

Milt shook his head. He knew that only God could now help Baylis.

It was the ninth of December when they departed. After a single mile of travel the third storm in forty-three days broke. In those days they had only seen the sun for twenty of them. It took Milt and Noah nearly ten hours to make the last four miles to the Donner camp. The snowshoe party were planning on making five miles a day up through the pass. Milt and Noah would not get back to warn them of the struggle they had had even at this lower elevation.

It snowed for five days. The Donner and Reed teamsters couldn't even gather the materials, let alone start making them. Fuel for survival was more important than snowshoes. Wagon canvas tents didn't hold in the heat as well as the logs of the cabins.

The day after the storm Milt sent Antonio back with the word that it would take the Donner people at least a week to ten days to prepare. Because the small-boned man was down to a hundred pounds he had very little difficulty keeping on top of the under-crust from the previous storm and so failed to report the difficulties that Milt and Noah had encountered.

The mild-mannered Charles Stanton flew into a rage. He had counted so on food supplies from the Donners, and Antonio had come without even food for himself. He didn't even ask if the Mexican wished to go along. He just pointed at a pair of snowshoes, told him to make plans with the Spanish-speaking Indians, and stormed across the snowdrifts that hid the Breen cabin and Keseberg lean-to from view.

"Can't let you in," John Breen said through the crack in the door. "Paw is right sick again."

Stanton could hear him moaning dreadfully, not knowing it was Spitzer, but it mattered not to him.

"Look, tell him we are going for the good of all. I need some meat for myself, the Indian guides and the Mexican."

"Not likely you'll get much from Paw."

John was pushed aside and Patrick Dolan opened the door halfway.

"Half the cattle we got through to here were mine,

Stanton. Dig into the stack and take a quarter of jerky. Then count on me going along."

The door was quickly closed and Stanton plowed to the snow heaped stack beside the cabin. Dutch Charley came out of the lean-to to help.

"Lewis is still bad off. I'll be going to bring back food for this family. Phillipine has prepared me enough jerky for the six days. Don't leave her much, but she'll make do till I return."

Stanton nearly cried as they dug out the frozen hindquarter of oxen. Margaret Reed, who was worse off than anyone, had offered a portion of her skimpy supplies. Now Phillipine Keseberg would short herself for Dutch Charley, while next to the greedy Breen cabin were stacked the frozen quarters of a good dozen cattle and oxen.

He knew it wasn't fair, but he was at least thankful that he would have two men like Dutch Charley and Patrick Dolan along.

Even though some were dipping toward the point of starvation, and this party would be going out with most skimpy supplies, it never crossed a single mind how easy it would have been to steal from Paddy Breen's pile. They were not that kind of thinking people, as yet.

Peggy Breen waited until she heard the two men leave the side of the cabin.

"Patrick, why must you go?"

"Paddy can't. John's strong, but too young. I'm it to get us back something other than beef."

"Which you just gave some away without cash in return!" Paddy snarled.

Quietly the clown became serious as he turned. "And I intend on taking a few more quarters over to Mrs. Reed before I depart."

"Like hell you will!" Paddy exploded. "What will she use to pay you for it?"

"The full belly I had after we started carrying some of their supplies. Did they ask for pay?"

"We cared for them for the pay!"

"And ate it all up, too."

"What in the hell is the matter with you?"

"What in the hell is the matter with you?" Dolan snapped right back. "You refused Eddy water for his children. Peggy refused them food. You charged Foster twenty-five dollars for a quarter of beef. Peggy, have you ever paid back a damn thing you ever borrowed from Lavina? Paddy, how many of these men helped get your wagons and cattle through? Perhaps, because I am a bachelor, you don't think my property rights stand for much. Well, I've just changed my mind on something. I'm going to tell Mrs. Reed that she and her children can have all of my share of cattle that is left."

"Like hell," Paddy repeated. "I will see you dead first!"

Patrick Dolan grinned evilly. On his horse-like face, grown gaunt from nothing but a meat diet, it became an ugly mask.

"Spitzer mumbles in his delirium," he said cunningly. "You think I don't know about that necklace you clutch under the blanket. It has Wolfinger's blood on it. If you wish to add mine to it, go right ahead. I don't think I know you anymore, so it will only be a stranger killing me."

"No," Paddy glowered, "I will leave that damn pass to kill you and all the other foolhardy ones."

Then a coughing spell put him flat back on the bed. It was echoed by Spitzer from his corner.

Peggy Breen quickly crossed herself, as though to ward off all this evil talk of death.

John Breen stood a little puzzled. Both men were like fathers to him, but which one was really right in this matter?

12

THEIR SIXTH DAY was the twenty-first of December—
the shortest day of the year.

Charles Stanton sat by the campfire smoking his
pipe. It was his last pinch of tobacco. The summit
had been reached but before them were heavily for-
ested mountains, so deep in snow that he did not
recognize them.

Hardly the five miles a day that they had planned.
Hardly the departure they had planned, or the personnel.

Baylis Williams died the night before they left. It
put Mary Ann Graves into such a despondent mood
that her father decided she should go along. Because
Sarah Graves Fosdick did not trust her husband Jay
alone with her sister, she, too, decided to go.

Something akin to this had happened in the Murphy clan. Foster was determined to go, along with

Lem and William, but when the widow Harriet Murphy Pike determined she was strong enough to go, "Sour Sarah" determined the same. This made Amanda McCutchen demand to be taken along.

This left Lavina with quite a parcel of children to mother.

Nothing had gone as Charles Stanton had planned. The first night they could still see the smoke from the cabins and Dutch Charley had been forced to turn back with a totally worn out William Murphy. The snowshoes were cumbersome and sometimes better left off than on.

Appreciation of Stanton was renewed when the pass was reached the next day, as he had done twice before. It held as the third day was an easy downhill course. But the treeless expanse introduced them to a seemingly endless field of dazzling whiteness in the heavy sunlight. Their pale skin turned pink from burning and Stanton, himself, suffered the worst from snow-blindness.

By late afternoon they were almost grateful for the snow flurries that broke out. By nighttime they regretted such thoughts as the flurries brought with them furiously blowing freezing winds.

The next day the flurries had become fierce squalls with the party stretching out and Stanton the laggard. He could barely see and left the Indians to get them down into the Yuba Bottoms. The landmark should have been the high dome of Cisco Butte. He could not see it due to snow-blindness. They could not see it because of the storm. He almost stumbled through the camp without seeing them.

The next day was clear, but a four mile uphill struggle that took the whole day. The same followed for the next day, but with the growing realization that the snow was deeper on this side of the divide and would remain so till Bear Valley or beyond.

Mary Ann approached the pipe-smoking man.

"What are you thinking?"

Stanton smiled to himself. "Of the valley of the Sacramento. As it is eternal winter here, it is eternal summer there. Strange what a difference a few miles can make."

"Are you coming? We are ready."

"Yes," he smiled, "I am coming soon."

Antonio headed out, jabbering away at the Indians, who spoke Spanish almost as well as he did himself. The others followed.

That was the last they saw of Charles Stanton.

He was a victim of the few miles difference of which he spoke. Where he sat smoking his last drags of tobacco was not far from the spot where James Frazier and Mac McCutchen had been turned back by a storm five weeks before. A spot where they had cached beef jerky and flour and carefully marked it. It could not be missed if the party came along the trail.

But the Indians, with Antonio jabbering away, did not keep to the trail. They made a fatal mistake by turning downhill into the uncharted, look-alike canyon maze of the American River. They headed away from Bear Valley with their last day's provision of food.

"What do you think you are doing?"

Doolittle Thornburg sat and looked at Mary Florence MacDuff as though she were the last person in the world who had the right to ask him such a question. Beneath the quilt he knew he was as naked as a jay-bird and equally knew that she would be responsible.

"I am reaching about for my clothing," he said, embarrassed that Tamsen and the children sat close by and George Donner lay on the other side of the fire. If Mary Florence had done to him, what he suspected she had done to him, in front of all these eyes he was really going to be embarrassed.

"You are still too weak to have need of them, so just lie back down."

"But . . . but . . ." he tried to protest.

Tamsen came and squatted down beside him.

"You've been very sick, Doolittle. Now don't start being an unruly patient. Mary Florence and I have had our hands full between you and my husband."

Doolittle turned scarlet. "You saw me like this?"

"Oh, Doolittle," she chuckled, "I hardly found you any different from my own husband. Mary Florence, see to him, while I dish him up a bowl of soup from Margaret Reed's Christmas present."

"Christmas?" he asked in surprise.

"Well," Mary Florence laughed, "actually a few days before, but already snowing, as though we really needed a white Christmas. A few days ago Margaret Reed sent down two quarters of beef by Lavina Murphy. Lord knows where she got them, but those are her Christmas presents to everyone. One was sent over for the teamsters. Tamsen, being Tamsen, had to gather up some things and send Sol back with Lavina."

"Christmas," he repeated, but this time almost on a note of puzzlement and he laid back down. "I had almost forgotten that it could make people different for a single day out of the year."

"Tamsen," she laughed, "is the same all the time."

"And you?"

Tears sprang to her eyes. "Hearing you be snotty again was all the Christmas I prayed for, Thorny."

"Thorny? No more Doo or Doolittle?"

"Well," she sniffed, "Thorny does rhyme better with what you usually are."

He reached out and took her hand. "I can't think

of a thing that would rhyme with Mary Florence—
except love."

Margaret Reed turned back, having gotten her emotions under control. She waved Elizabeth Graves and
her children over from their half of the cabin to
view the marvelous Christmas basket Sol Hook had
brought from the Donners. They hung back a little
hesitantly, although Billy was dying to pump Sol
for every last bite of information he had about
Elitha.

"I am sure that it is meant for us all," Margaret
said generously. "The gifts of the Magi, really."

"I'm not so sure about one of the articles," Sol said,
a little dubiously. "I forgot about it being in the
wagon until the other day. Cattle didn't really need
to lick on it across the desert and it was put away.
Aunt Tammy broke it up and shared."

He gingerly lifted up the little bag and held it
out as though Margaret Reed would dash it from
his hand with a stinging insult.

She took it in trembling hands. "Lizzy Graves,
would you come look. Tamsen has sent us enough
flour to make dumplings for that beef broth. Three
potatoes, from God knows where, a loaf of sugar,
two jars of strawberry preserves and this most precious gift of all. Salt!"

"Been licked upon," Sol warned.

"My dear boy," Margaret roared with laughter, "I
could hardly care less if they used their other end
upon it! It will add some savor we haven't had for
a long, long time. Oh, I know it is still three days
till Chirstmas. But it is snowing, the presents have
come, and what does the day mean anyhow. Sol, you
will stay for our Christmas supper. Lizzy, come to
help me. No, Eliza, you stay and chat with the young

folk. You work hard enough as it is. Oh, Merry Christmas, everyone!"

Less than thirty miles over the mountains from them no such cheer rang out. No one brought a basket of Christmas goodies. Eleanor Eddy had put an extra pound of bear meat in Bill's pack, but even in depriving herself to see that her husband got through, it was gone and he had not made it.

By an odd quirk of fate the people back at the camp had lost a day. Those on the mountainside had not. As they laid green wood down upon the snow to build a fire upon, they were most aware that it was Christmas eve. They were also most aware of a most strange conversation that had been popping up during the last three days in which they had eaten nothing. Conversation, but no final conclusion, although the meaning was obvious.

"Man, over the centuries has eaten almost everything on earth."

"To stay alive, I guess that he has."

"But he has had to kill it first. We have not even seen a coyote or owl to kill."

"No, but we have. . . ." Eddy did not finish and the pause lengthened.

"Each other," Patrick Dolan closed the pause reluctantly.

They sat in stunned and disbelieving silence. Dolan, even though he might have lost, had been willing to suggest a drawing of lots, so that the body of one might provide survival for the others. Eddy had been thinking of a much more dramatic event. A duel between the two weakest. Then he reasoned differently. The weak were going to fall soon enough as it was.

But the idea had been planted, and as the fire

roared up no one knew for sure if the one sitting next to them wished to butcher them like an ox, or cut their throat in their sleep like a sheep. Even family members began to question the look in the eyes of their kin.

Without saying it aloud, everyone knew it was a draw between Antonio and Uncle Billy Graves. They were both failing fast, but neither one would give in.

The fire was warming, piled upon the green logs, but it did little to soothe their starving bellies. They had experienced hallucinations from the snow-blindness, near as much as they had gone through on the desert. But half-mad with hunger this aroma was maniacal to taunt their craving for food. Roasting meat when there was none?

Eddy had watched Antonio's arm and hand fall into the fire. When it had not been instantly pulled back he had drawn it forth. A moment later the young Mexican made a rattling sound in his throat and the arm was flung out again. Eddy was cold, fatigued and perplexed. Logic told him that it no longer mattered to Antonio as the flames began to shrivel his hand to a burned coal. Suddenly, that seemed a horrible waste to his gnawing belly and he put out his foot to thrust more of the arm and body in for roasting. Here was food for all of the camp.

The others looked on in anxiety, despair, confusion, hopefulness, disbelief, hunger, madness and even a desire to not think on it at all.

A moment later every thinking process was reversed. Wind, hail, and snow beat down on them so suddenly and with such incredible force that it jolted their minds away from Antonio. The only way to keep themselves from freezing was to pile more and more wood upon the fire.

The heat became so intense that it not only burned Antonio to a cinder, but ate into the green foundation of logs and began to melt the snow—which went unnoticed.

Like mad creatures they kept the altar fire alight until they were wading about in ice-cold water eight feet below the surface of the snow outside.

"Got to get out of here," Uncle Billy mumbled, starting to fall into a stupor.

"Everybody out!" Eddy barked.

One of the Sutter Indians roused himself and clumsily tried to scale the snow wall. Half-frozen and starved, he fell back against the green wood pyre and upset it. Before anyone could react the burning logs were hissing in the water and winking out.

"You stupid heathen!" Jay Fosdick screeched, jumping the man and trying to choke him.

"Stop it!" Eddy commanded, wading over and pulling them apart. It was a strange command for a man who had earlier considered that two of them should duel to supply food. "Now get out of here, both of you."

Mary Ann already had helped to hoist her father and self from the pit. Then she reached back to give a hand up to her sister and Jay.

Eddy was out and spreading their blankets on the snow.

"Sit close together in a circle and I will cover us with blankets. It will be the only warmth we have until we find dry wood in the morning."

They heard his words, but to scale the eight feet was like climbing the pass all over again. The Murphy sisters had to overcome Foster's apathy and bodily drag him up and onto the blankets.

Not strong to begin with, Amanda McCutchen pleaded with the other women to come and help her get up the other men.

"A moment first," Uncle Billy wheezed. "Girls, use me to save yourselves."

They considered his words came from a delirious state and went to help. When they returned he was dead.

They sat under the tent-like blankets in stunned grief—their starved bodies giving some warmth as the storm roared on through the night and Christmas Day.

"Eddy," Patrick Dolan mumbled, "I have just talked with the Blessed Virgin about my plan."

Bill Eddy ignored him. Dolan had been mumbling strange, disconnected things for hours.

"You are our leader," he said, trying to get himself out from under the blanekts. "You and I can make it to the settlement in a few hours."

"Sit down, Patrick! You're sifting snow in!"

But Dolan was already crawling out from under and Eddy felt responsible to get him back. But by the time Eddy had wormed his way out, Dolan had taken off his boots and was discarding his clothing.

"What the hell?"

"The Mother of us all told me we could go faster this way. Disrobe so we can be off!"

Eddy picked up the clothes and tried to force them back into Dolan's arms. Deranged, he would not accept them and began pelting Eddy with his fists. Eddy had to back away from his delirious strength.

"If you cannot hear Her speak in the wind, then you are the fool," he screamed and began running through the snow.

Eddy knew he would be a fool to try and chase him down, but had enough of his own wits still about him to take the clothing back under the blankets.

They might help Lem Murphy, if nothing else. The thirteen-year-old could not overcome the shakes and shivering. Falling into his own delirious state he could only talk wildly about food. It did not help the mental condition of anyone.

The silence that Patrick had broken seemed to give them all voice to wail and shriek at Lem for further silence.

"Here, darling, let your sister hold you in her arms."

Sarah Foster held him close, nestling his head upon her breast, rocking gently and singing softly. For once she really had something to be sour against the world about, but was a calming influence for all.

So calming that when they heard Patrick come crawling back they pulled him back under the blankets without comment. His run had exhausted his strength and his voice. As calm as the rest, he laid down in the center of the circle and was almost instantly asleep. His final sleep.

That night they all tried to sleep somewhat as the storm still raged.

"*Caramba!*" the Indian screamed, then began to curse in his own tongue, as he looked at the deep tooth marks on the back of his hand.

"I was dreaming," Harriet Pike whimpered. "I was a child again and didn't have to fight anyone for a drumstick. There were so many and I grabbed the first one."

"Did you have to pick a live one?" Foster chuckled.

Half comatose, the joke was not appreciated by the survivors. Nor was the storm. Only because they could make out figures a little better did they know it was the day after Christmas. They had been under the blankets now for over thirty hours. Most weren't even aware any longer that their limbs were numbed to non feeling.

"It is still impossible to build a fire outside," Eddy said.

No one answered him.

Perhaps he was suffering from a bit of delirium himself at that moment. He put Patrick Dolan's boots down in the center of the circle where the clown had slept his last. He sprinkled them, as though it were seasoning, with gun-powder from his tinder. Foolishly, he did not recap the powderhorn and in the awkward position he was forced to work in, his knee knocked it closer to the boots and sprinkled out another line of dry powder.

The first strike of the flint on steel jumped a spark right down onto the line. With a roar and flash the powderhorn exploded right up into Eddy's face, sending flying particles to cut a gash in Amanda McCutchen's forehead and a half dozen cuts in Sarah's hands that she used to protect Lem's head.

It was unneeded protection. He had breathed his last before the accident.

"No!" Eddy bellowed, but not because of his badly burned face and hands. He would not let the storm outlast him. Forgetting his pain he struggled from under the blankets and was determined to get wood for a fire.

The pound of bear meat gave him just that much more strength than the others, but it had gone through his body a long time before.

After two hours he was nearly exhausted and had found nothing but storm-soaked wood.

He stood by the snow-covered mound of people and wanted to cry. Was this to be their communal burial site? At first he thought the warmth on his face was from the powder burn and he gritted his teeth against the pain. Then he had to blink his eyes against another pain. It was bright, dazzling and brought black specks before his eyes.

Then he did weep. "The sun! It is still snowing, but the sun is breaking through the clouds. Oh, my dear God, does it feel good!"

What came out from beneath the blankets was more animal than human. They stank, but they were not smelling. Their eyes were near maniacal, but they were not looking at each other. They were near blinded themselves by staring up at the sun and capturing some of its warm rays on their gaunt faces.

Five days they had been without food, but now the sun renewed their will to live.

As they had done before they found a dead pine that was full of pitch, but had no more tinder to ignite it. Everything about them, and upon them, was wet or damp.

"My mantle," Harriet Pike mused, "it is cotton-fleece-lined and has been keeping me dry."

Again they were sharing. The cotton was damp, but held to the sun it was soon dry enough to take a flint spark that could be gently blown into a flame.

The pitch refused to believe that it was damp and roared up to dry the bark and burn higher. They gathered around its warmth. Now all they lacked was food.

As weak as the rest, the Indians climbed into other dead trees and knocked down branches. The first load they hauled back the emigrants used to build a fire closer to the ground. The second load they quietly took a little distance away to ignite their own fire.

While they had been gathering dead branches they had seen Foster take his knife to cut green branches and whittle their ends to points. Then they had seen him stand silently for a long time over the near-nude body of Patrick Dolan.

Stoically they sat by their fire with their backs turned so they would not have to see any more.

The spitted strips of flesh sizzled and popped as they thawed and cooked.

Others took knives and cut spitting sticks. Then, averting the faces of the others, approached the frozen carcass—for through their weeping eyes it had to cease to have human form.

"I think," Eddy said weakly, refusing to participate even though he had been one of the original suggestors of this course, "that I best go and find more wood. This won't last long."

It was not the manner of meal one sat and chatted over. Each cut more branches and made crude beds under the burning tree. No one spoke as they made trip after trip back to the cooking fire and then back to their boughs.

Sparks and burned-through branches fell about them and they paid them no mind. They were primeval people just learning the value of fire and what it could do to change the taste of raw flesh. Primeval enough that they had not as yet learned the art of communication.

A fourth did not eat. Lem Murphy was too far sunk into a stupor. Throughout the rest of the day and evening Sarah sat rocking and soothing him.

The tree continued to burn into the night as though wishing to be an eternal flame for this spot.

Eddy finally gave in as a quarter moon began to swing through the cloudless sky, but as though he had brought this upon Patrick Dolan, he would not eat of that flesh. Neither would the Graves girls and Jay Fosdick touch of Uncle Billy, even though he had ordered it.

The Indian war-party of two finally finished their long and deliberate council near midnight. Unless they wished to be next on the spits, they needed food to stay as strong or stronger than the white men and women.

At moon-set Lem died. They gently took him from Sarah's arms. She fell into the first sleep she had allowed herself in forty hours.

Sunday morning came bright and dazzling. It was the twenty-seventh. They had been gone for twelve days—twice the time they had allotted. Refreshed by food and undisturbed prone sleep, they had to reestablish communications among themselves and a systematic manner for what they were about.

"The first thing we have to realize," Eddy said, taking command, "is that we are lost and Stanton had the only compass. The powder is gone for the rifle and we don't have too many shots left for the pistols. We will have to get quite close for any game. One meal isn't going to strengthen us, so we had best rest here for a couple more days. We will also need that time to roast and dry every bit of available food to take with us."

Sarah Foster came awake during the bustle of activity. Coming out of such a deep sleep she was chilled and rose to go warm herself by the fire. Still benumbed by sleep she stood and watched a spitted heart broil over the coals. Then she turned and was violently ill. No one had to tell her that it was Lem Murphy's little heart.

13

WHEN THE STORM continued Margaret realized the mistake she had made. It had been a marvellous Christmas party, but she could have the one she had planned for her children anyway. Beneath the jewels in her case had been carefully hoarded away some tripe, a cupful of white beans, half a cup of rice, a few dried apples, and a piece of bacon two inches square.

With the hides from Patrick Dolan she felt most wealthy again.

"Sol, you will just have to stay through the storm and have a second Christmas with us."

"Of course he will stay," Eliza chirped, coming to twist a finger through his hair until it left a curl.

Sol blushed. The last two nights had been almost unbearable in embarrassment for him. The death of Baylis had made Eliza almost as childish as her

brother had been. One moment she would be kitten-
ish and the next almost sultry. Margaret didn't let
it worry her, because in such crowded conditions
it couldn't grow into a real embarrassment.

But before Sol could really answer the hide flapped
back from the doorway and Milt Elliott stomped in,
his beard powdered with snow.

He looked at them as though he couldn't believe
his eyes and then sighed.

"I thought to find you all sick and dying. That's
why I rushed back through the storm."

"Milt, what are you talking about?"

He looked as though he wished Sol Hook wasn't
there. "Some of the meat—tainted right bad. Made
the teamsters real sick. Noah James is still down with
it. Afraid Sam Shoemaker and James Smith were just
too weak to stand all that retching. Took them both
about an hour apart."

"And my family?" Sol gulped.

"They were saving theirs for Christmas, except for
soup. They be fine except . . . well, it's your . . .
well, Uncle Jake just didn't wake up yesterday morning. Went, peaceful-like."

Sol gulped again, this time to hold down the tears.
It was not as if he hadn't expected it. Jacob Donner
had been failing by the day, but he had somehow
expected the bad news to be about Uncle George.
He, too, was in a bad way because of the unhealing
hand.

"Guess I better tell you the other, too," Milt went
on. "Reinhardt came back, a raving lunatic. He confessed to killing Wolfinger and then killed himself.
Instead of going to pieces, Mrs. Wolfinger then confessed to all the stores they had in their wagon. As
soon as the storm passes, Thornburg is going to use
the snowshoes to go search it out."

It was almost too much bad news to absorb at

once and they stood strangely silent. And just as strangely, it was Elizabeth Graves, in her corner of the cabin who began to softly cry, as though the premonition she'd had since the departure of her husband had been confirmed.

The silence was broken by the flap being pushed back again and the fearful face of John Breen poked in.

"Paw says any who can help, come quick. No men at the other cabin and Dutch Charley is down sick."

He vanished without further comment. Milt Elliott immediately thought the help was needed because of the tainted meat, but this group had been eating it with apparently no ill-effects.

"I'll get help," Eliza said unexpectedly. "I will get help from my husband, who was not mentioned as ill."

She pulled a shawl over her head and darted out the door. Sol and Milt went after her. John Breen was plowing the half mile back as though his life depended upon it and Eliza was jumping into his tracks as though playing a game of hop-scotch.

"What in the hell got into her?"

"Baylis's death. She talks sometimes like they were back in Ireland as children and he was still alive. This latest notion is something new."

"Amazed more of us aren't foaming at the mouth, Sol. Now we best set our minds to finding a few more dead ones."

They found no human dead, although Dutch Charley was failing fast. Upon returning Bill Murphy to Lavina he felt a failure in not bringing back food for Phillipine and her children. In the night he had stolen one of the quarters, but Lewis turned moralistic and refused any portion of it for his family. The starved Karl Burger had eaten and grown ill.

They found one dead wolf, clubbed to death by Paddy Breen's homemade crutch.

They found Paddy Breen ranting and raving and waving the crutch at a pack of ten to twelve other wolves who were dragging away the rest of his carcasses.

"Stop them!" he screamed, turning his wrath on them. "That fool of a son used up all my ammunition and didn't hit a one."

"I tried, Paw," John wailed.

Across the snowfield was a strange sight. The rest of the wolf pack were proving smarter than man. They would gnaw into a frozen carcass until they had it a bit thawed and the meat juices flowing. Some were backing away from their stolen bad quarters and snarling and fighting with those who stayed haunched down and gnawing.

"Well? Well?" Paddy demanded.

"Some of that meat has cost lives," Milt declared drily.

"Nonsense!"

"Made Dutch Charley right sick," Phillipine declared from the flap of the lean-to.

"I have sold him none!" Breen flared.

The wolves barked at his loud voice. Then they whimpered as they sniffed at the rest of the pile and left almost in disgust.

"What are those that are left?" Milt demanded.

Peggy Breen answered, for she had slaughtered them. "The oxen that weakened and died from their arrow wounds."

"Then the Diggers must have used something on their arrows to make them sick and the people sick who eat of them. It is all a horrible waste."

"But it is all I have left," Paddy cried.

He had nothing left. The milch cattle had been

on top. They had been sold off, with some going to Stanton, a good quarter to Margaret, and less than a quarter thawing in his cabin. Then there would be none.

"We have plenty left," Eliza giggled, "and gold plates to serve it upon."

For the moment she was ignored because of a ghost-like figure that had pulled himself to the door of the Breen cabin.

"And I know where there is a treasure trove of food," Spitzer called out in German and then collapsed again.

"Peggy, see to the poor man," Paddy said, in almost too gentle a manner, then lamely added: "He wandered in, and we have been seeing to him."

"Poor, poor dear," Eliza clucked. "I will just have to have Lewis tell me what he said."

Milt went and took her by the arm. The sight of Spitzer had almost unnerved him. Reinhardt had claimed to have killed the man. "We will take care of her, Mrs. Keseberg, thank you."

She nodded curtly, her mind still on Spitzer's words. She would just have to get Lewis on his feet to talk with the German if he knew where there was food to be had.

Eliza smiled sweetly at Milt. "Where are we going?"

"It's time for you to get back to fix dinner, Eliza."

"Oh, yes, Baylis will be in soon with the cattle to help me set up the table."

He nodded and whispered to Sol. "Can you get back to Doolittle in this storm?"

"I can try."

"He must know about Spitzer, Keseberg's wife understood his German and I think it had to do with the Wolfinger's food. I have a hunch the German's wagon is closer to this camp than the one below. If

murder was done for it one time, then murder could
be done for it again."

Strange words for Milt Elliott, who had almost
murdered twice on the trail.

The children had their fine Christmas dinner. With
fine dignity the adults refused to join in. With the
Dolan beef now known to be useless, her hoard used
up, Margaret was reduced to two final choices. The
hides which had been used to roof the cabin and
the children's pet dog.

On the trail, as it turned into a new year, they had
feasted on a deer that Eddy had shot—and then
they feasted on Jay Fosdick. But it was not enough.
Schemes came out of their madness and starvation.
They began to look upon the two Indians as little
more than animals like the deer. The attempt to murder them was a disaster and left only a trail of tan-
talizing blood to follow. But the Indians refused to
die and so the weakest among them began to plot
the next meal.

"Amanda," Foster giggled inanely. "She is a nui-
sance and holds us back."

Eddy had an ounce of civilization left in him.
"Good God, man, she is a wife and mother."

Foster shrugged. "The Graves sisters are no longer
wife or mother."

A shout rang out. The Indians had collapsed on
the trail. Foster ran forward and two shots echoed
through the woods.

They had been twenty-five days on the trail. William Foster, his face haggard, his beard matted, his
eyes hot with frenzy, had just dipped to a level
lower than the caveman.

Sarah Fosdick, Mary Ann Graves and Eddy now

camped a little away from Foster, his wife and sister-in-law. He was no longer sane and who would be next in his maniacal mind when the Indians were fully consumed?

Because they were slowly coming down out of the snow country, the three began to fill their bellies with grass in a self-preservation move to allow Foster his full ration of meat.

They still had eight days before they would make it to the first settlement on the edge of the Sacramento Valley. Seven out of fifteen.

At the camps, they still buried their dead under the snow:

Dutch Charley—four days after Christmas.

The Keseberg's young son Lewis.

Young Landrum Murphy.

At the upper camp that wasn't all of their woes. Lavina Murphy went blind and the Reed's pet dog went into the stew pot. John Breen took sick and Spitzer seemed to get better.

Desperate, Margaret made a heroic gamble that was a near disaster. Shepherding out the younger children, she took Milt, Eliza and Virginia to assault the pass and find rescuers.

Eliza turned back the first night, more addlepated than ever. Four days later they were all back, frostbitten, starved and driven out of the Sierras by yet another five-day storm.

Having fought the mountain and lost, they now had to fight for shelter—and again they lost. Elizabeth Graves, now sure that her family members had perished, held them out of the cabin at gun point, for what roof hides remained over the rear half she would boil down for her own children and no other.

Ironically, although Lavina had ample room and

could have used the help, Peggy Breen, as though trying to appease God, took them in to make fifteen within that cabin.

It would have been sixteen, but Paddy Breen flatly refused to have Milt Elliott.

He found refuge with Lavina Murphy. Throughout the rest of January and early February he became as good a servant to her and the children as he had been to the Reeds.

Unable to write words on paper Lavina coached eleven-year-old Simon as to the message to carry across to Margaret:

"Our dear friend and trusted servant has departed us to his maker."

None were aware that all manner of relief parties had been formed to reach them since the half-crazed Eddy had made it to the Johnston ranch, and that James Frazier and Mac McCutchen were again attempting to get back to their families.

Communications over the Sierras were nearly as impossible as communications with the Donners five miles to the east.

Fortunately, except for a slim diet, matters had stayed much the same there since Christmas. George Donner held onto a thread of life, Noah James with the Hook brothers did the chores, Elizabeth glowered at Johanna's skirts, Leanna Donner took down with a bad cold, and, when able, Doolittle went in search of the Reinhardt wagon.

It was most like a Yuletide message home full of the little nothings of each day.

Then a single event took place that gave them several hours of turmoil and conflict.

"I found it," Doolittle said sadly. "I couldn't tell if they had left it in such a shambles or if bears had gotten into the wagon. Stores of food? I hardly had enough to get me back here without anything from there. Nothing!"

Elizabeth Donner had waited long and patiently for this moment. With lightning speed, despite her weakness, she put out her hands and tried to tear away Johanna's skirt. The raw-boned woman, her jowls now nothing but deflated sacks, fought her off. They swayed back and forth, splintering a pine bough bed until Elizabeth was aware suddenly of other hands tugging feebly at her shoulders. She released Johanna, and turned her attention to an age-old opponent. Her big hands encircled Tamsen's thin throat and squeezed hard, her voice a maniacal shriek:

"She has food! Damn you, she has food under her skirt!"

"I have not!" Johanna wailed.

Before Doolittle and Mary Florence could pull Elizabeth away, she turned Tamsen loose and spun back on Johanna.

"Liar! I saw! You have little parcels of food attached to your petticoat."

"No!" Johanna wailed even louder. "It is all gone."

"Gone!" Elizabeth screeched. "You mean you ate it all, you greedy, fat old cow?"

"She gave it to me," Tamsen cried, her own nerves on a raw edge. "She gave it to me over a month ago."

"And you ate it all?" Elizabeth shot acidly. "What happened to my share?"

"Of course I ate it all," Tamsen retorted bitterly. "That's why Johanna gave it to me, can't you see? So that I could sit in a corner and secretly nibble on it each night."

Elizabeth grew so hysterical that it took every ounce of energy Doolittle and Mary Florence could muster to hold her back from clawing at Tamsen's face.

Tamsen felt a slow sickness spreading through her middle, as she realized what she must do. She stepped forward and slapped Elizabeth three times, back and forth across the cheeks.

"Get hold of yourself," she said sternly, "and stop playing your idiot role. Your children may still be alive because Johanna acted unselfishly. When you decide to act like a lady again, I pray she has the heart to forgive you."

Elizabeth glowered, her eyes blinded by all the hatred she still possessed for Tamsen, then in her customary way, she crushed herself onto Johanna, weeping and wailing and begging forgiveness.

"I don't see how you put up with her," Mary Florence said. "I would have smacked her weeks ago when she accused you of letting Uncle Jake die just to keep George alive."

Tamsen sighed. "Elizabeth's tongue always speaks before her mind can catch up to it. She will now have a good gossipy chat with Johanna and feel quite chipper again. Sometimes I envy her ability to close all of this worry out of her mind. Well, this time I guess we should thank her for bringing things into a sharp focus. Doo, I have maybe an impossible favor to ask of you and Mary Florence."

"Name it."

"Leave, while you can."

"I can't do that," Mary Florence protested.

"Listen to me," she growled. "This time no news does not mean good news. I have given up hope that Stanton got through to bring help. The mice that Elizabeth used to scream about—the boys can no longer find to put into the pot. The hides we cut off of the slaughtered cattle and threw aside I now have Sol and Noah dig into the snow to find so that they can be boiled."

"All the more reason for me to stay," Doolittle insisted, "so that I can start hunting game instead of that damn wagon."

"All the more reason for you to leave, Doolittle. I am not being brave about this, I am being sensible. Even if rescue came this very minute, what could I do about George? He couldn't go a mile without being transported. That's my favor. You two are young, and still fairly strong. Mary Florence can soon learn to use the snowshoes Milt made."

"I already know. We used them in Canada."

"One problem solved. I have a compass, a hidden parcel of jerky and Luke Halloran's money. It's already February. If you fight your way through, you could purchase a team and wagon and be back for George by early spring."

Bitter laughter rumbled in Doolittle's throat, but he kept his mouth closed so she would not hear it. She was thinking in terms of Illinois where in a good year the fields could be plowed by mid-March or early April. Here, where winter had come in September, it might last until May or June. But she was not giving up, that was the important thing.

"But one more thing," she went on, "that you must promise me. If it takes too long, or the storms continue at such a regular interval, stay in California and use the money to start your lives over again."

They both stood silent, with bands of iron wrapped around their hearts, welded there by all those months of struggle. She was being so practical about the matter that they wanted to cry. It was a favor they could not possibly turn down.

On the eighteenth of February the seven men of the Aquilla Glover rescue party, still haunted by the tales heard from Bill Eddy, were a mile away and five hundred feet below the gap through the jagged Sierras. Like the Eddy group, they had lost their way and had spent a week of sleepless struggle against the snow and storms. They had had to lighten their packs and cache the supplies to survive themselves.

Now, that tantalizingly close, Glover feared that he and young Daniel Rhoads would not make it. The others relieved them of their packs and began the triple work of climbing up through the light snow.

They had left the Johnson's ranch on the fourth. It had taken them fourteen days.

James Frazier Reed had left Yerba Buena, which the American settlers called San Francisco, with supplies and a rescue team on the seventh. They would not make it to the ranch until the twenty-second, because of flood conditions, but kept sending messages ahead.

Doolittle and Mary Florence had left the Donner camp on the fourteenth. They saved time by not going by the northern camp and snowshoed right across the frozen surface of the lake.

He as a mountain man and she as a northwoods woman were better suited to the journey than any one who had gone before, or any coming their way. They had kept their packs small, their clothing warm but light—Mary Florence decked out in garments borrowed from Sol Hook—and paced themselves against fatigue. Doolittle had fashioned poles so that their arms could do some of the work, pushing them along on some of the harder surfaces.

There was no need to waste time in hunting for wood and building a fire. Doolittle knew how to sleep warmly and comfortably under the snow—and they would only sleep for two hours, push on for six and then sleep two more.

As the Glover party made it over the pass and started their descent down toward the lake, Doolittle and Mary Florence were walking into Johnson's ranch. It had taken just four incredible days!

As James Frazier was expected momentarily, they waited.

"Halloooo!"

There was no response. The cabins stood silent and smokeless.

Glover, in his exhaustion, almost wept. "After all this, have we failed?"

To stamp the thought out of their own minds the others began halloing together.

A cabin door creaked open. An unkempt and filthy creature timidly came forth.

Peggy Breen blinked and her voice cracked with emotion:

"Be ye men from California, or be ye coming from heaven?"

"From the one, but sent by the other," Glover cried, his own emotions unnerved at the sight of the flesh wasted on her large body.

His cry brought weeping and hysterically laughing people from the cabins and lean-to. They were like children receiving their first visit from Santa Claus. But it was a prudent Santa Claus who distributed food only in such quantities that would not make them sick. All they asked in return was information.

Paddy Breen, hobbling on his crutch, began reciting the dead from his diary.

"We are more interested in the living," Glover said gently.

Breen pursed his lips. "Well now, ain't had Billy Graves around here trying to borrow for two or three weeks. They be a half mile that way. Ain't heard tell of the Donner folk since around Christmas, I'd say. They be stubbornly five miles that away."

"Tucker take your pack to that nearer cabin. It's too late in the day to make the five miles. We will tackle it after some sleep and then start laying plans to get some of these people out of here."

The "some" caught Paddy Breen's ear. He began laying plans on who the "some" should be, but his famished and half-crazed mind kept getting confused on who was still alive and who was dead. He had to rifle through his diary to reacquaint himself on some matters.

Spitzer he knew had died on the seventh. As the man had started to get stronger from his frost-bite—and John Breen weaker—Paddy had cut down on Spitzer's ration to reverse the process. And on that day he had recorded that the Eddy baby had died in the morning and Eleanor Eddy that evening. Jimmy Eddy had been put in the care of the blind Lavina Murphy.

One too young and one too feeble to leave, in Breen's opinion.

By the time he had sorted it out in his opinionated mind, only the nine members of the Breen family would have been leaving.

The next day, after his first sleep in a week, Aquilla Glover could look at the matter as prudently as he had passed out the food. After sending three men to the Donner camp, he was able to size up the very weak from the not-too-strong, the young from the old and those just overwrought emotionally from those who seemed mentally unbalanced.

Paddy Breen didn't like it from the first. He was considered too ill and lame at this time, with enough food to last his family until the Reed relief supplies arrived. That Reed would be bringing them put Paddy into such a rage that Glover considered him mentally unbalanced. Still, John and Eddie Breen would be taken out.

The Reeds, with Eliza, would have to go because

they had been totally without supplies for the past week. Virginia was failing and the jewels Margaret had in the little case now fully belonged to Paddy Breen.

Elizabeth Graves took the news of the death of her husband and Jay Fosdick bitterly. She would send out Eleanor and Lavina, but keep Billy to help her with the other four.

Lavina Murphy decided that Mary and William, of twelve and eleven years, deserved to live. She had already given up to the grave Pike, John, Lemuel, Foster and a grandchild.

Lewis Keseberg lay on his back unable to move.

"It would be inhumane to leave me here all alone," he pleaded.

"I have made arrangements for you to be moved over to the Murphy cabin," Phillipine answered, preparing a harness to strap three-year-old Ada across her back.

"Where will I meet you?" he nearly cried.

"Probably in hell," she said coldly.

It was a strange assortment the three rescuers brought back from the Donner camp. As they passed the Graves cabin Billy ran out to Elitha.

"My Paw is bad off and Tamsen will not leave him."

What wasn't said was more factual. James Denton and Noah James had demanded to go. Tamsen had agreed only if Jean Baptiste stayed to help her. He was not about to be left behind, until Tamsen bribed him with one thousand dollars from the quilt. Leanna had to be gotten out because she was failing daily. Sol and Bill Hook were sent to care for her. Johanna was going because she was strong enough to make the trip.

Elizabeth was also strong enough to go, as Tamsen did most of the minding of their combined eight younger children, but as long as George Donner was alive Elizabeth reverted to type and refused to leave her true love.

It was love and a sworn secret that kept Billy from telling Elitha the fate of some of his family members. Glover and his men had carefully concealed the fate of the Stanton party except from Lavina Murphy and Elizabeth Graves. Lavina had no one to share it with and Mrs. Graves poured her bitterness out on his eighteen-year-old shoulders.

"I am going with you," he said tenderly, "to see you through. Don't let them leave without me."

At his request Elizabeth Graves's bitterness turned to gall. She accused him of almost every sin under the sun.

"I love her, mother, and plan to marry her. Please, can't you see that she needs me at this time?"

"And I don't, I suppose? Who is to chop wood for me and the children your foolish father has left behind? Tell me that?"

"Mother," he pleaded further, "they said that Mary Ann and Sarah were at that ranch just waiting for the next relief group. It's only a matter of days."

"Days?" she scoffed. "You sound just like your father. What did that man say? Thirty-three days."

"They were lost."

"All right, you smart-ass," she sniffed. "If you want to leave so badly, cut me a month's supply of wood before you depart."

It was a near impossible challenge she had presented. Glover had made it clear he wished to depart on Monday morning. That gave Billy two and a quarter days. In spite of his own starved condition he set to work.

Not including Billy Graves, Glover had twenty-three people selected to go with the relief party and a problem that had never been considered when they left the Johnson ranch. To get this many back would require the greater portion of food that they had brought with them. For the seventeen staying at the lake-camp, and twelve at the Donner camp, they could leave very little.

Sol Hook, looking at Virginia, thought she should be left behind, food or no food. She was so gaunt and pale that she almost looked ethereal. There was no sparkle to her eyes and her voice was soft and near haunting.

"We have been there before, you know."

"Yes, your mother told me. I am most sorry to hear about Milt. I got so I really liked him."

"Milt . . ." she said vaguely. "Almost like my grandmother."

"I don't understand."

"Of course you do, Sol. That day we talked about Luke Halloran's death. That was death. I tried, then, not to think of my grandmother as having died before that. As long as I thought it, she wasn't dead. I was always mean and spiteful to her. I was also mean and spiteful to Milt. That's why I try not to think of them as dead. I shall have to face them soon and I don't know how to apologize."

"You apologized to me once, Virginia."

She smiled weakly. "Yes, I suppose that I did. I was mean and spiteful to you, too."

He patted her hand. "Don't worry about that and don't worry about the trip. I will see you through."

She clutched his hand as though it would be the last thing on earth she would feel. "Thank you, Sol, but Eliza will need more help than I. Poor dear, she's sometimes just like a little baby."

Tears welled in Sol's eyes. It was the second time he had come near to crying that day. The first had been in saying good-bye to Tamsen. She had all but forced him to leave, as though knowing full well the terrible days she still had ahead. Those had been tears of love. These were now tears of love every bit as true. Virginia Reed had at last thought of someone else before herself.

14

"WHAT? Gone less than a day and back already?"

"It is two of the Reed children, Mrs. Breen," Glover said. "Tommy and Patty just aren't going to make it. Moultry and I have brought them back."

"To what?" Paddy Breen screamed, from inside the cabin. "We cannot care for them."

"I shall care for Tommy," eight-year-old Patty said stoically. Her clear eyes had already seen too much for one so young. "This man is a Mason like my father and shall return for me, even if my father does not."

"And what shall you eat in the meantime?" Peggy asked coldly.

"I shall leave my own ration," Moultry growled angrily.

"Take them back to their mother," Paddy screamed again.

The little girl looked at Peggy Breen with a look that was pure Margaret Reed. "My mother, Mrs. Breen, is going to do the best that she can, although I never expect to see her again. If we are to be a bother, Tommy and I shall walk down to Mrs. Donner. She has always struck me as a most charitable lady."

It was said with such childish, matter-of-fact truthfulness that Peggy Breen blanched. She felt what had once been apple cheeks smart at the insult.

"I'll take them," she whispered, knowing she would still have to battle Paddy's ill grace over the matter.

As Glover and Moultry turned to leave Billy Graves came plodding up from the lower cabin. His pack was pretty thin, a hunting knife his only weapon, and he looked already fully fatigued. But when he saw them he broke into a broad grin and his shoulders went back proudly. He had done the impossible and would not have to catch up with the others alone.

Aquilla Glover nearly wept again. This was the type of person one did not mind risking their life to rescue.

"Poppa?"

Virginia leapt in the air, tried to run toward the approaching men and fell in the snow from weakness.

"Sol," Margaret gasped. "What did the man say?"

"That Mr. Reed is here!"

Overcome, Margaret slumped down in the snow.

Sol handed Jimmy Reed to Eliza and stepped back from the family reunion. He hardly recognized the man who scooped Virginia up in his arms. The mustache was bushy and unkempt, the hair shot through with gray, and the handsome face lined and haggard.

"Your mother, dear one, your mother!" he cried. "Where is *she*?"

Virginia pointed and James Frazier called for a young man to bring his daughter bread they had baked during the night. Then he put her down and went toward the almost skeletal woman.

He slumped down beside her, took up her hands and buried his face in them.

"Husband," she said quietly, "our Patty and Tommy are still back at the lake."

"Oh, no," he moaned.

"Not dead," she soothed. "Just not strong enough to walk with the other children."

"Thank God! We shall go for them. Is everyone else of this party safe?"

"We've lost two," she sighed. "James Denton and Mrs. Keseberg's daughter Ada."

"Don't fret, my dear. You have never seen anything as heart-warming as this whole mission. Down at Mule Springs are horses and supplies. There is more at the fort and a relay camp set up by Captain Kern. I have seen some of our people at Johnson's place. Oh, Sol, you will be happy to hear that Thornburg and Mrs. MacDuff have some men building a sort of sled for Mr. Donner. Everyone seems to be taking a hand in the relief work, even Governor Hull. But enough of this, we have matters to attend."

Nearby there was a violent fit of coughing and choking. William Hook had eaten too fast and too much of the bread given him. He was violently ill and the young rescuer who had given Virginia the bread was pounding him on the back.

"That helps naught!" Glover roared, jawing a plug of tobacco. As the Reeds prepared to separate again, Glover forced Bill to swallow the tobacco juice and empty his stomach.

"He is now too weak to go on. Moultry, build a fire and keep him here for awhile. God-speed James

Frazier. I will get them down to Bear Valley and beyond."

Billy Graves frost-bitten feet were almost as bad as Bill Hook's stomach. It was decided he should rest for awhile too. By stopping, his feet swelled past the point of walking, and Moultry determined that they should stay the night.

While they slept the empty stomach became uncontrollably ravenous. Bill Hook stole to the tree where Moultry had stored his provision pack out of the reach of bears. It was more than enough to get the three to Bear Valley. It was too much for a starving twelve-year-old to fully consume and not be sick again.

When they found him in the morning he was too far gone for tobacco-juice. What he had not been able to cram into his stomach and mouth, he had hidden in his pockets. It wasn't much, but they put it back in the pack and buried him.

Billy Graves decided that he could walk on his feet rather than die of starvation. He could hardly recall the names of the twenty-eight who were already dead.

The nine that pushed on with Reed were mainly trappers, hunters, and mountain men except for one. Mac McCutchen was still a giant in strength, but no longer jolly. His child was dead, and from Amanda he had heard the tale of the snowshoers. He had also heard of Pike and Lavina's blindness. These were the people who had taken in his family and shared their food. No man alive could have kept him from not going back with relief.

Their arrival came just a week after the departure of Glover. No one had died in the lake cabins, but the seven days had been like seventy.

Nauseated, James Frazier found Patty sitting on a snowbank outside the Breen cabin eating vermin she picked out of her hair.

"Did they not leave you food, little sparrow?" he asked gently.

"Mr. Breen ate most of it," she said matter-of-factly. "Then he shot and dressed Towser, but refused to give any of it to Mrs. Graves. That's why he's abed. She got so mad she took his crutch away from him and broke it into splinters over her knee."

"Tommy?" he asked warily.

"Sleeping. I let him sleep all he wants so he won't cry for food."

The Breens hardly looked at him when he went in to pick up the mere skeleton of his son. Peggy Breen's eyes were averted from guilt. Paddy kept his down on his lap and kept petting the dressed fur of Towser, his sheepdog.

Fires were built on the paths between the cabins and kettles found to heat water. Charley Stone, the rough frontiersman, took away the children's clothes to wash them. Patty and Tommy might be cold for a little while for a soaping and washing, but it would be a cold that the vermin couldn't take.

The Breen cabin was a palace next to the Murphys'. James Frazier could not find words to describe it in his mind.

Just in pushing back the hide door covering for his first look in left him in amazement. He shook his hand, but the black swarm of jumping fleas had found a new home. He brushed them off with snow.

"Mac, best we fully undress and leave our clothes out here."

First they got out the younger children of Pike and Foster. One of the other rescuers had been going through the snow-laden wagons for dry clothing and had found two bolts of flannel.

Lavina, grown childish, refused to be budged and sat giggling and weeping. Peggy Breen, fearing that James Frazier might leave them behind again, finally came to help clean Lavina up somewhat.

Beds were pulled forth, dumped in the snowbanks and replaced by pine boughs.

"God!" Mac gasped, starting to lift up a pile of rags and discarded clothing. "There's something alive under here!"

"Keseberg," ten-year-old Simon Murphy said, as though it didn't really matter.

What they found under the pile of filth was almost unspeakable.

"Roll him onto those pine boughs and shred away the clothes. Lord, I can hardly see him for the mass of crawling things. We will have to wash him in here."

Lewis Keseberg, who had learned to keep his eyes tightly closed against the vermin, recognized the voice and instantly feared. This was the man he was going to hang from his wagon-tongue.

"Not him," he muttered. "Please not him to wash me."

Reed ignored him as he came to help Mac. He didn't want to think at that moment at all. He had moments before taken the cooking pot out of the cabin. It smelled worse than some of the people.

"What's in here?" he had asked Simon.

"What mother sent me up the bank to get out of the snow," he answered, pointing to the far outside corner of the cabin. James Frazier had started through the snow and stopped short. It was propped up on the snowbank in plain view, but no one had seen it. The flesh had been torn away and an arm and leg were missing, but the head and face of his faithful Milt had not been touched.

"Charley," he had called softly to Stone, "a little snow to cover him, please."

Oddly, he felt no grief. He had felt that upon first hearing the news of Milt's death. Strangely, he felt pride. Milt Elliott had continued serving others even after death.

Oddly, again, he didn't have quite the same feeling the next day as he, Cady and Clark approached the Donner camp.

Jean Baptiste jumped from a hole in the snow, the leg of a man, cut off at the thigh, tucked under his arm. Upon seeing them he quickly threw it back in the hole and stood hesitantly.

"What are you about, Jean Baptiste?"

"A chore, Mr. Reed. The George Donners sent me to borrow this food supply, for it is the property of the Jacob Donners."

Passing the hole Cady and Clark nearly gagged. The head of Jacob Donner had been cut off, but the features preserved by the cold. The limbless trunk was little more than back and a quarter of rib cage.

"Which tent is which?"

"Aunt Betsy first. I take care her and children, mostly. Aunt Tammy next."

"And Uncle George?" Reed felt foolish. He had never called Donner that ever before.

"Same, same."

Nor had he ever heard anyone call Elizabeth Donner. "Aunt Betsy." Nor did he hardly recognize the wasted, gaunt and prostrate woman, who had refused to eat the flesh of her husband. The Jacob Donner children were so sunk into the apathy of starvation that they paid no attention to Reed's approach to Elizabeth's bed. Cady and Clark had to turn quickly back from the tent flap. The children sat innocently by the fire, their chins and breasts smeared bloodily, as they tore and ate at a half-roasted liver and heart.

"Elizabeth," Reed said gently, "we have come for you."

She opened her eyes and blinked. "Why, James Frazier, I told you that I have not ridden double on a horse for years. I will just wait until Margaret comes along and I can ride amidship with her."

At one time the woman's chatter would have driven him nearly crazy. Now he heard in it nothing but death.

He heard it again, a few seconds later, but in the voice of George Donner.

Amazingly, he found Tamsen Donner to be still healthy, as strong as could be expected and cheerful. Her three little daughters sat on a Navajo blanket, which Jean Baptiste had carried all the way from New Mexico, playing with rag dolls. Something boiled in the pot, but it was only strips of hide.

James Frazier looked at it so strangely that Tamsen blushed.

"I know what you are thinking," she whispered. "I sent Jean Baptiste to borrow. Those are the last of my hides he can find. George and the girls don't know what I was about to do, so please, say nothing."

"Then how do you stay so healthy?"

She shrugged. "On the good days I get the girls out in the air to exercise. I tell them that, but it is really to burrow down in the snow to find the old pine cones. Dried and roasted you can get a most tasty little nut out of each little spine." Then she laughed. "Of course it takes a heap to even fill a tooth cavity."

"Tamsen, Thornburg is through and building a sled. There is another relief party also on its way. I can leave a couple of men to see after George and Elizabeth, but I think you should take all the children and go with me."

"Thank you, James, but I will stay with George. And as long as it will probably only be a few more days I will keep the girls with me, but except for Elizabeth's two little ones, I think the others should go."

As long as relief was that close at hand Jean Baptiste decided he could stay and take care of Aunt Betsy and the little ones.

Again a walk was to be made away from the cabins, but not for all. Charley Stone would remain behind to care for Lewis Keseberg, Lavina Murphy, her son Simon and grandson George Foster. Also, because few gave him a chance for survival, three-year-old James Eddy was left.

The banished man had returned for them. It was a bitter pill for a Paddy Breen and an Elizabeth Graves to swallow. In their minds they gave the credit to Mac McCutchen.

Weary minds and bodies produced little vigor. They would not be hurried along and it took the whole first day just to get halfway along the lake.

The second day saw them only to the foot of the pass.

Reed was getting nervous. Woodworth was nowhere in sight and they had food for only another day and a half. It had not stormed in a month and clouds were piling up in the peaks. He would have to send men ahead to the next cache for food.

The third day, the clouds hung heavy. The men went ahead for food, leaving few able-bodied ones to help with the seventeen emigrants. They would have to make the summit that day, for there was no camping on the treeless, windswept pass.

The refugees finally came to the full realization that they must make it or die. They made it by noon and by mid-afternoon were at the head of the Yuba where the first relief party had made camp.

Still the mountain men did not return from the cache.

The storm broke during the night. Winter would not relent. It was fierce and howling, the snow crystals so biting that a man could not keep his eyes open to the blast.

Already exhausted from getting the emigrants up the pass, the mountain men were valiant in making a wind-break of branches and keeping the fire high.

A ration of a spoonful of flour each was supper.

"Reed probably has us lost again," Breen sniffed. How quickly one forgets. A few hours before, because of his weak leg, James Frazier had time and time again helped him up the pass.

In the morning it was worse and much colder. To keep the fires high required a lot of work. The searchers found they could not stay away from the fire for longer than ten minutes or they would be frost-bitten and frozen.

The whole day brought no improvement, except for increased cries of hunger from the children.

James Frazier, who had started keeping a diary again, wrote ominously: "Night closing fast, and with it the hurricane increases."

They could rail against it, but that did not decrease hunger or cold.

On the third morning they found five-year-old Isaac Donner dead from exposure.

"The wind is letting up, if not the whole storm. To wait longer for Woodworth is to lean upon a broken stick. We must move on to find the cache ourselves."

"Not with you!" Breen bellowed. "All you have ever done is lead us from one disaster to another. God is punishing you for the death of John Snyder and we are being made to suffer right along. My family and I stay."

The memory of it enraged Mrs. Graves as well. "We stay, too!"

"The rest go!" Reed stormed. "And may God hear this, Patrick Breen! If any Breen or Graves child thus dies, then the blood is upon your head." Then he whispered softly to the mountain men. "Fetch them at least three days supply of firewood. Mary, come here. Why are you limping?"

"I burned my foot in the fire, Mr. Reed."

"Can you walk on it?"

"I can try, sir."

She hobbled. Sadly, he realized he must leave her behind with people who didn't like a Donner any better than they did a Reed.

He was no longer thinking of Woodworth, just the cache. Some link in the carefully thought-out relief chain had somehow broken. But to worry on it only used up energy. How different things might have been had he not wasted so much energy months before.

If he left behind enemies, he walked with a friend. Mac McCutchen was well aware that James Frazier had never once before the camp people taken credit for the endless hours of pleading, begging and recruiting he had done for the relief effort. It wasn't just for his family, it was for all the families.

Charley Stone had fumed over the emigrants only making it half-way across the lake that first day. He had helped Mac McCutchen cache some of the refugees' personal things until spring. He had been with Mac when they had to help Mrs. Graves take some spikes out of the table legs that held it firm on the floor of one wagon. Beneath the legs were bored holes full of coins. At the time Elizabeth Graves had scoffed that it was little in comparison to what the Donners must have carried along.

That certainly tied in with what he had heard at Sutter's Fort. James Frazier Reed was considered wealthy and allowed Captain Sutter to know that the Donners would also help in paying for any supplies advanced. But supplies for over eighty people? That took a bigger heap of money than Charley's mind could fathom.

Finally he could wait no longer and left for the Donner camp.

"Where's Clark?"

"Sent him off with the Mex to chase a she-bear I winged yesterday."

"Learn anything?"

Cady grinned. "Some things. That one is real poorly and that one is having second thoughts because her old man is much worse. Heard her talking with the Mex about taking her girls away."

"Money mentioned?"

"The Mex said the thousand was enough," Cady chuckled.

"*Thousand?*" Stone gulped. "I think we'd best talk to her fast before Clark and the Mex get back."

C.L. Cady had almost heard right. Jean Baptiste had said that the one thousand dollars already given would be quite enough—money he had left in Tamsen's care—but that the bear meat for supplies would also be needed.

They found Tamsen already preparing the girls for travel, on the expectation that the bear would be shot that morning. For one who seldom changed her mind, this was not sudden. After Reed had departed, George Donner just seemed to give up all hope. He was failing so fast, she knew it was just a matter of a day or two. But a day or two might put James Reed out of reach to send the girls to Elitha and Leanna. And being Tamsen Donner she would not leave Elizabeth and her children behind.

"Still at the lake?" she nearly giggled. "Oh, if only Jean Baptiste would get back. It is shorter to the lake and pass from here, I have been told."

Cady shrugged shrewdly. "Once Nick Clark starts after a bear no telling when he will get back."

"Mr. Stone, would you be willing to take them to the party?"

Charley looked sad. "I'm supposed to be looking out for the people at the lake-cabins and it's a big chore for just one man with three that young."

"Mr. Cady, I can look out for things here, if you could help. If they are still that close you would neither one be gone for more than a day. I would be willing to pay."

"How much?" they both almost echoed together.

Tamsen's mind was so worried over George that she didn't hear the greed in their voices. Still, she couldn't go and rifle through the quilt that lay atop him for money—and in front of them. Her ready money she had given to Thornburg. Then she thought of the money she had given Jean Baptiste.

"Five hundred . . . I can give you five hundred apiece."

Charley Stone's eyes bulged. He never had more than ten dollars put together at one time. "We sure better get started."

"Oh, one other thing. This pack for my step-daughters. It has a note for them and some silver spoons and jewelry, so that they can establish some credit until I get there."

Charley took the pack and motioned Cady outside. "Go get your foodpack and Clark's."

"Just for a day?"

"Damnit, man, who is coming back?"

The children were dressed warm and bright, as though for church. They also said good-bye to George Donner as though they were to be gone but an hour for church.

For once the three behaved without raising a fuss. It had been so long since they had been so finely dressed that they had taken Tamsen's lie that they were going to the other camp for a children's party without question.

She turned back into the tent quickly, praying she had done the right thing.

They were finally taken to the other camp, but not until after a near murderous argument.

"Didn't you hear her? 'Credit until she got there.' That means she's got a helluva lot more."

"No! Let's just leave the brats to get lost in the woods and take off with this."

"Charley, look at it two different ways. The kids think that they are going to the other camp, right? So we take them and drop them on the old blind gal. That way we don't have to think that we left them here to die—and dead they ain't no good to us for the other way. We'll be able to see Woodworth coming down and can make it back there to get more ransom money out of her before he gets here."

Reluctantly, Charley agreed.

They didn't count on the storm and the non-arrival of Woodworth.

In the dark, smoky hovel it was no party. In her childish way Lavina thought they were just three of her own. Keseberg only growled at them when they cried too much, and Simon tried to make the rations stretch three more ways. Holed up in the Breen cabin, the two men had never thought to leave food for their "kidnap" victims.

There was no bear shot and no provisions left for Nick Clark. He suspected the worst upon hearing the story, but held his silence. The next day he would have to get the bear. The next day it was snowing. And the next and next.

What food there had been was gone—even Jacob.

The wind was so fierce they could hear tree branches cracked off and crashed down. Jean Baptiste got his Navajo blanket back to shiver under. But that didn't help three-year-old Lewis Donner. The death of her baby put Elizabeth into a semi-coma of grief.

The storm seemed to cease around the lake before higher up. Strong, comparatively well fed, and now fearful after several days to think over their plot, Stone and Cady decided to leave with just the money and silver spoons.

Ironically, later on, they skirted the Breen-Graves camp and overcame the exhausted, struggling Reed group. There was no need for suspicious glances, for logic would have suggested that they needed food from the cache for the camps as desperately as did these people. Because they shared some of their food, Reed thought nothing of their pressing right on. They were still hale and hearty, so why not?

The next morning Reed did worry about one of them. They left a trail of blood from a cracked, open, frost-bitten foot.

A queer pair had helped build the sled and get it on a wagon for Bear Valley. Eddy and Foster had stood two months before ready to kill each other— Foster still not knowing that he had been confused by some with Fosdick and had been declared dead. Now, with Doolittle, they stood ready to kill another.

On the ninth of March, Woodworth still sat in the Bear Valley camp, surrounded by men, horses, mules and supplies. As Reed had taken away his best mountain man guides, he sat like a general-of-the-army waiting for them to return.

"But before the storm you would have had their trails to follow."

"Possibly," he said arrogantly, "but it was not for me to attempt, and I would not advise it for you."

"Advise," Doolittle growled. "Are you aware to whom you speak, you rum-sotted bastard. They have passed over under vastly more difficult circumstances, and they will certainly attempt it again. Now, break out some flat-shoed mules to pull this sled and get your do-nothing men to fill it with supplies. Each of these men still have family over there."

"You will have nothing."

With a single movement Doolittle had his knife at the man's throat and his other hand twisting back his hair.

"When you came through Johnson's I had some respect for you. It just oozed out like your blood will soon be doing. This is not the military, you're no damn commander, and these supplies were raised to help those people, not feed these three-dollar-a-day fortune hunters. Do I make myself clear!"

Wishing political fortune in California, Woodworth not only quickly agreed, but also agreed to go with them with some other men. It was a pure political move. He figured the parties would be on their way down already anyway.

They were, but in no order he had ever expected. The mountain men sent for food had found the first cache robbed by martens, and the storm had delayed them to the second. Nearly starved themselves they had taken some and left some for others. Reed had found it and was the next found. No one could answer his question about Cady and Stone, although they had pushed on ahead.

Then Cady came down the trail, seven toes having already dropped off. He was too overcome by exposure to worry about the vanishing Stone and the money.

356 Lee Davis Willoughby

But no one else? James Frazier was haunted by
the memory of having left the Breens and Graves and
Mary Donner. He and his family were safe, if not
yet wholly sound, but he had to raise the question.

Woodworth was quick to ask for volunteers, but
uttered no word as a leader.

Eddy and Foster were ready to go and Doolittle
had his contraption that could sled back down. The
spirit that had moved them this far for rescue would
move them no farther. James Frazier tiredly said he
would return.

"No," Doolittle heard himself shouting, "You and
Mac have done enough these last few days while
these lard-asses have sat around. We three will go!"

Embarrassed, Woodworth had to open up the purse
strings of the relief fund that James Frazier had
been responsible raising.

"All right, I will offer three-a-day per man and a
fifty dollar bonus for each child carried out by hand."

"I'll go," Charley Stone said, stepping forth from
the group. No one had seen him arrive and Cady
was off having his frostbite taken care of. "I passed
where they were camped and know the spot."

Because the frontiersman was willing to go back,
others agreed. They were not as greedy as Stone to
get every last dollar they could out of this venture.

But things did not go fully as Charley had expected. He hardly thought anyone out of that camp
could still be alive—or at the other camps—and really
wanted to get back to find nothing more than the
rest of the Donner money—after he had taken the
money he was well aware Elizabeth Graves had taken
from the bored holes in the wagon.

But atfer the first night out, Doolittle seemed to
take command and felt they stood a better chance
to save the majority by splitting the eight men into

two groups. With seven against him Charley had to agree, but because the Graves money was closer, he went with that group.

He found Elizabeth Graves, but not the money. She lay mutilated in the snow, her breasts, liver and heart gone, and year-old Elizabeth, the baby, wailing with a tiny hand upon the mangled body of its mother. About them were the corpses of two other Graves children.

Just beyond was a great cup, twenty-five feet deep, melted into the snow. Smoke rose from it, and the aroma of cooking. Cautiously, John Starks, a two hundred pound recruit, crawled to the brink and peered down.

At the bottom, on the burned down to ground, a fire blazed beneath a boiling pot, and in the room-sized area people lounged about on blankets as though sunning themselves on a fine summer afternoon.

Patrick Breen let out an enormous burp. "Damn, heart burn! Towser didn't do that. If that stupid baby would stop wailing it wouldn't either."

He crawled back. He had never expected to see so many alive. It was embarrassing. Four of them for so many? Well, one way or another they would have to do it.

Eddy, Foster, and Doolittle had been through storms before—desert, mountain and personal. But to go back over the mountain pass again was nothing less than raw gut courage. There was no leader behind them. Woodworth was a hopeless waste, Reed spent. Ironically, they were men who could still laugh at themselves. The sled was fine for something other than mules. They released the animals and pulled the vehicle to a spot where Eddy remembered, then caching some of the food under the sled, took up packs with the other recruit.

Fatigue didn't seem to grip them, for three were held in suspense of what they would find. Two fathers and a man who had come to feel like a Donner family member.

Sunrise found them ready to slide down the snow wall of the eastern slope and by mid-morning coming close to the cabins. If Doolittle and Mary Florence had set a record going over the pass, these men had broken it with spirited audacity.

But again they split. Doolittle wanted to take the short cut to the Donner camp. How could they refuse him?

Death had also kept pace with their rhythm.

These two Williams, Eddy and Foster, sat without the filth and mutilation to hear confusing and conflicting story after story.

Every ounce of Lewis Keseberg's education came forth in elegant style, although so gaunt and heavily bearded, that his height now seemed doubled.

"Stick with the exact fact, girl," he chided Georgia Donner. "I took the Foster child to bed for warmth on a most cold and stormy night. Poor child died. Grandmother Murphy was most grieved."

"Then why did you take him away from her and hang him up?"

"Gentlemen," Keseberg said smoothly, "hunger tends to bring on the same delusions we underwent in the desert. The woman accused me of choking the child to death on my penis. The woman was failing and I took the dead child from her and did tie its swaddling clothes to the rafters so that she could not cuddle it and fuss."

"But it didn't stay there long."

"Naturally not," Keseberg said with a sort of perverted bravado, "as soon as she lapsed back into one of her snoring sleeps we needed him for the pot. The other child had been nothing but skin and bones."

Each father was enraged enough to kill, just as Keseberg seemed to have killed and forfeited his rights as a human being. Then as William Foster looked at the pitiable blind creature who had once been the strength of the Murphy clan, he shuddered.

"Eddy," he said pitifully, "look at the German Does not that horrible and emaciated figure remind you of where we have been and what we have done? We have not the right to cast the first stone."

"But they were our children!" Eddy cried.

"And these are mine!"

They turned, surprised to find Tamsen Donner in the path. Her daughters let out a shriek of greeting, but she coldly waved them to silence. In her hand was a bullwhip, as though she intended using it for more than bringing silence.

"I am glad to see you," she said curtly. "The storm made me fear for my daughters and I sent Clark here for news. You have just heard the same news that I have heard. The question now, as it is near noonday, is how soon will you be ready to leave with those able?"

Her eyes were too glassy and her voice too even-tempered. Not angry, but dully curt. She could have been more feared than Keseberg.

"Mrs. Donner," Eddy said quietly, "Doolittle Thornburg has come back for you and your husband."

"That is a matter I shall discuss with Doolittle. Elizabeth gave me fifteen hundred in silver. It is yours for taking the children out."

"I would not want to burden the load with even a hundred dollars of the weight, Mrs. Donner. Besides, the other Mrs. Donner will be needing it."

"Elizabeth needs nothing now. She is at rest and little Sammie is soon to follow."

"I will take the children, of course. But what of yourself?"

She smiled but did not answer. No use repeating what she had so often repeated before. No use saying good-bye to the children again either. She turned to go back through the forest to George's death-bed. Straight-backed, assured and determined, she did not once look back.

It was a time when some men did things as they saw were necessary and other men did things as they saw personal.

It was necessary to cut wood to make Lavina comfortable, although they could leave her no food supply.

It was not necessary, in the opinion of Eddy and Foster, to do a thing for Lewis Keseberg.

At the foot of the pass they were surprised to find Jean Baptiste and Nick Clark. They were disgusted that they had left a dying man and child.

It was the claim of Jean Baptiste that George Donner had ordered him to go. It was doubted, but perhaps most true. He had come away without getting his one thousand dollars again from Tamsen.

Such was not the case of Nick Clark. Like his friends before him, he came away with a forty-pound pack of booty he felt was his due. Had he waited, Tamsen might have given him silver or paper money worth a great deal more than the loot.

15

THE REFUGEES, until the last man was out, were taken in by various families from Johnson's ranch to Sutter's fort. As became their aristocracy, the Reeds and Mrs. MacDuff were taken in by the Alcalde Sinclair family. Kindly little Mrs. Sinclair did her best to keep their hopes alive for those still on the other side of the mountain.

But throughout the end of March and into early April it rained in Sacramento Valley. They were now seasoned pioneers of this new land and knew that rain in the valley meant more deep winter snow in the Sierras.

A month evaporated, with only one small, futile attempt at rescue. Then, in mid-April, another party was formed. It could hardly be called relief, going after just five remaining. No one really held out any hope of still finding Lavina Murphy alive, and cared less about Lewis Keseberg. If George Donner still held on it would have been a miracle, and the same went for little Sammie.

Tamsen had been given opportunity after opportunity to leave, they reasoned, and now had the mountain man who could have brought her out at any time. Oddly, because he had been in and out, no one included Doolittle in the five to still be rescued.

Perhaps not odd considering that the majority of the men who signed up for this crossing were really going as a salvage team to pick over the wealth the emigrants had left behind.

Only Phillipine Keseberg, William Foster, the Donner children, Mary Florence and the Reeds really wished word back from them. There was no Reed still left behind, but James Frazier felt responsible as the man who had put together the relief effort. But the relief chain was now many broken links. No more relay camps and messengers riding back and forth. They would just have to be patient until the party returned with the final news.

But they did not just stand and wait. There was much activity brewing for the future.

"Dearest Helen," Virginia Reed wrote back to her cousin in Springfield:

"Tell the girls that this is the greatest place for marrying they ever saw, and that they must come to California if they want to marry. I know for a fact, even though I am just turning fourteen. Once we were ahorse, for our last leg of the journey, a gallant swain tried to press his suit. The proposal was very funny, he a total stranger and all, although at long last I have made Sol Hook jealous. He is my love, Helen, and from experience I can say that honestly. However, we shall wait for a proper age.

"Others of near my age are not waiting. Mary Ann Graves is to be married here in May to Captain Perry McCoon. He being the man who ferried my father and the relief party across the flooded Sacramento. He is most handsome. Also most handsome is Billy Graves, although much too old for me. He had had only one true love this whole journey—Elitha Donner, a year my senior. They marry in June.

"Tell your mother's Irish maid not to give up heart because even our Eliza is engaged to be married. You may all think this is a joke, but I tell you 'tis the truth. He is really not all that handsome a man, Helen, but I now think of him as most a hero. Someday I must tell you the whole tale of this William Eddy. He will make Eliza a most stout husband, I am sure.

"Now, I suppose I should tell you about the journey and why it has taken so long. . . ."

"It is remarkable," Mary Florence laughed, sprinkling a bit of salt from the cellar onto her food. "Before we never gave salt a second thought. Now, it is the most precious gift that I can think of."

Margaret Reed sat silent. She knew exactly why Mary Florence was being jovial and keeping the conversation away from what she really wished to be discussing.

An hour before breakfast they had seen the returning party head for the fort. The count was not good. Only one refugee was among them. James Frazier had gone at once to learn the news and the identity.

Mary Florence didn't need to be told. The image of Doolittle Thornburg aboard a horse was burned into her memory. Even at a distance this man was too tall, too wild of hair, too unkempt of clothing.

"Ah, James Frazier," Mrs. Sinclair chirped, "back just in time to sit the table."

He looked from woman to woman, from child's face to child's face, then slowly sat.

"Keseberg," he said simply and accepted a steaming plate from a Spanish maid.

The adults had heard enough about the man from Eddy and Foster to let the simple statement stand until the meal was over and the children out of earshot.

Under the table Mary Florence pressed her hands together so tightly that her knuckles went white. A cold dread gripped at her heart.

"Children," Margaret said quickly, knowing how unfair this was to the woman, "you may be excused."

With glee they raced away. The Sinclair ranch was really a marvel to them.

"Thank you, my dear, for I would not have been able to eat, anyhow. The tale from Keseberg is almost as crazy as the man himself. If Bill Foster had not been in the Fallon party, I might be tempted to believe none of it. With Keseberg's past I don't think we need dwell on what became of Foster's mother-in-law. The same could be said of George Donner, who was found wrapped in a fine linen shroud, and not but a couple of days dead. But I get ahead of myself."

"James Frazier," Margaret said sternly, "just get to the part that will interest Mrs. MacDuff."

He hung his head. "I wish that I could. I wish that I could make sense out of it all, but I can't. It even started oddly for the Fallon men at the lakecamp. Deserted and strewn about like a ship-wreck. Then a scream that even gave the mountain men a creeping horror.

"The Diggers had finally made it to the lake. They fled in equal terror down the trail. The men found Lavina Murphy's remains, so to speak, a boiling stew pot, but containing only a young child's bones and no Keseberg.

"They pushed on after the Indians toward the Donner camp. Following a blood trail, but no Indian had been shot. It was in an even greater shambles. As I said, George was wrapped in linen, with only his heart missing. In the tent they found a large kettle containing the heart, cut up. Nearby was a chair upon which were three legs of ox that had been buried under the snow all winter. Their centers were still frozen hard.

"There was no trace of Tamsen or Doolittle. No trace of Keseberg and no trace of the Donner money. The quilt Jean Baptiste told about was not there. The silver that Eddy told about was not there.

"They camped the night and got some of their answers the next morning. The cut up heart was gone from the pot and there was a new bloody trail back toward the lake. Returning, they found Keseberg calmly eating his breakfast, with one foot bare and bleeding.

"Now his story is most crazy and confusing. He claimed not to have ransacked the camps for the money, and indeed had hidden only $216. But, and I am sorry I must say this, he claimed that Tamsen came to the lake a few days after the death of Lavina, told of George's death and then died herself. Disgustedly, he repeated that not over a half hour ago and claims she was the most tender meal he had ever eaten."

"But it doesn't make sense," he hurried on, before he thought too much on that picture. "Lavina's remains, according to Fallon, were a month old and George's no more than four to five days. Nor was there any evidence of Tamsen's body and Keseberg swears he never saw Thornburg."

"Doolittle would not have left Tamsen alone with just George," Mary Florence insisted.

"Agreed," James Frazier sighed. "And there are the ox legs that Keseberg says he never saw in the tent. Hardly put there by the Diggers, if they were the ones who ransacked the camp. Well, again the Fallon men went back to search out this mystery. They sorted and dried out the valuables remaining to find a clue. They tramped the woods in all directions, but found no boot prints in among the Diggers's tracks. The track from the Donner tents to the lake had not been rebroken since the last storm.

"Whatever happened there, had to have taken place in the four to five days after George's death and before Keseberg came to take out his heart. Little Sammie is also a mystery, except for the bones in the pot. But when did Keseberg get hold of that body? I don't have any other answers, and only a personal theory. Fallon's men did not see the fleeing Diggers carry off anything. In his mind I think Keseberg is right about Tamsen coming to tell of George's death. I would go farther to say that Doolittle was with her and they were on their way over the pass with the quilt and silver. From there my theory runs into a blank wall. It has been well over a month."

Mary Florence rose slowly and went from the dining room to the living room. From there she could look out across the valley, over the foothills and to the high Sierras still mantled in white. It was his theory, but one she could hardly accept. He was saying they were lost up there somewhere. That was hard for her to accept, knowing that she and Doolittle had made it in four days, in much worse weather.

"Mrs. MacDuff."

She turned away from the scene slowly. "Isn't it time that it became Mary Florence . . . Margaret?"

"Past time, my dear. Come and sit with me a moment. I, more than any, know this moment for you. I lived through many hellish months not knowing if my husband was alive or dead. It was torture of the worst kind possible."

"But you never gave up hope, did you?"

Margaret smiled and tapped her heart. "Something in here kept telling me that he was alive."

Mary Florence sat down slowly, unable to tap her heart. It held a feeling, a feeling that had been there before. A feeling that made her be honest with herself and with Margaret.

"It is not there for me, Margaret. Tamsen was with me when I finally came to the realization that my husband was dead. Today, when I realized it was Keseberg on the horse, I also realized I would never see Tamsen again. All morning I have put out of my mind that also meant I would not see Doolittle again." She laughed weakly. "I just know that they are dead, but am strangely warmed by it. We don't know how they died, but maybe God wanted to leave us with this final mystery. Whatever became of the last of the Donner people?"

Margaret didn't answer. What was to answer? Her heart had told her the same all morning. Tamsen had always been somewhat of a mystery to her—too strong, too self-assured, too much a survivor. If God had now taken her in a mysterious way, who were they to question?

"I wonder," she said, at last, "if people will even ask that question of us?"

Mary Florence looked at her strangely. "If they are sensible, Margaret, they should learn from the causes of our many mistakes. It is not, depending upon the time of year, the nearest route to this valley. Not if you have to leave half of your party behind as corpses."

There was a long pause.

"What will you do now?" Margaret asked quietly.

"Be a Selkirk," she said, slowly rising and going back to the window. "They are survivors. Beyond the snows I left everything I owned or hoped to own. It matters little. I also left good friends in Charley Stanton and Jimmy Smith. . . . and Doolittle. But others will come just like them, because they blazed the trail."

Margaret shuddered. "No one will ever come that way again, Mary Florence."

"Not come?" she laughed. "They will come by the thousands and tramp up over the pass where Donner blood was spilled. The majority of them won't even know of us or care. But come as they will, they will never be able to take one thing away from us."

"What is that?"

Again she turned slowly. Like so many of the party she was again quite alone in the world. But that, *alone*, could not erase the determination from her face of the love she'd been given.

"We were the first!"